From the Pages of
King Solomon's Mines

"A sharp spear," runs the Kukuana saying, "needs no polish;" and on the same principle I venture to hope that a true story, however strange it may be, does not require to be decked out in fine words.

(page 8)

There, there, it is a cruel and a wicked world, and for a timid man I have been mixed up in a deal of slaughter. (page 10)

"I am a fatalist, and believe that my time is appointed to come quite independently of my own movements, and that if I am to go to Suliman's Mountains to be killed, I shall go there and shall be killed there. God Almighty, no doubt, knows His mind about me, so I need not trouble on that point." (page 30)

"There is no journey upon this earth that a man may not make if he sets his heart to it." (page 49)

"If we cannot find water we shall all be dead before the moon rises to-morrow." (page 58)

There he sat, a sad memento of the fate that so often overtakes those who would penetrate into the unknown; and there probably he will still sit, crowned with the dread majesty of death, for centuries yet unborn, to startle the eyes of wanderers like ourselves, if any such should ever come again to invade his loneliness. (page 70)

"The diamonds are surely there, and you shall have them since you white men are so fond of toys and money." (page 92)

"The sun is dying—the wizards have killed the sun." (page 124)

I shook my head and looked again at the sleeping men, and to my tired and yet excited imagination it seemed as though death had already touched them. My mind's eye singled out those who were sealed to slaughter, and there rushed in upon my heart a great sense of the mystery of human life, and an overwhelming sorrow at its futility and sadness. To-night these thousands slept their healthy sleep, to-morrow they, and many others with them, ourselves perhaps among them, would be stiffening in the cold; their wives would be widows, their children fatherless, and their place know them no more for ever. (page 131)

Suddenly, with a bound and a roar, they sprang forward with uplifted spears, and the two regiments met in deadly strife. Next second, the roll of the meeting shields came to our ears like the sound of thunder, and the whole plain seemed to be alive with flashes of light reflected from the stabbing spears. To and fro swung the heaving mass of struggling, stabbing humanity. (page 146)

"We are the richest men in the whole world," I said. "Monte Christo is a fool to us." (page 183)

There around us lay treasures enough to pay off a moderate national debt, or to build a fleet of ironclads, and yet we would gladly have bartered them all for the faintest chance of escape. (page 188)

King Solomon's Mines

H. Rider Haggard

With an Introduction and Notes
by Benjamin Ivry

George Stade
Consulting Editorial Director

BARNES & NOBLE CLASSICS
NEW YORK

ℬ
BARNES & NOBLE CLASSICS
NEW YORK

Published by Barnes & Noble Books
122 Fifth Avenue
New York, NY 10011

www.barnesandnoble.com/classics

King Solomon's Mines was first published in 1885.

Published in 2004 by Barnes & Noble Classics with new Introduction,
Notes, Biography, Chronology, Inspired By, Comments & Questions,
and For Further Reading.

King Solomon's Mines
ISBN 1-59308-275-4
LC Control Number 2004110078

Produced and published in conjunction with:
Fine Creative Media, Inc.
322 Eighth Avenue
New York, NY 10001
Michael J. Fine, President and Publisher

Printed in the United States of America
QM
1   3   5   7   9   10   8   6   4   2
FIRST PRINTING

H. Rider Haggard

H. Rider Haggard wrote *King Solomon's Mines*, the story goes, after his brother bet him he couldn't pen a book as exotic, thrilling, and commercially successful as Robert Louis Stevenson's 1883 adventure novel *Treasure Island*. Haggard succeeded, and went on to write dozens more best-selling tales. Though his family initially had low expectations for him, Haggard not only made a living as an author; he also learned Zulu, brokered peace treaties, took part in the annexing of territories, and acted as the British Empire's right-hand man in the diamond- and gold-rich colonies of South Africa.

Born on June 22, 1856, in Norfolk, England, Henry Rider Haggard was the eighth of ten children. His father was a country squire and barrister; his mother was an Englishwoman raised in India. Haggard exhibited little academic ambition during his youth and did not attend university. After he failed the army entrance exam, he was sent to London to prepare for a post in the Foreign Office. In 1875 family connections secured him a job as secretary to Governor Henry Bulwer in Britain's Natal colony in South Africa. For the next four years, Haggard served the British Empire in various capacities, storing in his mind settings and events he would later use in his novels. He witnessed tense rebellions and outright war, served as a diplomat and aide, and hunted big game for sport—the stuff of his countrymen's wildest imaginings. However modern society may interpret the ideas expressed in *King Solomon's Mines*, Haggard's tale is an imaginatively embellished reflection of direct experience, one that gives us a window into the British colonial mind.

In 1879 Haggard returned briefly to England, where he met an heiress from Norfolk, Louisa Margitson; they married the next year. The couple returned to Africa, but their stay was brief; in 1881 they returned to England, where Haggard read for the bar and began to write fiction. *King Solomon's Mines*, published in 1885, was Haggard's third novel and his first popular success. He followed up the best-seller with a string of other novels, including a wildly popular tale of a 2,000-year-old queen, *She: A History of Adventure* (1887).

Personal suffering muted Haggard's success when his nine-year-old son died in 1891. A daughter, Lilias, was born the next year; she would eventually publish a biography of her father.

Although he maintained a farm and country house in Norfolk, Haggard traveled to Egypt, Mexico, Canada, the United States, and South Africa. He lectured and published reports on agriculture, one of his fields of expertise. His work was often in the service of the British government, which honored him with a knighthood in 1912 and made him a Knight Commander of the British Empire in 1919.

Haggard authored more than fifty works of fiction and nonfiction in his lifetime. His psychologically complex novels about distant lands influenced writers from Sigmund Freud and Carl Jung to Joseph Conrad, C. S. Lewis, and Henry Miller. H. Rider Haggard died on May 14, 1925, in London.

Table of Contents

The World of H. Rider Haggard
and King Solomon's Mines

1856   Henry Rider Haggard is born the eighth of ten children on June 22 in Norfolk, England. His father, William, is a country squire and barrister; his mother, Ella Doveton, is an amateur writer who was raised in India. Great Britain establishes a crown colony in Natal, South Africa.

1857   The Boers (South Africans of Dutch or Huguenot descent) establish the South African Republic in the region known as the Transvaal.

1859   Charles Darwin publishes *On the Origin of Species by Means of Natural Selection*.

1865   Lewis Carroll's *Alice's Adventures in Wonderland* appears.

1867   A diamond field is discovered in South Africa. Alfred Nobel invents dynamite.

1873   Haggard fails the army entrance exams; his family sends him to London to be trained to join the Foreign Office.

1875   While in London, Haggard experiments with spiritualism. His father arranges for him to go to South Africa, where he works as a secretary to the governor of Britain's colony in Natal, Sir Henry Bulwer.

1877   Haggard joins the staff of special commissioner Sir Theophilus Shepstone and hoists the flag at the British annexation of the Transvaal.

1878   Haggard's service earns him the position of master and registrar of the High Court in the Transvaal.

1879   On January 22 Zulu King Cetshwayo's army wipes out a British regiment that includes many of Haggard's friends. In May Haggard resigns his post and returns to England.

1880   Haggard marries a Norfolk heiress, Louisa Margitson; in November the two sail to Africa to live on a farm near the Transvaal border. Émile Zola publishes *Nana*, whose realism Haggard will later denounce.

1881   Jock, the Haggards' first child, is born in May. When the Transvaal is ceded to the Boers, Haggard and his wife return to England, where Haggard reads for the bar.

1882   Haggard publishes *Cetywayo and His White Neighbours; or, Remarks on Recent Events in Zululand, Natal, and the Transvaal*, a nonfiction work that examines colonial relations in South Africa.

1883   Robert Louis Stevenson's *Treasure Island* is published.

1884   Haggard is admitted to the bar and also publishes his first novel, *Dawn*, which is neither a commercial nor a critical success. Hiram Maxim invents the recoil-operated machine gun.

1885   Haggard's second novel, *The Witch's Head*, is published but receives little notice. A five-shilling bet with his brother prompts Haggard to write *King Solomon's Mines*; it is a huge commercial success and makes Haggard a household name.

1887   Haggard publishes "About Fiction" in the February issue of the *Contemporary Review*. His popular novel *She: A History of Adventure*, about a 2,000-year-old white queen named Ayesha, is released; the book enthralls psychoanalysts Sigmund Freud and Carl Jung. Three other novels set in South Africa—*Jess, Allan Quatermain* (the first of many sequels to *King Solomon's Mines*), and *A Tale of Three Lions*—are also published. Queen Victoria celebrates her Golden Jubilee, marking fifty years as ruler of the United Kingdom.

1888   Haggard travels to Iceland to gather material for a novel about the Vikings. *Maiwa's Revenge, Colonel Quaritch, V.C., My Fellow Labourer and the Wreck of the Copeland*, and *Mr. Meeson's Will* are published.

1889   The novels *Allan's Wife* and *Cleopatra* are released.

1890   *Beatrice*, a novel, is published. Haggard and Andrew Lang collaborate on the novel *The World's Desire*, about Helen of Troy. Haggard travels to Mexico.

1891   *Eric Brighteyes*, a Viking romance set in Iceland, is published. When his nine-year-old son Jock dies, Haggard is grief-stricken.

1892   *Nada the Lily* is published. Haggard's daughter Lilias, his future biographer, is born, raising his spirits.

1893   The novel *Montezuma's Daughter* is published. Natal becomes a self-governing British colony.

1894   *The People of the Mist* appears. Rudyard Kipling's *The Jungle Book* is published.

1895   *Joan Haste* and *Heart of the World* are published. Haggard is narrowly defeated in his bid for a seat in Parliament. H. G. Wells's *The Time Machine* is published.

1896   *The Wizard* is published.

1898   *Doctor Therne* is published.

1899   Two Boer territories—the South African Republic (Transvaal) and the Orange Free State—declare war on Britain, thus beginning the South African War (Boer War). Haggard's novel *The Spring of Lion* is published, as well as *The Last Boer War* and *A Farmer's Year*, both works of nonfiction. Sigmund Freud publishes his *Interpretation of Dreams*, in which he describes a fascination with Haggard's *She*.

1900   Haggard travels through Italy, Palestine, and Cyprus. *A History of the Transvaal* is released.

1901   Haggard's reflections on his recent travels are published in *A Winter Pilgrimage*. *Lysbeth*, a novel, is also published. Queen Victoria dies.

1902   The Boer War ends, with the Boers accepting British sovereignty. Haggard publishes *Rural England*, a two-volume study of the problem of depopulation. Joseph Conrad publishes his novella *Heart of Darkness* in book form.

1903   Haggard's *Pearl-Maiden*, a novel about the fall of Jerusalem, is released.

1904   Haggard travels to Egypt. The historical novels *Stella Fregelius* and *The Brethren* are published.

1905   *Ayesha: The Return of She*, a sequel to *She*, is published, as is the nonfiction *A Gardener's Year*. Haggard is sent by the Rhodes Trust to research Salvation Army settlements in the western United States, with an eye to opening similar settlements in South Africa. His report on his research is published under the title *The Poor and the Land*.

1906   *Benita: An African Romance* and *The Way of the Spirit* are published. Haggard joins the Royal Commission on Coast Erosion.

1907   *Fair Margaret,* a novel, is published. Kipling wins the Nobel Prize for Literature.

1908   *The Ghost Kings* is published.

1909   *The Yellow God* and *The Lady of Blossholme* are released. *Queen Sheba's Ring,* a novel based on Haggard's research in Egypt, is published.

1910   *Morning Star,* another novel about Egypt, is published.

1911   *Rural Denmark and Its Lessons,* Haggard's study of Danish farms, is published.

1912   *Marie,* the first volume in Haggard's fictionalized history of the Zulu people, is published. Haggard is knighted for his contributions to agricultural advancement. Sir Arthur Conan Doyle publishes *The Lost World.*

1913   *Child of Storm,* the second volume in Haggard's Zulu trilogy, is published.

1914   World War I begins.

1915   *The Holy Flower* is published.

1916   *The Ivory Child* is published. *Finished,* the last volume of Haggard's Zulu trilogy, is published.

1919   Haggard is named a Knight Commander of the British Empire (KBE) as a reward for his service on government commissions concerned with agriculture.

1920   *The Ancient Allan* is published.

1921   *She and Allan,* a sequel to *She,* is published.

1923   *Wisdom's Daughter,* another *She* sequel, is published.

1924   *Heu-Heu; or, The Monster* is published.

1925   Henry Rider Haggard dies on May 14 in London.

1926   *The Days of My Life: An Autobiography of Sir H. Rider Haggard* is released, as is another Quatermain adventure, *The Treasure of the Lake.*

1927   *Allan and the Ice-Gods* is published.

1937   A British film version of *King Solomon's Mines* is made, with Paul Robeson as Umbopa and Sir Cedric Hardwicke as Allan Quatermain; some scenes are filmed on location in Natal.

1950   Metro-Goldwyn-Mayer makes a film version of *King Solomon's Mines* starring Deborah Kerr and Stewart Granger.

1959   *Watusi: Guardians of King Solomon's Mines*, a film based on Haggard's novel, is released; it stars George Montgomery.

1980   Haggard's private diaries are published.

1985   Sharon Stone, John Rhys-Davies, and Richard Chamberlain star in a film remake of *King Solomon's Mines*, proving the enduring popularity of the 100-year-old novel.

Introduction

Haggard's Way

"GRIP" IS A QUALITY H. Rider Haggard aimed for in his novels, and the best of them, especially *King Solomon's Mines* (1885), remain compulsively readable as popular literature. The adventure of the elephant hunter Allan Quatermain in his quest for King Solomon's treasure in Africa remains an addictive page-turner, despite some aspects that have inevitably dated the book. The story of the voyage to the fictional kingdom of Kukuanaland has lasting resonances for the book's intended readers: "all the big and little boys," as Haggard's dedication puts it. Modern critics have made much of the sexist implications of Haggard's dedication to the "boys." In her introduction to the recent reprint edition of Robert Baden-Powell's *Scouting for Boys*, editor Elleke Boehmer points out that this Victorian classic of civic education for boys was an "immediate success amongst young audiences, male and female alike" (Oxford: Oxford University Press, 2004, p. xi). Baden-Powell's book, so expressly intended (and entitled) for boys, was also devoured by Victorian girls. Haggard's dedication probably did not scare off girl readers of his day either. Nor should it make today's reader jump to conclusions about the book's audience and intent. Haggard admitted he wrote *King Solomon's Mines* in direct competition with a recent bestseller, Robert Louis Stevenson's *Treasure Island*, also a book ostensibly for boys but one that has always been read by girls—and adults of both sexes.

Prefiguring Edgar Rice Burrough's Tarzan books and other popular literature, *King Solomon's Mines* is genuinely involved with Africa, however consciously Haggard mythicizes the subject matter. This is only to be expected in an author for whom Africa was a subject of lasting preoccupation. Born in West Bradenham Hall, Norfolk, England, in 1856, the son of a country squire, Henry Rider Haggard was seen as unpromising by his family. When young Henry failed to get an army commission, he was sent off to Natal, South Africa, in 1875 as secretary to the governor of Britain's Natal colony.

His career advanced, and in 1877 he transferred jobs, to work for the special commissioner. The following year he became master and registrar of the High Court in the Transvaal. His six years in Africa would provide inspiration for the rest of his writing life.

His friend Andrew Lang would later write that Haggard had "found himself" by writing *King Solomon's Mines.* One might add that Haggard found himself even before, by going to Africa, which transformed a rather muddled civil servant into a decisive and productive Victorian writer. This metamorphosis is akin to the change experienced by another Victorian novelist, Anthony Trollope (1815–1882), after Trollope landed a job as post-office inspector in Ireland, which awakened his own latent talents.

Haggard was deeply involved with public service, and published many books of history and advocacy, most of which are unread today. He never took his adventure stories as seriously as his nonfiction books, such as *Cetywayo and His White Neighbours; Or, Remarks on Recent Events in Zululand, Natal, and the Transvaal* (London: Trübner and Company, 1882); *The Last Boer War* (London: Kegan Paul and Company, 1899); and *A History of the Transvaal,*(New York: New Amsterdam Book Company, 1900). Obsessed with the fate of poor rural communities, he published studies like *A Farmer's Year: Being His Commonplace Book for 1898* (London: Longmans and Company, 1899; *The Poor and the Land: Being a Report on the Salvation Army Colonies in the United States and at Hadleigh, England, with Scheme of National Land Settlement, and an Introduction* (London, New York: Longmans, Green, 1905); *Rural Denmark and Its Lessons* (London, New York: Longmans, Green, 1911); *Regeneration: Being an Account of the Social Work of the Salvation Army in Great Britain* (London: Longmans, Green, 1910); and *Rural England: Being an Account of Agricultural and Social Researches Carried Out in the Years 1901 & 1902* (London, New York: Longmans, Green, 1902). Haggard also wrote extensively about World War I: *A Call to Arms to the Men of East Anglia* (London: R. Clay, 1914), and *The After-War Settlement and Employment of Ex-Servicemen in the Oversea Dominions* (London: Published for the Royal Colonial Institute by the Saint Catherine Press, 1916).

Although few fans of Haggard's novels today have read these hard-to-find nonfiction texts, Haggard himself felt they represented his highest achievements. Unlike Sir Arthur Conan Doyle, who valued his own eccentric writings on spiritualism over his immortal Sherlock Holmes stories, Haggard may have been at least partly right in his evaluation of his own work. The myths so abundant in *King Solomon's Mines* and *She* are bolstered by factual material, hard-won life experience of the kind detailed in Haggard's books about history, agriculture, and war, as well as in his private diaries and letters. The latter are better known since Denys Edwin Whatmore self-published a series of short books containing excerpts from Haggard's letters about activities for the public good. Three of these titles are: *Deeds for the Church: Rider Haggard* (Cheltenham: D. E. Whatmore, 1995); *Deeds for Children and Young People: Rider Haggard* (Cheltenham: D. E. Whatmore, 1996); and *Deeds for the Salvation Army: Rider Haggard* (Cheltenham: D. E. Whatmore, 1996). In addition, the Rider Haggard Society (www.riderhaggardsociety.org.uk), a British organization, has through its occasional journal worked since 1985 to propagate a more rounded view of Haggard. Even so, the only two texts by Haggard that are still widely read remain and look likely to remain—*She* and *King Solomon's Mines.*

Rapid Writing

Haggard admitted he wrote *King Solomon's Mines* in six weeks, a quickness that surprised his writer friends like Andrew Lang and Robert Louis Stevenson. The latter sent Haggard a letter cautioning him about excessive haste. Yet the famed Belgian-born detective storywriter Georges Simenon (1903–1989) often wrote entire books even faster. The French novelist Stendhal (Marie Henri Beyle, 1783–1842) typically completed novels in a matter of weeks. Speed in writing per se is not necessarily a threat to quality; adventure writers in particular can be like the journalists of whom the noted critic Karl Kraus (1874–1936) wrote, "They write worse when they have time." Pacing was essential for Haggard, who claimed that writing a text fast helped to energize it, making it irresistibly readable. He described his approach with typical dash in his autobiography, *The Days of My Life* (1926; see "For Further Reading"): "Such work should be written rapidly and, if possible, not rewritten, since wine of this character loses its bouquet when it is poured from glass to glass."

The speed of writing translates to speed of reading, with as few impediments as possible to the reader's momentum. Although there are a number of exotic words in *King Solomon's Mines* that require annotation, their frequency decreases as the book advances, and Haggard often provides his own, perfectly serviceable translation of local terms. As a result, the reader does not need to pause to understand the reference, but can plunge ahead to find out what happens next, which is essential for the enjoyment of a real page-turner like *King Solomon's Mines*.

Despite Haggard's speed and occasional carelessness about details, *King Solomon's Mines* shows some real control of structural and stylistic elements, which is part of its lasting power. To cite one stylistic aspect used coherently throughout the book, Haggard used italics almost always to convey the horror of death, such as when an elephant picked up a servant "*and tore him in two*" (p. 46). In a cave discovered along his trip, Quatermain finds that a servant who was alive the night before is now "*stone dead*" (p. 68). These italics denoting urgent shock in relation to death recur throughout the story, like underlining in a letter excitedly dashed off to a friend.

One of Haggard's goals, as expressed in "About Fiction" (*Contemporary Review*, February 1887), was to create an interesting book, as he felt the Anglo-American novel had declined into a series of dull domestic dramas. Haggard alluded to William Dean Howells (1837–1920), who wrote novels like *A Woman's Reason* (1883), *A Modern Instance* (1882), and *The Rise of Silas Lapham* (1885), as an example. By focusing on the imaginative and fantastic domains, Haggard aimed at exciting the reader in the way that he felt naturalistic nineteenth-century fiction had ceased to do. In this goal he succeeded brilliantly, as generations of readers have conceded.

In *King Solomon's Mines*, with a dour feeling of fatalism, the elephant hunter Allan Quatermain agrees to join a dangerous treasure hunt. Quatermain is presented as an amateur author, whose first statement at the beginning of the book is one of modesty, of being aware of his book's "shortcomings." As narrator, Quatermain dithers over lore and legends that he might have included in *King Solomon's Mines* had he "given way to [his] own impulses" (p. 7). Authorship as a form of discipline and control is also expressed at the end of the story, when Quatermain announces, "And here, at this point, I think

I shall end this history" (p. 207). The reader is reminded that the story does not end by itself; the writer ends it. Control and consciousness were keywords for Quatermain as an author—and quite possibly for Haggard as well.

Haggard's protagonist Quatermain describes himself as a 55-year-old man who has survived the job of elephant hunter much longer than most of his colleagues. Quatermain explains at the start of his tale, "I am a timid man, and don't like violence," (p. 9) and near the end, after many heroics, he reiterates, "I never had any great pretensions to be brave" (p. 188). Such self-definitions are repeated throughout the book until the narrative itself begins to seem like a means of self-definition. The effort to write, as well as the events narrated, define the narrator.

There may not be much progression of character in *King Solomon's Mines*, but Quatermain rings true precisely because of his lack of grandiose pretensions. Quatermain's self-deflating tone may include something of Haggard's own ironic self-regard. When Haggard traveled to Africa in 1914 and his photo was plastered on the local newspaper *Natal Witness*, Haggard noted in his diary that his image looked "exactly like that of the mummy of Rameses the Second," a recently disinterred Pharaoh. This lack of vanity or vaingloriousness is unusual in a generation of writers on Africa that included such egomaniacs as Sir Richard Burton, translator of *The Arabian Nights*.

At the start of chapter 1, Quatermain informs us: "I am not a literary man, though very devoted to the Old Testament and also to the 'Ingoldsby Legends'" (p. 9); the latter is an early Victorian compilation of odd and grotesque jokes in prose and verse by Richard Harris Barham (1788–1845). Mention of *The Ingoldsby Legends* is a running gag throughout the *King Solomon's Mines*. Quatermain misattributes lines from Walter Scott to "Ingoldsby" in a jape that resulted in a chiding letter from Robert Louis Stevenson, who thought the error was Haggard's own, rather than his protagonist Quatermain's. Reflecting its narrator's literary tastes, *King Solomon's Mines* veers in tone between the Victorian jokes of *The Ingoldsby Legends* and the sober majesty of the Old Testament. As the story advances, the Bible and *The Ingoldsby Legends* are repeatedly invoked until they are yoked together in an unlikely identification. During one potentially tragic moment in chapter 6 when Quatermain and his friends are dying of thirst, the narrator decides to read the poem "The Jackdaw of Rheims" from *The Ingoldsby Legends* (p. 59). Later, at the height of battle, Quatermain states: "Warlike fragments from the 'Ingoldsby Legends,' together with numbers of sanguinary verses from the Old Testament, sprang up in my brain like mushrooms in the dark" (p. 148). The disparate texts join as inspiration for the bloodbath to come.

The influence of the Bible on *King Solomon's Mines* can hardly be overstated, starting with the title itself, which honors a biblical monarch renowned both for his wisdom and his wealth. Aside from many explicit references, there are also many biblical allusions, such as when Sir Henry Curtis convinces Quatermain to join the expedition to Africa. Curtis explains that the company will search for his lost brother Neville: "We had quarrelled bitterly, and I behaved very unjustly to my brother in my anger" (p.16). This description echoes the prose cadences of the King James Bible; the fratricidal story of Cain and Abel from the Bible is surely not far behind. This richness of reference is part of the lasting fascination of *King Solomon's Mines*.

When the travelers arrive at the Hall of the Dead to discover the beheaded, mummified corpse of a Zulu king, Quatermain likens this horrific image to Hamilton Tighe, a beheaded sailor who in *The Ingoldsby Legends* appears carrying his own head (p. 176).

Racism and Sexism

The depiction of Africans in *King Solomon's Mines* has rightly attracted much condemnation in recent years. At the start of the book, Quatermain announces that he doesn't like calling natives by the term that today has become known as "the n-word" and yet he abundantly uses another term, *kafir*, which in South Africa is hardly less offensive (p. 11). The villainous king Twala is introduced as having "the most entirely repulsive countenance we had ever beheld. The lips were as thick as a negro's, the nose was flat, it had but one gleaming black eye . . . and its whole expression was cruel and sensual to a degree" (p. 96).

It is true that Quatermain says some Africans are gentlemen, while some "mean whites with lots of money" are not (p. 10). Still, the book contains some mean-spirited jokes against Africans, such as when some natives sample champagne belonging to their employers and Quatermain tells them that it is medicine and they are "as good as dead men. They went on to the shore in a very great fright, and I do not think that they will touch champagne again" (p. 27). Presumably this joke was intended as punishment for stealing champagne, but it seems unjustified all the same.

Africans are also the subject of some bluff, gross-out humor, such as the gratuitous account of a native whose toe amputation "was a pleasure to see," followed by the "Kafir" asking after the operation for a white toe to be attached in place of the missing one (p. 33). Perhaps the most low-minded instance of racism in the book occurs when Umbopa, eventually revealed as exiled royalty whose real name is Ignosi, states that "black people" do not "hold life so high as [whites]" (p. 118). By having an African say this, Haggard lends extra authority to this dehumanizing notion. Similarly, the native maiden Foulata declares herself opposed to miscegenation: " 'Can the sun mate with the darkness, or the white with the black?' " (p. 197). Putting racist sentiments in the mouths of African characters is a particularly insidious form of racist discourse.

Yet the nobility of Umbopa/Ignosi as depicted in *King Solomon's Mines* is undeniable. Haggard does not have a uniformly low opinion of Africans, at least not much lower than his view of humanity in general. Elephants stampeding during a hunt are described as pushing one another "in their selfish panic, just like so many human beings" (p. 44). Haggard is suggesting that animals at their worst can be as bestial as humans. Africans who are spared the impediments of modern Western culture might be noble, but they can sometimes reveal character flaws as bad as Western man's.

Similarly, Quatermain's translations of what certain Africans say in the narrative reflect his view of Africa and Africans. Umpoba speaks of the mountains leading to the treasure as "a strange land there, a land of witchcraft and beautiful things; a land of brave people, and of trees, and streams, and white mountains, and of a great white road" (p. 50). The noble Umbopa's prose cadences seem to prefigure the style of Ernest Hemingway. Yet elsewhere the ancient, evil African crone Gagaoola intones: "*Blood! blood! blood! rivers of blood; blood everywhere . . . Footsteps! footsteps! footsteps!* the tread of the white man coming from afar" (p. 100). The thrice-repeated rhythmic incantations are comparable to the Civil War tune, "Tramp! Tramp! Tramp! The boys are marching," by George Frederick Root (1820–1895), as well as ballads by Haggard's friend Rudyard Kipling, like "Gunga Din": "It was 'Din! Din! Din! / 'Ere's a beggar with a bullet through 'is spleen.'"

Haggard applies European history—and not just English prosody—to Africa by having Captain Good, a friend of Sir Henry Curtis, refer to the murderous King Twala as "just like a black Madame Defarge" (p. 110). The French Revolutionary character Madame Defarge in Charles Dickens' *A Tale of Two Cities* (1859) is ferociously vengeful and knits the names of her intended victims. Yet in *King Solomon's Mines* Quatermain and his party, not Africa and King Twala, are, in their plot to overthrow a cruel king, the real revolutionary participants. This curiously layered simile is typical of the complexity and contradictions of *King Solomon's Mines.*

Women too are treated roughly in *King Solomon's Mines.* Quatermain informs the reader almost casually that "women bring trouble as surely as the night follows the day" (p. 119). Shortly after this misogynistic statement, murder is described as a kind of symbolic rape, when the young maiden Foulata is threatened with ritual execution by a leering aggressor who taps his spear and cries, "She shrinks from the sight of my little plaything even before she has tasted it" (p. 121).

King Solomon's Mines reflects an awareness of what may be called the Eros of otherness. In a running gag repeated *ad nauseum*, Captain Good's bare white legs are the objects of admiration for Africans who "satisfy their æsthetic longings" (p. 127) by staring at them, as Quatermain puts it with heavy ironic humor. Descriptions of Kukuana women fall into racial stereotypes: "the lips are not unpleasantly thick as is the case in most African races" (p. 88). Umbopa is described as a "tall, handsome-looking man, somewhere about thirty years of age, and very light-coloured for a Zulu" (p. 35). Haggard accepts the racist notion that lighter skin is handsomer than dark, and Africans are most beautiful when they look less African and more European in appearance.

Even beautiful Africans are not described in any great admiring detail. Umbopa gets only a passing reference about a period of famine during which he wore "a leather belt strapped so tight round his stomach . . . that his waist looked like a girl's" (p. 67). This mild observation scarcely has the erotic charge of the words describing a dead athlete who wears a "garland briefer than a girl's" in A. E. Housman's "To An Athlete Dying Young," in his classic 1896 collection *A Shropshire Lad*. Some critics have written about homoerotic aspects of *King Solomon's Mines*, but in truth they are difficult to find.

Still, the descriptions of sexuality in *King Solomon's Mines* have attracted much critical comment. One critic even noted that H. Rider Haggard and Sigmund Freud were born in the same year, 1856. Thus, when Haggard is described by other critics as "pre-Freudian," this is not strictly true. Extra-Freudian or Super-Freudian might be a more apt term, as Haggard's directness in sexual matters almost makes Freudian interpretation seem obsolete.

Instead of being buried in the unconscious, sexuality is right on the surface in Haggard's world, as in the map leading to King Solomon's Mines, which names mountains known as Sheba's Breasts that are on the way to the treasure (p. 22). An accompanying text supposedly written in 1590 by the Portuguese adventurer José da Silvestra when he was "dying of hunger," also refers to "the north side of the nipple of the southernmost of the two mountains I have named Sheba's Breasts" (p. 23). Da Silvestra adds that any future treasure seeker must "climb the snow of Sheba's left breast till he comes to the nipple" (p. 23). In Victorian England, where in sitting rooms, piano legs were prudishly covered by rugs and referred to coyly as "limbs," this frank description of female body parts must have been powerful. The impact must have been something close to the impact on later generations of nude photographs of African women in *National Geographic* magazines. Elizabeth Bishop's poem "In the Waiting Room" describes a young girl sitting in a dentist's office circa 1918, waiting for her Aunt, who is being treated. She looks at the photographs in a *National Geographic* magazine: "black, naked women with necks / wound round and round with wire / like the necks of light bulbs. / Their breasts were horrifying." Likewise, Haggard's young readers, boys and girls both, were confronted by unexpected references to the unadorned female body in *King Solomon's Mines*.

Critical Reaction

King Solomon's Mines was an impressive popular success, with more than 30,000 copies sold in Britain in its first year of publication, 1885. Among its enthusiastic readers were the future American president Theodore Roosevelt (1858–1919), Britain's prime minister William Ewart Gladstone (1809–1898), and a precocious English eleven-year-old, Winston Churchill (1874–1965). *King Solomon's Mines* also received generally glowing reviews. The poet and scholar Andrew Lang (1844–1912) in the *Saturday Review* praised Haggard's "very remarkable and uncommon powers of invention and the gift of 'vision.'" Lang separated Haggard from the "hack book-makers for boys" who wrote books based on other books they had read, instead of real-life experience. However, the London *Church Quarterly Review* dissented, complaining about the narrative, which "trembles on the verge of sensuality" and contains "indiscriminate and individual slaughter, whole corpses and dismembered limbs, skulls and bones, duels and suicide, torture and treachery, witchcraft and madness."

Some reviews of the American edition of the book, which appeared in 1886, were even more equivocal. *The Dial*, while appreciating the excitement of the tale, complained about the "crudeness of many of Mr. Haggard's sentences." A Boston publication, *Literary World*, even made a punning reference to the novelist's name: "The book reeks with brutality and suffering, and enough to make the reader as haggard as its author." Affectionate joshing and parodies by Haggard's friends and readers appeared as a sign of the book's striking novelty. The minor nineteenth-century poet James Kenneth Stephen (1859–1892) penned "To R. K." some humorous doggerel that was published in the *Cambridge Review* and later collected in his *Lapsus Calami* (Cambridge: Macmillan and Bowes, 1891):

> When mankind shall be delivered
> From the clash of magazines,
> And the inkstand shall be shivered
> Into countless smithereens:
> When there stands a muzzled stripling,
> Mute, beside a muzzled bore:
> When the Rudyards cease from kipling
> And the Haggards Ride no more.

Rudyard Kipling himself, a friend to both Haggard and Andrew Lang, also penned a humorous verse in 1889 in homage to them. As reprinted in *The Letters of Rudyard Kipling* (Vol. 1, *1872–1889*, Iowa City: University of Iowa Press, 1990), Kipling's verse, written in the style of the American western author Bret Harte (1836–1902), conjured up the notion of a lecture tour that Haggard and Lang might one day make to the United States:

> I reside at Table Mountain and my name is Truthful James
> I am not versed in lecturin' or other sinful games.
> You will please refrain from shooting while my simple lyre I twang
> To the tale of Mister Haggard and his partner Mister Lang. . . .
> In the ears of Mister Haggard whom they hailed as Mister Lang
> The societies of Boston ethnologically sang
> And they spoke of creature-legends, and of totem, myth, and sign
> And the stricter laws of Metre — Mister Haggard answered '*Nein.*'

Sir Henry Chartres Biron (1863–1940) wrote a more ambitious, book-length parody, *King Solomon's Wives; or, The Phantom Mines*, under the pseudonym Hyder Ragged (London: Vizetelly and Company, 1887). The Hyder Ragged parody describes a trip across a desert and an encounter with King Twosh. *King Solomon's Treasures*, John De Morgan's American parody, also appeared in 1887 (New York: N. L. Munro). These and other parodies were reprinted in *King Solomon's Children* (New York: Arno Press, 1978). Their existence is evidence of the strong and immediate impact of *King Solomon's Mines* on readers on two continents and beyond.

After King Solomon's Mines

Haggard quickly found himself a genuine literary celebrity after the success of *King Solomon's Mines*. He hobnobbed with other literary personalities in London, attending tea parties and dinners at the home of the English poet, author, and critic Sir Edmund William Gosse (1849–1928). A preserved guest book attests that at one such gathering, Haggard rubbed elbows with such literary immortals as Thomas Hardy, Henry James, Walter Pater, and Robert Bridges. At another event at the Gosse home, Haggard was a guest alongside Sir

Max Beerbohm, Aubrey Beardsley, and the painter Sir Lawrence Alma-Tadema.

Haggard did not permit his renown to interfere with his productivity, and he churned out a series of bestsellers. A partial list of novels he subsequently published includes *She* (1887), *Jess* (1887), *Allan Quatermain* (1887), *A Tale of Three Lions* (1887), *Mr. Meeson's Will* (1888), *Maiwa's Revenge* (1888), *My Fellow Labourer and the Wreck of the Copeland* (1888), *Colonel Quaritch, V.C.* (1888), *Allan's Wife* (1889), *Beatrice* (1890), *Eric Brighteyes* (1891), *Nada the Lily* (1892), *Montezuma's Daughter* (1893), *The People of the Mist* (1894), *Joan Haste* (1895), *Heart of the World* (1895), *The Wizard* (1896), *Doctor Therne* (1898), *The Spring of Lion* (1899), *Lysbeth* (1901), *Pearl-Maiden* (1903), *Stella Fregelius* (1904), *Ayesha: The Return of She* (1905), *Benita: An African Romance* (1906), *Fair Margaret* (1907), *The Ghost Kings* (1908), *The Yellow God* (1909), *The Lady of Blossholme* (1909), and *Queen Sheba's Ring* (1909).

Despite his continued activity, Haggard's latter years were not joyful. His nine-year-old son Jock died in 1891, and Haggard's ensuing depression led to permanent respiratory and digestive problems. In his memoir *The Days of My Life* Haggard admitted that his best novels were "among the first dozen or so" he wrote between *King Solomon's Mines* and *Montezuma's Daughter*. Haggard ascribes a falling off in quality of his output to the shock of his son's death and his own subsequent bad health: "Although from necessity I went on with the writing of stories, and do so still, it has not been with the same zest. Active rather than imaginative life has appealed to me more."

Part of this active life was a careful study of farming conditions in Britain, which resulted in books like *A Farmer's Year* (1899) and *Rural England* (1902), as mentioned earlier. In 1902 Haggard was asked to become a commissioner for the British government and report on agricultural labor colonies that had been established in the United States. On his return from America and Canada, he began to concentrate on such agricultural issues as soil erosion. He experimented successfully on his own estate, Kessingland Grange, situated beside the North Sea. Joining the Royal Commission on Coast Erosion and Afforestation, he was also active in helping the Salvation Army and its founder, General William Booth (1829–1912). Bad health after 1909 slowed him down, despite the honor of a knighthood, bestowed in 1912 for services to the British Empire, rather than for literary achievement. A sense of duty made Haggard accept membership on a six-person Royal Commission to visit the various dominions of the British Empire. Starting in 1912, this commission's activities necessitated trips to Australia and Africa during which Haggard energetically gathered material for future books. As Haggard's biographer Morton Cohen aptly puts it, "His holidays were inspection tours of the world."

No sooner had Haggard returned to England than he leapt into action to support England's entry into World War I in 1914. During the war, he would travel again to South Africa, Australia, New Zealand, and Canada. By the war's end his chronic bronchitis had developed into emphysema. By the mid-1920s he was fighting what he called in a diary entry "a losing battle with pain, weakness, and depression." Operated on for an abscess, he did not recover, and he died on May 14, 1925. His grave is in Ditchingham, a small town in Norfolk, England, where he has been honored with a street named after him, Rider Haggard Way. In St. Mary's Church, Ditchingham, a stained-glass window that pays tribute to Haggard includes images of his farm in South Africa and of the Egyptian pyramids. Carved in marble, above a vault containing his remains, are the words:

> Here lie the ashes of Henry Rider Haggard
> Knight Bachelor
> Knight of the British Empire
> Who with a Humble Heart Strove to Serve his Country.

Later generations of readers have retained their affection for the author of *King Solomon's Mines*. In *The Lost Childhood and Other Essays* (London: Eyre and Spottiswoode, 1951), the noted British novelist Graham Greene (1904–1991) praises the "poetic elements" of Haggard's books, which according to Greene "live today with undiminished vitality." The great British critic and literary historian George Saintsbury (1845–1933) ranked *King Solomon's Mines* alongside *Treasure Island* and stated he wished he had written "the fight between Twala and Sir Henry." Other adventure writers from Haggard's era, including A. E. W. Mason, Stanley Mason, Anthony Hope-Hawkins, and H. B. Marriott-Watson are in the oubliettes of literary history, whereas Haggard's best books have remained in print continuously since they first appeared.

King Solomon's Mines has been translated into African languages (among its dozens of foreign editions). Its Portuguese translation was done by the eminent novelist and short-story writer José Maria Eça de Queirós (1845–1900). Eça de Queirós was no slouch—Émile Zola called him "greater than Flaubert"—and by translating Haggard into Portuguese in 1891 (as *As Minas de Salomão*), he added to the European prestige of the book. Perhaps most curiously, *King Solomon's Mines* has been abridged and edited for wide use not just as a text for learning English as a foreign language in Africa, China, and elsewhere, but also for young readers.

Authors as diverse as C. S. Lewis, D. H. Lawrence, and Gilbert Murray fell under the spell of Haggard's adventure stories. Today, the British writer John Mortimer continues to pay wry tribute to Haggard in the popular series of mystery stories featuring a British barrister, Rumpole of the Bailey. The aging Rumpole refers to his daunting wife with affectionate irony as "She Who Must Be Obeyed," a takeoff of Haggard's *She* novels. Despite the unamusing ways in which parts of Haggard's books have dated, most readers still feel affection for *King Solomon's Mines* and *She*.

Targets of Loathing

Haggard did not single out Africans for despising, according to the informative *Rider Haggard and the Fiction of Empire*, by Wendy R. Katz. His other novels and private writings also express disdain for "Jews, communists, trade unionists, Irish, Quebecois, and Indian nationalists." Jews and Communists, according to Katz, were the special targets of Haggard's loathing, far more than any other category of people, and as he aged, the intensity of his hatred increased. Although not present in *King Solomon's Mines*, Jews are portrayed unattractively in *She, The World's Desire, The People of the Mist,* and others among Haggard's novels. In later private writings, Haggard blamed the Russian Revolution on Jews, and after the Romanov family was killed by the revolutionary forces, Haggard noted with extreme bigotry in his diary for 1920: "The tendency of the Jew to torture before he kills is a curious indication of his character which apparently has not varied since the days of Pontius Pilate" (Katz, p. 150). Katz concludes that Haggard was "an imperial propagandist, a man who made use of every opportunity to advance matters relating to Empire. . . . Through his fiction, the ideas and attitudes that accrue to imperialism were conveyed almost effortlessly to the largely uncritical and accepting reader. . . . His fiction, only superficially innocuous, contributed generously to the process of shaping the imperial mentality" (p. 153).

One of the advantages of historical hindsight is that we may read *King Solomon's Mines* today as a period piece, with a conscious awareness of its imperialist messages. No matter how much Haggard may seem to be a critic of Victorian society, in many ways *King Solomon's Mines* at its most sincere reinforces the deepest beliefs of its day. Thus, when Sir Henry offers to Umbopa a cherished credo without a trace of irony and it is wholly accepted by the noble African, the words seem to come from Haggard's own heart:

> "But there is no journey upon this earth that a man may not make if he sets his heart to it. There is nothing, Umbopa, that he cannot do, there are no mountains he may not climb, there are no deserts he cannot cross . . . if love leads him and he holds his life in his hand counting it as nothing, ready to keep it or to lose it as Providence may order" (p. 49).

In this declaration, Haggard is close to Baden-Powell's exhortations in his scouting guide, as well as literary friends like the poet William Ernest Henley (1849–1903). Henley's most famous poem, "Invictus" (written in 1875), is a forthright assertion of Victorian self-possession: "It matters not how strait the gate, / How charged with punishments the scroll, / I am the master of my fate: / I am the captain of my soul."

Unlike the reader of 1885, we do not need to accept the underlying political, social, gender, and racial theories of *King Solomon's Mines* as self-evident. Bolstered with recent publications by such excellent researchers as Stephen Coan, Gerald Monsman, and James Danly, among others (see "For Further Reading"), we may appreciate what is still effective and exciting in Haggard's book, while discarding what is obsolete, or even potentially perilous.

Benjamin Ivry is the author of biographies of Arthur Rimbaud (Absolute Press), Francis Poulenc (Phaidon), and Maurice Ravel (Welcome Rain Publishers). His poetry collection *Paradise for the Portuguese Queen* (Orehises) appeared in 1998. He has also translated many books from the French by such authors as André Gide, Jules Verne, and Balthus.

King Solomon's Mines

Contents

Introduction

NOW THAT THIS BOOK is printed, and about to be given to the world, the sense of its shortcomings, both in style and contents, weighs very heavily upon me. As regards the latter, I can only say that it does not pretend to be a full account of everything we did and saw. There are many things connected with our journey into Kukuanaland[1] which I should have liked to dwell upon at length, and which have, as it is, been scarcely alluded to. Amongst these are the curious legends which I collected about the chain armour that saved us from destruction in the great battle of Loo, and also about the "silent ones" or colossi at the mouth of the stalactite cave. Again, if I had given way to my own impulses, I should have liked to go into the differences, some of which are to my mind very suggestive, between the Zulu and Kukuana dialects. Also a few pages might profitably have been given up to the consideration of the indigenous flora and fauna of Kukuanaland.* Then there remains the most interesting subject—that, as it is, has only been incidentally alluded to—of the magnificent system of military organisation in force in that country, which is, in my opinion, much superior to that inaugurated by Chaka[2] in Zululand, inasmuch as it permits of even more rapid mobilisation, and does not necessitate the employment of the pernicious system of forced celibacy. And, lastly, I have scarcely touched on the domestic and family customs of the Kukuanas, many of which are exceedingly quaint, or on their proficiency in the art of smelting and welding metals. This last they carry to considerable perfection, of which a good example is to be seen in their "tollas," or heavy throwing knives, the backs of these knives being made of hammered iron, and the edges of beautiful steel welded with great skill on to the iron backs. The fact of the matter is, that I thought (and so did Sir Henry Curtis and Captain Good) that the best plan

---

*I discovered eight varieties of antelope, with which I was previously totally unacquainted, and many new species of plants, for the most part of the bulbous tribe.—A.Q. [Haggard's note]

would be to tell the story in a plain, straightforward manner, and leave these matters to be dealt with subsequently in whatever way may ultimately appear to be desirable. In the meanwhile I shall, of course, be delighted to give any information in my power to anybody interested in such things.

And now it only remains for me to offer my apologies for my blunt way of writing. I can only say in excuse for it that I am more accustomed to handle a rifle than a pen, and cannot make any pretence to the grand literary flights and flourishes which I see in novels—for I sometimes like to read a novel. I suppose they—the flights and flourishes—are desirable, and I regret not being able to supply them; but at the same time I cannot help thinking that simple things are always the most impressive, and books are easier to understand when they are written in plain language, though I have perhaps no right to set up an opinion on such a matter. "A sharp spear," runs the Kukuana saying, "needs no polish;" and on the same principle I venture to hope that a true story, however strange it may be, does not require to be decked out in fine words.

ALLAN QUATERMAIN.

Chapter 1

I Meet Sir Henry Curtis

IT IS A CURIOUS thing that at my age—fifty-five last birthday—I should find myself taking up a pen to try and write a history. I wonder what sort of a history it will be when I have done it, if I ever come to the end of the trip! I have done a good many things in my life, which seems a long one to me, owing to my having begun so young, perhaps. At an age when other boys are at school, I was earning my living as a trader in the old Colony.[1] I have been trading, hunting, fighting, or mining ever since. And yet it is only eight months ago that I made my pile. It is a big pile now I have got it—I don't yet know how big—but I don't think I would go through the last fifteen or sixteen months again for it; no, not if I knew that I should come out safe at the end, pile and all. But then I am a timid man, and don't like violence, and am pretty sick of adventure. I wonder why I am going to write this book: it is not in my line. I am not a literary man, though very devoted to the Old Testament and also to the "Ingoldsby Legends."[2] Let me try and set down my reasons, just to see if I have any.

First reason: Because Sir Henry Curtis and Captain John Good asked me to.

Second reason: Because I am laid up here at Durban with the pain and trouble in my left leg. Ever since that confounded lion got hold of me I have been liable to it, and its being rather bad just now makes me limp more than ever. There must be some poison in a lion's teeth, otherwise how is it that when your wounds are healed they break out again, generally, mark you, at the same time of year that you got your mauling? It is a hard thing that when one has shot sixty-five lions as I have in the course of my life, that the sixty-sixth should chew your leg like a quid of tobacco. It breaks the routine of the thing, and putting other considerations aside, I am an orderly man and don't like that. This is by the way.

Third reason: Because I want my boy Harry, who is over there at the hospital in London studying to become a doctor, to have something to amuse him and keep him out of mischief for a week or so. Hospital work must sometimes pall and get rather dull, for even of cutting up dead bodies there must come satiety, and as this history won't be dull, whatever else it may be, it may put a little life into things for a day or two while he is reading it.

Fourth reason and last: Because I am going to tell the strangest story that I know of. It may seem a queer thing to say that, especially considering that there is no woman in it—except Foulata. Stop, though! there is Gagaoola, if she was a woman and not a fiend. But she was a hundred at least, and therefore not marriageable, so I don't count her. At any rate, I can safely say that there is not a *petticoat* in the whole history. Well I had better come to the yoke. It's a stiff place, and I feel as though I were bogged up to the axle. But "sutjes, sutjes,"* as the Boers say (I'm sure I don't know how they spell it), softly does it. A strong team will come through at last, that is if they ain't too poor. You will never do anything with poor oxen. Now to begin.

I, Allan Quatermain, of Durban, Natal, Gentleman, make oath and say—That's how I began my deposition before the magistrate, about poor Khiva's and Ventvögel's sad deaths;[3] but somehow it doesn't seem quite the right way to begin a book. And, besides, am I a gentleman? What is a gentleman? I don't quite know, and yet I have had to do with niggers—no, I'll scratch that word "niggers" out, for I don't like it. I've known natives who *are*, and so you'll say, Harry, my boy, before you're done with this tale, and I have known mean whites with lots of money and fresh out from home, too, who *ain't*. Well, at any rate, I was born a gentleman, though I've been nothing but a poor travelling trader and hunter all my life. Whether I have remained so I know not, you must judge of that. Heaven knows I've tried. I've killed many men in my time, but I have never slain wantonly or stained my hand in innocent blood, only in self-defence. The Almighty gave us our lives, and I suppose he meant us to defend them, at least I have always acted on that, and I hope it won't be brought up against me when my clock strikes. There, there, it is a cruel and a wicked world, and for a timid man I have been mixed up

---

*Or *suetjies*; softly, gently, slowly (Afrikaans).

in a deal of slaughter. I can't tell the rights of it, but at any rate I have never stolen, though I once cheated a Kafir* out of a herd of cattle. But then he had done me a dirty turn, and it has troubled me ever since into the bargain.

Well it's eighteen months or so ago since I first met Sir Henry Curtis and Captain Good, and it was in this way. I had been up elephant hunting beyond Bamangwato,[4] and had had bad luck. Everything went wrong that trip, and to top up with I got the fever badly. So soon as I was well enough I trekked down to the Diamond Fields,[5] sold such ivory as I had, and also my waggon and oxen, discharged my hunters, and took the post-cart to the Cape. After spending a week in Cape Town, finding that they overcharged me at the hotel, and having seen everything there was to see, including the botanical gardens, which seem to me likely to confer a great benefit on the country, and the new Houses of Parliament, which I expect will do nothing of the sort, I determined to go on back to Natal by the *Dunkeld*, then lying in the docks waiting for the *Edinburgh Castle* due in from England. I took my berth and went aboard, and that afternoon the Natal passengers from the *Edinburgh Castle* transhipped, and we weighed and put out to sea.

Among the passengers who came on board there were two who excited my curiosity. One, a man of about thirty, was one of the biggest-chested and longest-armed men I ever saw. He had yellow hair, a big yellow beard, clear-cut features, and large grey eyes set deep into his head. I never saw a finer-looking man, and somehow he reminded me of an ancient Dane. Not that I know much of ancient Danes, though I remember a modern Dane who did me out of ten pounds; but I remember once seeing a picture of some of those gentry, who, I take it, were a kind of white Zulus. They were drinking out of big horns, and their long hair hung down their backs, and as I looked at my friend standing there by the companion-ladder, I thought that if one only let his hair grow a bit, put one of those chain shirts on to those great shoulders of his, and gave him a big battle-axe and a horn mug, he might have sat as a model for that picture. And by the way it is a curious thing, and just shows how the blood will show out, I found out afterwards that Sir Henry Curtis,

---

*Also spelled *kaffir*; derogatory South African term for a black person.

for that was the big man's name, was of Danish blood.* He also reminded me strongly of somebody else, but at the time I could not
remember who it was.

The other man who stood talking to Sir Henry was short, stout,
and dark, and of quite a different cut. I suspected at once that he was
a naval officer. I don't know why, but it is difficult to mistake a navy
man. I have gone on shooting trips with several of them in the
course of my life, and they have always been just the best and bravest
and nicest fellows I ever met, though given to the use of profane language.

I asked a page or two back, what is a gentleman? I'll answer it
now: a Royal Naval officer is, in a general sort of a way, though, of
course, there may be a black sheep among them here and there. I
fancy it is just the wide sea and the breath of God's winds that
washes their hearts and blows the bitterness out of their minds and
makes them what men ought to be. Well, to return, I was right again;
I found out that he *was* a naval officer, a lieutenant of thirty-one,
who, after seventeen years' service, had been turned out of her
Majesty's employ with the barren honour of a commander's rank,
because it was impossible that he should be promoted. That is what
people who serve the Queen have to expect: to be shot out into the
cold world to find a living just when they are beginning to really understand their work, and to get to the prime of life. Well, I suppose
they don't mind it, but for my part I had rather earn my bread as a
hunter. One's halfpence are as scarce perhaps, but you don't get so
many kicks. His name I found out—by referring to the passengers'
list—was Good—Captain John Good. He was broad, of medium
height, dark, stout, and rather a curious man to look at. He was so
very neat and so very clean shaved, and he always wore an eye-glass
in his right eye. It seemed to grow there, for it had no string, and he
never took it out except to wipe it. At first I thought he used to sleep
in it, but I afterwards found that this was a mistake. He put it in his
trousers pocket when he went to bed, together with his false teeth, of
which he had two beautiful sets that have often, my own being none

---

*Mr. Quatermain's ideas about ancient Danes seem to be rather confused; we have
always understood that they were dark-haired people. Probably he was thinking of
Saxons.—*Editor*. [Haggard's note]

of the best, caused me to break the tenth commandment.[6] But I am anticipating.

Soon after we had got underway evening closed in, and brought with it very dirty weather. A keen breeze sprang up off land, and a kind of aggravated Scotch mist soon drove everybody from the deck. And as for that *Dunkeld*, she is a flat-bottomed punt, and going up light as she was, she rolled very heavily. It almost seemed as though she would go right over, but she never did. It was quite impossible to walk about, so I stood near the engines where it was warm, and amused myself with watching the pendulum,* which was fixed opposite to me, swinging slowly backwards and forwards as the vessel rolled, and marking the angle she touched at each lurch.

"That pendulum's wrong; it is not properly weighted," suddenly said a voice at my shoulder, somewhat testily. Looking round I saw the naval officer I had noticed when the passengers came aboard.

"Indeed, now what makes you think so?" I asked.

"Think so. I don't think at all. Why there"—as she righted herself after a roll—"if the ship had really rolled to the degree that thing pointed to then she would never have rolled again, that's all. But it is just like these merchant skippers, they always are so confoundedly careless."

Just then the dinner-bell rang, and I was not sorry, for it is a dreadful thing to have to listen to an officer of the Royal Navy when he gets on to that subject. I only know one worse thing, and that is to hear a merchant skipper express his candid opinion of officers of the Royal Navy.

Captain Good and I went down to dinner together, and there we found Sir Henry Curtis already seated. He and Captain Good sat together, and I sat opposite to them. The captain and I soon got into talk about shooting and what not; he asking me many questions, and I answering as well as I could. Presently he got on to elephants.

"Ah, sir," called out somebody who was sitting near me, "you've got to the right man for that; Hunter Quatermain should be able to tell you about elephants if anybody can."

---

*A chronometer, a device invented by British scientist John Harrison (1693–1776) to measure longitude when ships are at sea.

Sir Henry, who had been sitting quite quiet listening to our talk, started visibly.

"Excuse me, sir," he said, leaning forward across the table, and speaking in a low, deep voice, a very suitable voice it seemed to me, to come out of those great lungs. "Excuse me, sir, but is your name Allan Quatermain?"

I said it was.

The big man made no further remark, but I heard him mutter "fortunate" into his beard.

Presently dinner came to an end, and as we were leaving the saloon Sir Henry came up and asked me if I would come into his cabin and smoke a pipe. I accepted, and he led the way to the *Dunkeld* deck cabin, and a very good cabin it was. It had been two cabins, but when Sir Garnet[7] or one of those big swells went down the coast in the *Dunkeld*, they had knocked away the partition and never put it up again. There was a sofa in the cabin, and a little table in front of it. Sir Henry sent the steward for a bottle of whisky, and the three of us sat down and lit our pipes.

"Mr. Quatermain," said Sir Henry Curtis, when the steward had brought the whisky and lit the lamp, "the year before last about this time you were, I believe, at a place called Bamangwato, to the north of the Transvaal."

"I was," I answered, rather surprised that this gentleman should be so well acquainted with my movements, which were not, so far as I was aware, considered of general interest.

"You were trading there, were you not?" put in Captain Good, in his quick way.

"I was. I took up a wagon load of goods, and made a camp outside the settlement, and stopped till I had sold them."

Sir Henry was sitting opposite to me in a Madeira chair,[8] his arms leaning on the table. He now looked up, fixing his large grey eyes full upon my face. There was a curious anxiety in them I thought.

"Did you happen to meet a man called Neville there?"

"Oh, yes; he outspanned* alongside of me for a fortnight to rest his oxen before going on to the interior. I had a letter from a lawyer

---

*Unyoked or disengaged oxen from a wagon.

a few months back asking me if I knew what had become of him, which I answered to the best of my ability at the time."

"Yes," said Sir Henry, "your letter was forwarded to me. You said in it that the gentleman called Neville left Bamangwato in the beginning of May in a waggon with a driver, a voorlooper,* and a Kafir hunter called Jim, announcing his intention of trekking if possible as far as Inyati,[9] the extreme trading post in the Matabele country, where he would sell his wagon and proceed on foot. You also said that he did sell his waggon, for six months afterwards you saw the waggon in the possession of a Portuguese trader, who told you that he had bought it at Inyati from a white man whose name he had forgotten, and that the white man with a native servant had started off for the interior on a shooting trip, he believed."

"Yes."

Then came a pause.

"Mr. Quatermain," said Sir Henry, suddenly, "I suppose you know or can guess nothing more of the reasons of my—of Mr. Neville's journey to the northward, or as to what point that journey was directed?"

"I heard something," I answered, and stopped. The subject was one which I did not care to discuss.

Sir Henry and Captain Good looked at each other, and Captain Good nodded.

"Mr. Quatermain," said the former, "I am going to tell you a story, and ask your advice, and perhaps your assistance. The agent who forwarded me your letter told me that I might implicitly rely upon it, as you were," he said, "well known and universally respected in Natal, and especially noted for your discretion."

I bowed and drank some whisky and water to hide my confusion, for I am a modest man—and Sir Henry went on.

"Mr. Neville was my brother."

"Oh," I said, starting, for now I knew who Sir Henry had reminded me of when I first saw him. His brother was a much smaller man and had a dark beard, but now I thought of it, he possessed eyes

---

*Boy who leads the front oxen of a herd (Afrikaans).

of the same shade of grey and with the same keen look in them, and the features too were not unlike.

"He was," went on Sir Henry, "my only and younger brother, and till five years ago I do not suppose we were ever a month away from each other. But just about five years ago a misfortune befell us, as sometimes does happen in families. We had quarrelled bitterly, and I behaved very unjustly to my brother in my anger." Here Captain Good nodded his head vigorously to himself. The ship gave a big roll just then, so that the looking-glass, which was fixed opposite us to starboard, was for a moment nearly over our heads, and as I was sitting with my hands in my pockets and staring upwards, I could see him nodding like anything.

"As I daresay you know," went on Sir Henry, "if a man dies intestate, and has no property but land, real property it is called in England, it all descends to his eldest son. It so happened that just at the time when we quarrelled our father died intestate. He had put off making his will until it was too late. The result was that my brother, who had not been brought up to any profession, was left without a penny. Of course it would have been my duty to provide for him, but at the time the quarrel between us was so bitter that I did not—to my shame I say it (and he sighed deeply) offer to do anything. It was not that I grudged him anything, but I waited for him to make advances, and he made none. I am sorry to trouble you with all this, Mr. Quatermain, but I must to make things clear, eh, Good?"

"Quite so, quite so," said the captain. "Mr. Quatermain will, I am sure, keep this history to himself."

"Of course," said I, for I rather pride myself on my discretion.

"Well," went on Sir Henry, "my brother had a few hundred pounds to his account at the time, and without saying anything to me he drew out this paltry sum, and, having adopted the name of Neville, started off for South Africa in the wild hope of making a fortune. This I heard afterwards. Some three years passed, and I heard nothing of my brother, though I wrote several times. Doubtless the letters never reached him. But as time went on I grew more and more troubled about him. I found out, Mr. Quatermain, that blood is thicker than water."

"That's true," said I, thinking of my boy Harry.

"I found out, Mr. Quatermain, that I would have given half my fortune to know that my brother George, the only relation I have, was safe and well, and that I should see him again."

"But you never did, Curtis," jerked out Captain Good, glancing at the big man's face.

"Well, Mr. Quatermain, as time went on, I became more and more anxious to find out if my brother was alive or dead, and if alive to get him home again. I set inquiries on foot, and your letter was one of the results. So far as it went it was satisfactory, for it shewed that till lately George was alive, but it did not go far enough. So, to cut a long story short, I made up my mind to come out and look for him myself, and Captain Good was so kind as to come with me."

"Yes," said the captain; "nothing else to do, you see. Turned out by my Lords of the Admiralty to starve on half pay. And now perhaps, sir, you will tell us what you know or have heard of the gentleman called Neville."

Chapter 2

The Legend of Solomon's Mines[1]

"WHAT WAS IT THAT you heard about my brother's journey at Bamangwato?" said Sir Henry, as I paused to fill my pipe before answering Captain Good.

"I heard this," I answered, "and I have never mentioned it to a soul till to-day. I heard that he was starting for Solomon's Mines."

"Solomon's Mines!" ejaculated both my hearers at once. "Where are they?"

"I don't know," I said; "I know where they are said to be. I once saw the peaks of the mountains that border them, but there was a hundred and thirty miles of desert between me and them, and I am not aware that any white man ever got across it save one. But perhaps the best thing I can do is to tell you the legend of Solomon's Mines as I know it, you passing your word not to reveal anything I tell you without my permission. Do you agree to that? I have my reasons for asking it."

Sir Henry nodded, and Captain Good replied, "Certainly, certainly."

"Well," I began, "as you may guess, in a general way, elephant hunters are a rough set of men, and don't trouble themselves with much beyond the facts of life and the ways of Kafirs. But here and there you meet a man who takes the trouble to collect traditions from the natives, and tries to make out a little piece of the history of this dark land. It was such a man as this who first told me the legend of Solomon's Mines, now a matter of nearly thirty years ago. It was when I was on my first elephant hunt in the Matabele country. His name was Evans, and he was killed next year, poor fellow, by a wounded buffalo, and lies buried near the Zambesi Falls.[2] I was telling Evans one night, I remember, of some wonderful workings I had found whilst hunting koodoo* and eland in what is now the Lydenburg district of the Transvaal. I see they have come across these

---

*Large African antelope with a brown coat and vertical white stripes; variant of *kudu*, from *koedoe* (Afrikaans) and *i-qudu* (Xhosa, the local language).

workings again lately in prospecting for gold, but I knew of them years ago. There is a great wide waggon road cut out of the solid rock, and leading to the mouth of the working or gallery. Inside the mouth of this gallery are stacks of gold quartz piled up ready for crushing, which shows that the workers, whoever they were, must have left in a hurry, and about twenty paces in the gallery is built across, and a beautiful bit of masonry it is.

"'Ay,' said Evans, 'but I will tell you a queerer thing than that;' and he went on to tell me how he had found in the far interior a ruined city, which he believed to be the Ophir of the Bible,[3] and, by the way, other more learned men have said the same long since poor Evans' time. I was, I remember, listening open-eared to all these wonders, for I was young at the time, and this story of an ancient civilisation and of the treasure which those old Jewish or Phœnician adventurers used to extract from a country long since lapsed into the darkest barbarism took a great hold upon my imagination, when suddenly he said to me, "Lad, did you ever hear of the Suliman Mountains up to the north-west of the Mashukulumbwe country?" I told him I never had. "Ah, well," he said, "that was where Solomon really had his mines, his diamond mines, I mean."

"'How do you know that?' I asked.

"'Know it; why what is "Suliman" but a corruption of Solomon!* and, besides, an old Isanusi (witch doctor) up in the Manica country[5] told me all about it. She said that the people who lived across those mountains were a branch of the Zulus, speaking a dialect of Zulu, but finer and bigger men even; that there lived among them great wizards, who had learnt their art from white men when 'all the world was dark,' and who had the secret of a wonderful mine of "bright stones."'

"Well, I laughed at this story at the time, though it interested me, for the diamond fields were not discovered then, and poor Evans went off and got killed, and for twenty years I never thought any more of the matter. But just twenty years afterwards—and that is a long time, gentlemen, an elephant hunter does not often live for twenty years at his business—I heard something more definite about Suliman's Mountains and the country which lies beyond it. I was up beyond the

---

*Suliman is the Arabic form of Solomon.—*Editor*. [Haggard's note]

Manica country at a place called Sitanda's Kraal,* and a miserable place it was, for one could get nothing to eat there, and there was but little game about. I had an attack of fever, and was in a bad way generally, when one day a Portugee arrived with a single companion—a half-breed. Now I know your Delagoa Portugee[6] well. There is no greater devil unhung in a general way, battening as he does upon human agony and flesh in the shape of slaves. But this was quite a different type of man to the low fellows I had been accustomed to meet; he reminded me more of the polite dons I have read about. He was tall and thin, with large dark eyes and curling grey moustachios. We talked together a little, for he could speak broken English, and I understood a little Portugee, and he told me that his name was José Silvestre, and that he had a place near Delagoa Bay; and when he went on next day with his half-breed companion, he said, 'Good-bye,' taking off his hat quite in the old style. 'Good-bye, senor,' he said; 'if ever we meet again I shall be the richest man in the world, and I will remember you.' I laughed a little—I was too weak to laugh much—and watched him strike out for the great desert to the west, wondering if he was mad, or what he thought he was going to find there.

"A week passed, and I got the better of my fever. One evening I was sitting on the ground in front of the little tent I had with me, chewing the last leg of a miserable fowl I had bought from a native for a bit of cloth worth twenty fowls, and staring at the hot red sun sinking down into the desert, when suddenly I saw a figure, apparently that of a European, for it wore a coat, on the slope of the rising ground opposite to me, about three hundred yards away. The figure crept along on its hands and knees, then it got up and staggered along a few yards on its legs, only to fall and crawl along again. Seeing that it must be somebody in distress, I sent one of my hunters to help him, and presently he arrived, and who do you suppose it turned out to be?"

"José Silvestre, of course," said Captain Good.

"Yes, José Silvestre, or rather his skeleton and a little skin. His face was bright yellow with bilious fever, and his large, dark eyes stood nearly out of his head, for all his flesh had gone. There was nothing

---

*Native village surrounded by a mud wall or other fence; refers as well to the community living within (Afrikaans).

but yellow parchment-like skin, white hair, and the gaunt bones sticking up beneath.

"'Water! for the sake of Christ, water!' he moaned. I saw that his lips were cracked, and his tongue, which protruded between them, swollen and blackish.

"I gave him water with a little milk in it, and he drank it in great gulps, two quarts or more, without stopping. I would not let him have any more. Then the fever took him again, and he fell down and began to rave about Suliman's Mountains, and the diamonds, and the desert. I took him into the tent and did what I could for him, which was little enough; but I saw how it must end. About eleven o'clock he got quieter, and I lay down for a little rest and went to sleep. At dawn I woke again, and saw him in the half light sitting up, a strange, gaunt form, and gazing out towards the desert. Presently the first ray of the sun shot right across the wide plain before us till it reached the far-away crest of one of the tallest of the Suliman Mountains more than a hundred miles away.

"'There it is!' cried the dying man in Portuguese, stretching out his long, thin arm, 'but I shall never reach it, never. No one will ever reach it!'

"Suddenly he paused, and seemed to take a resolution. 'Friend,' he said, turning towards me, 'are you there? My eyes grow dark.'

"'Yes,' I said; 'yes, lie down now, and rest.'

"'Ay,' he answered, 'I shall rest soon, I have time to rest—all eternity. Listen, I am dying! You have been good to me. I will give you the paper. Perhaps you will get there if you can live through the desert, which has killed my poor servant and me.'

"Then he groped in his shirt and brought out what I thought was a Boer tobacco pouch[7] of the skin of the Swart-vet-pens (sable antelope). It was fastened with a little strip of hide, what we call a rimpi, and this he tried to untie, but could not. He handed it to me. 'Untie it,' he said. I did so, and extracted a bit of torn yellow linen, on which something was written in rusty letters. Inside was a paper.

"Then he went on feebly, for he was growing weak: 'The paper has it all, that is on the rag. It took me years to read. Listen: my ancestor, a political refugee from Lisbon, and one of the first Portuguese who landed on these shores, wrote that when he was dying on those mountains which no white foot ever pressed before or since. His

name was José da Silvestra, and he lived three hundred years ago. His
slave, who waited for him on this side the mountains, found him
dead, and brought the writing home to Delagoa. It has been in the
family ever since, but none have cared to read it till at last I did. And
I have lost my life over it, but another may succeed, and become the
richest man in the world—the richest man in the world. Only give it
to no one; go yourself!' Then he began to wander again, and in an
hour it was all over.

"God rest him! he died very quietly, and I buried him deep, with
big boulders on his breast; so I do not think that the jackals can have
dug him up. And then I came away."

"Ay, but the document," said Sir Henry, in a tone of deep interest.

"Yes, the document; what was in it?" added the captain.

"Well, gentlemen, if you like I will tell you. I have never showed it
to anybody yet except my dear wife, who is dead, and she thought it
was all nonsense, and a drunken old Portuguese trader who translated it for me, and had forgotten all about it next morning. The
original rag is at my home in Durban, together with poor Dom José's
translation, but I have the English rendering in my pocket-book, and a
facsimile of the map, if it can be called a map. Here it is."

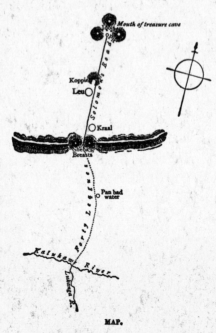

MAP.

"I, José da Silvestra, who am now dying of hunger in the little cave where no snow is on the north side of the nipple of the southernmost of the two mountains I have named Sheba's Breasts, write this in the year 1590 with a cleft bone upon a remnant of my raiment, my blood being the ink. If my slave should find it when he comes, and should bring it to Delagoa, let my friend (name illegible) bring the matter to the knowledge of the king, that he may send an army which, if they live through the desert and the mountains, and can overcome the brave Kukuanes and their devilish arts, to which end many priests should be brought, will make him the richest king since Solomon. With my own eyes have I seen the countless diamonds stored in Solomon's treasure chamber behind the white Death; but through the treachery of Gagool the witch-finder I might bring nought away, scarcely my life. Let him who comes follow the map, and climb the snow of Sheba's left breast till he comes to the nipple, on the north side of which is the great road Solomon made, from whence three days' journey to the King's Place. Let him kill Gagool. Pray for my soul. Farewell.

"José da Silvestra."*

When I had finished reading the above and shewn the copy of the map, drawn by the dying hand of the old Dom with his blood for ink, there followed a silence of astonishment.

"Well," said Captain Good, "I have been round the world twice, and put in at most ports, but may I be hung if I ever heard a yarn like that out of a story book, or in it either, for the matter of that."

---

*Eu José de Silvestra que estou morrendo de fome ná pequena cova onde não ha neve ao lado norte do bico mais ao sul das duas montanhas que chamei seio de Sheba; escrevo isto no anno 1590; escrevo isto com um pedaço d ôsso n' um farrapo de minha roupa e com sangue meu por tinta; se o meu escravo dér com isto quando venha ao levar para Lourenzo Marquez, que o meu amigo (———) leve a cousa ao conhecimento d' El Rei, para que possa mandar um exercito que, se desfiler pelo deserto e pelas montanhas e mesmo sobrepujar os bravos Kukuanes e suas artes diabolicas, pelo que se deviam trazer muitos padres Fara o Rei mais rico depois de Salomão. Com meus proprios olhos vé os di amantes sem conto guardados nas camaras do thesouro de Salomão a traz da morte branca, mas pela traição de Gagoal a feiticeira achadora, nada poderia levar, e apenas a minha vida. Quem vier siga o mappa e trepe pela neve de Sheba peito à esquerda até chegar ao bico, do lado norte do qual está a grande estrada do Salomão por elle feita, donde ha tres dias de jornada até ao Palacio do Rei. Mate Gagoal. Reze por minha alma. Adeos. José da Silvestra. [Haggard's note]

"It's a queer story, Mr. Quatermain," said Sir Henry. "I suppose you are not hoaxing us? It is, I know, sometimes thought allowable to take a greenhorn in."

"If you think that, Sir Henry," I said, much put out, and pocketing my paper, for I do not like to be thought one of those silly fellows who consider it witty to tell lies, and who are for ever boasting to new comers of extraordinary hunting adventures which never happened, "why there is an end of the matter," and I rose to go.

·   Sir Henry laid his large hand upon my shoulder. "Sit down, Mr. Quatermain," he said, "I beg your pardon; I see very well you do not wish to deceive us, but the story sounded so extraordinary that I could hardly believe it."

"You shall see the original map and writing when we reach Durban," I said, somewhat mollified, for really when I came to consider the matter it was scarcely wonderful that he should doubt my good faith. "But I have not told you about your brother. I knew the man Jim who was with him. He was a Bechuana[8] by birth, a good hunter, and for a native a very clever man. The morning Mr. Neville was starting, I saw Jim standing by my waggon and cutting up tobacco on the disselboom.*

" 'Jim,' said I, 'where are you off to this trip? Is it elephants?'

" 'No, Baas,'† he answered, 'we are after something worth more than ivory.'

" 'And what might that be?' I said, for I was curious. 'Is it gold?'

" 'No, Baas, something worth more than gold,' and he grinned.

"I did not ask any more questions, for I did not like to lower my dignity by seeming curious, but I was puzzled. Presently Jim finished cutting his tobacco.

" 'Baas,' said he.

"I took no notice.

" 'Baas,' said he again.

"Eh, boy, what is it?' said I.

" 'Baas, we are going after diamonds.'

" 'Diamonds! why, then, you are going in the wrong direction; you should head for the Fields.'

---

*Central shaft on a wagon or cart (Afrikaans).
†Boss; form of address used by nonwhites to show respect to white males.

"'Baas, have you ever heard of Suliman's Berg?' (Solomon's Mountains).

"'Ay!'

"'Have you ever heard of the diamonds there?'

"'I have heard a foolish story, Jim.'

"'It is no story, Baas. I once knew a woman who came from there, and got to Natal with her child, she told me:—she is dead now.'

"'Your master will feed the aasvogels (vultures), Jim, if he tries to reach Suliman's country, and so will you if they can get any pickings off your worthless old carcass,' said I.

"He grinned. 'Mayhap, Baas. Man must die; I'd rather like to try a new country myself; the elephants are getting worked out about here.'

"'Ah! my boy,' I said, 'you wait till the "pale old man" (death) gets a grip of your yellow throat, and then we'll hear what sort of a tune you sing.'

"Half an hour after that I saw Neville's waggon move off. Presently Jim came running back. 'Good-bye, Baas,' he said. 'I didn't like to start without bidding you good-bye, for I daresay you are right, and we shall never come back again.'

"'Is your master really going to Suliman's Berg, Jim, or are you lying?'

"'No,' says he; 'he is going. He told me he was bound to make his fortune somehow, or try to; so he might as well try the diamonds.'

"'Oh!' said I; 'wait a bit, Jim; will you take a note to your master, Jim, and promise not to give it to him till you reach Inyati?' (which was some hundred miles off).

"'Yes,' said he.

"So I took a scrap of paper, and wrote on it, 'Let him who comes . . . climb the snow of Sheba's left breast, till he comes to the nipple, on the north side of which is Solomon's great road.'

"'Now, Jim,' I said, 'when you give this to your master, tell him he had better follow the advice implicitly. You are not to give it to him now, because I don't want him back asking me questions which I won't answer. Now be off, you idle fellow, the waggon is nearly out of sight.'

"Jim took the note and went, and that is all I know about your brother, Sir Henry; but I am much afraid——"

"Mr. Quatermain," said Sir Henry, "I am going to look for my brother; I am going to trace him to Suliman's Mountains, and over them if necessary, till I find him, or till I know that he is dead. Will you come with me?"

I am, as I think I have said, a cautious man, indeed a timid one, and I shrunk from such an idea. It seemed to me that to start on such a journey would be to go to certain death, and putting other things aside, as I had a son to support, I could not afford to die just then.

"No, thank you, Sir Henry, I think I had rather not," I answered. "I am too old for wild-goose chases of that sort, and we should only end up like my poor friend Silvestre. I have a son dependent on me, so cannot afford to risk my life."

Both Sir Henry and Captain Good looked very disappointed.

"Mr. Quatermain," said the former, "I am well off, and I am bent upon this business. You may put the remuneration for your services at whatever figure you like, in reason, and it shall be paid over to you before we start. Moreover, I will, before we start, arrange that in the event of anything happening to us or to you, that your son shall be suitably provided for. You will see from this how necessary I think your presence. Also if by any chance we should reach this place, and find diamonds, they shall belong to you and Good equally. I do not want them. But of course the chance is as good as nothing, though the same thing would apply to any ivory we might get. You may pretty well make your own terms with me, Mr. Quatermain; and of course I shall pay all expenses."

"Sir Henry," said I, "this is the most liberal offer I ever had, and one not to be sneezed at by a poor hunter and trader. But the job is the biggest I ever came across, and I must take time to think it over. I will give you my answer before we get to Durban."

"Very good," answered Sir Henry, and then I said good-night and turned in, and dreamt about poor long-dead Silvestre and the diamonds.

Chapter 3

Umbopa Enters Our Service

It TAKES FROM FOUR to five days, according to the vessel and the state of the weather, to run up from the Cape to Durban. Sometimes, if the landing is bad at East London,[1] where they have not yet got that wonderful harbour they talk so much of, and sink such a mint of money in, one is delayed for twenty-four hours before the cargo boats can get out to take the goods off. But on this occasion we had not to wait at all, for there were no breakers on the Bar* to speak of, and the tugs came out at once with their long strings of ugly flat-bottomed boats, into which the goods were bundled with a crash. It did not matter what they were, over they went slap bang; whether they were china or woollen goods they met with the same treatment. I saw one case containing four dozen of champagne smashed all to bits, and there was the champagne fizzing and boiling about in the bottom of the dirty cargo boat. It was a wicked waste, and so evidently the Kafirs in the boat thought, for they found a couple of unbroken bottles, and knocking the tops off drank the contents. But they had not allowed for the expansion caused by the fizz in the wine, and feeling themselves swelling, rolled about in the bottom of the boat, calling out that the good liquor was "tagati" (bewitched). I spoke to them from the vessel, and told them that it was the white man's strongest medicine, and that they were as good as dead men. They went on to the shore in a very great fright, and I do not think that they will touch champagne again.

Well, all the time we were running up to Natal I was thinking over Sir Henry Curtis' offer. We did not speak any more on the subject for a day or two, though I told them many hunting yarns, all true ones. There is no need to tell lies about hunting, for so many curious

---

*Breaker: large white-capped wave that breaks against a shoreline; bar: ridge of sand formed by the action of the tide against the shore.

things happen within the knowledge of a man whose business it is to hunt; but this is by the way.

At last, one beautiful evening in January, which is our hottest month, we steamed along the coast of Natal, expecting to make Durban Point by sunset. It is a lovely coast all along from East London, with its red sandhills and wide sweeps of vivid green, dotted here and there with Kafir kraals, and bordered by a ribbon of white surf, which spouts up in pillars of foam where it hits the rocks. But just before you get to Durban there is a peculiar richness about it. There are the deep kloofs* cut in the hills by the rushing rains of centuries, down which the rivers sparkle; there is the deepest green of the bush, growing as God planted it, and the other greens of the mealie† gardens and the sugar patches, while here and there a white house, smiling out at the placid sea, puts a finish and gives an air of homeliness to the scene. For to my mind, however beautiful a view may be, it requires the presence of man to make it complete, but perhaps that is because I have lived so much in the wilderness, and therefore know the value of civilisation, though to be sure it drives away the game. The Garden of Eden, no doubt, was fair before man was, but I always think it must have been fairer when Eve was walking about it. But we had miscalculated a little, and the sun was well down before we dropped anchor off the Point, and heard the gun which told the good folk that the English Mail[2] was in. It was too late to think of getting over the Bar that night, so we went down comfortably to dinner, after seeing the Mails carried off in the lifeboat.

When we came up again the moon was up, and shining so brightly over sea and shore that she almost paled the quick large flashes from the lighthouse. From the shore floated sweet spicy odours that always remind me of hymns and missionaries, and in the windows of the houses on the Berea[3] sparkled a hundred lights. From a large brig lying near came the music of the sailors as they worked at getting the anchor up to be ready for the wind. Altogether it was a perfect night, such a night as you only get in Southern Africa, and it threw a garment of peace over everybody as the moon threw a garment of silver over everything. Even the great bulldog,

---

*Ravines (Afrikaans).

†Afrikaans term for an ear of maize (American corn).

belonging to a sporting passenger, seemed to yield to the gentle influences, and giving up yearning to come to close quarters with the baboon in a cage on the foc'sle, snored happily in the door of the cabin, dreaming no doubt that he had finished him, and happy in his dream.

We all—that, is Sir Henry Curtis, Captain Good, and myself—went and sat by the wheel, and were quiet for a while.

"Well, Mr. Quatermain," said Sir Henry, presently, "have you been thinking about my proposals?"

"Ay," echoed Captain Good, "what do you think of them, Mr. Quatermain? I hope you are going to give us the pleasure of your company as far as Solomon's Mines, or wherever the gentleman you knew as Neville may have got to."

I rose and knocked out my pipe before I answered. I had not made up my mind, and wanted the additional moment to complete it. Before the burning tobacco had fallen into the sea it was completed; just that little extra second did the trick. It is often the way when you have been bothering a long time over a thing.

"Yes, gentlemen," I said, sitting down again, "I will go, and by your leave I will tell you why and on what terms. First for the terms which I ask.

"1. You are to pay all expenses, and any ivory or other valuables we may get is to be divided between Captain Good and myself.

"2. That you pay me £500 for my services on the trip before we start, I undertaking to serve you faithfully till you choose to abandon the enterprise, or till we succeed, or disaster overtakes us.

"3. That before we start you execute a deed agreeing, in the event of my death or disablement, to pay my boy Harry, who is studying medicine over there in London at Guy's Hospital, a sum of £200 a year for five years, by which time he ought to be able to earn a living for himself. That is all, I think, and I daresay you will say quite enough too."

"No," answered Sir Henry, "I accept them gladly. I am bent upon this project, and would pay more than that for your help, especially considering the peculiar knowledge you possess."

"Very well. And now that I have made my terms I will tell you my reasons for making up my mind to go. First of all, gentlemen, I have been observing you both for the last few days, and if you will not think me impertinent I will say that I like you, and think that we shall come up well to the yoke together. That is something, let me tell you, when one has a long journey like this before one.

"And now as to the journey itself, I tell you flatly, Sir Henry and Captain Good, that I do not think it probable that we can come out of it alive, that is, if we attempt to cross the Suliman Mountains. What was the fate of the old Dom da Silvestra three hundred years ago? What was the fate of his descendant twenty years ago? What has been your brother's fate? I tell you frankly, gentlemen, that as their fate was so I believe ours will be."

I paused to watch the effect of my words. Captain Good looked a little uncomfortable; but Sir Henry's face did not change. "We must take our chance," he said.

"You may perhaps wonder," I went on, "why, if I think this, I, who am, as I told you, a timid man, should undertake such a journey. It is for two reasons. First I am a fatalist, and believe that my time is appointed to come quite independently of my own movements, and that if I am to go to Suliman's Mountains to be killed, I shall go there and shall be killed there. God Almighty, no doubt, knows His mind about me, so I need not trouble on that point. Secondly, I am a poor man. For nearly forty years I have hunted and traded, but I have never made more than a living. Well, gentlemen, I don't know if you are aware that the average life of an elephant hunter from the time he takes to the trade is from four to five years. So you see I have lived through about seven generations of my class, and I should think that my time cannot be far off anyway. Now, if anything were to happen to me in the ordinary course of business, by the time my debts were paid there would be nothing left to support my son Harry whilst he was getting in the way of earning a living, whereas now he would be provided for for five years. There is the whole affair in a nutshell."

"Mr. Quatermain," said Sir Henry, who had been giving me the most serious attention; "your motives for undertaking an enterprise which you believe can only end in disaster reflect a great deal of credit on you. Whether or not you are right, time and the event of course alone can show. But whether you are right or wrong, I may as well tell you at once that I am going through with it to the end, sweet or bitter. If we are going to be knocked on the head, all I have to say is that I hope we shall get a little shooting first, eh, Good?"

"Yes, yes," put in the captain. "We have all three of us been accustomed to face danger, and hold our lives in our hands in various ways, so it is no good turning back now."

"And now I vote we go down to the saloon and take an observation, just for luck, you know." And we did—through the bottom of a tumbler.

Next day we went ashore, and I put Sir Henry and Captain Good up at the little shanty I have on the Berea, and which I call my home. There are only three rooms and a kitchen in it, and it is built of green brick with a galvanised iron roof, but there is a good garden with the best loquot* trees in it that I know, and some nice young mangoes, of which I hope great things. The curator of the botanical gardens gave them to me. It is looked after by an old hunter of mine, named Jack, whose thigh was so badly broken by a buffalo cow in Sikukuni's⁴ country, that he will never hunt again. But he can potter about and garden, being a Griqua⁵ by birth. You can never get your Zulu to take much interest in gardening. It is a peaceful art, and peaceful arts are not in his line.

Sir Henry and Good slept in a tent pitched in my little grove of orange trees at the end of the garden (for there was no room for them in the house), and what with the smell of the bloom and the sight of the green and golden fruit—for in Durban you will see all three on the tree together—I daresay it is a pleasant place enough (for we have few mosquitoes here unless there happens to come an unusually heavy rain).

Well, to get on—for unless I do you will be tired of my story before ever we fetch up at Suliman's Mountains—having once made up my mind to go I set about making the necessary preparations. First I got the deed from Sir Henry, providing for my boy in case of accidents. There was some little difficulty about getting this legally executed, as Sir Henry was a stranger here, and the property to be charged was over the water, but it was ultimately got over with the help of a lawyer, who charged £20 for the job—a price that I thought outrageous. Then I got my cheque for £500. Having paid this tribute

---

*Also spelled loquat. Small, large-leaved evergreen tree (*Eriobotrya japonica*) that yields golden, pear-shaped fruit with a sweet but acidic taste; native to China, it was transported to Japan and later grown in Africa.

to my bump of caution,[6] I bought a waggon and a span of oxen on
Sir Henry's behalf, and beauties they were. It was a twenty-two-foot
waggon with iron axles, very strong, very light, and built throughout
of stink wood.* It was not quite a new one, having been to the Diamond Fields and back, but in my opinion it was all the better for
that, for one could see that the wood was well seasoned. If anything
is going to give in a waggon, or if there is green wood in it, it will
show out on the first trip. It was what we call a "half-tented" waggon, that is to say, it was only covered in over the after twelve feet,
leaving all the front part free for the necessaries we had to carry with
us. In this after part was a hide "cartle," or bed, on which two people
could sleep, also racks for rifles, and many other little conveniences.
I gave £125 for it, and think it was cheap at the price. Then I bought
a beautiful team of twenty salted Zulu oxen, which I had had my eye
on for a year or two. Sixteen oxen are the usual number for a team,
but I had four extra to allow for casualties. These Zulu oxen are
small and light, not more than half the size of the Africander oxen,
which are generally used for transport purposes; but they will live
where the Africanders will starve, and with a light load will make five
miles a day better going, being quicker and not so liable to get foot-
sore. What is more, this lot were thoroughly "salted," that is, they had
worked all over South Africa, and so had become proof (comparatively speaking) against red water,[†] which so frequently destroys
whole teams of oxen when they get on to strange "veldt" (grass
country). As for "lung sick," which is a dreadful form of pneumonia,
very prevalent in this country, they had all been inoculated against
it. This is done by cutting a slit in the tail of an ox, and binding in a
piece of the diseased lung of an animal which has died of the sick-
ness. The result is that the ox sickens, takes the disease in a mild
form, which causes its tail to drop off, as a rule about a foot from the
root, and becomes proof against future attacks. It seems cruel to rob
the animal of his tail, especially in a country where there are so many

---

*South African evergreen (*Ocotea bullata*); also called stinkhout, cape walnut, cape
laurel, and laurel wood; its dark-colored wood is as strong and durable as teak and
has a very fine grain; when freshly cut, it emits a strong odor.
†Highly fatal disease (*bacillary hemoglobinuria*) in cattle or sheep; caused by the bac-
teria *Clostridium haemolyticum*, found in soil. The scientific name derives from the
red urine afflicted animals excrete as a result of ruptured red blood cells.

flies, but it is better to sacrifice the tail and keep the ox than to lose both tail and ox, for a tail without an ox is not much good except to dust with. Still it does look odd to trek along behind twenty stumps, where there ought to be tails. It seems as though nature had made a trifling mistake, and stuck the stern ornaments of a lot of prize bull-dogs on to the rumps of the oxen.

Next came the question of provisioning and medicines, one which required the most careful consideration, for what one had to do was to avoid lumbering the waggon up, and yet take everything absolutely necessary. Fortunately, it turned out that Good was a bit of a doctor, having at some period in his previous career managed to pass through a course of medical and surgical instruction, which he had more or less kept up. He was not, of course, qualified, but he knew more about it than many a man who could write M.D. after his name, as we found out afterwards, and he had a splendid travel-ling medicine chest and a set of instruments. Whilst we were at Dur-ban he cut off a Kafir's big toe in a way which it was a pleasure to see. But he was quite flabbergasted when the Kafir, who had sat stolidly watching the operation, asked him to put on another, saying that a "white one" would do at a pinch.

There remained, when these questions were satisfactorily settled, two further important points for consideration, namely, that of arms and that of servants. As to the arms I cannot do better than put down a list of those we finally decided on from among the ample store that Sir Henry had brought with him from England, and those which I had. I copy it from my pocket-book, where I made the entry at the time.

"Three heavy breechloading double-eight elephant guns, weigh-ing about fifteen pounds each, with a charge of eleven drachms* of black powder." Two of these were by a well-known London firm, most excellent makers, but I do not know by whom mine, which was not so highly finished, was made. I had used it on several trips, and shot a good many elephants with it, and it had always proved a most superior weapon, thoroughly to be relied on.

"Three double .500 expresses, constructed to carry a charge of six

*Also spelled dram; a drachm was a British imperial unit of measurement equiva-lent to 60 minims or 3.5516 cubic centimeters.

drachms," sweet weapons, and admirable for medium-sized game, such as eland or sable antelope, or for men, especially in an open country and with the semi-hollow bullet.

"One double No. 12 central-fire Keeper's shotgun, full choke both barrels."[7] This gun proved of the greatest service to us afterwards in shooting game for the pot.

"Three Winchester repeating rifles (not carbines), spare guns.

"Three single-action Colt's revolvers, with the heavier pattern of cartridge."

This was our total armament, and the reader will doubtless observe that the weapons of each class were of the same make and calibre, so that the cartridges were interchangeable, a very important point. I make no apology for detailing it at length, for every experienced hunter will know how vital a proper supply of guns and ammunition is to the success of an expedition.

Now as to the men who were to go with us. After much consultation we decided that their number should be limited to five, namely, a driver, a leader, and three servants.

The driver and leader I got without much difficulty, two Zulus, named respectively Goza and Tom; but the servants were a more difficult matter. It was necessary that they should be thoroughly trustworthy and brave men, as in a business of this sort our lives might depend upon their conduct. At last I secured two, one a Hottentot* called Ventvögel (wind-bird), and one a little Zulu named Khiva, who had the merit of speaking English perfectly. Ventvögel I had known before; he was one of the most perfect "spoorers" (game trackers) I ever had to do with, and tough as whipcord. He never seemed to tire. But he had one failing, so common with his race, drink. Put him within reach of a bottle of grog and you could not trust him. But as we were going beyond the region of grog-shops this little weakness of his did not so much matter.

Having got these two men I looked in vain for a third to suit my purpose, so we determined to start without one, trusting to luck to find a suitable man on our way up country. But on the evening be-

---

*Offensive Afrikaans term for a Khoikhoi, a member of a pastoral people of southern Africa.

fore the day we had fixed for our departure the Zulu Khiva informed
me that a man was waiting to see me. Accordingly when we had
done dinner, for we were at table at the time, I told him to bring him
in. Presently a very tall, handsome-looking man, somewhere about
thirty years of age, and very light-coloured for a Zulu, entered, and,
lifting his knob-stick by way of salute, squatted himself down in the
corner on his haunches, and sat silent. I did not take any notice of
him for a while, for it is a great mistake to do so. If you rush into
conversation at once, a Zulu is apt to think you a person of little dignity or consideration. I observed, however, that he was a "Keshla"
(ringed man), that is, that he wore on his head the black ring, made
of a species of gum polished with fat and worked in with the hair,
usually assumed by Zulus on attaining a certain age or dignity. Also
it struck me that his face was familiar to me.

"Well," I said at last, "what is your name?"

"Umbopa," answered the man in a slow, deep voice.

"I have seen your face before."

"Yes; the Inkoosi (chief) saw my face at the place of the Little
Hand (Isandhlwana) the day before the battle."

Then I remembered. I had been one of Lord Chelmsford's guides
in that unlucky Zulu War,[8] and had had the good fortune to leave
the camp in charge of some waggons the day before the battle. While
I had been waiting for the cattle to be inspanned I had fallen into
conversation with this man, who held some small command among
the native auxiliaries, and he had expressed to me his doubts of the
safety of the camp. At the time I had told him to hold his tongue,
and leave such matters to wiser heads; but afterwards I thought of
his words.

"I remember," I said; "what is it you want?"

"It is this, 'Macumazahn' (that is my Kafir name, and means the
man who gets up in the middle of the night, or, in vulgar English, he
who keeps his eyes open). I hear that you go on a great expedition
far into the North with the white chiefs from over the water. Is it a
true word?"

"It is."

"I hear that you go even to the Lukanga River,[9] a moon's journey
beyond the Manica country. Is this so also, 'Macumazahn?' "

"Why do you ask whither we go? What is it to thee?" I answered, suspiciously, for the objects of our journey had been kept a dead secret.

"It is this, O white men, that if indeed you travel so far I would travel with you."

There was a certain assumption of dignity in the man's mode of speech, and especially in his use of the words "O white men," instead of "O Inkosis" (chiefs), which struck me.

"You forget yourself a little," I said. "Your words come out unawares. That is not the way to speak. What is your name, and where is your kraal? Tell us, that we may know with whom we have to deal."

"My name is Umbopa. I am of the Zulu people, yet not of them. The house of my tribe is in the far North; it was left behind when the Zulus came down here a 'thousand years ago,' long before Chaka reigned in Zululand. I have no kraal. I have wandered for many years. I came from the North as a child to Zululand. I was Cetywayo's man[*] in the Nkomabakosi Regiment. I ran away from Zululand and came to Natal because I wanted to see the white man's ways. Then I served against Cetywayo in the war. Since then I have been working in Natal. Now I am tired, and would go North again. Here is not my place. I want no money, but I am a brave man, and am worth my place and meat. I have spoken."

I was rather puzzled at this man and his way of speech. It was evident to me from his manner that he was in the main telling the truth, but he was somehow different from the ordinary run of Zulus, and I rather mistrusted his offer to come without pay. Being in a difficulty, I translated his words to Sir Henry and Good, and asked them their opinion. Sir Henry told me to ask him to stand up. Umbopa did so, at the same time slipping off the long military great coat he wore, and revealing himself naked except for the moocha[10] round his centre and a necklace of lions' claws. He certainly was a magnificent-looking man; I never saw a finer native. Standing about six foot three high he was broad in proportion, and very shapely. In that light, too, his skin looked scarcely more than dark, except here and there where deep black scars marked old assegai wounds. Sir Henry walked up to him and looked into his proud, handsome face.

---

*See endnote 8, chapter 3.

"They make a good pair, don't they?" said Good; "one as big as the other."

"I like your looks, Mr. Umbopa, and I will take you as my servant," said Sir Henry in English.

Umbopa evidently understood him, for he answered in Zulu, "It is well;" and then with a glance at the white man's great stature and breadth, "we are men, thou and I."

Chapter 4

An Elephant Hunt

NOW I DO NOT propose to narrate at full length all the incidents of our long journey up to Sitanda's Kraal, near the junction of the Lukanga and Ralukwe Rivers, a journey of more than a thousand miles from Durban, the last three hundred or so of which, owing to the frequent presence of the dreadful "tsetse" fly, whose bite is fatal to all animals except donkeys and men, we had to make on foot.

We left Durban at the end of January, and it was in the second week of May that we camped near Sitanda's Kraal. Our adventures on the way were many and various, but as they were of the sort which befall every African hunter, I shall not—with one exception to be presently detailed—set them down here, lest I should render this history too wearisome.

At Inyati, the outlying trading station in the Matabele country, of which Lobengula[1] (a great scoundrel) is king, we with many regrets parted from our comfortable waggon. Only twelve oxen remained to us out of the beautiful span of twenty which I had bought at Durban. One we had lost from the bite of a cobra, three had perished from poverty and the want of water, one had been lost, and the other three had died from eating the poisonous herb called "tulip."[2] Five more sickened from this cause, but we managed to cure them with doses of an infusion made by boiling down the tulip leaves. If administered in time this is a very effective antidote. The waggon and oxen we left in the immediate charge of Goza and Tom, the driver and leader, both of them trustworthy boys, requesting a worthy Scotch missionary who lived in this wild place to keep an eye to it. Then, accompanied by Umbopa, Khiva, Ventvögel, and half a dozen bearers whom we hired on the spot, we started off on foot upon our wild quest. I remember we were all a little silent on the occasion of that departure, and I think that each of us was wondering if we should ever see that waggon again; for my part I never expected to. For a while we tramped on in silence, till Umbopa, who was marching in front, broke into a Zulu chant about how some brave men, tired of life and the tameness of things, started off into a great wilderness to find new things or die, and how, lo, and behold! when they had got far into the wilderness, they found it was not a wilderness at all, but a beautiful place full of young wives and fat cattle, of game to hunt and enemies to kill.

Then we all laughed and took it for a good omen. He was a cheerful savage was Umbopa, in a dignified sort of a way, when he had not got one of his fits of brooding, and had a wonderful knack of keeping one's spirits up. We all got very fond of him.

And now for the one adventure I am going to treat myself to, for I do dearly love a hunting yarn.

About a fortnight's march from Inyati, we came across a peculiarly beautiful bit of fairly-watered wooded country. The kloofs in the hills were covered with dense bush, "idoro" bush as the natives call it, and in some places, with the "wacht-een-beche" (wait-a-little) thorn,* and there were great quantities of the beautiful "machabell" tree, laden with refreshing yellow fruit with enormous stones. This tree is the elephant's favourite food, and there were not wanting signs that the great brutes were about, for not only was their spoor frequent, but in many places the trees were broken down and even up-rooted. The elephant is a destructive feeder.

One evening, after a long day's march, we came to a spot of peculiar loveliness. At the foot of a bush-clad hill was a dry river-bed, in which, however, were to be found pools of crystal water all trodden round with the hoof-prints of game. Facing this hill was a park-like plain, where grew clumps of flat-topped mimosa, varied with occasional glossy-leaved machabells, and all round was the great sea of pathless, silent bush.

As we emerged into this river-bed path we suddenly started a troop of tall giraffes, who galloped, or rather sailed off, with their strange gait, their tails screwed up over their backs, and their hoofs rattling like castanets. They were about three hundred yards from

---

*Haggard's spelling of *wag 'n bietjie*, the Afrikaans name for a species of acacia tree (*Acacia caffra*); also called common hook-thorn or cat thorn. It is distinguished by bright green, feathery leaves; its wood, resistant to fire, is used for fence posts and tobacco pipes.

us, and therefore practically out of shot, but Good, who was walking ahead, and had an express loaded with solid ball in his hand, could not resist, but upped gun and let drive at the last, a young cow. By some extraordinary chance the ball struck it full on the back of the neck, shattering the spinal column, and that giraffe went rolling head over heels just like a rabbit. I never saw a more curious thing.

"Curse it!" said Good—for I am sorry to say he had a habit of using strong language when excited—contracted, no doubt, in the course of his nautical career; "curse it! I've killed him."

"Ou, Bougwan," ejaculated the Kafirs; "ou! ou!"

They called Good "Bougwan." (glass eye) because of his eyeglass.

"Oh, 'Bougwan!'" re-echoed Sir Henry and I, and from that day Good's reputation as a marvellous shot was established, at any rate among the Kafirs. Really he was a bad one, but whenever he missed we overlooked it for the sake of that giraffe.

Having set some of the "boys" to cut off the best of the giraffe meat, we went to work to build a "scherm"* near one of the pools about a hundred yards to the right of it. This is done by cutting a quantity of thorn bushes and laying them in the shape of a circular hedge. Then the space enclosed is smoothed, and dry tambouki grass,[3] if obtainable, is made into a bed in the centre, and a fire or fires lighted.

By the time the "scherm" was finished the moon was coming up, and our dinner of giraffe steaks and roasted marrow bones was ready. How we enjoyed those marrow-bones, though it was rather a job to crack them! I know no greater luxury than giraffe marrow, unless it is elephant's heart, and we had that on the morrow. We ate our simple meal, pausing at times to thank Good for his wonderful shot, by the light of the full moon, and then we began to smoke and yarn, and a curious picture we must have made squatted there round the fire. I, with my short grizzled hair sticking up straight, and Sir Henry with his yellow locks, which were getting rather long, were rather a contrast, especially as I am thin, and short, and dark, weighing only nine stone and a half, and Sir Henry is tall, and broad, and fair, and weighs fifteen. But perhaps the most curious looking of the three, taking all the circumstances of the case into consideration,

---

*Shield or screen (Afrikaans).

was Captain John Good, R.N, There he sat upon a leather bag, looking just as though he had come in from a comfortable day's shooting in a civilised country, absolutely clean, tidy, and well dressed. He
had on a shooting suit of brown tweed, with a hat to match, and neat
gaiters. He was, as usual, beautifully shaved, his eyeglass and his false
teeth appeared to be in perfect order, and altogether he was the neat-
est man I ever had to do with in the wilderness. He even had on a
collar, of which he had a supply, made of white guttapercha.*

"You see, they weigh so little," he said to me, innocently, when I
expressed my astonishment at the fact; "I always like to look like a
gentleman."

Well, there we all sat yarning away in the beautiful moonlight,
and watching the Kafirs a few yards off sucking their intoxicating
"daccha"[4] in a pipe of which the mouthpiece was made of the horn
of an eland, till they one by one rolled themselves up in their blankets and went to sleep by the fire, that is, all except Umbopa, who sat
a little apart (I noticed he never mixed much with the other Kafirs),
his chin resting on his hand, apparently thinking deeply.

Presently, from the depths of the bush behind us, came a loud
"woof, woof!" "That's a lion," said I, and we all started up to listen.
Hardly had we done so, when from the pool, about a hundred yards
off, came the strident trumpeting of an elephant. "Unkungunklovo!
Unkungunklovo!" (elephant! elephant!) whispered the Kafirs; and a
few minutes afterwards we saw a succession of vast shadowy forms
moving slowly from the direction of the water towards the bush. Up
jumped Good, burning for slaughter, and thinking, perhaps, that it
was as easy to kill elephant as he had found it to shoot giraffe, but I
caught him by the arm and pulled him down.

"It's no good," I said, "let them go."

"It seems that we are in a paradise of game. I vote we stop here a
day or two, and have a go at them," said Sir Henry, presently.

I was rather surprised, for hitherto Sir Henry had always been for
pushing on as fast as possible, more especially since we had ascertained at Inyati that about two years ago an Englishman of the name

---

*Natural latex from the sap or resin of the *Isonandra gutta, Palaquium gutta*, and
other evergreen trees; has a texture similar to that of rubber, though is not as elastic;
since 1845, used to insulate marine and underground cables.

of Neville *had* sold his waggon there, and gone on up country; but I suppose his hunter instincts had got the better of him.

Good jumped at the idea, for he was longing to have a go at those elephants; and so, to speak the truth, did I, for it went against my conscience to let such a herd as that escape without having a pull at them.

"All right, my hearties," said I. "I think we want a little recreation. And now let's turn in, for we ought to be off by dawn, and then perhaps we may catch them feeding before they move on."

The others agreed, and we proceeded to make preparations. Good took off his clothes, shook them, put his eyeglass and his false teeth into his trousers pocket, and folding them all up neatly, placed them out of the dew under a corner of his mackintosh sheet. Sir Henry and I contented ourselves with rougher arrangements, and were soon curled up in our blankets, and dropping off into the dreamless sleep that rewards the traveller.

Going, going, go—What was that?

Suddenly from the direction of the water came a sound of violent scuffling, and next instant there broke upon our ears a succession of the most awful roars. There was no mistaking what they came from; only a lion could make such a noise as that. We all jumped up and looked towards the water, in the direction of which we saw a confused mass, yellow and black in colour, staggering and struggling towards us. We seized our rifles, and slipping on our veldtschoons (shoes made of untanned hide), ran out of the scherm towards it. By this time it had fallen, and was rolling over and over on the ground, and by the time we reached it it struggled no longer, but was quite still.

And this was what it was. On the grass there lay a sable antelope bull—the most beautiful of all the African antelopes—quite dead, and transfixed by its great curved horns was a magnificent black-maned lion, also dead. What had happened evidently was this. The sable antelope had come down to drink at the pool where the lion—no doubt the same we had heard—had been lying in wait. While the antelope was drinking the lion had sprung upon him, but was received upon the sharp curved horns and transfixed. I once saw the same thing happen before. The lion, unable to free himself, had torn and bitten at the back and neck of the bull, which, maddened with fear and pain, had rushed on till it dropped dead.

As soon as we had sufficiently examined the dead beasts we called the Kafirs, and between us managed to drag their carcasses up to the scherm. Then we went in and laid down, to wake no more till dawn.

With the first light we were up and making ready for the fray. We took with us the three eight-bore rifles, a good supply of ammunition, and our large water-bottles, filled with weak, cold tea, which I have always found the best stuff to shoot on. After swallowing a little breakfast we started, Umbopa, Khiva, and Ventvögel accompanying us. The other Kafirs we left with instructions to skin the lion and the sable antelope, and cut up the latter.

We had no difficulty in finding the broad elephant trail, which Ventvögel, after examination, pronounced to have been made by between twenty and thirty elephants, most of them full-grown bulls. But the herd had moved on some way during the night, and it was nine o'clock, and already very hot, before, from the broken trees, bruised leaves and bark, and smoking dung, we knew we could not be far off them.

Presently we caught sight of the herd, numbering, as Ventvögel had said, between twenty and thirty, standing in a hollow, having finished their morning meal, and flapping their great ears. It was a splendid sight.

They were about two hundred yards from us. Taking a handful of dry grass I threw it into the air to see how the wind was; for if once they winded us I knew they would be off before we could get a shot. Finding that, if anything, it blew from the elephants to us, we crept stealthily on, and thanks to the cover managed to get within forty yards or so of the great brutes. Just in front of us and broadside on stood three splendid bulls, one of them with enormous tusks. I whispered to the others that I would take the middle one; Sir Henry covered the one to the left, and Good the bull with the big tusks.

"Now," I whispered.

Boom! boom! boom! went the three heavy rifles, and down went Sir Henry's elephant dead as a hammer, shot right through the heart. Mine fell on to its knees, and I thought he was going to die, but in another moment he was up and off, tearing along straight past me. As he went I gave him the second barrel in the ribs, and this brought him down in good earnest. Hastily slipping in two fresh cartridges, I ran close up to him, and a ball through the brain put an end to the poor brute's struggles. Then I turned to see how Good had fared with the big bull, which I had heard screaming with rage and pain as I gave mine its quietus.[5] On reaching the captain I found him in a great state of excitement. It appeared that on receiving the bullet the bull had turned and come straight for his assailant, who had barely time to get out of his way, and then charged blindly on past him, in the direction of our encampment. Meanwhile the herd had crashed off in wild alarm in the other direction.

For a while we debated whether to go after the wounded bull or follow the herd, and finally decided for the latter alternative, and departed thinking that we had seen the last of those big tusks. I have often wished since that we had. It was easy work to follow the elephants, for they had left a trail like a carriage road behind them, crushing down the thick bush in their furious flight as though it were tambouki grass.

But to come up with them was another matter, and we had struggled on under a broiling sun for over two hours before we found them. They were, with the exception of one bull, standing together, and I could see, from their unquiet way and the manner in which they kept lifting their trunks to test the air, that they were on the look out for mischief. The solitary bull stood fifty yards or so this side of the herd, over which he was evidently keeping sentry, and about sixty yards from us. Thinking that he would see or wind us, and that it would probably start them all off again if we tried to get nearer, especially as the ground was rather open, we all aimed at this bull, and at my whispered word fired. All three shots took effect, and down he went dead. Again the herd started on, but unfortunately for them about a hundred yards farther on was a nullah, or dried water track, with steep banks, a place very much resembling the one the Prince Imperial[6] was killed in in Zululand. Into this the elephants plunged, and when we reached the edge we found them struggling in wild confusion to get up the other bank, and filling the air with their screams, and trumpeting as they pushed one another aside in their selfish panic, just like so many human beings. Now was our opportunity, and firing away as quick as we could load we killed five of the poor beasts, and no doubt should have bagged the whole herd had they not suddenly given up their attempts to climb the bank and rushed headlong down the nullah. We were too tired to follow them, and perhaps also a little sick of slaughter, eight elephants being a pretty good bag for one day.

So after we had rested a little, and the Kafirs had cut out the hearts of two of the dead elephants for supper, we started homewards, very well pleased with ourselves, having made up our minds to send the bearers on the morrow to chop out the tusks.

Shortly after we had passed the spot where Good had wounded the patriarchal bull we came across a herd of eland, but did not shoot at them, as we had already plenty of meat. They trotted past us, and then stopped behind a little patch of bush about a hundred yards away and wheeled round to look at us. As Good was anxious to get a near view of them, never having seen an eland close, he handed his rifle to Umbopa, and, followed by Khiva, strolled up to the patch of bush. We sat down and waited for him, not sorry of the excuse for a little rest.

The sun was just going down in its reddest glory, and Sir Henry and I were admiring the lovely scene, when suddenly we heard an elephant scream, and saw its huge and charging form with uplifted trunk and tail silhouetted against the great red globe of the sun. Next second we saw something else, and that was Good and Khiva tearing back towards us with the wounded bull (for it was he) charging after them. For a moment we did not dare to fire—though it would have been little use if we had at that distance—for fear of hitting one of them, and the next a dreadful thing happened—Good fell a victim to his passion for civilised dress. Had he consented to discard his trousers and gaiters as we had, and hunt in a flannel shirt and a pair of veldtschoons, it would have been all right, but as it was his trousers cumbered him in that desperate race, and presently, when he was about sixty yards from us, his boot, polished by the dry grass, slipped, and down he went on his face right in front of the elephant.

We gave a gasp, for we knew he must die, and ran as hard as we could towards him. In three seconds it had ended, but not as we thought. Khiva, the Zulu boy, had seen his master fall, and brave lad that he was, had turned and flung his assegai* straight into the elephant's face. It stuck in his trunk.

---

*Spear or lance with a long blade used by Bantu fighters.

With a scream of pain the brute seized the poor Zulu, hurled him to the earth, and placing his huge foot on to his body about the middle, twined his trunk round his upper part and *tore him in two*.

We rushed up mad with horror, and fired again, and again, and presently the elephant fell upon the fragments of the Zulu.

As for Good, he got up and wrung his hands over the brave man who had given his life to save him, and myself, though an old hand, I felt a lump in my throat. Umbopa stood and contemplated the huge dead elephant and the mangled remains of poor Khiva.

"Ah well," he said presently, "he is dead, but he died like a man."

Chapter 5

Our March into the Desert

WE HAD KILLED NINE elephants, and it took us two days to cut out the tusks and get them home and bury them carefully in the sand under a large tree, which made a conspicuous mark for miles round. It was a wonderfully fine lot of ivory. I never saw a better, averaging as it did between forty and fifty pounds a tusk. The tusks of the great bull that killed poor Khiva scaled one hundred and seventy pounds the pair, as nearly as we could judge.

As for Khiva himself, we buried what remained of him in an ant-bear[1] hole, together with an assegai to protect himself with on his journey to a better world. On the third day we started on, hoping that we might one day return to dig up our buried ivory, and in due course, after a long and wearisome tramp, and many adventures which have not space to detail, reached Sitanda's Kraal, near the Lukanga River, the real starting-point of our expedition. Very well do I recollect our arrival at that place. To the right was a scattered native settlement with a few stone cattle kraals and some cultivated lands down by the water, where these savages grew their scanty supply of grain, and beyond it great tracts of waving "veldt" covered with tall grass, over which herds of the smaller game were wandering. To the left was the vast desert. This spot appeared to be the outpost of the fertile country, and it would be difficult to say to what natural causes such an abrupt change in the character of the soil was due. But so it was. Just below our encampment flowed a little stream, on the farther side of which was a stony slope, the same down which I had twenty years before seen poor Silvestre creeping back after his attempt to reach Solomon's Mines, and beyond that slope began the waterless desert covered with a species of karoo shrub.[2] It was evening when we pitched our camp, and the great fiery ball of the sun was sinking into the desert, sending glorious rays of many-coloured light flying over all the vast expanse. Leaving Good to superintend the arrangement of our little camp, I took Sir Henry with

47

me, and we walked to the top of the slope opposite and gazed out across the desert. The air was very clear, and far, far away I could distinguish the faint blue outlines here and there capped with white of the great Suliman Berg.

"There," I said, "there is the wall of Solomon's Mines, but God knows if we shall ever climb it."

"My brother should be there, and if he is, I shall reach him somehow," said Sir Henry, in that tone of quiet confidence which marked the man.

"I hope so," I answered, and turned to go back to the camp, when I saw that we were not alone. Behind us, also gazing earnestly towards the far-off mountains, stood the great Zulu Umbopa.

The Zulu spoke when he saw that I had observed him, but addressed himself to Sir Henry, to whom he had attached himself.

"Is it to that land that thou wouldst journey, Incubu?" (a native word meaning, I believe, an elephant, and the name given to Sir Henry by the Kafirs) he said, pointing towards the mountains with his broad assegai.

I asked him sharply what he meant by addressing his master in that familiar way. It is very well for natives to have a name for one among themselves, but it is not decent that they should call one by their heathenish appellations to one's face. The man laughed a quiet little laugh which angered me.

"How dost thou know that I am not the equal of the Inkosi I serve?" he said. "He is of a royal house, no doubt; one can see it in his size and in his eye; so, mayhap, am I. At least I am as great a man. Be my mouth, oh Macumazahn, and say my words to the Inkoos Incubu, my master, for I would speak to him and to thee."

I was angry with the man, for I am not accustomed to be talked to in that way by Kafirs, but somehow he impressed me, and besides I was curious to know what he had to say, so I translated, expressing my opinion at the same time that he was an impudent fellow, and that his swagger was outrageous.

"Yes, Umbopa," answered Sir Henry, "I would journey there."

"The desert is wide and there is no water, the mountains are high and covered with snow, and man cannot say what is beyond them behind the place where the sun sets; how shalt thou come thither, Incubu, and wherefore dost thou go?"

I translated again.

"Tell him," answered Sir Henry, "that I go because I believe that a man of my blood, my brother, has gone there before me, and I go to seek him."

"That is so, Incubu; a man I met on the road told me that a white man went out into the desert two years ago towards those mountains with one servant, a hunter. They never came back."

"How do you know it was my brother?" asked Sir Henry.

"Nay, I know not. But the man, when I asked what the white man was like, said that he had thine eyes and a black beard. He said, too, that the name of the hunter with him was Jim, that he was a Bechuana hunter and wore clothes."

"There is no doubt about it," said I; "I knew Jim well."

Sir Henry nodded. "I was sure of it," he said. "If George set his mind upon a thing he generally did it. It was always so from his boyhood. If he meant to cross the Suliman Berg he has crossed it, unless some accident has overtaken him, and we must look for him on the other side."

Umbopa understood English, though he rarely spoke it.

"It is a far journey, Incubu," he put in, and I translated his remark.

"Yes," answered Sir Henry, "it is far. But there is no journey upon this earth that a man may not make if he sets his heart to it. There is nothing, Umbopa, that he cannot do, there are no mountains he may not climb, there are no deserts he cannot cross; save a mountain and a desert of which you are spared the knowledge, if love leads him and he holds his life in his hand counting it as nothing, ready to keep it or to lose it as Providence may order."

I translated.

"Great words, my father," answered the Zulu (I always called him a Zulu, though he was not really one), "great swelling words fit to fill the mouth of a man. Thou art right, my father Incubu. Listen! What is Life? It is a feather, it is the seed of the grass, blown hither and thither, sometimes multiplying itself and dying in the act, sometimes carried away into the heavens. But if the seed be good and heavy it may perchance travel a little way on the road it wills. It is well to try and journey one's road and to fight with the air. Man must die. At the worst he can but die a little sooner. I will go with thee across the desert and over the mountains, unless perchance I fall to the ground on the way, my father."

He paused awhile, and then went on with one of those strange bursts of rhetorical eloquence which Zulus sometimes indulge in, and which to my mind, full as they are of vain repetitions, show that the race is by no means devoid of poetic instinct and of intellectual power.

"What is life? Tell me, O white men, who are wise, who know the secrets of the world, and the world of stars, and the world that lies above and around the stars; who flash their words from afar without a voice; tell me, white men, the secret of our life—whither it goes and whence it comes!

"Ye cannot answer; ye know not. Listen, I will answer. Out of the dark we came, into the dark we go. Like a storm-driven bird at night we fly out of the Nowhere; for a moment our wings are seen in the light of the fire, and, lo! we are gone again into the Nowhere. Life is nothing. Life is all. It is the hand with which we hold off Death. It is the glow-worm that shines in the night-time and is black in the morning; it is the white breath of the oxen in winter; it is the little shadow that runs across the grass and loses itself at sunset."

"You are a strange man," said Sir Henry, when he ceased.

Umbopa laughed. "It seems to me that we are much alike, Incubu. Perhaps I seek a brother over the mountains."

I looked at him suspiciously. "What dost thou mean?" I asked; "what dost thou know of the mountains?"

"A little; a very little. There is a strange land there, a land of witchcraft and beautiful things; a land of brave people, and of trees, and streams, and white mountains, and of a great white road. I have heard of it. But what is the good of talking? it grows dark. Those who live to see will see."

Again I looked at him doubtfully. The man knew too much.

"Ye need not fear me, Macumazahn," he said interpreting my look. "I dig no holes for ye to fall in. I make no plots. If ever we cross those mountains behind the sun, I will tell what I know. But Death sits upon them. Be wise and turn back. Go and hunt elephant. I have spoken."

And without another word he lifted his spear in salutation, and returned towards the camp, where shortly afterwards we found him cleaning a gun like any other Kafir.

"That is an odd man," said Sir Henry.

"Yes," answered I, "too odd by half. I don't like his little ways. He knows something, and won't speak out. But I suppose it is no use quarrelling with him. We are in for a curious trip, and a mysterious Zulu won't make much difference one way or another."

Next day we made our arrangements for starting. Of course it was impossible to drag our heavy elephant rifles and other kit with us across the desert, so dismissing our bearers we made an arrangement with an old native who had a kraal close by to take care of them till we returned. It went to my heart to leave such things as those sweet tools to the tender mercies of an old thief, of a savage whose greedy eyes I could see gloating over them. But I took some precautions.

First of all I loaded all the rifles, and informed him that if he touched them they would go off. He instantly tried the experiment with my eight bore, and it did go off, and blew a hole right through one of his oxen, which were just then being driven up to the kraal, to say nothing of knocking him head over heels with the recoil. He got up considerably startled, and not at all pleased at the loss of the ox, which he had the impudence to ask me to pay for, and nothing would induce him to touch them again.

"Put the live devils up there in the thatch," he said, "out of the way, or they will kill us all."

Then I told him that if, when we came back, one of those things was missing I would kill him and all his people by witchcraft; and if we died and he tried to steal the things I would come and haunt him and turn his cattle mad and his milk sour till life was a weariness, and make the devils in the guns come out and talk to him in a way he would not like, and generally gave him a good idea of judgment to come. After that he swore he would look after them as though they were his father's spirit. He was a very superstitious old Kafir and a great villain.

Having thus disposed of our superfluous gear we arranged the kit we five—Sir Henry, Good, myself, Umbopa, and the Hottentot Ventvögel—were to take with us on our journey. It was small enough, but do what we would we could not get it down under about forty pounds a man. This is what it consisted of;—

The three express rifles and two hundred rounds of ammunition.

The two Winchester repeating rifles (for Umbopa and Ventvögel), with two hundred rounds of cartridge.

Three "Colt" revolvers and sixty rounds of cartridge.

Five Cochrane's water-bottles, each holding four pints.

Five blankets.

Twenty-five pounds' weight of biltong (sun-dried game flesh).

Ten pounds' weight of best mixed beads for gifts.

A selection of medicine, including an ounce of quinine, and one or two small surgical instruments.

Our knives, a few sundries, such as a compass, matches, a pocket filter,* tobacco, a trowel, a bottle of brandy, and the clothes we stood in.

This was our total equipment, a small one indeed for such a venture, but we dared not attempt to carry more. As it was that load was a heavy one per man to travel across the burning desert with, for in such places every additional ounce tells upon one. But try as we would we could not see our way to reducing it. There was nothing but what was absolutely necessary.

With great difficulty, and by the promise of a present of a good hunting knife each, I succeeded in persuading three wretched natives from the village to come with us for the first stage, twenty miles, and to carry each a large gourd holding a gallon of water. My object was to enable us to refill our water-bottles after the first night's march, for we determined to start in the cool of the night. I gave out to these natives that we were going to shoot ostriches, with which the desert abounded. They jabbered and shrugged their shoulders, and said we were mad and should perish of thirst, which I must say seemed very probable; but being desirous of obtaining the knives, which were almost unknown treasures up there, they consented to come, having probably reflected that, after all, our subsequent extinction would be no affair of theirs.

---

*Water filter. Thomas Cook (1808–1892), inventor of the guided tour and founder of a major British travel agency, advised travelers in his *Cook's Tourist's Handbook for Palestine and Syria* (1911) to carry "a leather drinking cup and a pocket filter."

All next day we rested and slept, and at sunset ate a hearty meal of fresh beef washed down with tea, the last, as Good sadly remarked, we were likely to drink for many a long day. Then, having made our final preparations, we lay down and waited for the moon to rise. At last about nine o'clock up she came in all her chastened glory, flooding the wild country with silver light, and throwing a weird sheen on the vast expanse of rolling desert before us, which looked as solemn and quiet and as alien to man as the star-studded firmament above. We rose up, and in a few minutes were ready, and yet we hesitated a little, as human nature is prone to hesitate on the threshold of an irrevocable step. We three white men stood there by ourselves. Umbopa, assegai in hand and the rifle across his shoulders, a few paces ahead of us, looked out fixedly across the desert; the three hired natives, with the gourds of water, and Ventvögel, were gathered in a little knot behind.

"Gentlemen," said Sir Henry, presently, in his low, deep voice, "we are going on about as strange a journey as men can make in this world. It is very doubtful if we can succeed in it. But we are three men who will stand together for good or for evil to the last. And now before we start let us for a moment pray to the Power who shapes the destinies of men, and who ages since has marked out our paths, that it may please Him to direct our steps in accordance with His will."

Taking off his hat he, for the space of a minute or so, covered his face with his hands, and Good and I did likewise.

I do not say that I am a first-rate praying man, few hunters are, and as for Sir Henry I never heard him speak like that before, and only once since, though deep down in his heart I believe he is very religious. Good too is pious, though very apt to swear. Anyhow I do not think I ever, excepting on one single occasion, put in a better prayer in my life than I did during that minute, and somehow I felt the happier for it. Our future was so completely unknown, and I think the unknown and the awful always bring a man nearer to his Maker.

"And now," said Sir Henry, "*trek.*"

So we started.

We had nothing to guide ourselves by except the distant mountains and old José da Silvestra's chart, which, considering that it was drawn by a dying and half distraught man on a fragment of linen three centuries ago, was not a very satisfactory sort of thing to work on. Still, such as it was, our sole hope of success depended on it. If we failed in finding that pool of bad water which the old Dom marked as being situated in the middle of the desert, about sixty miles from our starting-point, and as far from the mountains, we must in all probability perish miserably of thirst. And to my mind the chances of our finding it in that great sea of sand and karoo scrub seemed almost infinitesimal. Even supposing da Silvestra had marked it right, what was there to prevent its having been generations ago dried up by the sun, or trampled in by game, or filled with the drifting sand?

On we tramped silently as shades through the night and in the heavy sand. The karoo bushes caught our shins and retarded us, and the sand got into our veldtschoons and Good's shooting boots, so that every few miles we had to stop and empty them; but still the night was fairly cool, though the atmosphere was thick and heavy, giving a sort of creamy feel to the air, and we made fair progress. It was very still and lonely there in the desert, oppressively so indeed. Good felt this, and once began to whistle the "Girl I left behind me,"[3] but the notes sounded lugubrious in that vast place, and he gave it up. Shortly afterwards a little incident occurred which, though it made us jump at the time, gave rise to a laugh. Good, as the holder of the compass, which being a sailor, of course he thoroughly understood, was leading, and we were toiling along in single file behind him, when suddenly we heard the sound of an exclamation, and he vanished. Next second there arose all round us a most extraordinary hubbub, snorts, groans, wild sounds of rushing feet. In the faint light too we could descry dim galloping forms half hidden by wreaths of sand. The natives threw down their loads and prepared to bolt, but remembering that there was nowhere to bolt, cast themselves upon the ground and howled out that it was the devil. As for Sir Henry and myself we stood amazed; nor was our amazement lessened when we perceived the form of Good careering off in the direction of the mountains, apparently mounted on the back of a horse and halloaing like mad. In another second he threw up his arms, and we heard him come to the earth with a thud. Then I saw what had happened; we had stumbled right on to a herd of sleeping quagga,[4] on to the back of one of which Good had actually fallen, and the brute had naturally enough got up and made off with him. Singing out to the others that it was all right I ran towards Good, much afraid lest he should be hurt, but to my great relief found him sitting in the sand, his eye-glass still fixed firmly in his eye, rather shaken and very much startled, but not in any way injured.

After this we travelled on without any further misadventure till after one o'clock, when we called a halt, and having drunk a little water, not much, for water was precious, and rested for half an hour, started on again.

On, on we went, till at last the east began to blush like the cheek of a girl. Then there came faint rays of primrose light, that changed presently to golden bars, through which the dawn glided out across the desert. The stars grew pale and paler still till at last they vanished; the golden moon waxed wan, and her mountain ridges stood out clear against her sickly face like the bones on the face of a dying man; then came spear upon spear of glorious light flashing far away across the boundless wilderness, piercing and firing the veils of mist, till the desert was draped in a tremulous golden glow, and it was day.

Still we did not halt, though by this time we should have been glad enough to do so, for we knew that when once the sun was fully up it would be almost impossible for us to travel in it. At length, about six o'clock, we spied a little pile of rocks rising out of the plain, and to this we dragged ourselves. As luck would have it here we found an overhanging slab of rock carpeted beneath with smooth sand, which afforded a most grateful shelter from the heat. Underneath this we crept, and having drunk some water each and eaten a bit of biltong, we laid down and were soon sound asleep.

It was three o'clock in the afternoon before we woke, to find our three bearers preparing to return. They had already had enough of the desert, and no number of knives would have tempted them to come a step farther, So we had a hearty drink, and having emptied our water bottles filled them up again from the gourds they had brought with them, and then watched them depart on their twenty miles' tramp home.

At half-past four we also started on. It was lonely and desolate work, for with the exception of a few ostriches there was not a single living creature to be seen on all the vast expanse of sandy plain. It was evidently too dry for game, and with the exception of a deadly-looking cobra or two we saw no reptiles. One insect, however, was abundant, and that was the common or house fly. There they came, "not as single spies, but in battalions,"[5] as I think the Old Testament says somewhere. He is an extraordinary animal is the house fly. Go where you will you find him, and so it must always have been. I have seen him enclosed in amber, which must, I was told, have been half a million years old, looking exactly like his descendant of to-day, and I have little doubt but that when the last man lies dying on the earth he will be buzzing round—if that event should happen to occur in summer—watching for an opportunity to settle on his nose.

At sunset we halted, waiting for the moon to rise. At ten she came up beautiful and serene as ever, and with one halt about two o'clock in the morning, we trudged wearily on through the night, till at last the welcome sun put a period to our labours. We drank a little and flung ourselves down, thoroughly tired out, on the sand, and were soon all asleep. There was no need to set a watch, for we had nothing to fear from anybody or anything in that vast untenanted plain. Our only enemies were heat, thirst, and flies, but far rather would I have faced any danger from man or beast than that awful trinity. This time we were not so lucky as to find a sheltering rock to guard us from the glare of the sun, with the result that about seven o'clock we woke up experiencing the exact sensations one would attribute to a beefsteak on a gridiron. We were literally being baked through and through. The burning sun seemed to be sucking our very blood out of us. We sat up and gasped.

"Phew," said I, grabbing at the halo of flies, which buzzed cheerfully round my head. The heat did not affect them.

"My word," said Sir Henry.

"It *is* hot!" said Good.

It was hot, indeed, and there was not a bit of shelter to be had. Look where we would there was no rock or tree, nothing but an unending glare, rendered dazzling by the hot air which danced over the surface of the desert as it does over a red-hot stove.

"What is to be done?" asked Sir Henry; "we can't stand this for long."

We looked at each other blankly.

"I have it," said Good, "we must dig a hole and get in it, and cover ourselves with the karoo bushes."

It did not seem a very promising suggestion, but at least it was better than nothing, so we set to work, and with the trowel we had brought with us and our hands succeeded in about an hour in delving out a patch of ground about ten foot long by twelve wide to the depth of two feet. Then we cut a quantity of low scrub with our hunting knives, and creeping into the hole pulled it over us all, with the exception of Ventvögel, on whom, being a Hottentot, the sun had no particular effect. This gave us some slight shelter from the burning rays of the sun, but the heat in that amateur grave can be better imagined than described. The Black Hole of Calcutta[6] must have been a fool to it; indeed, to this moment I do not know how we lived through the day. There we lay panting, and every now and again moistening our lips from our scanty supply of water. Had we followed our inclinations we should have finished all we had off in the first two hours, but we had to exercise the most rigid care, for if our water failed us we knew that we must quickly perish miserably.

But everything has an end, if only you live long enough to see it, and somehow that miserable day wore on towards evening. About three o'clock in the afternoon we determined that we could stand it no longer. It would be better to die walking than to be slowly killed by heat and thirst in that dreadful hole. So taking each of us a little drink from our fast diminishing supply of water, now heated to about the same temperature as a man's blood, we staggered on.

We had now covered some fifty miles of desert. If my reader will refer to the rough copy and translation of old da Silvestra's map, he will see that the desert is marked as being forty leagues across, and the "pan bad water" is set down as being about in the middle of it. Now forty leagues is one hundred and twenty miles, consequently we ought at the most to be within twelve or fifteen miles of the water if any should really exist.

Through the afternoon we crept slowly and painfully along, scarcely doing more than a mile and a half an hour. At sunset we again rested, waiting for the moon, and after drinking a little managed to get some sleep.

Before we lay down Umbopa pointed out to us a slight and indistinct hillock on the flat surface of the desert about eight miles away. At the distance it looked like an ant-hill, and as I was dropping off to sleep I fell to wondering what it could be.

With the moon we started on again, feeling dreadfully exhausted, and suffering tortures from thirst and prickly heat. Nobody who has not felt it can know what we went through. We no longer walked, we staggered, now and again falling from exhaustion, and being obliged to call a halt every hour or so. We had scarcely energy left in us to speak. Up to now Good had chatted, and joked, for he was a merry fellow; but now he had not a joke left in him.

At last, about two o'clock, utterly worn out in body and mind, we came to the foot of this queer hill, or sand koppie,* which did at first sight resemble a gigantic ant-heap about a hundred feet high, and covering at the base nearly a morgen (two acres) of ground.

Here we halted, and driven by our desperate thirst sucked down our last drops of water. We had but half a pint a head, and we could each have drunk a gallon.

Then we lay down. Just as I was dropping off to sleep I heard Umbopa remark to himself in Zulu—

"If we cannot find water we shall all be dead before the moon rises to-morrow."

I shuddered, hot as it was. The near prospect of such an awful death is not pleasant, but even the thought of it could not keep me from sleeping.

---

*Also spelled *kopje*, small hill (South African).

Chapter 6

Water! Water!

IN TWO HOURS TIME, about four o'clock, I woke up. As soon as the first heavy demand of bodily fatigue had been satisfied, the torturing thirst from which I was suffering asserted itself. I could sleep no more. I had been dreaming that I was bathing in a running stream, with green banks and trees upon them, and I awoke to find myself in that arid wilderness, and to remember that, as Umbopa had said, if we did not find water that day we must certainly perish miserably. No human creature could live long without water in that heat. I sat up and rubbed my grimy face with my dry and horny hands. My lips and eyelids were stuck together, and it was only after some rubbing and with an effort that I was able to open them. It was not far off the dawn, but there was none of the bright feel of dawn in the air, which was thick with a hot murkiness I cannot describe. The others were still sleeping. Presently it began to grow light enough to read, so I drew out a little pocket copy of the "Ingoldsby Legends" I had brought with me, and read the "Jackdaw of Rheims."[1] When I got to where

> "A nice little boy held a golden ewer,
> Embossed, and filled with water as pure
> As any that flows between Rheims and Namur,"

I literally smacked my cracked lips, or rather tried to smack them. The mere thought of that pure water made me mad. If the Cardinal had been there with his bell, book, and candle, I would have whipped in and drank his water up, yes, even if he had already filled it with the suds of soap worthy of washing the hands of the Pope, and I knew that the whole concentrated curse of the Catholic Church should fall upon me for so doing. I almost think I must have been a little light-headed with thirst and weariness and want of food; for I fell to thinking how astonished the Cardinal and his nice little boy and the jackdaw would have looked to see a burnt up, brown-eyed, grizzled-haired little elephant hunter suddenly bound in and put his dirty face into the basin, and swallow every drop of the precious water. The idea amused me so that I laughed or rather cackled aloud, which woke the others up, and they began to rub *their* dirty faces and get *their* gummed-up lips and eyelids apart.

As soon as we were all well awake, we fell to discussing the situation, which was serious enough. Not a drop of water was left. We turned the water-bottles upside down, and licked the tops, but it was a failure, they were as dry as a bone. Good, who had charge of the bottle of brandy, got it out and looked at it longingly; but Sir Henry promptly took it away from him, for to drink raw spirit would only have been to precipitate the end.

"If we do not find water we shall die," he said.

"If we can trust to the old Don's map there should be some about," I said; but nobody seemed to derive much satisfaction from that remark. It was so evident that no great faith could be put in the map. It was now gradually growing light, and as we sat blankly staring at each other, I observed the Hottentot Ventvögel rise and begin to walk about with his eyes on the ground. Presently he stopped short, and uttering a guttural exclamation, pointed to the earth.

"What is it?" we exclaimed; and simultaneously rose and went to where he was standing pointing at the ground.

"Well," I said, "it is pretty fresh Springbok spoor;[2] what of it?"

"Sprinbucks do not go far from water," he answered in Dutch.

"No," I answered, "I forgot; and thank God for it."

This little discovery put new life into us; it is wonderful how, when one is in a desperate position, one catches at the slightest hope, and feels almost happy in it. On a dark night a single star is better than nothing.

Meanwhile Ventvögel was lifting his snub nose, and sniffing the hot air for all the world like an old Impala ram who scents danger. Presently he spoke again.

"I *smell* water," he said.

Then we felt quite jubilant, for we knew what a wonderful instinct these wild-bred men possess.

Just at that moment the sun came up gloriously, and revealed so grand a sight to our astonished eyes that for a moment or two we even forgot our thirst.

For there, not more than forty or fifty miles from us, glittering like silver in the early rays of the morning sun, were Sheba's breasts; and stretching away for hundreds of miles on each side of them was the great Suliman Berg. Now that I, sitting here, attempt to describe the extraordinary grandeur and beauty of that sight language seems to fail me. I am impotent even before its memory. There, straight before us, were two enormous mountains, the like of which are not, I believe, to be seen in Africa, if, indeed, there are any other such in the world, measuring each at least fifteen thousand feet in height, standing not more than a dozen miles apart, connected by a precipitous cliff of rock, and towering up in awful white solemnity straight into the sky. These mountains standing thus, like the pillars of a gigantic gateway, are shaped exactly like a woman's breasts. Their bases swelled gently up from the plain, looking, at that distance, perfectly round and smooth; and on the top of each was a vast round hillock covered with snow, exactly corresponding to the nipple on the female breast. The stretch of cliff which connected them appeared to be some thousand feet in height, and perfectly precipitous, and on each side of them, as far as the eye could reach, extended similar lines of cliff, broken only here and there by flat table-topped mountains, something like the world-famed one at Cape Town;[3] a formation, by the way, very common in Africa.

To describe the grandeur of the whole view is beyond my powers. There was something so inexpressibly solemn and overpowering about those huge volcanoes—for doubtless they are extinct volcanoes—that it fairly took our breath away. For awhile the morning lights played upon the snow and the brown and swelling masses beneath, and then, as though to veil the majestic sight from our curious eyes, strange mists and clouds gathered and increased around them, till presently we could only trace their pure and gigantic outline swelling ghostlike through the fleecy envelope. Indeed, as we afterwards discovered, they were normally wrapped in this curious gauzy mist, which doubtless accounted for one not having made them out more clearly before.

Scarcely had the mountains vanished into cloud-clad privacy before our thirst—literally a burning question—reasserted itself.

It was all very well for Ventvögel to say he smelt water, but look which way we would we could see no signs of it. So far as the eye could reach there was nothing but arid sweltering sand and karoo scrub. We walked round the hillock and gazed about anxiously on the other side, but it was the same story, not a drop of water was to be seen; there was no indication of a pan, a pool, or a spring.

"You are a fool," I said, angrily, to Ventvögel; "there is no water."

But still he lifted his ugly snub nose and sniffed.

"I smell it, Baas" (master), he answered; "it is somewhere in the air."

"Yes," I said, "no doubt it is in the clouds, and about two months hence it will fall and wash our bones."

Sir Henry stroked his yellow beard thoughtfully. "Perhaps it is on the top of the hill," he suggested.

"Rot," said Good; "whoever heard of water being found on the top of a hill!"

"Let us go and look," I put in, and hopelessly enough we scrambled up the sandy sides of the hillock, Umbopa leading. Presently he stopped as though he was petrified.

"Nanzia manzie!" (here is water), he cried with a loud voice.

We rushed up to him, and there, sure enough, in a deep cup or indentation on the very top of the sand koppie was an undoubted pool of water. How it came to be in such a strange place we did not stop to inquire, nor did we hesitate at its black and uninviting appearance. It was water, or a good imitation of it, and that was enough for us. We gave a bound and a rush, and in another second were all down on our stomachs sucking up the uninviting fluid as though it were nectar fit for the gods. Heavens, how we did drink! Then when we had done drinking we tore off our clothes and sat down in it, absorbing the moisture through our parched skins. You, my reader, who have only to turn on a couple of taps and summon "hot" and "cold" from an unseen vasty boiler, can have little idea of the luxury of that muddy wallow in brackish tepid water.

After awhile we arose from it, refreshed indeed, and fell to on our "biltong,"[4] of which we had scarcely been able to touch a mouthful for twenty-four hours, and ate our fill. Then we smoked a pipe, and lay down by the side of that blessed pool under the overhanging shadow of the bank, and slept till mid-day.

All that day we rested there by the water, thanking our stars that we had been lucky enough to find it, bad as it was, and not forgetting to render a due share of gratitude to the shade of the long-departed da Silvestra, who had corked it down so accurately on the tail of his shirt. The wonderful thing to us was that it should have lasted so long, and the only way that I can account for it is by the supposition that it is fed by some spring deep down in the sand.

Having filled both ourselves and our water-bottles as full as possible, in far better spirits we started off again with the moon. That night we covered nearly five-and-twenty miles, but, needless to say, found no more water, though we were lucky enough on the following day to get a little shade behind some ant-heaps. When the sun rose and, for awhile, cleared away the mysterious mists, Suliman's Berg and the two majestic breasts, now only about twenty miles off, seemed to be towering right above us, and looked grander than ever. At the approach of evening we started on again, and, to cut a long story short, by daylight next morning found ourselves upon the lowest slopes of Sheba's left breast, for which we had been steadily steering. By this time our water was again exhausted and we were suffering severely from thirst, nor indeed could we see any chance of relieving it till we reached the snow line far far above us. After resting an hour or two, driven to it by our torturing thirst, we went on again, toiling painfully in the burning heat up the lava slopes, for we found that the huge base of the mountain was composed entirely of lava beds belched out in some far past age.

By eleven o'clock we were utterly exhausted, and were, generally speaking, in a very bad way indeed. The lava clinker,* over which we had to make our way, though comparatively smooth compared with some clinker I have heard of, such as that on the Island of Ascension[5] for instance, was yet rough enough to make our feet very sore, and this, together with our other miseries, had pretty well finished us. A few hundred yards above us were some large lumps of lava, and towards these we made with the intention of lying down beneath their shade. We reached them, and to our surprise, so far as we had a capacity for surprise left in us, on a little plateau or ridge close by we saw that the lava was covered with a dense green growth. Evidently

---

*Coarse, irregular surface layer of lava.

soil formed from decomposed lava had rested there, and in due course had become the receptacle of seeds deposited by birds. But we did not take much further interest in the green growth, for one cannot live on grass like Nebuchadnezzar.[6] That requires a special dispensation of Providence and peculiar digestive organs. So we sat down under the rocks and groaned, and I for one heartily wished that we had never started on this fool's errand. As we were sitting there I saw Umbopa get up and hobble off towards the patch of green, and a few minutes afterwards, to my great astonishment, I perceived that usually uncommonly dignified individual dancing and shouting like a maniac, and waving something green. Off we all scrambled towards him as fast as our wearied limbs would carry us, hoping that he had found water.

"What is it, Umbopa, son of a fool?" I shouted in Zulu.

"It is food and water, Macumazahn," and again he waved the green thing.

Then I saw what he had got. It was a melon. We had hit upon a patch of wild melons, thousands of them, and dead ripe.

"Melons!" I yelled to Good, who was next me; and in another second he had his false teeth fixed in one.

I think we ate about six each before we had done, and, poor fruit as they were, I doubt if I ever thought anything nicer.

But melons are not very satisfying, and when we had satisfied our thirst with their pulpy substance, and set a stock to cool by the simple process of cutting them in two and setting them end on in the hot sun to get cold by evaporation, we began to feel exceedingly hungry. We had still some biltong left, but our stomachs turned from biltong, and besides we had to be very sparing of it, for we could not say when we should get more food. Just at this moment a lucky thing happened. Looking towards the desert I saw a flock of about ten large birds flying straight towards us.

"Skit, Baas, skit!" (shoot, Master, shoot!), whispered the Hottentot, throwing himself on his face, an example which we all followed.

Then I saw that the birds were a flock of pauw (bustards),* and

---

*The heaviest bird in Africa, the great paauw or kori bustard (*Ardeotis kori*) can weigh more than 40 pounds; an omnivore, it sometimes eats carrion or hares found on shortgrass plains.

that they would pass within fifty yards of my head. Taking one of the repeating Winchesters I waited till they were nearly over us, and then jumped on to my feet. On seeing me the pauw bunched up together, as I expected they would, and I fired two shots straight into the thick of them, and, as luck would have it, brought one down, a fine fellow, that weighed about twenty pounds. In half an hour we had a fire made of dry melon stalks, and he was toasting over it, and we had such a feed as we had not had for a week. We ate that pauw; nothing was left of him but his bones and his beak, and we felt not a little the better afterwards.

That night we again went on with the moon, carrying as many melons as we could with us. As we got higher up we found the air grew cooler and cooler, which was a great relief to us, and at dawn, so far as we could judge, were not more than about a dozen miles from the snow line. Here we found more melons, so had no longer any anxiety about water, for we knew that we should soon get plenty of snow. But the ascent had now become very precipitous, and we made but slow progress, not more than a mile an hour. Also that night we ate our last morsel of biltong. As yet, with the exception of the pauw, we had seen no living thing on the mountain, nor had we come across a single spring or stream of water, which struck us as very odd, considering all the snow above us, which must, we thought, melt sometimes. But as we afterwards discovered, owing to some cause, which it is quite beyond my power to explain, all the streams flowed down upon the north side of the mountains.

We now began to grow very anxious about food. We had escaped death by thirst, but it seemed probable that it was only to die of hunger. The events of the next three miserable days are best described by copying the entries made at the time in my note-book.

21st May.—Started 11 a.m., finding the atmosphere quite cold enough to travel by day, carrying some watermelons with us. Struggled on all day, but saw no more melons, having, evidently, passed out of their district. Saw no game of any sort. Halted for the night at sundown, having had no food for many hours. Suffered much during the night from cold.

22nd.—Started at sunrise again, feeling very faint and weak. Only made five miles all day; found some patches of snow, of which we ate, but nothing else. Camped at night under the edge of a great

plateau. Cold bitter. Drank a little brandy each, and huddled ourselves together, each wrapped up in our blanket to keep ourselves
alive. Are now suffering frightfully from starvation and weariness.
Thought that Ventvögel would have died during the night.

23rd.—Struggled forward once more as soon as the sun was well
up, and had thawed our limbs a little. We are now in a dreadful
plight, and I fear that unless we get food this will be our last day's
journey. But little brandy left. Good, Sir Henry, and Umbopa bear
up wonderfully, but Ventvögel is in a very bad way. Like most Hot-
tentots, he cannot stand cold. Pangs of hunger not so bad, but have
a sort of numb feeling about the stomach. Others say the same. We
are now on a level with the precipitous chain, or wall of lava, con-
necting the two breasts, and the view is glorious. Behind us the great
glowing desert rolls away to the horizon, and before us lies mile
upon mile of smooth hard snow almost level, but swelling gently
upwards, out of the centre of which the nipple of the mountain,
which appears to be some miles in circumference, rises about four
thousand feet into the sky. Not a living thing is to be seen. God help
us, I fear our time has come.

And now I will drop the journal, partly because it is not very interesting reading, and partly because what follows requires perhaps
rather more accurate telling.

All that day (the 23rd May) we struggled slowly on up the incline
of snow, lying down from time to time to rest. A strange, gaunt crew
we must have looked, as, laden as we were, we dragged our weary
feet over the dazzling plain, glaring round us with hungry eyes. Not
that there was much use in glaring, for there was nothing to eat. We
did not do more than seven miles that day. Just before sunset we
found ourselves right under the nipple of Sheba's left breast, which
towered up thousands of feet into the air above us, a vast, smooth
hillock of frozen snow. Bad as we felt we could not but appreciate
the wonderful scene, made even more wonderful by the flying rays
of light from the setting sun, which here and there stained the snow
blood red, and crowned the towering mass above us with a diadem
of glory.

"I say," gasped Good, presently, "we ought to be somewhere near
the cave the old gentleman wrote about."

"Yes," said I, "if there is a cave."

"Come, Quatermain," groaned Sir Henry, "don't talk like that; I have every faith in the Dom; remember the water. We shall find the place soon."

"If we don't find it before dark we are dead men, that is all about it," was my consolatory reply.

For the next ten minutes we trudged on in silence, when suddenly Umbopa, who was marching along beside me, wrapped up in his blanket, and with a leather belt strapped so tight round his stomach to "make his hunger small," as he said, that his waist looked like a girl's, caught me by the arm.

"Look!" he said, pointing towards the springing slope of the nipple.

I followed his glance, and perceived some two hundred yards from us what appeared to be a hole in the snow.

"It is the cave," said Umbopa.

We made the best of our way to the spot, and found sure enough that the hole was the mouth of a cave, no doubt the same as that of which da Silvestra wrote. We were none too soon, for just as we reached shelter the sun went down with startling rapidity, leaving the whole place nearly dark. In these latitudes there is but little twilight. We crept into the cave, which did not appear to be very big, and huddling ourselves together for warmth, swallowed what remained of our brandy—barely a mouthful each—and tried to forget our miseries in sleep. But this the cold was too intense to allow us to do. I am convinced that at that great altitude the thermometer cannot have been less than fourteen or fifteen degrees below freezing point. What this meant to us, enervated as we were by hardship, want of food, and the great heat of the desert, my reader can imagine better than I can describe. Suffice it to say that it was something as near death from exposure as I have ever felt. There we sat hour after hour through the bitter night, feeling the frost wander round and nip us now in the finger, now in the foot, and now in the face. In vain did we huddle up closer and closer; there was no warmth in our miserable starved carcasses. Sometimes one of us would drop into an uneasy slumber for a few minutes, but we could not sleep long, and perhaps it was fortunate, for I doubt if we should ever have woke again. I believe it was only by force of will that we kept ourselves alive at all.

Not very long before dawn I heard the Hottentot Ventvögel, whose teeth had been chattering all night like castanets, give a deep sigh, and then his teeth stopped chattering. I did not think anything of it at the time, concluding that he had gone to sleep. His back was resting against mine, and it seemed to grow colder and colder, till at last it was like ice.

At length the air began to grow grey with light, then swift golden arrows came flashing across the snow, and at last the glorious sun peeped up above the lava wall and looked in upon our half-frozen forms and upon Ventvögel, sitting there amongst us *stone dead*. No wonder his back had felt cold, poor fellow. He had died when I heard him sigh, and was now almost frozen stiff. Shocked beyond measure we dragged ourselves from the corpse (strange the horror we all have of the companionship of a dead body), and left it still sitting there, with its arms clasped round its knees.

By this time the sunlight was pouring its cold rays (for here they were cold) straight in at the mouth of the cave. Suddenly I heard an exclamation of fear from some one, and turned my head down the cave.

And this was what I saw. Sitting at the end of it, for it was not more than twenty feet long, was another form, of which the head rested on the chest and the long arms hung down. I stared at it, and saw that it too was a *dead man*, and what was more, a white man.

The others saw it too, and the sight proved too much for our shattered nerves. One and all we scrambled out of the cave as fast as our half-frozen limbs would allow.

Chapter 7

Solomon's Road

OUTSIDE THE CAVE WE halted, feeling rather foolish.

"I am going back," said Sir Henry.

"Why?" asked Good.

"Because it has struck me that—what we saw—may be my brother."

This was a new idea, and we re-entered the cave to put it to the proof. After the bright light outside, our eyes, weak as they were with staring at the snow, could not for awhile pierce the gloom of the cave. Presently however we grew accustomed to the semi-darkness, and advanced on the dead form.

Sir Henry knelt down and peered into its face.

"Thank God," he said, with a sigh of relief, "it is not my brother."

Then I went and looked. The corpse was that of a tall man in middle life with aquiline features, grizzled hair, and a long black moustache. The skin was perfectly yellow, and stretched tightly over the bones. Its clothing, with the exception of what seemed to be the remains of a woollen pair of hose, had been removed, leaving the skeleton-like frame naked. Round the neck hung a yellow ivory crucifix. The corpse was frozen perfectly stiff.

"Who on earth can it be?" said I.

"Can't you guess?" asked Good.

I shook my head.

"Why, the old Dom, José da Silvestra, of course—who else?"

"Impossible," I gasped, "he died three hundred years ago."

"And what is there to prevent his lasting for three thousand years in this atmosphere I should like to know?" asked Good. "If only the air is cold enough flesh and blood will keep as fresh as New Zealand mutton for ever, and Heaven knows it is cold enough here. The sun never gets in here; no animal comes here to tear or destroy. No doubt his slave, of whom he speaks on the map, took off his clothes and left him. He could not have buried him alone. Look here," he went on, stooping down and picking up a queer shaped bone scraped at the end into a sharp point, "here is the 'cleft-bone' that he used to draw the map with."

We gazed astonished for a moment, forgetting our own miseries in this extraordinary and, as it seemed to us, semi-miraculous sight.

"Ay," said Sir Henry, "and here is where he got his ink from," and he pointed to a small wound on the dead man's left arm. "Did ever man see such a thing before?"

There was no longer any doubt about the matter, which I confess for my own part perfectly appalled me. There he sat, the dead man, whose directions, written some ten generations ago, had led us to this spot. There in my own hand was the rude pen with which he had written them, and there round his neck was the crucifix his dying lips had kissed. Gazing at him my imagination could reconstruct the whole scene, the traveller dying of cold and starvation, and yet striving to convey the great secret he had discovered to the world:—the awful loneliness of his death, of which the evidence sat before us. It even seemed to me that I could trace in his strongly marked features a likeness to those of my poor friend Silvestre his descendant, who had died twenty years ago in my arms, but perhaps that was fancy. At any rate, there he sat, a sad memento of the fate that so often overtakes those who would penetrate into the unknown; and there probably he will still sit, crowned with the dread majesty of death, for centuries yet unborn, to startle the eyes of wanderers like ourselves, if any such should ever come again to invade his loneliness. The thing overpowered us, already nearly done to death as we were with cold and hunger.

"Let us go," said Sir Henry, in a low voice; "stay, we will give him a companion," and lifting up the dead body of the Hottentot Ventvögel, he placed it near that of the old Dom. Then he stooped down, and with a jerk broke the rotten string of the crucifix round his neck, for his fingers were too cold to attempt to unfasten it. I believe that he still has it. I took the pen, and it is before me as I write—sometimes I sign my name with it.

Then leaving those two, the proud white man of a past age, and the poor Hottentot, to keep their eternal vigil in the midst of the eternal snows, we crept out of the cave into the welcome sunshine and resumed our path, wondering in our hearts how many hours it would be before we were even as they are.

When we had gone about half a mile we came to the edge of the plateau, for the nipple of the mountain did not rise out of its exact centre, though from the desert side it seemed to do so. What lay below us we could not see, for the landscape was wreathed in billows of morning mist. Presently, however, the higher layers of mist cleared a little, and revealed some five hundred yards beneath us, at the end of a long slope of snow, a patch of green grass, through which a stream was running. Nor was this all. By the stream, basking in the morning sun, stood and lay a group of from ten to fifteen *large antelopes*—at that distance we could not see what they were.

The sight filled us with an unreasoning joy. There was food in plenty if only we could get it. But the question was how to get it. The beasts were fully six hundred yards off, a very long shot, and one not to be depended on when one's life hung on the results.

Rapidly we discussed the advisability of trying to stalk the game, but finally reluctantly dismissed it. To begin with the wind was not favourable, and further, we should be certain to be perceived, however careful we were, against the blinding background of snow, which we should be obliged to traverse.

"Well, we must have a try from where we are," said Sir Henry. "Which shall it be, Quatermain, the repeating rifles or the expresses?"

Here again was a question. The Winchester repeaters—of which we had two, Umbopa carrying poor Ventvögel's as well as his own—were sighted up to a thousand yards, whereas the expresses were only sighted to three hundred and fifty, beyond which distance shooting with them was more or less guess work. On the other hand, if they did hit, the express bullets being expanding, were much more likely to bring the game down. It was a knotty point, but I made up my mind that we must risk it and use the expresses.

"Let each of us take the buck opposite to him. Aim well at the point of the shoulder, and high up," said I; "and Umbopa do you give the word, so that we may all fire together."

Then came a pause, each man aiming his level best, as indeed one is likely to do when one knows that life itself depends upon the shot.

"Fire!" said Umbopa, in Zulu, and at almost the same instant the three rifles rang out loudly; three clouds of smoke hung for a moment before us, and a hundred echoes went flying away over the silent snow. Presently the smoke cleared, and revealed—oh, joy!—a great buck lying on its back and kicking furiously in its death agony. We gave a yell of triumph—we were saved, we should not starve. Weak as we were, we rushed down the intervening slope of snow, and in ten minutes from the time of firing the animal's heart and liver were lying smoking before us. But now a new difficulty arose, we had no fuel, and therefore could make no fire to cook them at. We gazed at each other in dismay.

"Starving men must not be fanciful," said Good; "we must eat raw meat."

There was no other way out of the dilemma, and our gnawing hunger made the proposition less distasteful than it would otherwise have been. So we took the heart and liver and buried them for a few minutes in a patch of snow to cool them. Then we washed them in the ice-cold water of the stream, and lastly ate them greedily. It sounds horrible enough, but honestly, I never tasted anything so good as that raw meat. In a quarter of an hour we were changed men. Our life and our vigour came back to us, our feeble pulses grew strong again, and the blood went coursing through our veins. But mindful of the results of over-feeding on starving stomachs, we were careful not to eat too much, stopping whilst we were still hungry.

"Thank God!" said Sir Henry; "that brute has saved our lives. What is it, Quatermain?"

I rose and went to look at the antelope, for I was not certain. It was about the size of a donkey, with large curved horns. I had never seen one like it before, the species was new to me. It was brown, with faint red stripes, and a thick coat. I afterwards discovered that the natives of that wonderful country called the species "Inco." It was very rare, and only found at a great altitude where no other game would live. The animal was fairly shot high up in the shoulder, though whose bullet it was that brought it down we could not, of course, discover. I believe that Good, mindful of his marvellous shot at the giraffe, secretly set it down to his own prowess, and we did not contradict him.

We had been so busy satisfying our starving stomachs that we had hitherto not found time to look about us. But now, having set Umbopa to cut off as much of the best meat as we were likely to be able to carry, we began to inspect our surroundings. The mist had now cleared away, for it was eight o'clock, and the sun had sucked it up, so we were able to take in all the country before us at a glance. I know not how to describe the glorious panorama which unfolded itself to our enraptured gaze. I have never seen anything like it before, nor shall, I suppose, again.

Behind and over us towered Sheba's snowy breasts, and below, some five thousand feet beneath where we stood, lay league on league of the most lovely champaign country.[1] Here were dense patches of lofty forest, there a great river wound its silvery way. To the left stretched a vast expanse of rich undulating veldt or grass land, on which we could just make out countless herds of game or cattle, at that distance we could not tell which. This expanse appeared to be ringed in by a wall of distant mountains. To the right the country was more or less mountainous, that is, solitary hills stood up from its level, with stretches of cultivated lands between, amongst which we could distinctly see groups of dome-shaped huts. The landscape lay before us like a map, in which rivers flashed like silver snakes, and Alp-like peaks crowned with wildly twisted snow wreaths rose in solemn grandeur, whilst over all was the glad sunlight and the wide breath of Nature's happy life.

Two curious things struck us as we gazed. First, that the country before us must lie at least five thousand feet higher than the desert we had crossed, and secondly, that all the rivers flowed from south to north. As we had painful reason to know, there was no water at all on the southern side of the vast range on which we stood, but on the northern side were many streams, most of which appeared to unite with the great river we could trace winding away farther than we could follow it.

We sat down for a while and gazed in silence at this wonderful view. Presently Sir Henry spoke.

"Isn't there something on the map about Solomon's Great Road?" he said.

I nodded, my eyes still looking out over the far country.

"Well, look; there it is!" and he pointed a little to our right.

Good and I looked accordingly, and there, winding away towards the plain, was what appeared to be a wide turnpike road. We had not seen it at first because it, on reaching the plain, turned behind some broken country. We did not say anything, at least not much; we were beginning to lose the sense of wonder. Somehow it did not seem particularly unnatural that we should find a sort of Roman road in this strange land. We accepted the fact, that was all.

"Well," said Good, "it must be quite near us if we cut off to the right. Hadn't we better be making a start?"

This was sound advice, and so soon as we had washed our faces and hands in the stream, we acted on it. For a mile or so we made our way over boulders and across patches of snow, till suddenly, on reaching the top of the little rise, there lay the road at our feet. It was a splendid road cut out of the solid rock, at least fifty feet wide, and apparently well kept; but the odd thing about it was that it seemed to begin there. We walked down and stood on it, but one single hundred paces behind us, in the direction of Sheba's breasts, it vanished, the whole surface of the mountain being strewn with boulders interspersed with patches of snow.

"What do you make of that, Quatermain?" asked Sir Henry.

I shook my head, I could make nothing of it.

"I have it!" said Good; "the road no doubt ran right over the range and across the desert the other side, but the sand of the desert has covered it up, and above us it has been obliterated by some volcanic eruption of molten lava."

This seemed a good suggestion; at any rate, we accepted it, and proceeded down the mountain. It was a very different business travelling along down hill on that magnificent pathway with full stomachs to what it had been travelling up hill over the snow quite starved and almost frozen. Indeed, had it not been for melancholy recollections of poor Ventvögel's sad fate, and of that grim cave where he kept company with the old Don, we should have been positively cheerful, notwithstanding the sense of unknown dangers before us. Every mile we walked the atmosphere grew softer and balmier, and the country before us shone with a yet more luminous beauty. As for the road itself, I never saw such an engineering work, though Sir Henry said that the great road over the St. Gothard in

Switzerland[2] was very like it. No difficulty had been too great for the Old World engineer who designed it. At one place we came to a great ravine three hundred feet broad and at least a hundred deep. This vast gulf was actually filled in, apparently with huge blocks of dressed stone, with arches pierced at the bottom for a water-way, over which the road went sublimely on. At another place it was cut in zigzags out of the side of a precipice five hundred feet deep, and in a third it tunnelled right through the base of an intervening ridge a space of thirty yards or more.

Here we noticed that the sides of the tunnel were covered with quaint sculptures mostly of mailed figures driving in chariots. One, which was exceedingly beautiful, represented a whole battle scene with a convoy of captives being marched off in the distance.

"Well," said Sir Henry, after inspecting this ancient work of art, "it is very well to call this Solomon's Road, but my humble opinion is that the Egyptians have been here before Solomon's people ever set a foot on it. If that isn't Egyptian handiwork, all I have to say is it is very like it."

By midday we had advanced sufficiently far down the mountain to reach the region where wood was to be met with. First we came to scattered bushes which grew more and more frequent, till at last we found the road winding through a vast grove of silver trees similar to those which are to be seen on the slopes of Table Mountain at Cape Town. I had never before met with them in all my wanderings, except at the Cape, and their appearance here astonished me greatly.

"Ah!" said Good, surveying these shining-leaved trees with evident enthusiasm, "here is lots of wood, let us stop and cook some dinner; I have about digested that raw meat."

Nobody objected to this, so leaving the road we made our way to a stream which was babbling away not far off, and soon had a goodly fire of dry boughs blazing. Cutting off some substantial hunks from the flesh of the inco which we had brought with us, we proceeded to toast them on the end of sharp sticks, as one sees the Kafirs do, and ate them with relish. After filling ourselves, we lit our pipes and gave ourselves up to enjoyment, which, compared to the hardships we had recently undergone, seemed almost heavenly.

The brook, of which the banks were clothed with dense masses of a gigantic species of maidenhair fern* interpersed with feathery tufts of wild asparagus, babbled away merrily at our side, the soft air murmured through the leaves of the silver trees, doves cooed around, and bright-winged birds flashed like living gems from bough to bough. It was like Paradise.

The magic of the place, combined with the overwhelming sense of dangers left behind, and of the promised land reached at last, seemed to charm us into silence. Sir Henry and Umbopa sat conversing in a mixture of broken English and Kitchen Zulu in a low voice, but earnestly enough, and I lay, with my eyes half shut, upon that fragrant bed of fern and watched them. Presently I missed Good, and looked to see what had become of him. As I did so I observed him sitting by the bank of the stream, in which he had been bathing. He had nothing on but his flannel shirt, and his natural habits of extreme neatness having reasserted themselves, was actively employed in making a most elaborate toilet. He had washed his guttapercha collar, thoroughly shaken out his trousers, coat, and waistcoat, and was now folding them up neatly till he was ready to put them on, shaking his head sadly as he did so over the numerous rents and tears in them, which had naturally resulted from our frightful journey. Then he took his boots, scrubbed them with a handful of fern, and finally rubbed them over with a piece of fat, which he had carefully saved from the inco meat, till they looked, comparatively speaking, respectable. Having inspected them judiciously through his eye-glass, he put them on and began a fresh operation. From a little bag he carried he produced a pocket comb in which was fixed a tiny looking-glass, and in this he surveyed himself. Apparently he was not satisfied, for he proceeded to do his hair with great care. Then came a pause whilst he again contemplated the effect; still it was not satisfactory. He felt his chin, on which was now the accumulated scrub of a ten days' beard. "Surely," thought I, "he is not going to try and shave." But so it was. Taking the piece of fat with which he had greased his boots he washed it carefully in the stream. Then diving again into the bag he brought out a little pocket razor with a guard to it, such as are sold to people afraid of cutting themselves, or to those about to undertake

---

*This fern (*Adiantum pedatum*) has dainty, feathery fronds and often grows on limestone soil in rich woodlands.

a sea voyage. Then he vigorously scrubbed his face and chin with the fat and began. But it was evidently a painful process, for he groaned very much over it, and I was convulsed with inward laughter as I watched him struggling with that stubbly beard. It seemed so very odd that a man should take the trouble to shave himself with a piece of fat in such a place and under such circumstances. At last he succeeded in getting the worst of the scrub off the right side of his face and chin, when suddenly I, who was watching, became aware of a flash of light that passed just by his head.

Good sprang up with a profane exclamation (if it had not been a safety razor he would certainly have cut his throat), and so did I, without the exclamation, and this was what I saw. Standing there, not more than twenty paces from where I was, and ten from Good, were a group of men. They were very tall and copper-coloured, and some of them wore great plumes of black feathers and short cloaks of leopard skins; this was all I noticed at the moment. In front of them stood a youth of about seventeen, his hand still raised and his body bent forward in the attitude of a Grecian statue of a spear thrower. Evidently the flash of light had been a weapon, and he had thrown it.

As I looked an old soldier-like looking man stepped forward out of the group, and catching the youth by the arm said something to him. Then they advanced upon us.

Sir Henry, Good, and Umbopa had by this time seized their rifles and lifted them threateningly. The party of natives still came on. It struck me that they could not know what rifles were, or they would not have treated them with such contempt.

"Put down your guns!" I hallooed to the others, seeing that our only chance of safety lay in conciliation. They obeyed, and walking to the front I addressed the elderly man who had checked the youth.

"Greeting," I said, in Zulu, not knowing what language to use. To my surprise I was understood.

"Greeting," answered the man, not, indeed, in the same tongue, but in a dialect so closely allied to it, that neither Umbopa or myself had any difficulty in understanding it. Indeed, as we afterwards found out, the language spoken by this people was an old-fashioned form of the Zulu tongue, bearing about the same relationship to it that the English of Chaucer does to the English of the nineteenth century.

"Whence come ye?" he went on, "what are ye? and why are the

faces of three of ye white, and the face of the fourth as the face of our mother's sons?" and he pointed to Umbopa. I looked at Umbopa as he said it, and it flashed across me that he was right. Umbopa was like the faces of the men before me, so was his great form. But I had not time to reflect on this coincidence.

"We are strangers, and come in peace," I answered, speaking very slow, so that he might understand me, "and this man is our servant."

"Ye lie," he answered, "no strangers can cross the mountains where all things die. But what do your lies matter, if ye are strangers then ye must die, for no strangers may live in the land of the Kukuanas. It is the king's law. Prepare then to die, O strangers!"

I was slightly staggered at this, more especially as I saw the hands of some of the party of men steal down to their sides, where hung on each what looked to me like a large and heavy knife.

"What does that beggar say?" asked Good.

"He says we are going to be scragged," I answered grimly.

"Oh, Lord," groaned Good; and, as was his way when perplexed, put his hand to his false teeth, dragging the top set down and allowing them to fly back to his jaw with a snap. It was a most fortunate move, for next second the dignified crowd of Kukuanas gave a simultaneous yell of horror, and bolted back some yards.

"What's up?" said I.

"It's his teeth," whispered Sir Henry, excitedly. "He moved them. Take them out, Good, take them out!"

He obeyed, slipping the set into the sleeve of his flannel shirt.

In another second curiosity had overcome fear, and the men advanced slowly. Apparently they had now forgotten their amiable intentions of doing for us.

"How is it, O strangers," asked the old man solemnly, "that the teeth of the man (pointing to Good, who had nothing on but a flannel shirt, and had only half finished his shaving) whose body is clothed, and whose legs are bare, who grows hair on one side of his sickly face and not on the other, and who has one shining and transparent eye, and teeth that move of themselves, coming away from the jaws and returning of their own will?"

"Open your mouth," I said to Good, who promptly curled up his lips and grinned at the old gentleman like an angry dog, revealing to their astonished gaze two thin red lines of gum as utterly innocent of ivories as a new-born elephant. His audience gasped.

"Where are his teeth?" they shouted; "with our eyes we saw them."

Turning his head slowly and with a gesture of ineffable contempt, Good swept his hand across his mouth. Then he grinned again, and lo, there were two rows of lovely teeth.

The young man who had flung the knife threw himself down on the grass and gave vent to a prolonged howl of terror; and as for the old gentleman his knees knocked together with fear.

"I see that ye are spirits," he said, falteringly; "did ever man born of woman have hair on one side of his face and not on the other, or a round and transparent eye, or teeth which moved and melted away and grew again? Pardon us, O my lords."

Here was luck indeed, and, needless to say, I jumped at the chance.

"It is granted," I said, with an imperial smile. "Nay, ye shall know the truth. We come from another world, though we are men such as ye; we come," I went on, "from the biggest star that shines at night."

"Oh! oh!" groaned the chorus of astonished aborigines.

"Yes," I went on, "we do, indeed;" and I again smiled benignly as I uttered that amazing lie. "We come to stay with you a little while, and bless you by our sojourn. Ye will see, O friends, that I have prepared myself by learning your language."

"It is so, it is so," said the chorus.

"Only, my lord," put in the old gentleman, "thou hast learnt it very badly."

I cast an indignant glance at him, and he quailed.

"Now, friends," I continued, "ye might think that after so long a journey we should find it in our hearts to avenge such a reception, mayhap to strike cold in death the impious hand that—that, in short—threw a knife at the head of him whose teeth come and go."

"Spare him, my lords," said the old man in supplication; "he is the king's son, and I am his uncle. If anything befalls him his blood will be required at my hands."

"Yes, that is certainly so," put in the young man with great emphasis.

"You may perhaps doubt our power to avenge," I went on, heedless of this by-play. "Stay, I will show you. Here, you dog and slave (addressing Umbopa in a savage tone), give me the magic tube that speaks;" and I tipped a wink towards my express rifle.

Umbopa rose to the occasion, and with something as nearly resembling a grin as I have ever seen on his dignified face, handed me the rifle.

"It is here, O lord of lords," he said, with a deep obeisance.

Now, just before I asked for the rifle I had perceived a little klipspringer antelope* standing on a mass of rock about seventy yards away, and determined to risk a shot at it.

"Ye see that buck," I said, pointing the animal out to the party before me. "Tell me, is it possible for man, born of woman, to kill it from here with a noise?"

"It is not possible, my lord," answered the old man.

"Yet shall I kill it," said I, quietly.

The old man smiled. "That my lord cannot do," he said.

I raised the rifle, and covered the buck. It was a small animal, and one which one might well be excused for missing, but I knew that it would not do to miss.

I drew a deep breath, and slowly pressed on the trigger. The buck stood still as stone.

"Bang! thud!" The buck sprang into the air and fell on the rock dead as a door nail.

A groan of terror burst from the group before us.

"If ye want meat," I remarked coolly, "go fetch that buck."

The old man made a sign, and one of his followers departed, and presently returned bearing the klipspringer. I noticed, with satisfaction, that I had hit it fairly behind the shoulder. They gathered round the poor creature's body, gazing at the bullet hole in consternation.

"Ye see," I said, "I do not speak empty words."

There was no answer.

"If ye yet doubt our power," I went on, "let one of ye go stand upon that rock that I may make him as this buck."

None of them seemed at all inclined to take the hint, till at last the king's son spoke.

"It is well said. Do thou, my uncle, go stand upon the rock. It is but a buck that the magic has killed. Surely it cannot kill a man."

---

*Hoofed mammal (*Oreotragus oreotragus*) that thrives in African mountains and gorges, and whose coarse yellow and gray coat serves as camouflage. Its name derives from the Afrikaans for "rock leaper."

The old gentleman did not take the suggestion in good part. Indeed, he seemed hurt.

"No! no!" he ejaculated, hastily, "my old eyes have seen enough. These are wizards, indeed. Let us bring them to the king. Yet if any should wish a further proof, let *him* stand upon the rock, that the magic tube may speak with him."

There was a most general and hasty expression of dissent.

"Let not good magic be wasted on our poor bodies," said one, "we are satisfied. All the witchcraft of our people cannot show the like of this."

"It is so," remarked the old gentleman, in a tone of intense relief; "without any doubt it is so. Listen, children of the stars, children of the shining eye and the movable teeth, who roar out in thunder and slay from afar. I am Infadoos, son of Kafa, once King of the Kukuana people. This youth is Scragga."

"He nearly scragged me,"* murmured Good.

"Scragga, son of Twala, the great king—Twala, husband of a thousand wives, chief and lord paramount of the Kukuanas, keeper of the great road, terror of his enemies, student of the Black Arts, leader of an hundred thousand warriors, Twala the One-eyed, the Black, the Terrible."

"So," said I, superciliously, "lead us then to Twala. We do not talk with low people and underlings."

"It is well, my lords, we will lead you, but the way is long. We are hunting three days' journey from the place of the king. But let my lords have patience, and we will lead them."

"It is well," I said, carelessly, "all time is before us, for we do not die. We are ready, lead on. But Infadoos, and thou Scragga, beware! Play us no tricks, make for us no snares, for before your brains of mud have thought of them, we shall know them and avenge them. The light from the transparent eye of him with the bare legs and the half-haired face (Good) shall destroy you, and go through your land: his vanishing teeth shall fix themselves fast in you and eat you up, you and your wives and children; the magic tubes shall talk with you loudly, and make you as sieves. Beware!"

This magnificent address did not fail of its effect; indeed, it was

---

*Wrung my neck or strangled me (slang).

hardly needed, so deeply were our friends already impressed with
our powers.

The old man made a deep obeisance, and murmured the word
"Koom, Koom," which I afterwards discovered was their royal salute,
corresponding to the Bayéte of the Zulus,[3] and turning, addressed his
followers. These at once proceeded to lay hold of all our goods and
chattels, in order to bear them for us, excepting only the guns, which
they would on no account touch. They even seized Good's clothes,
which were, as the reader may remember, neatly folded up beside him.

He at once made a dive for them, and a loud altercation ensued.

"Let not my lord of the transparent eye and the melting teeth touch
them," said the old man. "Surely his slaves shall carry the things."

"But I want to put 'em on!" roared Good, in nervous English.

Umbopa translated.

"Nay, my lord," put in Infadoos, "would my lord cover up his
beautiful white legs (although he was so dark Good had a singularly
white skin) from the eyes of his servants? Have we offended my lord
that he should do such a thing?"

Here I nearly exploded with laughing; and meanwhile, one of the
men started on with the garments.

"Damn it!" roared Good, "that black villain has got my trousers."

"Look here, Good," said Sir Henry, "you have appeared in this
country in a certain character, and you must live up to it. It will
never do for you to put on trousers again. Henceforth you must live
in a flannel shirt, a pair of boots, and an eye-glass."

"Yes," I said, "and with whiskers on one side of your face and not
on the other. If you change any of these things they will think that
we are impostors. I am very sorry for you, but, seriously, you must
do it. If once they begin to suspect us, our lives will not be worth a
brass farthing."

"Do you really think so?" said Good, gloomily.

"I do, indeed. Your 'beautiful white legs' and your eye-glass are
now *the* feature of our party, and as Sir Henry says, you must live up
to them. Be thankful that you have got your boots on, and that the
air is warm."

Good sighed, and said no more, but it took him a fortnight to get
accustomed to his attire.

Chapter 8

We Enter Kukuanaland

ALL THAT AFTERNOON WE travelled on along the magnificent roadway, which headed steadily in a north-westerly direction. Infadoos and Scragga walked with us, but their followers marched about one hundred paces ahead.

"Infadoos," I said at length, "who made this road?"

"It was made, my lord, of old time, none know how or when, not even the wise woman Gagool, who has lived for generations. We are not old enough to remember its making. None can make such roads now, but the king lets no grass grow upon it."

"And whose are the writings on the walls of the caves through which we have passed on the road?" I asked, referring to the Egyptian-like sculptures we had seen.

"My lord, the hands that made the road wrote the wonderful writings. We know not who wrote them."

"When did the Kukuana race come into this country?"

"My lord, the race came down here like the breath of a storm ten thousand thousand moons ago, from the great lands which lie there beyond," and he pointed to the north. "They could travel no farther, so say the old voices of our fathers that have come down to us, the children, and so says Gagool, the wise woman, the smeller out of witches, because of the great mountains which ring in the land," and he pointed to the snow-clad peaks. "The country, too, was good, so they settled here and grew strong and powerful, and now our numbers are like the sea sand, and when Twala the king calls up his regiments their plumes cover the plain as far as the eye of man can reach."

"And if the land is walled in with mountains, who is there for the regiments to fight with?"

"Nay, my lord, the country is open there," and again he pointed towards the north, "and now and again warriors sweep down upon us in clouds from a land we know not, and we slay them. It is the third part of the life of a man since there was a war. Many thousands died in it, but we destroyed those who came to eat us up. So since then there has been no war."

"Your warriors must grow weary of resting on their spears."

"My Lord, there was one war, just after we destroyed the people that came down upon us, but it was a civil war,[1] dog eat dog."

"How was that?"

"My lord, the king, my half-brother, had a brother born at the same birth, and of the same woman. It is not our custom, my lord, to let twins live, the weakest must always die. But the mother of the king hid away the weakest child, which was born the last, for her heart yearned over it, and the child is Twala the king. I am his younger brother born of another wife."

"Well?"

"My lord, Kafa, our father, died when we came to manhood, and my brother Imotu was made king in his place, and for a space reigned and had a son by his favourite wife. When the babe was three years old, just after the great war, during which no man could sow or reap, a famine came upon the land, and the people murmured because of the famine, and looked round like a starved lion for something to rend. Then it was that Gagool, the wise and terrible woman, who does not die, proclaimed to the people, saying, 'The king Imotu is no king.' And at the time Imotu was sick with a wound, and lay in his hut not able to move.

"Then Gagool went into a hut and led out Twala, my half-brother, and the twin brother of the king, whom she had hidden since he was born among the caves and rocks, and stripping the 'moocha' (waist-cloth) off his loins, showed the people of the Kukuanas the mark of the sacred snake coiled round his waist, wherewith the eldest son of the king is marked at birth, and cried out loud, 'Behold, your king whom I have saved for you even to this day!' And the people being mad with hunger, and altogether bereft of reason and the knowledge of truth, cried out, '*The king! The king!*' but I knew that it was not so, for Imotu, my brother, was the elder of the twins, and was the lawful king. And just as the tumult was at its height Imotu the king, though he was very sick, came crawling from his hut holding his wife by the hand, and followed by his little son Ignosi (the lightning).

"'What is this noise?' he asked; 'Why cry ye *The king! The king?*'

"Then Twala, his own brother, born of the same woman and in the same hour, ran to him, and taking him by the hair stabbed him through the heart with his knife. And the people being fickle, and ever ready to worship the rising sun, clapped their hands and cried, *'Twala is king!* Now we know that Twala is king!'"

"And what became of his wife and her son Ignosi? Did Twala kill them too?"

"Nay, my lord. When she saw that her lord was dead, she seized the child with a cry, and ran away. Two days afterwards she came to a kraal very hungry, and none would give her milk or food, now that her lord the king was dead, for all men hate the unfortunate. But at nightfall a little child, a girl, crept out and brought her to eat, and she blessed the child, and went on towards the mountains with her boy before the sun rose again, where she must have perished, for none have seen her since, nor the child Ignosi."

"Then if this child Ignosi had lived, he would be the true king of the Kukuana people?"

"That is so, my lord; the sacred snake is round his middle. If he lives he is the king; but alas! he is long dead."

"See, my lord," and he pointed to a vast collection of huts surrounded with a fence, which was in its turn surrounded by a great ditch, that lay on the plain beneath us. "That is the kraal where the wife of Imotu was last seen with the child Ignosi. It is there that we shall sleep to-night, if, indeed," he added, doubtfully, "my lords sleep at all upon this earth."

"When we are among the Kukuanas, my good friend Infadoos, we do as the Kukuanas do," I said, majestically, and I turned round suddenly to address Good, who was tramping along sullenly behind, his mind fully occupied with unsatisfactory attempts to keep his flannel shirt from flapping up in the evening breeze, and to my astonishment butted into Umbopa, who was walking along immediately behind me, and had very evidently been listening with the greatest interest to my conversation with Infadoos. The expression on his face was most curious, and gave the idea of a man who was struggling with partial success to bring something long ago forgotten back into his mind.

All this while we had been pressing on at a good rate down towards the undulating plain beneath. The mountains we had crossed now loomed high above us, and Sheba's breasts were modestly veiled in diaphanous wreaths of mist. As we went on the country grew more and more lovely. The vegetation was luxuriant; without being tropical, the sun was bright and warm, but not burning, and a gracious breeze blew softly along the odorous slopes of the mountains. And, indeed, this new land was little less than an earthly paradise; in beauty, in natural wealth, and in climate I have never seen its like. The Transvaal is a fine country, but it is nothing to Kukuanaland.

So soon as we started, Infadoos had despatched a runner on to warn the people of the kraal, which, by the way, was in his military command, of our arrival. This man had departed at an extraordinary speed, which Infadoos had informed me he would keep up all the way, as running was an exercise much practised among his people.

The result of this message now became apparent. When we got within two miles of the kraal we could see that company after company of men was issuing from its gates and marching towards us.

Sir Henry laid his hand upon my arm, and remarked that it looked as though we were going to meet with a warm reception. Something in his tone attracted Infadoos' attention.

"Let not my lords be afraid," he said hastily, "for in my breast there dwells no guile. This regiment is one under my command, and comes out by my orders to greet you."

I nodded easily, though I was not quite easy in my mind.

About half a mile from the gates of the kraal was a long stretch of rising ground sloping gently upwards from the road, and on this the companies formed up. It was a splendid sight to see them, each company about three hundred strong, charging swiftly up the slope, with flashing spears and waving plumes, and taking their appointed place. By the time we came to the slope twelve such companies, or in all three thousand six hundred men, had passed out and taken up their positions along the road.

Presently we came to the first company, and were able to gaze in astonishment on the most magnificent set of men I have ever seen. They were all men of mature age, mostly veterans of about forty, and not one of them was under six feet in height, whilst many were six feet three or four. They wore upon their heads heavy black plumes of Sakabwla[2] feathers, like those which adorned our guides. Round their waists and also beneath the right knee were bound circlets of white ox tails, and in their left hands were round shields about twenty inches across. These shields were very curious. The framework consisted of an iron plate beaten out thin, over which was stretched milk-white ox hide. The weapons that each man bore were simple, but most effective, consisting of a short and very heavy two-edged spear with a wooden shaft, the blade being about six inches across at the widest part. These spears were not used for throwing, but like the Zulu "bangwan," or stabbing assegai, were for close quarters only, when the wound inflicted by them was terrible. In addition to these bangwans each man also carried three large and heavy knives, each knife weighing about two pounds. One knife was fixed in the ox tail girdle, and the other two at the back of the round shield. These knives, which are called "tollas" by the Kukuanas, take the place of the throwing assegai of the Zulus. A Kukuana warrior can throw them with great accuracy at a distance of fifty yards, and it is their custom on charging to hurl a volley of them at the enemy as they come to close quarters.

Each company stood like a collection of bronze statues till we were opposite to it, when at a signal given by its commanding officer who, distinguished by a leopard skin cloak, stood some paces in front, every spear was raised into the air, and from three hundred throats sprang forth with a sudden roar the royal salute of "*Koom.*" Then when we had passed the company formed up behind us, and followed us towards the kraal, till at last the whole regiment of the "Greys" (so called from their white shields), the crack corps of the Kukuana people, was marching behind us with a tread that shook the ground.

At length, branching off from Solomon's Great Road, we came to the wide fosse surrounding the kraal, which was at least a mile round, and fenced with a strong palisade of piles formed of the trunks of trees. At the gateway this fosse was spanned by a primitive drawbridge which was let down by the guard to allow us to pass in. The kraal was exceedingly well laid out. Through the centre ran a wide pathway intersected at right angles by other pathways so arranged as to cut the huts into square blocks, each block being the quarters of a company. The huts were dome-shaped, and built, like those of the Zulus, of a framework of wattle, beautifully thatched with grass; but, unlike the Zulu huts, they had doorways through which one could walk. Also they were much larger, and surrounded with a verandah about six feet wide, beautifully paved with powdered lime trodden hard. All along each side of the wide pathway that pierced the kraal were ranged hundreds of women, brought out by curiosity to look at us. These women are, for a native race, exceedingly handsome. They are tall and graceful, and their figures are wonderfully fine. The hair, though short, is rather curly than woolly, the features are frequently aquiline, and the lips are not unpleasantly thick as is the case in most African races. But what struck us most was their exceedingly quiet dignified air. They were as well-bred in their way as the habituées of a fashionable drawing-room, and in this respect differ from Zulu women, and their cousins the Masai who inhabit the district behind Zanzibar. Their curiosity had brought them out to see us, but they allowed no rude expressions of wonder or savage criticism to pass their lips as we trudged wearily in front of them. Not even when old Infadoos with a surreptitious motion of the hand pointed out the crowning wonder of poor Good's "beautiful white legs," did they allow the feeling of intense admiration which evidently mastered their minds to find expression. They fixed their dark eyes upon their snowy loveliness (Good's skin is exceedingly white), and that was all. But this was quite enough for Good, who is modest by nature.

When we got to the centre of the kraal, Infadoos halted at the door of a large hut, which was surrounded at a distance by a circle of smaller ones.

"Enter, sons of the stars," he said, in a magniloquent voice, "and deign to rest awhile in our humble habitations. A little food shall be brought to you, so that ye shall have no need to draw your belts tight from hunger; some honey and some milk, and an ox or two, and a few sheep; not much, my lords, but still a little food."

"It is good," said I, "Infadoos, we are weary with travelling through realms of air; now let us rest."

Accordingly we entered into the hut, which we found amply prepared for our comfort. Couches of tanned skins were spread for us to rest on, and water was placed for us to wash in.

Presently we heard a shouting outside; and stepping to the door, saw a line of damsels bearing milk and roasted mealies, and honey in a pot. Behind these were some youths driving a fat young ox. We received the gifts, and then one of the young men took the knife from his girdle and dexterously cut the ox's throat. In ten minutes it was dead, skinned, and cut up. The best of the meat was then cut off for us, and the rest I, in the name of our party, presented to the warriors round us, who took it off and distributed the "white men's gift."

Umbopa set to work, with the assistance of an extremely prepossessing young woman, to boil our portion in a large earthenware pot over a fire which was built outside the hut, and when it was nearly ready we sent a message to Infadoos, and asked him, and Scragga the king's son, to join us.

Presently they came, and sitting down upon little stools, of which there were several about the hut (for the Kukuanas do not in general squat upon their haunches like the Zulus), helped us to get through our dinner. The old gentleman was most affable and polite, but it struck us that the young one regarded us with suspicion. He had, together with the rest of the party, been overawed by our white appearance and by our magic properties; but it seemed to me that on discovering that we ate, drank, and slept like other mortals, his awe was beginning to wear off and be replaced by a sullen suspicion— which made us feel rather uncomfortable.

In the course of our meal Sir Henry suggested to me that it might be well to try and discover if our hosts knew anything of his brother's fate, or if they had ever seen or heard of him; but, on the whole, I thought that it would be wiser to say nothing of the matter at that time.

After supper we filled our pipes and lit them: a proceeding which filled Infadoos and Scragga with astonishment. The Kukuanas were evidently unacquainted with the divine uses of tobacco-smoke. The herb was grown among them extensively; but, like the Zulus, they only used it for snuff, and quite failed to identify it in its new form.

Presently I asked Infadoos when we were to proceed on our journey, and was delighted to learn that preparations had been made for us to leave on the following morning, messengers having already left to inform Twala the king of our coming. It appeared that Twala was at his principal place, known as Loo, making ready for the great annual feast which was held in the first week of June. At this gathering all the regiments, with the exception of certain detachments left behind for garrison purposes, were brought up and paraded before the king; and the great annual witch-hunt, of which more by-and-by, was held.

We were to start at dawn; and Infadoos, who was to accompany us, expected that we should, unless we were detained by accident or by swollen rivers, reach Loo on the night of the second day.

When they had given us this information our visitors bade us good night; and, having arranged to watch turn and turn about, three of us flung ourselves down and slept the sweet sleep of the weary, whilst the fourth sat up on the look-out for possible treachery.

Chapter 9

Twala the King

IT WILL NOT BE necessary for me to detail at length the incidents of our journey to Loo. It took two good days' travelling along Solomon's Great Road, which pursued its even course right into the heart of Kukuanaland. Suffice it to say that as we went the country seemed to grow richer and richer, and the kraals, with their wide surrounding belts of cultivation, more and more numerous. They were all built upon the same principles as the first one we had reached, and were guarded by ample garrisons of troops. Indeed, in Kukuanaland, as among the Germans, the Zulus, and the Masai, every able-bodied man is a soldier, so that the whole force of the nation is available for its wars, offensive or defensive. As we travelled along we were overtaken by thousands of warriors hurrying up to Loo to be present at the great annual review and festival, and a grander series of troops I never saw. At sunset on the second day we stopped to rest awhile upon the summit of some heights over which the road ran, and there on a beautiful and fertile plain before us was Loo itself. For a native town it was an enormous place, quite five miles round I should say, with outlying kraals jutting out from it, which served on grand occasions as cantonments for the regiments, and a curious horse-shoe-shaped hill, with which we were destined to become better acquainted, about two miles to the north. It was beautifully situated, and through the centre of the kraal, dividing it into two portions, ran a river, which appeared to be bridged at several places, the same perhaps that we had seen from the slopes of Sheba's Breasts. Sixty or seventy miles away three great snow-capped mountains, placed like the points of a triangle, started up out of the level plain. The conformation of these mountains was unlike that of Sheba's Breasts, being sheer and precipitous, instead of smooth and rounded.

Infadoos saw us looking at them and volunteered a remark—

"The road ends there," he said, pointing to the mountains known among the Kukuanas as the "Three Witches."

"Why does it end?" I asked.

"Who knows?" he answered, with a shrug; "the mountains are full of caves, and there is a great pit between them. It is there that the wise men of old time used to go to get whatever it was they came to this country for, and it is there now that our kings are buried in the Place of Death."

"What was it they came for?" I asked eagerly.

"Nay, I know not. My lords who come from the stars should know," he answered with a quick look. Evidently he knew more than he chose to say.

"Yes," I went on, "you are right, in the stars we know many things. I have heard, for instance, that the wise men of old came to those mountains to get bright stones, pretty playthings, and yellow iron."

"My lord is wise," he answered coldly, "I am but a child and cannot talk with my lord on such things. My lord must speak with Gagool the old, at the king's place, who is wise even as my lord," and he turned away.

As soon as he was gone, I turned to the others and pointed out the mountains. "There are Solomon's diamond mines," I said.

Umbopa was standing with them, apparently plunged in one of the fits of abstraction which were common to him, and caught my words.

"Yes, Macumazahn," he put in, in Zulu, "the diamonds are surely there, and you shall have them since you white men are so fond of toys and money."

"How dost thou know that, Umbopa?" I asked sharply, for I did not like his mysterious ways.

He laughed; "I dreamed it in the night, white men," and then he too turned upon his heel and went.

"Now what," said Sir Henry, "is our black friend at? He knows more than he chooses to say, that is clear. By the way, Quatermain, has he heard anything of—of my brother?"

"Nothing; he has asked every one he has got friendly with, but they all declare no white man has ever been seen in the country before."

"Do you suppose he ever got here at all?" suggested Good; "we have only reached the place by a miracle; is it likely he could have reached it at all without the map?"

"I don't know," said Sir Henry, gloomily, "but somehow I think that I shall find him."

Slowly the sun sank, and then suddenly darkness rushed down on the land like a tangible thing. There was no breathing-space between the day and the night, no soft transformation scene, for in these latitudes twilight does not exist. The change from day to night is as quick and as absolute the change from life to death. The sun sank and the world was wreathed in shadows. But not for long, for see in the east there is a glow, then a bent edge of silver light, and at last the full bow of the crescent moon peeps above the plain and shoots its gleaming arrows far and wide, filling the earth with a faint refulgence, as the glow of a good man's deeds shines for awhile upon his little world after his sun has set, lighting the faint-hearted travellers who follow on towards a fuller dawn.

We stood and watched the lovely sight, whilst the stars grew pale before this chastened majesty, and felt our hearts lifted up in the presence of a beauty we could not realise, much less describe. Mine has been a rough life, my reader, but there are a few things I am thankful to have lived for, and one of them is to have seen that moon rise over Kukuanaland. Presently our meditations were broken in upon by our polite friend Infadoos.

"If my lords are rested we will journey on to Loo, where a hut is made ready for my lords to-night. The moon is now bright, so that we shall not fall on the way."

We assented, and in an hour's time were at the outskirts of the town, of which the extent, mapped out as it was by thousands of camp fires, appeared absolutely endless. Indeed, Good, who was always fond of a bad joke, christened it "Unlimited Loo."[1] Presently we came to a moat with a drawbridge, where we were met by the rattling of arms and the hoarse challenge of a sentry. Infadoos gave some password that I could not catch, which was met with a salute, and we passed on through the central street of the great grass city. After nearly half an hour's tramp, past endless lines of huts, Infadoos at last halted at the gate of a little group of huts which surrounded a small courtyard of powdered limestone, and informed us that these were to be our "poor" quarters.

We entered, and found that a hut had been assigned to each of us. These huts were superior to any which we had yet seen, and in each was a most comfortable bed made of tanned skins spread upon mattresses of aromatic grass. Food too was ready for us, and as soon as we had washed ourselves with water, which stood ready in earthen-ware jars, some young women of handsome appearance brought us roasted meat and mealie cobs* daintily served on wooden platters, and presented it to us with deep obeisances.

We ate and drank, and then the beds having by our request been all moved into one hut, a precaution at which the amiable young ladies smiled, we flung ourselves down to sleep, thoroughly wearied out with our long journey.

When we woke, it was to find that the sun was high in the heavens, and that the female attendants, who did not seem to be troubled by any false shame, were already standing inside the hut, having been ordered to attend and help us to "make ready."

"Make ready, indeed," growled Good, "when one has only a flannel shirt and a pair of boots, that does not take long. I wish you would ask them for my trousers."

I asked accordingly, but was informed that these sacred relics had already been taken to the king, who would see us in the forenoon.

Having, somewhat to their astonishment and disappointment, requested the young ladies to step outside, we proceeded to make the best toilet that the circumstances admitted of. Good even went the length of again shaving the right side of his face; the left, on which now appeared a very fair crop of whiskers, we impressed upon him he must on no account touch. As for ourselves, we were contented with a good wash and combing our hair. Sir Henry's yellow locks were now almost down to his shoulders, and he looked more like an ancient Dane than ever, while my grizzled scrub was fully an inch long, instead of half an inch, which in a general way I considered my maximum length.

By the time that we had eaten our breakfasts, and smoked a pipe, a message was brought to us by no less a personage than Infadoos himself that Twala, the king, was ready to see us, if we would be pleased to come.

We remarked in reply that we should prefer to wait till the sun was a little higher, we were yet weary with our journey, &c. &c. It is always well, when dealing with uncivilised people, not to be in too great a hurry. They are apt to mistake politeness for awe or servility. So, al-

---

*Cobs of maize or, in American terms, corn (Afrikaans). During Nelson Mandela's impoverished childhood he stole mealie cobs from maize fields to stave off hunger.

though we were quite as anxious to see Twala as Twala could be to see us, we sat down and waited for an hour, employing the interval in preparing such presents as our slender stock of goods permitted—namely, the Winchester rifle which had been used by poor Ventvögel, and some beads. The rifle and ammunition we determined to present to his Royal Highness, and the beads were for his wives and courtiers. We had already given a few to Infadoos and Scragga, and found that they were delighted with them, never having seen anything like them before. At length we declared that we were ready, and guided by Infadoos, started off to the levee, Umbopa carrying the rifle and beads.

After walking a few hundred yards, we came to an enclosure, something like that which surrounded the huts that had been allotted to us, only fifty times as big. It could not have been less than six or seven acres in extent. All round the outside fence was a row of huts, which were the habitations of the king's wives. Exactly opposite the gateway, on the further side of the open space, was a very large hut, which stood by itself, in which his Majesty resided. All the rest was open ground; that is to say, it would have been open had it not been filled by company after company of warriors, who were mustered there to the number of seven or eight thousand. These men stood still as statues as we advanced through them, and it would be impossible to give an idea of the grandeur of the spectacle which they presented, in their waving plumes, their glancing spears, and iron-backed ox-hide shields.

The space in front of the large hut was empty, but before it were placed several stools. On three of these, at a sign from Infadoos, we seated ourselves, Umbopa standing behind us. As for Infadoos, he took up a position by the door of the hut. So we waited for ten minutes or more in the midst of a dead silence, but conscious that we were the object of the concentrated gaze of some eight thousand pairs of eyes. It was a somewhat trying ordeal, but we carried it off as best we could. At length the door of the hut opened, and a gigantic figure, with a splendid tiger-skin karross[2] flung over its shoulders, stepped out, followed by the boy Scragga, and what appeared to us to be a withered-up monkey, wrapped in a fur cloak. The figure seated itself upon a stool, Scragga took his stand behind it, and the withered-up monkey crept on all fours into the shade of the hut and squatted down.

Still there was silence.

Then the gigantic figure slipped off the karross and stood up before us, a truly alarming spectacle. It was that of an enormous man with the most entirely repulsive countenance we had ever beheld. The lips were as thick as a negro's, the nose was flat, it had but one gleaming black eye (for the other was represented by a hollow in the face), and its whole expression was cruel and sensual to a degree. From the large head rose a magnificent plume of white ostrich feathers, the body was clad in a shirt of shining chain armour, whilst round the waist and right knee was the usual garnish of white ox-tails. In the right hand was a huge spear. Round the neck was a thick torque of gold, and bound on to the forehead was a single and enormous uncut diamond.

Still there was silence; but not for long. Presently the figure, whom we rightly guessed to be the king, raised the great spear in its hand. Instantly eight thousand spears were raised in answer, and from eight thousand throats rang out the royal salute of "*Koom.*" Three times this was repeated, and each time the earth shook with the noise, that can only be compared to the deepest notes of thunder.

"Be humble, O people," piped out a thin voice which seemed to come from the monkey in the shade, "it is the king."

"*It is the king,*" boomed out eight thousand throats, in answer. "*Be humble, O people, it is the king.*"

Then there was silence again—dead silence. Presently, however, it was broken. A soldier on our left dropped his shield, which fell with a clatter on the limestone flooring.

Twala turned his one cold eye in the direction of the noise.

"Come hither, thou," he said, in a voice of thunder.

A fine young man stepped out of the ranks, and stood before him.

"It was thy shield that fell, thou awkward dog. Wilt thou make me a reproach in the eyes of strangers from the stars? What hast thou to say?"

And then we saw the poor fellow turn pale under his dusky skin.

"It was by chance, O calf of the black cow," he murmured.

"Then it is a chance for which thou must pay. Thou hast made me foolish; prepare for death."

"I am the king's ox," was the low answer.

"Scragga," roared the king, "let me see how thou canst use thy spear. Kill me this awkward dog."

Scragga stepped forward with an ill-favoured grin, and lifted his spear. The poor victim covered his eyes with his hand and stood still. As for us, we were petrified with horror.

Once, twice, he waved the spear and then struck, ah, God! right home—the spear stood out a foot behind the soldier's back. He flung up his hands and dropped dead. From the multitude around rose something like a murmur, it rolled round and round, and died away. The tragedy was finished; there lay the corpse, and we had not yet realised that it had been enacted. Sir Henry sprang up and swore a great oath, then, overpowered by the sense of silence, sat down again.

"The thrust was a good one," said the king; "take him away."

Four men stepped out of the ranks, and lifting the body of the murdered man, carried it away.

"Cover up the blood-stains, cover them up," piped out the thin voice from the monkey-like figure; "the king's word is spoken, the king's doom is done."

Thereupon a girl came forward from behind the hut, bearing a jar filled with powdered lime, which she scattered over the red mark, blotting it from sight.

Sir Henry meanwhile was boiling with rage at what had happened; indeed, it was with difficulty that we could keep him still.

"Sit down, for heaven's sake," I whispered; "our lives depend on it."

He yielded and remained quiet.

Twala sat still until the traces of the tragedy had been removed, then he addressed us.

"White people," he said, "who come hither, whence I know not, and why I know not, greeting."

"Greeting Twala, King of the Kukuanas," I answered.

"White people, whence come ye, and what seek ye?"

"We come from the stars, ask us not how. We come to see this land."

"Ye come from far to see a little thing. And that man with ye," pointing to Umbopa, "does he too come from the stars?"

"Even so; there are people of thy colour in the heavens above; but ask not of matters too high for thee, Twala, the king."

"Ye speak with a loud voice, people of the stars," Twala answered, in a tone which I scarcely liked. "Remember that the stars are far off, and ye are here. How if I make ye as him whom they bear away?"

I laughed out loud, though there was little laughter in my heart.

"O king," I said, "be careful, walk warily over hot stones, lest thou shouldst burn thy feet; hold the spear by the handle, lest thou shouldst cut thy hands. Touch but one hair of our heads, and destruction shall come upon thee. What, have not these," pointing to Infadoos and Scragga (who, young villain that he was, was employed in cleaning the blood of the soldier off his spear), "told thee what manner of men we are? Hast thou ever seen the like of us?" and I pointed to Good, feeling quite sure that he had never seen anybody before who looked in the least like *him* as he then appeared.

"It is true, I have not," said the king.

"Have they not told thee how we strike with death from afar?" I went on.

"They have told me, but I believe them not. Let me see you kill. Kill me a man among those who stand yonder"—and he pointed to the opposite side of the kraal—"and I will believe."

"Nay," I answered; "we shed no blood of man except in just punishment; but if thou wilt see, bid thy servants drive in an ox through the kraal gates, and before he has run twenty paces I will strike him dead."

"Nay," laughed the king, "kill me a man, and I will believe."

"Good, O king, so be it," I answered, coolly; "do thou walk across the open space, and before thy feet reach the gate thou shalt be dead; or if thou wilt not, send thy son Scragga" (whom at that moment it would have given me much pleasure to shoot).

On hearing this suggestion Scragga gave a sort of howl, and bolted into the hut.

Twala frowned majestically; the suggestion did not please him.

"Let a young ox be driven in," he said.

Two men at once departed, running swiftly.

"Now, Sir Henry," said I, "do you shoot. I want to show this ruffian that I am not the only magician of the party."

Sir Henry accordingly took the "express," and made ready.

"I hope I shall make a good shot," he groaned.

"You must," I answered. "If you miss with the first barrel, let him have the second. Sight for 150 yards, and wait till the beast turns broadside on."

Then came a pause, till presently we caught sight of an ox running straight for the kraal gate. It came on through the gate, and then, catching sight of the vast concourse of people, stopped stupidly, turned round, and bellowed.

"Now's your time," I whispered.

Up went the rifle.

Bang! thud! and the ox was kicking on his back, shot in the ribs. The semi-hollow bullet had done its work well, and a sigh of astonishment went up from the assembled thousands.

I turned coolly round—

"Have I lied, O king?"

"Nay, white man, it is a truth," was the somewhat awed answer.

"Listen, Twala," I went on. "Thou hast seen. Now know we come in peace, not in war. See here" (and I held up the Winchester repeater); "here is a hollow staff that shall enable you to kill even as we kill, only this charm I lay upon it, thou shalt kill no man with it. If thou liftest it against a man, it shall kill thee. Stay, I will show thee. Bid a man step forty paces and place the shaft of a spear in the ground so that the flat blade looks towards us."

In a few seconds it was done.

"Now, see, I will break the spear."

Taking a careful sight I fired. The bullet struck the flat of the spear, and broke the blade into fragments.

Again the sigh of astonishment went up.

"Now, Twala" (handing him the rifle), "this magic tube we give to thee, and by-and-by I will show thee how to use it; but beware how thou usest the magic of the stars against a man of earth," and I handed him the rifle. He took it very gingerly, and laid it down at his feet. As he did so I observed the wizened monkey-like figure creeping up from the shadow of the hut. It crept on all fours, but when it reached the place where the king sat, it rose upon its feet, and throwing the furry covering off its face, revealed a most extraordinary and weird countenance. It was (apparently) that of a woman of great age, so shrunken that in size it was no larger than that of a year-old child, and was made up of a collection of deep yellow wrinkles. Set in the wrinkles was a sunken slit, that represented the mouth, beneath which the chin curved outwards to a point. There was no nose to speak of; indeed, the whole countenance might have been taken for that of a sun-dried corpse had it not been for a pair of large black eyes, still full of fire and intelligence, which gleamed and played under the snow-white eyebrows, and the projecting parchment-coloured skull, like jewels in a charnel-house. As for the skull itself, it was perfectly bare, and yellow in hue, while its wrinkled scalp moved and contracted like the hood of a cobra.

The figure to whom this fearful countenance, which caused a shiver of fear to pass through us as we gazed on it, belonged, stood still for a moment, and then suddenly projected a skinny claw armed with nails nearly an inch long, and laid it on the shoulder of Twala, the king, and began to speak in a thin, piercing voice—

"Listen, O king! Listen, O people! Listen, O mountains and plains and rivers, home of the Kukuana race! Listen, O skies and sun, O rain and storm and mist! Listen, all things that live and must die! Listen, all dead things that must live again—again to die! Listen, the spirit of life is in me, and I prophesy. I prophesy! I prophesy!"

The words died away in a faint wail, and terror seemed to seize upon the hearts of all who heard them, including ourselves. The old woman was very terrible.

"*Blood! blood! blood!* rivers of blood; blood everywhere. I see it, I smell it, I taste it—it is salt; it runs red upon the ground, it rains down from the skies.

"*Footsteps! footsteps! footsteps!* the tread of the white man coming from afar. It shakes the earth; the earth trembles before her master.

"Blood is good, the red blood is bright; there is no smell like the smell of new-shed blood. The lions shall lap it and roar, the vultures shall wash their wings in it, and shriek in joy.

"I am old! I am old! I have seen much blood; ha, ha! but I shall see more ere I die, and be merry. How old am I, think ye? Your fathers knew me, and *their* fathers knew me, and *their* fathers' fathers. I have seen the white man, and know his desires. I am old, but the mountains are older than I. Who made the great road, tell me? Who wrote in pictures on the rocks, tell me? Who reared up the three silent ones yonder, who gaze across the pit, tell me?" (And she pointed towards the three precipitous mountains we had noticed on the previous night.)

"Ye know not, but I know. It was a white people who were before ye are, who shall be when ye are not, who shall eat ye up, and destroy ye. *Yea! yea! yea!*

"And what came they for, the white ones, the terrible ones, the skilled in magic and all learning, the strong, the unswerving? What is that bright stone upon thy forehead, O king? Whose hands made the iron garments upon thy breast, O king? Ye know not, but I know. I the old one, I the wise one, I the Isanusi!" (witch doctress.)

Then she turned her bald vulture-head towards us.

"What seek ye, white men of the stars—ah, yes, of the stars? Do ye seek a lost one? Ye shall not find him here. He is not here. Never for ages upon ages has a white foot pressed this land; never but once, and he left it but to die. Ye come for bright stones; I know it—I know it; ye shall find them when the blood is dry; but shall ye return whence ye came, or shall ye stop with me? Ha! ha! ha!

"And thou, thou with the dark skin and the proud bearing" (pointing her skinny finger at Umbopa), "who art *thou*, and what seekest *thou*? Not stones that shine, not yellow metal that gleams, that thou leavest to 'white men from the stars.' Methinks I know thee; methinks I can smell the smell of the blood in thy veins. Strip off the girdle——"

Here the features of this extraordinary creature became convulsed, and she fell to the ground foaming in an epileptic fit, and was carried off into the hut.

The king rose up trembling, and waved his hand. Instantly the regiments began to file off, and in ten minutes, save for ourselves, the king, and a few attendants, the great space was left clear.

"White people," he said, "it passes in my mind to kill ye. Gagool has spoken strange words. What say ye?"

I laughed. "Be careful, O king, we are not easy to slay. Thou hast seen the fate of the ox; wouldst thou be as the ox?"

The king frowned. "It is not well to threaten a king."

"We threaten not, we speak what is true. Try to kill us, O king, and learn."

The great man put his hand to his forehead.

"Go in peace," he said, at length. "To-night is the great dance. Ye shall see it. Fear not that I shall set a snare for ye. To-morrow I shall think."

"It is well, O king," I answered, unconcernedly, and then, accompanied by Infadoos, we rose, and went back to our kraal.

Chapter 10

The Witch-hunt

ON REACHING OUR HUT, I motioned to Infadoos to enter with us.

"Now, Infadoos," I said, "we would speak with thee."

"Let my lords say on."

"It seems to us, Infadoos, that Twala, the king, is a cruel man."

"It is so, my lords. Alas! the land cries out with his cruelties. To-night ye will see. It is the great witch-hunt, and many will be smelt out as wizards and slain. No man's life is safe. If the king covets a man's cattle, or a man's life, or if he fears a man that he should excite a rebellion against him, then Gagool, whom ye saw, or some of the witch-finding women whom she has taught, will smell that man out as a wizard, and he will be killed. Many will die before the moon grows pale to-night. It is ever so. Perhaps I too shall be killed. As yet I have been spared, because I am skilled in war, and beloved by the soldiers; but I know not how long I shall live. The land groans at the cruelties of Twala, the king; it is wearied of him and his red ways."

"Then why is it, Infadoos, that the people do not cast him down?"

"Nay, my lords, he is the king, and if he were killed Scragga would reign in his place, and the heart of Scragga is blacker than the heart of Twala, his father. If Scragga were king the yoke upon our neck would be heavier than the yoke of Twala. If Imotu had never been slain, or if Ignosi, his son, had lived, it had been otherwise; but they are both dead."

"How know you that Ignosi is dead?" said a voice behind us. We looked round with astonishment to see who spoke. It was Umbopa.

"What meanest thou, boy?" asked Infadoos; "who told thee to speak?"

"Listen, Infadoos," was the answer, "and I will tell thee a story. Years ago the King Imotu was killed in this country, and his wife fled with the boy Ignosi. Is it not so?"

"It is so."

"It was said that the woman and the boy died upon the mountains. Is it not so?"

"It is even so."

"Well, it came to pass that the mother and the boy Ignosi did not die. They crossed the mountains, and were led by a tribe of wandering desert men across the sands beyond, till at last they came to water and grass and trees again."

"How knowest thou that?"

"Listen. They travelled on and on, many months' journey, till they reached a land where a people called the Amazulu,[1] who too are of the Kukuana stock, live by war, and with them they tarried many years, till at length the mother died. Then the son, Ignosi, again became a wanderer, and went on into a land of wonders, where white people live, and for many more years learned the wisdom of the white people."

"It is a pretty story," said Infadoos, incredulously.

"For many years he lived there working as a servant and a soldier, but holding in his heart all that his mother had told him of his own place, and casting about in his mind to find how he might get back there to see his own people and his father's house before he died. For many years he lived and waited, and at last the time came, as it ever comes to him who can wait for it, and he met some white men who would seek this unknown land, and joined himself to them. The white men started and journeyed on and on, seeking for one who is lost. They crossed the burning desert, they crossed the snow-clad mountains, and reached the land of the Kukuanas, and there they met thee, oh Infadoos."

"Surely thou art mad to talk thus," said the astonished old soldier.

"Thou thinkest so; see, I will show thee, oh my uncle.

"*I am Ignosi, rightful king of the Kukuanas!*"

Then with a single movement he slipped off the "moocha" or girdle round his middle, and stood naked before us.

"Look," he said; "what is this?" and he pointed to the mark of a great snake tattooed in blue round his middle, its tail disappearing in its open mouth just above where the thighs are set into the body.

Infadoos looked, his eyes starting nearly out of his head, and then fell upon his knees.

"*Koom! Koom!*" he ejaculated; "it is my brother's son; it is the king."

"Did I not tell thee so, my uncle? Rise; I am not yet the king, but with thy help, and with the help of these brave white men, who are my friends, I shall be. But the old woman Gagool was right, the land shall run with blood first, and hers shall run with it, for she killed my father with her words, and drove my mother forth. And now, Infadoos, choose thou. Wilt thou put thy hands between my hands and be my man? Wilt thou share the dangers that lie before me, and help me to overthrow this tyrant and murderer, or wilt thou not? Choose thou."

The old man put his hand to his head and thought. Then he rose, and advancing to where Umbopa, or rather Ignosi, stood, knelt before him and took his hand.

"Ignosi, rightful king of the Kukuanas, I put my hand between thy hands, and am thy man till death. When thou wast a babe I dandled thee upon my knee, now shall my old arm strike for thee and freedom."

"It is well, Infadoos; if I conquer, thou shalt be the greatest man in the kingdom after the king. If I fail, thou canst only die, and death is not far off for thee. Rise, my uncle."

"And ye, white men, will ye help me? What have I to offer ye! The white stones, if I conquer and can find them, ye shall have as many as ye can carry hence. Will that suffice ye?"

I translated this remark.

"Tell him," answered Sir Henry, "that he mistakes an Englishman. Wealth is good, and if it comes in our way we will take it; but a gentleman does not sell himself for wealth. But, speaking for myself, I say this. I have always liked Umbopa, and so far as lies in me will stand by him in this business. It will be very pleasant to me to try and square matters with that cruel devil, Twala. What do you say, Good, and you, Quatermain?"

"Well," said Good, "to adopt the language of hyperbole, in which all these people seem to indulge, you can tell him that a row is surely good, and warms the cockles of the heart, and that so far as I am concerned I'm his boy. My only stipulation is, that he allows me to wear trousers."

I translated these answers.

"It is well, my friends," said Ignosi, late Umbopa; "and what say you, Macumazahn, art thou too with me, old hunter, cleverer than a wounded buffalo?"

I thought awhile and scratched my head.

"Umbopa, or Ignosi," I said, "I don't like revolutions. I am a man of peace, and a bit of a coward" (here Umbopa smiled), "but, on the other hand, I stick to my friends, Ignosi. You have stuck to us and played the part of a man, and I will stick to you. But mind you I am a trader, and have to make my living, so I accept your offer about those diamonds in case we should ever be in a position to avail ourselves of it. Another thing: we came, as you know, to look for Incubu's (Sir Henry's) lost brother. You must help us to find him."

"That will I do," answered Ignosi. "Stay, Infadoos, by the sign of the snake round my middle, tell me the truth. Has any white man to thy knowledge set his foot within the land?"

"None, oh Ignosi."

"If any white man had been seen or heard of, wouldst thou have known it?"

"I should certainly have known."

"Thou hearest, Incubu," said Ignosi to Sir Henry, "he has not been here."

"Well, well," said Sir Henry, with a sigh; "there it is; I suppose he never got here. Poor fellow, poor fellow! So it has all been for nothing. God's will be done."

"Now for business," I put in, anxious to escape from a painful subject. "It is very well to be a king by right divine, Ignosi, but how dost thou purpose to become a king indeed?"

"Nay, I know not. Infadoos, hast thou a plan?"

"Ignosi, son of the lightning," answered his uncle, "to-night is the great dance and witch-hunt. Many will be smelt out and perish, and in the hearts of many others there will be grief and anguish and anger against the King Twala. When the dance is over, then will I speak to some of the great chiefs, who in turn, if I can win them over, shall speak to their regiments. I shall speak to the chiefs softly at first, and bring them to see that thou art indeed the king, and I think that by tomorrow's light thou shall have twenty thousand spears at thy command. And now must I go and think, and hear, and make ready. After the dance is done I will, if I am yet alive, and we are all alive, meet thee here, and we will talk. At the best there will be war."

At this moment our conference was interrupted by the cry that messengers had come from the king. Advancing to the door of the hut we ordered that they should be admitted, and presently three men entered, each bearing a shining shirt of chain armour, and a magnificent battle-axe.

"The gifts of my lord the king to the white men from the stars!" exclaimed a herald who came with them.

"We thank the king," I answered; "withdraw."

The men went, and we examined the armour with great interest. It was the most beautiful chain work we had ever seen. A whole coat fell together so closely that it formed a mass of links scarcely too big to be covered with both hands.

"Do you make these things in this country, Infadoos?" I asked; "they are very beautiful."

"Nay, my lord, they come down to us from our forefathers. We know not who made them, and there are but few left. None but those of royal blood may wear them. They are magic coats through which no spear can pass. He who wears them is well-nigh safe in the battle. The king is well pleased or much afraid, or he would not have sent them. Wear them to-night, my lords."

The rest of the day we spent quietly resting and talking over the situation, which was sufficiently exciting. At last the sun went down, the thousand watchfires glowed out, and through the darkness we heard the tramp of many feet and the clashing of hundreds of spears, as the regiments passed to their appointed places to be ready for the great dance. About ten the full moon came up in splendour, and as we stood watching her ascent Infadoos arrived, clad in full war toggery, and accompanied by a guard of twenty men to escort us to the dance. We had already, as he recommended, donned the shirts of chain armour which the king had sent us, putting them on under our ordinary clothing, and finding to our surprise that they were neither very heavy nor uncomfortable. These steel shirts, which had evidently been made for men of a very large stature, hung somewhat loosely upon Good and myself, but Sir Henry's fitted his magnificent frame like a glove. Then strapping our revolvers round our waists, and taking the battle-axes which the king had sent with the armour in our hands, we started.

On arriving at the great kraal, where we had that morning been interviewed by the king, we found that it was closely packed with some twenty thousand men arranged in regiments round it. The regiments were in turn divided into companies, and between each company was a little path to allow free passage to the witch-finders to pass up and down. Anything more imposing than the sight that was presented by this vast and orderly concourse of armed men it is impossible for one to conceive. There they stood perfectly silent, and the moonlight poured its light upon the forest of their raised spears, upon their majestic forms, waving plumes, and the harmonious shading of their various-coloured shields. Wherever we looked was line upon line of set faces surmounted by range upon range of glittering spears.

"Surely," I said to Infadoos, "the whole army is here?"

"Nay, Macumazahn," he answered, "but a third part of it. One third part is present at this dance each year, another third part is mustered outside in case there should be trouble when the killing begins, ten thousand more garrison the outposts round Loo, and the rest watch at the kraals in the country. Thou seest it is a very great people."

"They are very silent," said Good; and indeed the intense stillness among such a vast concourse of living men was almost overpowering.

"What says Bougwan?" asked Infadoos.

I translated.

"Those over whom the shadow of Death is hovering are silent," he answered, grimly.

"Will many be killed?"

"Very many."

"It seems," I said to the others, "that we are going to assist at a gladiatorial show arranged regardless of expense."

Sir Henry shivered, and Good said that he wished that we could get out of it.

"Tell me," I asked Infadoos, "are we in danger?"

"I know not, my lords, I trust not; but do not seem afraid. If ye live through the night all may go well. The soldiers murmur against the king."

All this while we had been advancing steadily towards the centre of the open space, in the midst of which were placed some stools. As we proceeded we perceived another small party coming from the direction of the royal hut.

"It is the king, Twala, and Scragga his son, and Gagool the old, and see, with them are those who slay," and he pointed to a little group of about a dozen gigantic and savage-looking men, armed with spears in one hand and heavy kerries[2] in the other.

The king seated himself upon the centre stool, Gagool crouched at his feet, and the others stood behind.

"Greeting, white lords," he cried, as we came up; "be seated, waste not the precious time—the night is all too short for the deeds that must be done. Ye come in a good hour, and shall see a glorious show. Look round, white lords; look round," and he rolled his one wicked eye from regiment to regiment. "Can the stars show ye such a sight as this? See how they shake in their wickedness, all those who have evil in their hearts and fear in the judgment of 'Heaven above.'"

"*Begin! begin!*" cried out Gagool in her thin piercing voice; "the hyænas are hungry, they howl for food. *Begin! begin!*" Then for a moment there was intense stillness, made horrible by a presage of what was to come.

The king lifted his spear, and suddenly twenty thousand feet were raised, as though they belonged to one man, and brought down with a stamp upon the earth. This was repeated three times, causing the solid ground to shake and tremble. Then from a far point of the circle a solitary voice began a wailing song, of which the refrain ran something as follows:—

"*What is the lot of man born of woman?*"

Back came the answer rolling out from every throat in that vast company—

"*Death!*"

Gradually, however, the song was taken up by company after company, till the whole armed multitude were singing it, and I could no longer follow the words, except in so far as they appeared to represent various phases of human passions, fears, and joys. Now it seemed to be a love song, now a magestic swelling war chant, and last of all a death-dirge ending suddenly in one heartbreaking wail that went echoing and rolling away in a volume of blood-curdling sound. Again the silence fell upon the place, and again it was broken by the king lifting up his hand. Instantly there was a pattering of feet, and from out of the masses of the warriors strange and awful figures came running towards us. As they drew near we saw that they were those of women, most of them aged, for their white hair, ornamented with small bladders taken from fish, streamed out behind them. Their faces were painted in stripes of white and yellow; down their backs hung snake-skins, and round their waists rattled circlets of human bones, while each held in her shrivelled hand a small forked wand. In all there were ten of them. When they arrived in front of us they halted, and one of them, pointing with her wand towards the crouching figure of Gagool, cried out—

"Mother, old mother, we are here."

"*Good! good! good!*" piped out that aged iniquity. "Are your eyes keen, Isanusis (witch doctresses), ye seers in dark places?"

"Mother, they are keen."

"*Good! good! good!* Are your ears open, Isanusis, ye who hear words that come not from the tongue?"

"Mother, they are open."

"*Good! good! good!* Are your senses awake, Isanusis—can ye smell blood, can ye purge the land of the wicked ones who compass evil against the king and against their neighbours? Are ye ready to do the justice of 'Heaven above,' ye whom I have taught, who have eaten the bread of my wisdom and drunk of the water of my magic?"

"Mother, we can."

"Then go! Tarry not, ye vultures; see the slayers," pointing to the ominous group of executioners behind, "make sharp their spears; the white men from afar are hungry to see. *Go.*"

With a wild yell the weird party broke away in every direction, like fragments from a shell, the dry bones round their waists rattling as they ran, and made direct for various points of the dense human circle. We could not watch them all, so fixed our eyes upon the Isanusi nearest us. When she came within a few paces of the warriors, she halted and began to dance wildly, turning round and round with an almost incredible rapidity, and shrieking out sentences such as "I smell him, the evil-doer!" "He is near, he who poisoned his mother!" "I hear the thoughts of him who thought evil of the king!"

Quicker and quicker she danced, till she lashed herself into such a frenzy of excitement that the foam flew in flecks from her gnashing jaws, her eyes seemed to start from her head, and her flesh to quiver visibly. Suddenly she stopped dead, and stiffened all over, like a pointer dog when he scents game, and then with outstretched wand began to creep stealthily towards the soldiers before her. It seemed to us that as she came their stoicism gave way, and that they shrank from her. As for ourselves, we followed her movements with a horrible fascination. Presently, still creeping and crouching like a dog, she was before them. Then she stopped and pointed, and then again crept on a pace or two.

Suddenly the end came. With a shriek she sprang in and touched a tall warrior with the forked wand. Instantly two of his comrades, those standing immediately next to him, seized the doomed man, each by one arm, and advanced with him towards the king.

He did not resist, but we saw that he dragged his limbs as though they were paralysed, and his fingers, from which the spear had fallen, were limp as those of a man newly dead.

As he came, two of the villainous executioners stepped forward to meet him. Presently they met, and the executioners turned round towards the king as though for orders.

"*Kill!*" said the king.

"*Kill!*" squeaked Gagool.

"*Kill!*" re-echoed Scragga, with a hollow chuckle.

Almost before the words were uttered, the horrible deed was done. One man had driven his spear into the victim's heart, and to make assurance doubly sure, the other had dashed out his brains with his great club.

"*One,*" counted Twala the king, just like a black Madame Defarge,[3] as Good said, and the body was dragged a few paces away and stretched out.

Hardly was this done, before another poor wretch was brought up, like an ox to the slaughter. This time we could see, from the leopard-skin cloak, that the man was a person of rank. Again the awful syllables were spoken, and the victim fell dead.

"*Two,*" counted the king.

And so the deadly game went on, till some hundred bodies were stretched in rows behind us. I have heard of the gladiatorial shows of the Cæsars, and of the Spanish bull-fights, but I take the liberty of doubting if they were either of them half as horrible as this Kukuana witch hunt. Gladiatorial shows and Spanish bull-fights, at any rate, contributed to the public amusement, which certainly was not the case here. The most confirmed sensation-monger would fight shy of sensation if he knew that it was well on the cards that he would, in his own proper person, be the subject of the next "event."

Once we rose and tried to remonstrate, but were sternly repressed by Twala.

"Let the law take its course, white men. These dogs are magicians and evil-doers; it is well that they should die," was the only answer vouchsafed to us.

About midnight there was a pause. The witchfinders gathered themselves together, apparently exhausted with their bloody work, and we thought that the whole performance was done with. But it was not so, for presently, to our surprise, the old woman, Gagool, rose from her crouching position, and supporting herself with a stick, staggered off into the open space. It was an extraordinary sight to see this frightful vulture-headed old creature, bent nearly double with extreme age, gather strength by degrees till at last she rushed about almost as actively as her ill-omened pupils. To and fro she ran, chanting to herself, till suddenly she made a dash at a tall man standing in front of one of the regiments, and touched him. As she did so, a sort of groan went up from the regiment, which he evidently commanded. But all the same, two of its members seized him and brought him up for execution. We afterwards learned that he was a man of great wealth and importance, being, indeed, a cousin of the king's.

He was slain, and the king counted one hundred and three. Then Gagool again sprang to and fro, gradually drawing nearer and nearer to ourselves.

"Hang me if I don't believe she is going to try her games on us," ejaculated Good in horror.

"Nonsense!" said Sir Henry.

As for myself, as I saw that old fiend dancing nearer and nearer, my heart positively sank into my boots. I glanced behind us at the long rows of corpses, and shivered.

Nearer and nearer waltzed Gagool, looking for all the world like an animated crooked stick, her horrid eyes gleaming and glowing with a most unholy lustre.

Nearer she came, and nearer yet, every pair of eyes in that vast assemblance watching her movements with intense anxiety. At last she stood still and pointed.

"Which is it to be?" asked Sir Henry to himself.

In a moment all doubts were set at rest, for the old woman had rushed in and touched Umbopa, alias Ignosi, on the shoulder.

"I smell him out," she shrieked. "Kill him, kill him, he is full of evil; kill him, the stranger, before blood flows for him. Slay him, O king."

There was a pause, which I instantly took advantage of.

"O King," I called out, rising from my seat, "this man is the servant of thy guests, he is their dog; whosoever sheds the blood of our dog sheds our blood. By the sacred law of hospitality I claim protection for him."

"Gagool, mother of the witch doctors, has smelt him out; he must die, white men," was the sullen answer.

"Nay, he shall not die," I replied; "he who tries to touch him shall die indeed."

"Seize him!" roared Twala to the executioners, who stood around red to the eyes with the blood of their victims.

They advanced towards us, and then hesitated. As for Ignosi, he raised his spear, and raised it as though determined to sell his life dearly.

"Stand back, ye dogs," I shouted, "if ye would see to-morrow's light. Touch one hair of his head and your king dies," and I covered Twala with my revolver. Sir Henry and Good also drew their pistols, Sir Henry pointing his at the leading executioner, who was advancing to carry out the sentence, and Good taking a deliberate aim at Gagool.

Twala winced perceptibly, as my barrel came in a line with his broad chest.

"Well," I said, "what is it to be, Twala?"

Then he spoke.

"Put away your magic tubes," he said; "ye have adjured me in the name of hospitality, and for that reason, but not from fear of what ye can do, I spare him. Go in peace."

"It is well," I answered, unconcernedly; "we are weary of slaughter, and would sleep. Is the dance ended?"

"It is ended," Twala answered, sulkily. "Let these dogs," pointing to the long rows of corpses, "be flung out to the hyænas and the vultures," and he lifted his spear.

Instantly the regiments began in perfect silence to defile off through the kraal gateway, a fatigue party only remaining behind to drag away the corpses of those who had been sacrificed.

Then we too rose, and making our salaam* to his majesty, which he hardly deigned to acknowledge, departed to our kraal.

"Well," said Sir Henry, as we sat down, having first lit a lamp of the sort used by the Kukuanas, of which the wick is made of the fibre of a species of palm leaf, and the oil of clarified hippopotamus fat, "well, I feel uncommonly inclined to be sick."

"If I had any doubts about helping Umbopa to rebel against that infernal blackguard," put in Good, "they are gone now. It was as much as I could do to sit still while that slaughter was going on. I tried to keep my eyes shut, but they would open just at the wrong time. I wonder where Infadoos is. Umbopa, my friend, you ought to be grateful to us; your skin came near to having an air-hole made in it."

"I am grateful, Bougwan," was Umbopa's answer, when I had translated, "and I shall not forget. As for Infadoos, he will be here by-and-by. We must wait."

So we lit our pipes and waited.

---

*Peace (Arabic); respectful ceremonial Islamic greeting or blessing.

Chapter 11

We Give a Sign

FOR A LONG WHILE—two hours, I should think—we sat there in silence, for we were too overwhelmed by the recollection of the horrors we had seen to talk. At last, just as we were thinking of turning in—for already there were faint streaks of light in the eastern sky—we heard the sound of steps. Then came the challenge of the sentry, who was posted at the kraal gate, which was apparently answered, though not in an audible tone, for the steps came on; and in another second Infadoos had entered the hut, followed by some half-dozen stately-looking chiefs.

"My lords," he said, "I have come according to my word. My lords and Ignosi, rightful King of the Kukuanas, I have brought with me these men," pointing to the row of chiefs, "who are great men among us, having each one of them the command of three thousand soldiers, who live but to do their bidding, under the king's. I have told them of what I have seen, and what my ears have heard. Now let them also see the sacred snake around thee, and hear thy story, Ignosi, that they may say whether or no they will make cause with thee against Twala, the king."

For answer, Ignosi again stripped off his girdle, and exhibited the snake tattooed around him. Each chief in turn drew near and examined it by the dim light of the lamp, and without saying a word passed on to the other side.

Then Ignosi resumed his moocha, and addressing them, repeated the history he had detailed in the morning.

"Now ye have heard, chiefs," said Infadoos, when he had done, "what say ye; will ye stand by this man and help him to his father's throne, or will ye not? The land cries out against Twala, and the blood of the people flows like the waters in spring. Ye have seen to-night. Two other chiefs there were with whom I had it in my mind to speak, and where are they now? The hyænas howl over their corpses. Soon will ye be as they are if ye strike not. Choose then, my brothers."

The eldest of the six men, a short, thick-set warrior with white hair, stepped forward a pace and answered—

"Thy words are true, Infadoos; the land cries out. My own brother is among those who died to-night; but this is a great matter, and the thing is hard to believe. How know we that if we lift our spears it may not be for an impostor? It is a great matter, I say, and none may see the end of it. For of this be sure, blood will flow in rivers before the deed is done; many will still cleave to the king, for men worship the sun that still shines bright in the heavens, and not that which has not risen. These white men from the stars, their magic is great, and Ignosi is under the cover of their wing. If he be indeed the rightful king, let them give us a sign, and let the people have a sign, that all may see. So shall men cleave to us, knowing that the white man's magic is with them."

"Ye have the sign of the snake," I answered.

"My lord, it is not enough. The snake may have been placed there since the man's birth. Show us a sign. We will not move without a sign."

The others gave a decided assent, and I turned in perplexity to Sir Henry and Good, and explained the situation.

"I think I have it," said Good, exultingly; "ask them to give us a moment to think."

I did so, and the chiefs withdrew. As soon as they were gone, Good went to the little box in which his medicines were, unlocked it, and took out a note-book, in the front of which was an almanack. "Now, look here, you fellows, isn't to-morrow the fourth of June?"

We had kept a careful note of the days, so were able to answer that it was.

"Very good; then here we have it—'4 June, total eclipse of the sun commences at 11·15 Greenwich time, visible in these Islands—Africa, &c.' There's a sign for you. Tell them that you will darken the sun to-morrow."

The idea was a splendid one; indeed, the only fear about it was a fear lest Good's almanack might be incorrect. If we made a false prophecy on such a subject, our prestige would be gone for ever, and so would Ignosi's chance of the throne of the Kukuanas.

"Suppose the almanack is wrong," suggested Sir Henry to Good, who was busily employed in working out something on the fly-leaf of the book.

"I don't see any reason to suppose anything of the sort," was his answer. "Eclipses always come up to time; at least, that is my experience of them, and it especially states that it will be visible in Africa. I have worked out the reckonings as well as I can, without knowing our exact position; and I make out that the eclipse should begin here about one o'clock to-morrow, and last till half-past two. For half an hour or more there should be total darkness."

"Well," said Sir Henry, "I suppose we had better risk it."

I acquiesced, though doubtfully, for eclipses are queer cattle to deal with, and sent Umbopa to summon the chiefs back. Presently they came, and I addressed them thus—

"Great men of the Kukuanas, and thou, Infadoos, listen. We are not fond of showing our powers, since to do so is to interfere with the course of nature, and plunge the world into fear and confusion; but as this matter is a great one, and as we are angered against the king because of the slaughter we have seen, and because of the act of the Isanusi Gagool, who would have put our friend Ignosi to death, we have determined to do so, and to give such a sign as all men may see. Come hither," and I led them to the door of the hut and pointed to the fiery ball of the rising sun; "what see ye there?"

"We see the rising sun," answered the spokesman of the party.

"It is so. Now tell me, can any mortal man put out that sun, so that night comes down on the land at mid-day?"

The chief laughed a little. "No, my lord, that no man can do. The sun is stronger than man who looks on him."

"Ye say so. Yet I tell you that this day, one hour after mid-day, will we put out that sun for a space of an hour, and darkness shall cover the earth, and it shall be for a sign that we are indeed men of honour, and that Ignosi is indeed King of the Kukuanas. If we do this thing, will it satisfy ye?"

"Yea, my lords," answered the old chief with a smile, which was reflected on the faces of his companions; "*if* ye do this thing we will be satisfied indeed."

"It shall be done; we three, Incubu the Elephant, Bougwan the clear-eyed, and Macumazahn, who watches in the night, have said it, and it shall be done. Dost thou hear, Infadoos?"

"I hear, my lord, but it is a wonderful thing that ye promise, to put out the sun, the father of all things, who shines for ever."

"Yet shall we do it, Infadoos."

"It is well, my lords. To-day, a little after mid-day, will Twala send for my lords to witness the girls dance, and one hour after the dance begins shall the girl whom Twala thinks the fairest be killed by Scragga, the king's son, as a sacrifice to the silent stone ones, who sit and keep watch by the mountains yonder," and he pointed to the three strange-looking peaks where Solomon's road was supposed to end. "Then let my lords darken the sun, and save the maiden's life, and the people will indeed believe."

"Ay," said the old chief, still smiling a little, "the people will believe indeed."

"Two miles from Loo," went on Infadoos, "there is a hill curved like the new moon, a stronghold, where my regiment, and three other regiments which these men command, are stationed. This morning we will make a plan whereby other regiments, two or three, may be moved there also. Then if my lords can indeed darken the sun, in the darkness I will take my lords by the hand and lead them out of Loo to this place, where they shall be safe, and thence can we make war upon Twala, the king."

"It is good," said I. "Now leave us to sleep awhile and make ready our magic."

Infadoos rose, and, having saluted us, departed with the chiefs.

"My friends," said Ignosi, as soon as they were gone, "can ye indeed do this wonderful thing, or were ye speaking empty words to the men?"

"We believe that we can do it, Umbopa—Ignosi, I mean."

"It is strange," he answered, "and had ye not been Englishmen I would not have believed it; but English 'gentlemen' tell no lies. If we live through the matter, be sure I will repay ye!"

"Ignosi," said Sir Henry, "promise me one thing."

"I will promise, Incubu, my friend, even before I hear it," answered the big man with a smile. "What is it?"

"This: that if you ever come to be king of this people you will do away with the smelling out of witches such as we have seen last night; and that the killing of men without trial shall not take place in the land."

Ignosi thought for a moment, after I had translated this, and then answered—

"The ways of black people are not as the ways of white men, Incubu, nor do we hold life so high as ye. Yet will I promise it. If it be in my power to hold them back, the witch-finders shall hunt no more, nor shall any man die the death without judgment."

"That's a bargain, then," said Sir Henry; "and now let us get a little rest."

Thoroughly wearied out, we were soon sound asleep, and slept till Ignosi woke us about eleven o'clock. Then we got up, washed, and ate a hearty breakfast, not knowing when we should get any more food. After that we went outside the hut and stared at the sun, which we were distressed to observe presented a remarkably healthy appearance, without a sign of an eclipse anywhere about it.

"I hope it will come off," said Sir Henry, doubtfully. "False prophets often find themselves in painful positions."

"If it does not, it will soon be up with us," I answered, mournfully; "for so sure as we are living men, some of those chiefs will tell the whole story to the king, and then there will be another sort of eclipse, and one that we shall not like."

Returning to the hut we dressed ourselves, putting on the mail shirts which the king had sent us as before. Scarcely had we done so when a messenger came from Twala to bid us to the great annual "dance of girls" which was about to be celebrated.

Taking our rifles and ammunition with us so as to have them handy in case we had to fly, as suggested by Infadoos, we started boldly enough, though with inward fear and trembling. The great space in front of the king's kraal presented a very different appearance from what it had done on the previous evening. In the place of the grim ranks of serried warriors were company after company of Kukuana girls, not overdressed, so far as clothing went, but each crowned with a wreath of flowers, and holding a palm leaf in one hand and a tall white lily (the arum) in the other. In the centre of the open space sat Twala, the king, with old Gagool at his feet, attended by Infadoos, the boy Scragga, and about a dozen guards. There were also present about a score of chiefs, amongst whom I recongised most of our friends of the night before.

Twala greeted us with much apparent cordiality, though I saw him fix his one eye viciously on Umbopa.

"Welcome, white men from the stars," he said; "this is a different sight from what your eyes gazed on by the light of last night's moon, but it is not so good a sight. Girls are pleasant, and were it not for such as these" (and he pointed round him) "we should none of us be here to-day; but men are better. Kisses and the tender words of women are sweet, but the sound of the clashing of men's spears, and the smell of men's blood, are sweeter far! Would ye have wives from among our people, white men? If so, choose the fairest here, and ye shall have them, as many as ye will," and he paused for an answer.

As the prospect did not seem to be without attractions to Good, who was, like most sailors, of a susceptible nature, I, being elderly and wise, and foreseeing the endless complications that anything of the sort would involve (for women bring trouble as surely as the night follows the day), put in a hasty answer—

"Thanks, O king, but we white men wed only with white women like ourselves. Your maidens are fair, but they are not for us!"

The king laughed. "It is well. In our land there is a proverb which says, 'Woman's eyes are always bright, whatever the colour,' and another which says, 'Love her who is present, for be sure she who is absent is false to thee;' but perhaps these things are not so in the stars. In a land where men are white all things are possible. So be it, white men; the girls will not go begging! Welcome again; and welcome, too, thou black one; if Gagool here had had her way thou wouldst have been stiff and cold now. It is lucky that thou, too, camest from the stars; ha! ha!"

"I can kill thee before thou killest me, O king," was Ignosi's calm answer, "and thou shalt be stiff before my limbs cease to bend."

Twala started. "Thou speakest boldly, boy," he replied, angrily; "presume not too far."

"He may well be bold in whose lips are truth. The truth is a sharp spear which flies home and fails not. It is a message from 'the stars,' O king!"

Twala scowled, and his one eye gleamed fiercely, but he said nothing more.

"Let the dance begin," he cried, and next second the flower-crowned girls sprang forward in companies, singing a sweet song and waving the delicate palms and white flowers. On they danced, now whirling round and round, now meeting in mimic warfare, swaying, eddying here and there, coming forward, falling back in an ordered confusion delightful to witness. At last they paused, and a beautiful young woman sprang out of the ranks and began to pirouette in front of us with a grace and vigour which would have put most ballet girls to shame. At length she fell back exhausted, and another took her place, then another and another, but none of them, either in grace, skill, or personal attractions, came up to the first.

At length the king lifted his hand.

"Which think ye the fairest, white men?" he asked.

"The first," said I, unthinkingly. Next second I regretted it, for I remembered that Infadoos had said that the fairest woman was offered as a sacrifice.

"Then is my mind as your minds, and my eyes as your eyes. She is the fairest; and a sorry thing it is for her, for she must die!"

"*Ay, must die!*" piped out Gagool, casting a glance from her quick eyes in the direction of the poor girl, who, as yet ignorant of the awful fate in store for her, was standing some twenty yards off in front of a company of girls, engaged in nervously picking a flower from her wreath to pieces, petal by petal.

"Why, O king?" said I, restraining my indignation with difficulty; "the girl has danced well and pleased us; she is fair, too; it would be hard to reward her with death."

Twala laughed as he answered—

"It is our custom, and the figures who sit in stone yonder" (and he pointed towards the three distant peaks) "must have their due. Did I fail to put the fairest girl to death to-day misfortune would fall upon me and my house. Thus runs the prophecy of my people: 'If the king offer not a sacrifice of a fair girl on the day of the dance of maidens to the old ones who sit and watch on the mountains, then shall he fall and his house.' Look ye, white men, my brother who reigned before me offered not the sacrifice, because of the tears of the woman, and he fell, and his house, and I reign in his stead. It is finished; she must die!" Then turning to the guards—"Bring her hither; Scragga, make sharp thy spear."

Two of the men stepped forward, and as they did so, the girl, for the first time realising her impending fate, screamed aloud and turned to fly. But the strong hands caught her fast, and brought her, struggling and weeping, up before us.

"What is thy name, girl?" piped Gagool. "What! wilt thou not answer; shall the king's son do his work at once?"

At this hint Scragga, looking more evil than ever, advanced a step and lifted his great spear, and as he did so I saw Good's hand creep to his revolver. The poor girl caught the glint of the cold steel through her tears, and it sobered her anguish. She ceased struggling, but merely clasped her hands convulsively, and stood shuddering from head to foot.

"See," cried Scragga in high glee, "she shrinks from the sight of my little plaything even before she has tasted it," and he tapped the broad blade of the spear.

"If ever I get the chance, you shall pay for that, you young hound!" I heard Good mutter beneath his breath.

"Now that thou art quiet, give us thy name, my dear. Come, speak up, and fear not," said Gagool in mockery.

"Oh, mother," answered the girl in trembling accents, "my name is Foulata, of the house of Suko. Oh, mother, why must I die? I have done no wrong!"

"Be comforted," went on the old woman, in her hateful tone of mockery. "Thou must die indeed, as a sacrifice to the old ones who sit yonder" (and she pointed to the peaks); "but it is better to sleep in the night than to toil in the day-time; it is better to die than to live, and thou shalt die by the royal hand of the king's own son."

The girl Foulata wrung her hands in anguish, and cried out aloud: "Oh, cruel; and I so young! What have I done that I should never again see the sun rise out of the night, or the stars come following on his track in the evening: that I should no more gather the flowers when the dew is heavy, or listen to the laughing of the waters! Woe is me, that I shall never see my father's hut again, nor feel my mother's kiss, nor tend the kid that is sick! Woe is me, that no lover shall put his arm around me and look into my eyes, nor shall men children be born of me! Oh, cruel, cruel!" and again she wrung her hands and turned her tear-stained, flower-crowned face to Heaven, looking so lovely in her despair—for she was indeed a beautiful woman—that it would assuredly have melted the hearts of any one less cruel than the three fiends before us. Prince Arthur's appeal to the ruffians[1] who came to blind him was not more touching than this savage girl's.

But it did not move Gagool or Gagool's master, though I saw signs of pity among the guard behind, and on the faces of the chiefs; and as for Good, he gave a sort of snort of indignation, and made a motion as though to go to her. With all a woman's quickness, the doomed girl interpreted what was passing in his mind, and with a sudden movement flung herself before him, and clasped his "beautiful white legs" with her hands.

"Oh, white father from the stars!" she cried, "throw over me the mantle of thy protection; let me creep into the shadow of thy strength, that I may be saved. Oh, keep me from these cruel men and from the mercies of Gagool!"

"All right, my hearty, I'll look after you," sang out Good, in nervous Saxon.* "Come, get up, there's a good girl," and he stooped and caught her hand.

Twala turned and motioned to his son, who advanced with his spear lifted.

"Now's your time," whispered Sir Henry to me; "what are you waiting for?"

"I am waiting for the eclipse," I answered; "I have had my eye on the sun for the last half-hour, and I never saw it look healthier."

"Well, you must risk it now, or the girl will be killed. Twala is losing patience."

Recognising the force of the argument, having cast one more despairing look at the bright face of the sun, for never did the most ardent astronomer with a theory to prove await a celestial event with such anxiety, I stepped with all the dignity I could command between the prostrate girl and the advancing spear of Scragga.

"King," I said, "this shall not be; we will not tolerate such a thing; let the girl go in safety."

---

*Literally, the Germanic language of the Saxon people, but Haggard seems to be referring to English.

Twala rose from his seat in his wrath and astonishment, and from the chiefs and serried ranks of girls, who had slowly closed up upon us in anticipation of the tragedy, came a murmur of amazement.

"*Shall not be*, thou white dog, who yaps at the lion in his cave, *shall not be!* art thou mad? Be careful lest this chicken's fate overtakes thee, and those with thee. How canst thou prevent it? Who art thou that thou standest between me and my will? Withdraw, I say. Scragga, kill her. Ho, guards! seize these men."

At his cry armed men came running swiftly from behind the hut, where they had evidently been placed beforehand.

Sir Henry, Good, and Umbopa ranged themselves alongside of me, and lifted their rifles.

"Stop!" I shouted boldly, though at the moment my heart was in my boots. "Stop! we, the white men from the stars, say that it shall not be. Come but one pace nearer, and we will put out the sun and plunge the land in darkness. Ye shall taste of our magic."

My threat produced an effect; the men halted, and Scragga stood still before us, his spear lifted.

"Hear him! hear him!" piped Gagool; "hear the liar who says he will put out the sun like a lamp. Let him do it, and the girl shall be spared. Yes, let him do it, or die with the girl, he and those with him."

I glanced up at the sun, and to my intense joy and relief saw that we had made no mistake. On the edge of its brilliant surface was a faint rim of shadow.

I lifted my hand solemnly towards the sky, an example which Sir Henry and Good followed, and quoted a line or two of the "Ingoldsby Legends" at it in the most impressive tones I could command. Sir Henry followed suit with a verse out of the Old Testament, whilst Good addressed the King of Day in a volume of the most classical bad language that he could think of.

Slowly the dark rim crept on over the blazing surface, and as it did so I heard a deep gasp of fear rise from the multitude around.

"Look, O king! look, Gagool! Look, chiefs and people and women, and see if the white men from the stars keep their word, or if they be but empty liars!"

"The sun grows dark before your eyes; soon there will be night—ay, night in the noontime. Ye have asked for a sign; it is given to ye.

Grow dark, O sun! withdraw thy light, thou bright one; bring the proud heart to the dust, and eat up the world with shadows."

A groan of terror rose from the onlookers. Some stood petrified with fear, others threw themselves upon their knees, and cried out. As for the king, he sat still and turned pale beneath his dusky skin. Only Gagool kept her courage.

"It will pass," she cried; "I have seen the like before; no man can put out the sun; lose not heart; sit still—the shadow will pass."

"Wait, and ye shall see," I replied, hopping with excitement.

"Keep it up, Good, I can't remember any more poetry. Curse away, there's a good fellow."

Good responded nobly to the tax upon his inventive faculties. Never before had I the faintest conception of the breadth and depth and height of a naval officer's objurgatory powers. For ten minutes he went on without stopping, and scarcely ever repeated himself.

Meanwhile the dark ring crept on. Strange and unholy shadows encroached upon the sunlight, an ominous quiet filled the place, the birds chirped out frightened notes, and then were still; only the cocks began to crow.

On, yet on, crept the ring of darkness; it was now more than half over the reddening orb. The air grew thick and dusky. On, yet on, till we could scarcely see the fierce faces of the group before us. No sound rose now from the spectators, and Good stopped swearing.

"The sun is dying—the wizards have killed the sun," yelled out the boy Scragga at last. "We shall all die in the dark," and animated by fear or fury, or both, he lifted his spear, and drove it with all his force at Sir Henry's broad chest. But he had forgotten the mail shirts that the king had given us, and which we wore beneath our clothing. The steel rebounded harmless, and before he could repeat the blow Sir Henry had snatched the spear from his hand, and sent it straight through him. He dropped dead.

At the sight, and driven mad with fear at the gathering gloom, the companies of girls broke up in wild confusion, and ran screeching for the gateways. Nor did the panic stop there. The king himself, followed by the guards, some of the chiefs, and Gagool, who hobbled away after them with marvellous alacrity, fled for the huts, so that in another minute or so ourselves, the would-be victim Foulata, Infadoos, and some of the chiefs, who had interviewed us on the previous night, were left alone upon the scene with the dead body of Scragga.

"Now, chiefs," I said, "we have given you the sign. If ye are satisfied, let us fly swiftly to the place ye spoke of. The charm cannot now be stopped. It will work for an hour. Let us take advantage of the darkness."

"Come," said Infadoos, turning to go, an example which was followed by the awed chiefs, ourselves, and the girl Foulata, whom Good took by the hand.

Before we reached the gate of the kraal the sun went out altogether.

Holding each other by the hand we stumbled on through the darkness.

Chapter 12

Before the Battle

LUCKILY FOR US, INFADOOS and the chiefs knew all the pathways of the great town perfectly, so that notwithstanding the intense gloom we made fair progress.

For an hour or more we journeyed on, till at length the eclipse began to pass, and that edge of the sun which had disappeared the first, became again visible. In another five minutes there was sufficient light to see our whereabouts, and we then discovered that we were clear of the town of Loo, and approaching a large flat-topped hill, measuring some two miles in circumference. This hill, which was of a formation very common in Southern Africa, was not very high; indeed, its greatest elevation was not more than 200 feet, but it was shaped like a horse-shoe, and its sides were rather precipitous, and strewn with boulders. On the grass table-land at the top was ample camping ground, which had been utilised as a military cantonment of no mean strength. Its ordinary garrison was one regiment of three thousand men, but as we toiled up the steep side of the hill in the returning daylight, we perceived that there were many more warriors than that upon it.

Reaching the table-land at last, we found crowds of men huddled together in the utmost consternation at the natural phenomenon which they were witnessing. Passing through these without a word, we gained a hut in the centre of the ground, where we were astonished to find two men waiting, laden with our few goods and chattels, which of course we had been obliged to leave behind in our hasty flight.

"I sent for them," explained Infadoos; "also for these," and he lifted up Good's long-lost trousers.

With an exclamation of rapturous delight Good sprang at them, and instantly proceeded to put them on.

"Surely my lord will not hide his beautiful white legs!" exclaimed Infadoos, regretfully.

But Good persisted, and once only did the Kukuana people get the chance of seeing his beautiful legs again. Good is a very modest man. Henceforward they had to satisfy their æsthetic longings with his one whisker, his transparent eye, and his movable teeth.

Still gazing with fond remembrance at Good's trousers, Infadoos next informed us that he had summoned the regiments to explain to them fully the rebellion which was decided on by the chiefs, and to introduce to them the rightful heir to the throne, Ignosi.

In half an hour the troops, in all nearly twenty thousand men, constituting the flower of the Kukuana army, were mustered on a large open space, to which we proceeded. The men were drawn up in three sides of a dense square, and presented a magnificent spectacle. We took our station on the open side of the square, and were speedily surrounded by all the principal chiefs and officers.

These, after silence had been proclaimed, Infadoos proceeded to address. He narrated to them in vigorous and graceful language— for like most Kukuanas of high rank, he was a born orator—the history of Ignosi's father, how he had been basely murdered by Twala, the king, and his wife and child driven out to starve. Then he pointed out how the land suffered and groaned under Twala's cruel rule, instancing the proceedings of the previous night, when, under pretence of their being evil-doers, many of the noblest in the land had been hauled forth and cruelly done to death. Next he went on to say that the white lords from the stars, looking down on the land, had perceived its trouble, and determined, at great personal inconvenience, to alleviate its lot; how they had accordingly taken the real king of the country, Ignosi, who was languishing in exile, by the hand, and led him over the mountains; how they had seen the wickedness of Twala's doings, and for a sign to the wavering, and to save the life of the girl Foulata, had actually, by the exercise of their high magic, put out the sun, and slain the young fiend Scragga; and how they were prepared to stand by them, and assist them to overthrow Twala, and set up the rightful king, Ignosi, in his place.

He finished his discourse amidst a murmur of approbation, and then Ignosi stepped forward, and began to speak. Having reiterated all that Infadoos his uncle had said, he concluded a powerful speech in these words:—

"O chiefs, captains, soldiers, and people, ye have heard my words.

Now must ye make choice between me and him who sits upon my throne, the uncle who killed his brother, and hunted his brother's child forth to die in the cold and the night. That I am indeed the king these"—pointing to the chiefs—"can tell ye, for they have seen the snake about my middle. If I were not the king, would these white men be on my side, with all their magic? Tremble, chiefs, captains, soldiers, and people! Is not the darkness they have brought upon the land to confound Twala, and cover our flight, yet before your eyes?"

"It is," answered the soldiers.

"I am the king; I say to ye, I am the king," went on Ignosi, drawing up his great stature to its full, and lifting his broad-bladed battle-axe above his head. "If there be any man among ye who says that it is not so, let him stand forth, and I will fight him now, and his blood shall be a red token that I tell ye true. Let him stand forth, I say;" and he shook the great axe till it flashed in the sunlight.

As nobody seemed inclined to respond to this heroic version of "Dilly, Dilly, come and be killed,"[1] our late henchman proceeded with his address.

"I am indeed the king, and if ye do stand by my side in the battle, if I win the day ye shall go with me to victory and honour. I will give ye oxen and wives, and ye shall take place of all the regiments; and if ye fall I will fall with ye.

"And, behold, this promise do I give ye, that when I sit upon the seat of my fathers, bloodshed shall cease in the land. No longer shall ye cry for justice to find slaughter, no longer shall the witch-finder hunt ye out so that ye be slain without a cause. No man shall die save he who offendeth against the laws. The 'eating up' of your kraals shall cease; each shall sleep secure in his own hut and fear not, and justice shall walk blind throughout the land. Have ye chosen, chiefs, captains, soldiers, and people?"

"We have chosen, O king," came back the answer.

"It is well. Turn your heads and see how Twala's messengers go forth from the great town, east and west, and north and south, to gather a mighty army to slay me and ye, and these my friends and my protectors. To-morrow, or perchance the next day, will he come with all who are faithful to him. Then shall I see the man who is indeed my man, the man who fears not to die for his cause; and I tell ye he shall not be forgotten in the time of spoil. I have spoken, O chiefs, captains, soldiers, and people. Now go to your huts and make you ready for war."

There was a pause, and then one of the chiefs lifted his hand, and out rolled the royal salute, "Koom." It was a sign that the regiments accepted Ignosi as their king. Then they marched off in battalions.

Half an hour afterwards we held a council of war, at which all the commanders of regiments were present. It was evident to us that before very long we should be attacked in overwhelming force. Indeed, from our point of vantage on the hill we could see troops mustering, and messengers going forth from Loo in every direction, doubtless to summon regiments to the king's assistance. We had on our side about twenty thousand men, composed of seven of the best regiments in the country. Twala had, so Infadoos and the chiefs calculated, at least thirty to thirty-five thousand on whom he could rely at present assembled in Loo, and they thought that by midday on the morrow he would be able to gather another five thousand or more to his aid. It was, of course, possible that some of his troops would desert and come over to us, but it was not a contingency that could be reckoned on. Meanwhile, it was clear that active preparations were being made to subdue us. Already strong bodies of armed men were patrolling round and round the foot of the hill, and there were other signs of a coming attack.

Infadoos and the chiefs, however, were of opinion that no attack would take place that night, which would be devoted to preparation and to the removal by every possible means of the moral effect produced upon the minds of the soldiery by the supposed magical darkening of the sun. The attack would be on the morrow, they said, and they proved to be right.

Meanwhile, we set to work to strengthen the position as much as possible. Nearly the entire force was turned out, and in the two hours which yet remained to sundown wonders were done. The paths up the hill, which was rather a sanitarium than a fortress, being used generally as the camping place of regiments suffering from recent service in unhealthy portions of the country, were carefully blocked with masses of stones, and every other possible approach was made as impregnable as time would allow. Piles of boulders were collected at various spots to be rolled down upon an advancing enemy, stations were appointed to the different regiments, and every other preparation which our joint ingenuity could suggest was taken.

Just before sundown we perceived a small company of men advancing towards us from the direction of Loo, one of whom bore a palm leaf in his hand as a sign that he came as a herald.

As he came, Ignosi, Infadoos, one or two chiefs, and ourselves, went down to the foot of the mountain to meet him. He was a gallant-looking fellow, with the regulation leopard-skin cloak.

"Greeting!" he cried, as he came near; "the king's greeting to those who make unholy war against the king; the lion's greeting to the jackals who snarl around his heels."

"Speak," I said.

"These are the king's words. Surrender to the king's mercy ere a worse thing befall ye. Already the shoulder has been torn from the black bull, and the king drives him bleeding about the camp."*

"What are Twala's terms?" I asked for curiosity.

"His terms are merciful, worthy of a great king. These are the words of Twala, the one-eyed, the mighty, the husband of a thousand wives, lord of the Kukuanas, keeper of the great road (Solomon's Road), beloved of the strange ones who sit in silence at the mountains yonder (the Three Witches), calf of the black cow, elephant whose tread shakes the earth, terror of the evil-doer, ostrich whose feet devour the desert, huge one, black one, wise one, king from generation to generation! these are the words of Twala: 'I will have mercy and be satisfied with a little blood. One in every ten shall die, the rest shall go free; but the white man Incubu, who slew Scragga, my son, and the black man, his servant, who pretends to my throne, and Infadoos, my brother, who brews rebellion against me, these shall die by torture as an offering to the silent ones.' Such are the merciful words of Twala."

After consulting with the others a little, I answered him in a loud voice, so that the soldiers might hear, thus—

"Go back, thou dog, to Twala, who sent thee, and say that we, Ignosi, veritable king of the Kukuanas, Incubu, Bougwan, and

---

*This cruel custom is not confined to the Kukuanas, but is by no means uncommon amongst African tribes on the occasion of the outbreak of war or any other important public event. [Haggard's note]

Macumazahn, the wise white ones from the stars, who make dark the sun, Infadoos, of the royal house, and the chiefs, captains, and people here gathered, make answer and say, 'That we will not surrender; that before the sun has twice gone down Twala's corpse shall stiffen at Twala's gate, and Ignosi, whose father Twala slew, shall reign in his stead.' Now go, ere we whip thee away, and beware how ye lift a hand against such as we."

The herald laughed loud. "Ye frighten not men with such swelling words," he cried out. "Show yourselves as bold to-morrow, O ye who darken the sun. Be bold, fight, and be merry, before the crows pick your bones till they are whiter than your faces. Farewell; perhaps we may meet in the fight; wait for me, I pray, white men." And with this shaft of sarcasm he retired, and almost immediately the sun sank.

That night was a busy one for us, for as far as was possible by the moonlight all preparations for the morrow's fight were continued. Messengers were constantly coming and going from the place where we sat in council. At last, about an hour after midnight, everything that could be done was done, and the camp, save for the occasional challenge of a sentry, sank into sleep. Sir Henry and I, accompanied by Ignosi and one of the chiefs, descended the hill and made the round of the outposts. As we went, suddenly, from all sorts of unexpected places, spears gleamed out in the moonlight, only to vanish again as we uttered the password. It was clear to us that none were sleeping at their posts. Then we returned, picking our way through thousands of sleeping warriors, many of whom were taking their last earthly rest.

The moonlight flickered along their spears, and played upon their features and made them ghastly; the chilly night wind tossed their tall and hearse-like plumes. There they lay in wild confusion, with arms outstretched and twisted limbs; their stern, stalwart forms looking weird and unhuman in the moonlight.

"How many of these do you suppose will be alive at this time to-morrow?" asked Sir Henry.

I shook my head and looked again at the sleeping men, and to my tired and yet excited imagination it seemed as though death had already touched them. My mind's eye singled out those who were sealed to slaughter, and there rushed in upon my heart a great sense of the mystery of human life, and an overwhelming sorrow at its fu-

tility and sadness. To-night these thousands slept their healthy sleep,
to-morrow they, and many others with them, ourselves perhaps
among them, would be stiffening in the cold; their wives would be
widows, their children fatherless, and their place know them no
more for ever. Only the old moon would shine serenely on, the night
wind would stir the grasses, and the wide earth would take its happy
rest, even as it did æons before these were, and will do æons after
they have been forgotten.

Yet man dies not whilst the world, at once his mother and his
monument, remains. His name is forgotten, indeed, but the breath
he breathed yet stirs the pine-tops on the mountains, the sound of
the words he spoke yet echoes on through space; the thoughts his
brain gave birth to we have inherited to-day; his passions are our
cause of life; the joys and sorrows that he felt are our familiar
friends—the end from which he fled aghast will surely overtake us
also!

Truly the universe is full of ghosts, not sheeted churchyard spec-
tres, but the inextinguishable and immortal elements of life, which,
having once been, can never *die*, though they blend and change and
change again for ever.

All sorts of reflections of this sort passed through my mind—for
as I get older I regret to say that a detestable habit of thinking seems
to be getting a hold of me—while I stood and stared at those grim
yet fantastic lines of warriors sleeping, as their saying goes, "upon
their spears."

"Curtis," I said to Sir Henry, "I am in a condition of pitiable
funk."

Sir Henry stroked his yellow beard and laughed, as he answered—

"I've heard you make that sort of remark before, Quatermain."

"Well, I mean it now. Do you know, I very much doubt if one of
us will be alive to-morrow night. We shall be attacked in overwhelming force, and it is exceedingly doubtful if we can hold this
place."

"We'll give a good account of some of them, at any rate. Look
here, Quatermain, the business is a nasty one, and one with which,
properly speaking, we ought not to be mixed up, but we are in for it,
so we must make the best of it. Speaking personally, I had rather be

killed fighting than any other way, and now that there seems little chance of my finding my poor brother, it makes the idea easier to me. But fortune favours the brave, and we may succeed. Anyway, the slaughter will be awful, and as we have a reputation to keep up, we shall have to be in the thick of it."

Sir Henry made this last remark in a mournful voice, but there was a gleam in his eye which belied it. I have a sort of idea that Sir Henry Curtis actually likes fighting.

After this we went and slept for a couple of hours.

Just about dawn we were awakened by Infadoos, who came to say that great activity was to be observed in Loo, and that parties of the king's skirmishers were driving in our outposts.

We got up and dressed ourselves for the fray, each putting on our chain-armour shirt, for which at the present juncture we felt exceedingly thankful. Sir Henry went the whole length about the matter, and dressed himself like a native warrior. "When you are in Kukuanaland, do as the Kukuanas do," he remarked, as he drew the shining steel over his broad shoulders, which it fitted like a glove. Nor did he stop there. At his request, Infadoos had provided him with a complete set of war uniform. Round his throat he fastened the leopard-skin cloak of a commanding officer, on his brows he bound the plume of black ostrich feathers, worn only by generals of high rank, and round his centre a magnificent moocha of white ox-tails. A pair of sandals, a leglet of goats' hair, a heavy battle-axe, with a rhinoceros-horn handle, a round iron shield, covered with white ox-hide, and the regulation number of tollas, or throwing knives, made up his equipment, to which, however, he added his revolver. The dress was, no doubt, a savage one, but I am bound to say I never saw a finer sight than Sir Henry Curtis presented in this guise. It showed off his magnificent physique to the greatest advantage, and when Ignosi arrived presently, arrayed in similar costume, I thought to myself that I never before saw two such splendid men. As for Good and myself, the chain armour did not suit us nearly so well. To begin with, Good insisted upon keeping on his trousers, and a stout, short gentleman with an eye-glass, and one half of his face shaved, arrayed in a mail shirt carefully tucked into a very seedy pair of corduroys, looks more striking than imposing. As for myself, my chain shirt being too big for me, I put it on over all my clothes, which caused it to bulge out in a somewhat ungainly fashion. I discarded my trousers, however, determined to go into battle with bare legs, in order to be the lighter, in case it became necessary to retire quickly, retaining only my veldtschoons. This, a spear, a shield, which I did not know how to use, a couple of tollas, a revolver, and a huge plume, which I pinned into the top of my shooting hat, in order to give a bloodthirsty finish to my appearance, completed my modest equipment. In addition to all these articles, of course we had our rifles, but as ammunition was scarce, and they would be useless in case of a charge, we had arranged to have them carried behind us by bearers.

As soon as we had equipped ourselves, we hastily swallowed some food, and then started out to see how things were progressing. At one point in the table-land of the mountain there was a little koppie of brown stone, which served for the double purpose of headquarters and a conning tower. Here we found Infadoos surrounded by his own regiment, the Greys, which was undoubtedly the finest in the Kukuana army, and the same which we had first seen at the outlying kraal. This regiment, now three thousand five hundred strong, was being held in reserve, and the men were lying down on the grass in companies, and watching the king's forces creep out of Loo in long ant-like columns. There seemed to be no end to those columns—three in all, and each numbering at least eleven or twelve thousand men.

As soon as they were clear of the town, they formed up. Then one body marched off to the right, one to the left, and the third came slowly on towards us.

"Ah," said Infadoos, "they are going to attack us on three sides at once."

This was rather serious news, for as our position on the top of the mountain, which was at least a mile and a half in circumference, was an extended one, it was important to us to concentrate our comparatively small defending force as much as possible. But as it was impossible for us to dictate in what way we should be attacked, we had to make the best of it, and accordingly sent orders to the various regiments to prepare to receive the separate onslaughts.

Chapter 13

The Attack

SLOWLY, AND WITHOUT THE slightest appearance of haste or excitement, the three columns crept on. When within about five hundred yards of us, the main or centre column halted at the root of a tongue of open plain which ran up into the hill, to enable the other two to circumvent our position, which was shaped more or less in the form of a horse-shoe, the two points being towards the town of Loo, their object being, no doubt, that the threefold assault should be delivered simultaneously.

"Oh, for a gatling!"[1] groaned Good, as he contemplated the serried phalanxes beneath us. "I would clear the plain in twenty minutes."

"We have not got one, so it is no use yearning for it; but suppose you try a shot, Quatermain. See how near you can go to that tall fellow who appears to be in command. Two to one you miss him, and an even sovereign, to be honestly paid if ever we get out of this, that you don't drop the ball within ten yards."

This piqued me, so, loading the express with solid ball, I waited till my friend walked some ten yards out from his force, in order to get a better view of our position, accompanied only by an orderly, and then, lying down and resting the express upon a rock, I covered him. The rifle, like all expresses, was only sighted to three hundred and fifty yards, so to allow for the drop in trajectory I took him half-way down the neck, which ought, I calculated, to find him in the chest. He stood quite still and gave me every opportunity, but whether it was the excitement or the wind, or the fact of the man being a long shot, I don't know, but this was what happened. Getting dead on, as I thought, a fine sight, I pressed, and when the puff of smoke had cleared away, I, to my disgust, saw my man standing unharmed, whilst his orderly, who was at least three paces to the left, was stretched upon the ground, apparently dead. Turning swiftly, the officer I had aimed at began to run towards his force, in evident alarm.

"Bravo, Quatermain!" sang out Good; "you've frightened him."

This made me very angry, for if possible to avoid it, I hate to miss in public. When one can only do one thing well, one likes to keep up one's reputation in that thing. Moved quite out of myself at my failure, I did a rash thing. Rapidly covering the general as he ran, I let drive with the second barrel. The poor man threw up his arms, and fell forward on to his face. This time I had made no mistake; and— I say it as a proof of how little we think of others when our own pride or reputation are in question—I was brute enough to feel delighted at the sight.

The regiments who had seen the feat cheered wildly at this exhibition of the white man's magic, which they took as an omen of success, while the force to which the general had belonged—which, indeed, as we afterwards ascertained, he had commanded—began to fall back in confusion. Sir Henry and Good now took up their rifles, and began to fire, the latter industriously "browning" the dense mass before him with a Winchester repeater, and I also had another shot or two, with the result that so far as we could judge we put some eight or ten men *hors de combat** before they got out of range.

Just as we stopped firing there came an ominous roar from our far right, then a similar roar from our left. The two other divisions were engaging us.

At the sound, the mass of men before us opened out a little, and came on towards the hill up the spit of bare grass land at a slow trot, singing a deep-throated song as they advanced. We kept up a steady fire from our rifles as they came, Ignosi joining in occasionally, and accounted for several men, but of course produced no more effect upon that mighty rush of armed humanity than he who throws pebbles does on the advancing wave.

On they came, with a shout and the clashing of spears; now they were driving in the outposts we had placed among the rocks at the foot of the hill. After that the advance was a little slower, for though as yet we had offered no serious opposition, the attacking force had to come up hill, and came slowly to save their breath. Our first line

---

*Unfit for battle (French).

of defence was about half-way up the side, our second fifty yards further back, while our third occupied the edge of the plain.

On they came, shouting their war-cry, *"Twala! Twala! Chielé! Chielé!"* (Twala! Twala! Smite! Smite!). *"Ignosi! Ignosi! Chielé! Chielé!"* answered our people. They were quite close now, and the tollas, or throwing knives, began to flash backwards and forwards, and now with an awful yell the battle closed in.

To and fro swayed the mass of struggling warriors, men falling thick as leaves in an autumn wind; but before long the superior weight of the attacking force began to tell, and our first line of defence was slowly pressed back, till it merged into the second. Here the struggle was very fierce, but again our people were driven back and up, till at length, within twenty minutes of the commencement of the fight, our third line came into action.

But by this time the assailants were much exhausted, and had besides lost many men killed and wounded, and to break through that third impenetrable hedge of spears proved beyond their powers. For awhile the dense mass of struggling warriors swung backwards and forwards in the fierce ebb and flow of battle, and the issue was doubtful. Sir Henry watched the desperate struggle with a kindling eye, and then without a word he rushed off, followed by Good, and flung himself into the hottest of the fray. As for myself, I stopped where I was.

The soldiers caught sight of his tall form as he plunged into the battle, and there rose a cry of—

"Nanzia Incubu!" (Here is the Elephant!) *"Chielé! Chielé!"*

From that moment the issue was no longer in doubt. Inch by inch, fighting with desperate gallantry, the attacking force was pressed back down the hillside, till at last it retreated upon its reserves in something like confusion. At that moment, too, a messenger arrived to say that the left attack had been repulsed; and I was just beginning to congratulate myself that the affair was over for the present, when, to our horror, we perceived our men who had been engaged in the right defence being driven towards us across the plain, followed by swarms of the enemy, who had evidently succeeded at this point.

Ignosi, who was standing by me, took in the situation at a glance, and issued a rapid order. Instantly the reserve regiment round us (the Greys) extended itself.

Again Ignosi gave a word of command, which was taken up and repeated by the captains, and in another second, to my intense disgust, I found myself involved in a furious onslaught upon the advancing foe. Getting as much as I could behind Ignosi's huge frame, I made the best of a bad job, and toddled along to be killed, as though I liked it. In a minute or two—the time seemed all too short to me—we were plunging through the flying groups of our men, who at once began to re-form behind us, and then I am sure I do not know what happened. All I can remember is a dreadful rolling noise of the meeting of shields, and the sudden apparition of a huge ruffian, whose eyes seemed literally to be starting out of his head, making straight at me with a bloody spear. But—I say it with pride—I rose to the occasion. It was an occasion before which most people would have collapsed once and for all. Seeing that if I stood where I was I must be done for, I, as the horrid apparition came, flung myself down in front of him so cleverly, that, being unable to stop himself, he took a header right over my prostrate form. Before he could rise again, I had risen and settled the matter from behind with my revolver.

Shortly after this, somebody knocked me down, and I remember no more of the charge.

When I came to, I found myself back at the koppie, with Good bending over me with some water in a gourd.

"How do you feel, old fellow?" he asked, anxiously.

I got up and shook myself before answering.

"Pretty well, thank you," I answered.

"Thank Heaven! when I saw them carry you in I felt quite sick; I thought you were done for."

"Not this time, my boy. I fancy I only got a rap on the head, which knocked me out of time. How has it ended?"

"They are repulsed at every point for the time. The loss is dreadfully heavy; we have lost quite two thousand killed and wounded, and they must have lost three. Look, there's a sight!" and he pointed to long lines of men advancing by fours. In the centre of, and being borne by each group of four, was a kind of hide tray, of which a Kukuana force always carried a quantity, with a loop for a handle at each corner. On these trays—and their number seemed endless—lay wounded men, who as they arrived were hastily examined by the medicine men, of whom ten were attached to each regiment. If the wound was not of a fatal character, the sufferer was taken away and attended to as carefully as circumstances would allow. But if, on the other hand, the wounded man's condition was hopeless, what followed was very dreadful, though doubtless it was the truest mercy. One of the doctors, under pretence of carrying out an examination, swiftly opened an artery with a sharp knife, and in a minute or two the sufferer expired painlessly. There were many cases that day in which this was done. In fact, it was done in most cases when the wound was in the body, for the gash made by the entry of the enormously broad spears used by the Kukuanas generally rendered recovery hopeless. In most cases the poor sufferers were already unconscious, and in others the fatal "nick" of the artery was done so swiftly and painlessly that they did not seem to notice it. Still it was a ghastly sight, and one from which we were glad to escape; indeed, I never remember one which affected me more than seeing those gallant soldiers thus put out of pain by the red-handed medicine men, except, indeed, on an occasion when, after an attack, I saw a force of Swazis* burying their hopelessly wounded *alive*.

Hurrying from this dreadful scene to the further side of the koppie, we found Sir Henry (who still held a bloody battle-axe in his hand), Ignosi, Infadoos, and one or two of the chiefs in deep consultation.

"Thank heavens, here you are, Quatermain! I can't quite make out what Ignosi wants to do. It seems that, though we have beaten off the attack, Twala is now receiving large reinforcements, and is showing a disposition to invest us, with a view of starving us out."

"That's awkward."

"Yes; especially as Infadoos says that the water supply has given out."

"My lord, that is so," said Infadoos; "the spring cannot supply the wants of so great a multitude, and is failing rapidly. Before night we shall all be thirsty. Listen, Macumazahn. Thou art wise, and hast

---

*Bantu-speaking people of modern Swaziland and other areas of southeastern Africa; they live by farming and herding.

doubtless seen many wars in the lands from whence thou camest—
that is if, indeed, they make wars in the stars. Now tell us, what shall
we do? Twala has brought up many fresh men to take the place of
those who have fallen. But Twala has learnt a lesson; the hawk did
not think to find the heron ready; but our beak has pierced his
breast; he will not strike at us again. We too are wounded, and he
will wait for us to die; he will wind himself round us like a snake
round a buck, and fight the fight of 'sit down.'"

"I hear you," I said.

"So, Macumazahn, thou seest we have no water here, and but a
little food, and we must choose between these three things—to lan-
guish like a starving lion in his den, or to strive to break away towards the north, or"—and here he rose and pointed towards the
dense mass of our foes—"to launch ourselves straight at Twala's
throat. Incubu, the great warrior—for to-day he fought like a buffalo in a net, and Twala's soldiers went down before his axe like corn
before the hail; with these eyes I saw it—Incubu says 'Charge;' but
the Elephant is ever prone to charge. Now what says Macumazahn,
the wily old fox, who has seen much, and loves to bite his enemy
from behind? The last word is in Ignosi the king, for it is a king's
right to speak of war; but let us hear thy voice, O Macumazahn, who
watchest by night, and the voice too of him of the transparent eye."

"What sayest thou, Ignosi?" I asked.

"Nay, my father," answered our quondam servant, who now, clad
as he was in the full panoply of savage war, looked every inch a warrior king, "do thou speak, and let me, who am but a child in wisdom
beside thee, hearken to thy words."

Thus abjured, I, after taking hasty counsel with Good and Sir
Henry, delivered my opinion briefly to the effect that, being trapped,
our best chance, especially in view of the failure of our water supply,
was to initiate an attack upon Twala's forces, and then I recommended that the attack should be delivered at once, "before our
wounds grew stiff," and also before the sight of Twala's overpowering force caused the hearts of our soldiers "to wax small like fat before a fire." Otherwise, I pointed out, some of the captains might
change their minds, and, making peace with Twala, desert him, or
even betray us into his hands.

This expression of opinion seemed, on the whole, to be

favourably received; indeed, among the Kukuanas my utterances met with a respect which has never been accorded to them before or since. But the real decision as to our course lay with Ignosi, who, since he had been recognised as rightful king, could exercise the almost unbounded rights of sovereignty, including, of course, the final decision on matters of generalship, and it was to him that all eyes were now turned.

At length, after a pause, during which he appeared to be thinking deeply, he spoke:—

"Incubu, Macumazahn, and Bougwan, brave white men, and my friends; Infadoos, my uncle, and chiefs; my heart is fixed. I will strike at Twala this day, and set my fortunes on the blow, ay, and my life; my life and your lives also. Listen: thus will I strike. Ye see how the hill curves round like the half-moon, and how the plain runs like a green tongue towards us within the curve?"

"We see," I answered.

"Good; it is now mid-day, and the men eat and rest after the toil of battle. When the sun has turned and travelled a little way towards the dark, let thy regiment, my uncle, advance with one other down to the green tongue. And it shall be that when Twala sees it he shall hurl his force at it to crush it. But the spot is narrow, and the regiments can come against thee one at a time only; so shall they be destroyed one by one, and the eyes of all Twala's army shall be fixed upon a struggle the like of which has not been seen by living man. And with thee my uncle shall go Incubu my friend, that when Twala sees his battle-axe flashing in the first rank of the 'Greys' his heart may grow faint. And I will come with the second regiment, that which follows thee, so that if ye are destroyed, as it may happen, there may yet be a king left to fight for; and with me shall come Macumazahn the wise."

"It is well, O king," said Infadoos, apparently contemplating the certainty of the complete annihilation of his regiment with perfect calmness. Truly these Kukuanas are a wonderful people. Death has no terrors for them when it is incurred in the course of duty.

"And whilst the eyes of the multitude of Twala's regiments are thus fixed upon the fight," went on Ignosi, "behold, one-third of the men who are left alive to us (*i.e.*, about 6,000) shall creep along the right horn of the hill and fall upon the left flank of Twala's force, and one-third shall creep along the left horn and fall upon Twala's right flank. And when I see that the horns are ready to toss Twala, then will I, with the men who are left to me, charge home in Twala's face, and if fortune goes with us the day will be ours, and before Night drives her horses from the mountains to the mountains we shall sit in peace at Loo. And now let us eat and make ready; and, Infadoos, do thou prepare, that the plan be carried out; and stay, let my white father Bougwan go with the right horn, that his shining eye may give courage to the men."

The arrangements for attack thus briefly indicated were set in motion with a rapidity that spoke well for the perfection of the Kukuana military system. Within little more than an hour rations had been served out to the men and devoured, the three divisions were formed, the plan of attack explained to the leaders, and the whole force, with the exception of a guard left with the wounded, now numbering about 18,000 men in all, was ready to be put in motion.

Presently Good came up and shook hands with Sir Henry and myself.

"Good-bye, you fellows," he said, "I am off with the right wing according to orders; and so I have come to shake hands in case we should not meet again, you know," he added, significantly.

We shook hands in silence, and not without the exhibition of as much emotion as Englishmen are wont to show.

"It is a queer business," said Sir Henry, his deep voice shaking a little, "and I confess I never expect to see to-morrow's sun. As far as I can make out, the Greys, with whom I am to go, are to fight until they are wiped out in order to enable the wings to slip round unawares and outflank Twala. Well, so be it; at any rate, it will be a man's death! Good-bye, old fellow. God bless you! I hope you will pull through and live to collar the diamonds; but if you do, take my advice and don't have anything more to do with pretenders!"

In another second Good had wrung us both by the hand and gone; and then Infadoos came up and led off Sir Henry to his place in the forefront of the Greys, whilst, with many misgivings, I departed with Ignosi to my station in the second attacking regiment.

Chapter 14

The Last Stand of the Greys

IN A FEW MORE minutes the regiments destined to carry out the flanking movements had tramped off in silence, keeping carefully under the lee of the rising ground in order to conceal the movement from the keen eyes of Twala's scouts.

Half an hour or more was allowed to elapse between the setting out of the horns or wings of the army before any movement was made by the Greys and the supporting regiment, known as the Buffaloes, which formed its chest, and which were destined to bear the brunt of the battle.

Both of these regiments were almost perfectly fresh, and of full strength, the Greys having been in reserve in the morning, and having lost but a small number of men in sweeping back that part of the attack which had proved successful in breaking the line of defence, on the occasion when I charged with them and got knocked silly for my pains. As for the Buffaloes, they had formed the third line of defence on the left, and as the attacking force at that point had not succeeded in breaking through the second, had scarcely come into action at all.

Infadoos, who was a wary old general, and knew the absolute importance of keeping up the spirits of his men on the eve of such a desperate encounter, employed the pause in addressing his own regiment, the Greys, in poetical language: in explaining to them the honour that they were receiving in being put thus in the forefront of the battle, and in having the great white warrior from the stars to fight with them in their ranks, and in promising large rewards of cattle and promotion to all who survived in the event of Ignosi's arms being successful.

I looked down the long lines of waving black plumes and stern faces beneath them, and sighed to think that within one short hour most, if not all, of those magnificent veteran warriors, not a man of whom was under forty years of age, would be laid dead or dying in the dust. It could not be otherwise; they were being condemned, with that wise recklessness of human life that marks the great general, and often saves his forces and attains his ends, to certain slaughter, in order to give the cause and the remainder of the army a chance of success. They were foredoomed to die, and they knew it. It was to be their task to engage regiment after regiment of Twala's army on the narrow strip of green beneath us, till they were exterminated, or till the wings found a favourable opportunity for their onslaught. And yet they never hesitated, nor could I detect a sign of fear upon the face of a single warrior. There they were—going to certain death, about to quit the blessed light of day for ever, and yet able to contemplate their doom without a tremor. I could not even at that moment help contrasting their state of mind with my own, which was far from comfortable, and breathing a sigh of envy and admiration. Never before had I seen such an absolute devotion to the idea of duty, and such a complete indifference to its bitter fruits.

"Behold your king!" ended old Infadoos, pointing to Ignosi; "go fight and fall for him, as is the duty of brave men, and cursed and shameful for ever be the name of him who shrinks from death for his king, or who turns his back to his enemy. Behold your king! chiefs, captains, and soldiers; now do your homage to the sacred snake, and then follow on, that Incubu and I may show ye the road to the heart of Twala's forces."

There was a moment's pause, then suddenly there rose from the serried phalanxes before us a murmur, like the distant whisper of the sea, caused by the gentle tapping of the handles of six thousand spears against their holders' shields. Slowly it swelled, till its growing volume deepened and widened into a roar of rolling noise, that echoed like thunder against the mountains, and filled the air with heavy waves of sound. Then it decreased and slowly died away into nothing, and suddenly out crashed the royal salute.

Ignosi, I thought to myself, might well be a proud man that day, for no Roman emperor ever had such a salutation from gladiators "about to die."

Ignosi acknowledged this magnificent act of homage by lifting his battle-axe, and then the Greys filed off in a triple-line formation, each line containing about one thousand fighting men, exclusive of officers. When the last line had gone some five hundred yards, Ignosi put himself at the head of the Buffaloes, which regiment was drawn up in a similar three-line formation, and gave the word to march, and off we went, I, needless to say, uttering the most heartfelt prayers that I might come out of that job with a whole skin. Many a queer position have I found myself in, but never before in one quite so unpleasant as the present, or one in which my chance of coming off safe was so small.

By the time that we reached the edge of the plateau the Greys were already half-way down the slope ending in the tongue of grass land that ran up into the bend of the mountain, something as the frog of a horse's foot runs up into the shoe. The excitement in Twala's camp on the plain beyond was very great, and regiment after regiment were starting forward at a long swinging trot in order to reach the root of the tongue of land before the attacking force could emerge into the plain of Loo.

This tongue of land, which was some three hundred yards in depth, was even at its root or widest part not more than three hundred and fifty paces across, while at its tip it scarcely measured ninety. The Greys, who, in passing down the side of the hill and on to the tip of the tongue, had formed in column, on reaching the spot where it broadened out again reassumed their triple-line formation, and halted dead.

Then we—that is, the Buffaloes—moved down the tip of the tongue and took our stand in reserve, about one hundred yards behind the last line of the Greys, and on slightly higher ground. Meanwhile we had leisure to observe Twala's entire force, which had evidently been reinforced since the morning attack, and could not now, notwithstanding their losses, number less than forty thousand, moving swiftly up towards us. But as they drew near the root of the tongue they hesitated, having discovered that only one regiment could advance into the gorge at a time, and that there, some seventy yards from the mouth of it, unassailable except in front, on account of the high walls of boulder-strewn ground on either side, stood the famous regiment of Greys, the pride and glory of the Kukuana army, ready to hold the way against their forces as the three Romans[1] once held the bridge against thousands. They hesitated, and finally stopped their advance; there was no eagerness to cross spears with those three lines of grim warriors who stood so firm and ready.

Presently, however, a tall general, with the customary head-dress of nodding ostrich plumes, came running up, attended by a group of chiefs and orderlies, being, I thought, none other than Twala himself, and gave an order, and the first regiment raised a shout, and charged up towards the Greys, who remained perfectly still and silent till the attacking troops were within forty yards, and a volley of tollas, or throwing knives, came rattling among their ranks.

Then suddenly, with a bound and a roar, they sprang forward with uplifted spears, and the two regiments met in deadly strife. Next second, the roll of the meeting shields came to our ears like the sound of thunder, and the whole plain seemed to be alive with flashes of light reflected from the stabbing spears. To and fro swung the heaving mass of struggling, stabbing humanity, but not for long. Suddenly the attacking lines seemed to grow thinner, and then with a slow, long heave the Greys passed over them, just as a great wave heaves up and passes over a sunken ridge. It was done; that regiment was completely destroyed, but the Greys had but two lines left now; a third of their number were dead.

Closing up shoulder to shoulder once more, they halted in silence and awaited attack; and I was rejoiced to catch sight of Sir Henry's yellow beard as he moved to and fro, arranging the ranks. So he was yet alive!

Meanwhile we moved up on to the ground of the encounter, which was cumbered by about four thousand prostrate human beings, dead, dying, and wounded, and literally stained red with blood. Ignosi issued an order, which was rapidly passed down the ranks, to the effect that none of the enemies' wounded were to be killed, and so far as we could see this order was scrupulously carried out. It would have been a shocking sight, if we had had time to think of it.

But now a second regiment, distinguished by white plumes, kilts, and shields, was moving up to the attack of the two thousand remaining Greys, who stood waiting in the same ominous silence as before, till the foe was within forty yards or so, when they hurled themselves with irresistible force upon them. Again there came the awful roll of the meeting shields, and as we watched the grim tragedy repeated itself. But this time the issue was left longer in doubt; indeed, it seemed for awhile almost impossible that the Greys should again prevail. The attacking regiment, which was one formed of young men, fought with the utmost fury, and at first seemed by sheer weight to be driving the veterans back. The slaughter was something awful, hundreds falling every minute; and from among the shouts of the warriors and the groans of the dying, set to the clashing music of meeting spears, came a continuous hissing undertone of "*S'gee, s'gee,*" the note of triumph of each victor as he passed his spear through and through the body of his fallen foe.

But perfect discipline and steady and unchanging valour can do wonders, and one veteran soldier is worth two young ones, as soon became apparent in the present case. For just as we thought that it was all up with the Greys, and were preparing to take their place so soon as they made room by being destroyed, I heard Sir Henry's deep voice ringing out above the din, and caught a glimpse of his circling battle-axe as he waved it high above his plumes. Then came a change; the Greys ceased to give; they stood still as a rock, against which the furious waves of spearmen broke again and again, only to recoil. Presently they began to move again—forward this time; as they had no firearms, there was no smoke, so we could see it all. Another minute and the onslaught grew fainter.

"Ah, they are *men* indeed; they will conquer again," called out Ignosi, who was grinding his teeth with excitement at my side. "See, it is done!"

Suddenly, like puffs of smoke from the mouth of a cannon, the attacking regiment broke away in flying groups, their white headdresses streaming behind them in the wind, and left their opponents victors, indeed, but, alas! no more a regiment. Of the gallant triple line, which, forty minutes before, had gone into action three thousand strong, there remained at most some six hundred bloodbespattered men; the rest were under foot. And yet they cheered and waved their spears in triumph, and then, instead of falling back upon us as we expected, they ran forward, for a hundred yards or so, after the flying groups of foemen, took possession of a gently rising knoll of ground, and, resuming the old triple formation, formed a threefold ring around it. And then, thanks be to God, standing on the top of the mound for a minute, I saw Sir Henry, apparently unharmed, and with him our old friend Infadoos. Then Twala's regiments rolled down upon the doomed band, and once more the battle closed in.

As those who read this history will probably long ago have gathered, I am, to be honest, a bit of a coward, and certainly in no way given to fighting, though, somehow, it has often been my lot to get into unpleasant positions, and to be obliged to shed man's blood. But I have always hated it, and kept my own blood as undiminished in quantity as possible, sometimes by a judicious use of my heels. At this moment, however, for the first time in my life, I felt my bosom burn with martial ardour. Warlike fragments from the "Ingoldsby Legends," together with numbers of sanguinary verses from the Old Testament, sprang up in my brain like mushrooms in the dark; my blood, which hitherto had been half-frozen with horror, went beating through my veins, and there came upon me a savage desire to kill and spare not. I glanced round at the serried ranks of warriors behind us, and somehow, all in an instant, began to wonder if my face looked like theirs. There they stood, their heads craned forward over their shields, the hands twitching, the lips apart, the fierce features instinct with the hungry lust of battle, and in the eyes a look like the glare of a bloodhound when he sights his quarry.

Only Ignosi's heart seemed, to judge from his comparative self-possession, to all appearance, to beat as calmly as ever beneath his leopard-skin cloak, though even *he* still kept on grinding his teeth. I could stand it no longer.

"Are we to stand here till we put out roots, Umbopa—Ignosi, I mean—while Twala swallows our brothers yonder?" I asked.

"Nay, Macumazahn," was the answer; "see, now is the ripe moment: let us pluck it."

As he spoke, a fresh regiment rushed past the ring upon the little mound, and wheeling round, attacked it from the hither side.

Then, lifting his battle-axe, Ignosi gave the signal to advance, and, raising the Kukuana battle-cry, the Buffaloes charged home with a rush like the rush of the sea.

What followed immediately on this it is out of my power to tell. All I can remember is a wild yet ordered rushing, that seemed to shake the ground; a sudden change of front and forming up on the part of the regiment against which the charge was directed; then an awful shock, a dull roar of voices, and a continuous flashing of spears, seen through a red mist of blood.

When my mind cleared I found myself standing inside the remnant of the Greys near the top of the mound, and just behind no less a person than Sir Henry himself. How I got there I had, at the moment, no idea, but Sir Henry afterwards told me that I was borne up by the first furious charge of the Buffaloes almost to his feet, and then left, as they in turn were pressed back. Thereon he dashed out of the circle and dragged me into it.

As for the fight that followed, who can describe it? Again and again the multitudes surged up against our momentarily lessening circle, and again and again we beat them back.

> "The stubborn spearmen still made good
> The dark impenetrable wood;
> Each stepping where his comrade stood
> The instant that he fell,"

as I think the "Ingoldsby Legends" beautifully puts it.[2]

It was a splendid thing to see those brave battalions come on time after time over the barriers of their dead, sometimes holding corpses before them to receive our spear thrusts, only to leave their own corpses to swell the rising piles. It was a gallant sight to see that sturdy old warrior, Infadoos, as cool as though he were on parade, shouting out orders, taunts, and even jests, to keep up the spirit of his few remaining men, and then, as each charge rolled up, stepping forward to wherever the fighting was thickest, to bear his share in repelling it. And yet more gallant was the vision of Sir Henry, whose ostrich plumes had been shorn off by a spear stroke, so that his long yellow hair streamed out in the breeze behind him. There he stood, the great Dane, for he was nothing else, his hands, his axe, and his armour, all red with blood, and none could live before his stroke. Time after time I saw it come sweeping down, as some great warrior ventured to give him battle, and as he struck he shouted, *"O-hoy! O-hoy!"* like his Bersekir* forefathers, and the blow went crashing through shield and spear, through head-dress, hair, and skull, till at last none would of their own will come near the great white "tagati" (wizard), who killed and failed not.

---

*Usually spelled *berserker*; Old Norse warriors famed for their savagery.

But suddenly there rose a cry of "*Twala, y' Twala,*" and out of the press sprang forward none other than the gigantic one-eyed king himself, also armed with battle-axe and shield, and clad in chain armour.

"Where art thou, Incubu, thou white man, who slew Scragga, my son—see if thou canst kill me!" he shouted, and at the same time hurled a tolla straight at Sir Henry, who, fortunately, saw it coming, and caught it on his shield, which it transfixed, remaining wedged in the iron plate behind the hide.

Then, with a cry, Twala sprang forward straight at him, and with his battle-axe struck him such a blow upon the shield, that the mere force and shock of it brought Sir Henry, strong man as he was, down upon his knees.

But at the time the matter went no further, for at that instant there rose from the regiments pressing round us something like a shout of dismay, and on looking up I saw the cause.

To the right and to the left the plain was alive with the plumes of charging warriors. The outflanking squadrons had come to our relief. The time could not have been better chosen. All Twala's army had, as Ignosi had predicted would be the case, fixed their attention on the bloody struggle which was raging round the remnant of the Greys and the Buffaloes, who were now carrying on a battle of their own at a little distance, which two regiments had formed the chest of our army. It was not until the horns were about to close upon them that they had dreamed of their approach. And now, before they could even assume a proper formation for defence, the outflanking Impis had leapt, like greyhounds, on their flanks.

In five minutes the fate of the battle was decided. Taken on both flanks, and dismayed by the awful slaughter inflicted upon them by the Greys and Buffaloes, Twala's regiments broke into flight, and soon the whole plain between us and Loo was scattered with groups of flying soldiers, making good their retreat. As for the forces that had so recently surrounded us and the Buffaloes, they melted away as though by magic, and presently we were left standing there like a rock from which the sea has retreated. But what a sight it was! Around us the dead and dying lay in heaped-up masses, and of the gallant Greys there remained alive but ninety-five men. More than

2,900 had fallen in this one regiment, most of them never to rise again.

"Men," said Infadoos, calmly, as between the intervals of binding up a wound in his arm he surveyed what remained to him of his corps, "ye have kept up the reputation of your regiment, and this day's fighting will be spoken of by your children's children." Then he turned round and shook Sir Henry Curtis by the hand. "Thou art a great man, Incubu," he said, simply; "I have lived a long life among warriors, and known many a brave one, yet have I never seen a man like thee."

At this moment the Buffaloes began to march past our position on the road to Loo, and as they did so a message was brought to us from Ignosi requesting Infadoos, Sir Henry, and myself to join him. Accordingly, orders having been issued to the remaining ninety men of the Greys to employ themselves in collecting the wounded, we joined Ignosi, who informed us that he was pressing on to Loo to complete the victory by capturing Twala, if that should be possible. Before we had gone far we suddenly discovered the figure of Good sitting on an ant-heap about one hundred paces from us. Close beside him was the body of a Kukuana.

"He must be wounded," said Sir Henry, anxiously. As he made the remark, an untoward thing happened. The dead body of the Kukuana soldier, or rather what had appeared to be his dead body, suddenly sprang up, knocked Good head over heels off the ant-heap, and began to spear him. We rushed forward in terror, and as we drew near we saw the brawny warrior making dig after dig at the prostrate Good, who at each prod jerked all his limbs into the air. Seeing us coming, the Kukuana gave one final most vicious dig, and with a shout of "Take that, wizard," bolted off. Good did not move, and we concluded that our poor comrade was done for. Sadly we came towards him, and were indeed astonished to find him pale and faint indeed, but with a serene smile upon his face, and his eye-glass still fixed in his eye.

"Capital armour this," he murmured, on catching sight of our faces bending over him. "How cold he must have been," and then he fainted. On examination we discovered that he had been seriously wounded in the leg by a tolla in the course of the pursuit, but that the chain armour had prevented his last assailant's spear from doing anything more than bruise him badly. It was a merciful escape. As nothing could be done for him at the moment, he was placed on one of the wicker shields used for the wounded, and carried along with us.

On arriving before the nearest gate of Loo, we found one of our regiments watching it in obedience to orders received from Ignosi. The remaining regiments were in the same way watching the other exits to the town. The officer in command of this regiment coming up, saluted Ignosi as king, and informed him that Twala's army had taken refuge in the town, whither Twala himself had also escaped, but that he thought that they were thoroughly demoralised, and would surrender. Thereupon Ignosi, after taking counsel with us, sent forward heralds to each gate ordering the defenders to open, and promising on his royal word life and forgiveness to every soldier who laid down his arms. The message was not without its effect. Presently, amid the shouts and cheers of the Buffaloes, the bridge was dropped across the fosse, and the gates upon the further side flung open.

Taking due precautions against treachery, we marched on into the town. All along the roadways stood dejected warriors, their heads drooping, and their shields and spears at their feet, who, as Ignosi passed, saluted him as king. On we marched, straight to Twala's kraal. When we reached the great space, where a day or two previously we had seen the review and the witch hunt, we found it deserted. No, not quite deserted, for there, on the further side, in front of his hut, sat Twala himself, with but one attendant—Gagool.

It was a melancholy sight to see him seated there, his battle-axe and shield by his side, his chin upon his mailed breast, with but one old crone for companion, and notwithstanding his cruelties and misdeeds, a pang of compassion shot through me as I saw him thus "fallen from his high estate."[3] Not a soldier of all his armies, not a courtier out of the hundreds who had cringed round him, not even a solitary wife, remained to share his fate or halve the bitterness of his fall. Poor savage! he was learning the lesson that Fate teaches to most who live long enough, that the eyes of mankind are blind to the discredited, and that he who is defenceless and fallen finds few friends and little mercy. Nor, indeed, in this case did he deserve any.

Filing through the kraal gate, we marched straight across the open space to where the ex-king sat. When within about fifty yards the regiment was halted, and accompanied only by a small guard we advanced towards him, Gagool reviling us bitterly as we came. As we drew near, Twala, for the first time, lifted up his plumed head, and fixed his one eye, which seemed to flash with suppressed fury almost as brightly as the great diamond bound round his forehead, upon his successful rival—Ignosi.

"Hail, O king!" he said, with bitter mockery; "thou who hast eaten of my bread, and now by the aid of the white man's magic hast seduced my regiments and defeated mine army, hail! what fate hast thou for me, O king?"

"The fate thou gavest to my father, whose throne thou hast sat on these many years!" was the stern answer.

"It is well. I will show thee how to die, that thou mayest remember it against thine own time. See, the sun sinks in blood," and he pointed with his red battle-axe towards the fiery orb now going down; "it is well that my sun should sink with it. And now, O king! I am ready to die, but I crave the boon of the Kukuana royal house* to die fighting. Thou canst not refuse it, or even those cowards who fled to-day will hold thee shamed."

"It is granted. Choose—with whom wilt thou fight? Myself I cannot fight with thee, for the king fights not except in war."

Twala's sombre eye ran up and down our ranks, and I felt, as for a moment it rested on myself, that the position had developed a new horror. What if he chose to begin by fighting *me?* What chance should I have against a desperate savage six feet five high, and broad in proportion? I might as well commit suicide at once. Hastily I made up my mind to decline the combat, even if I were hooted out of Kukuanaland as a consequence. It is, I think, better to be hooted than to be quartered with a battle-axe.

Presently he spoke.

"Incubu, what sayest thou, shall we end what we began to-day, or shall I call thee coward, white—even to the liver?"

---

*It is a law amongst the Kukuanas that no man of the royal blood can be put to death unless by his own consent, which is, however, never refused. He is allowed to choose a succession of antagonists, to be approved by the king, with whom he fights, till one of them kills him. [Haggard's note]

"Nay," interposed Ignosi, hastily; "thou shalt not fight with Incubu."

"Not if he is afraid," said Twala.

Unfortunately Sir Henry understood this remark, and the blood flamed up into his cheeks.

"I will fight him," he said; "he shall see if I am afraid."

"For God's sake," I entreated, "don't risk your life against that of a desperate man. Anybody who saw you to-day will know that you are not a coward."

"I will fight him," was the sullen answer. "No living man shall call me a coward. I am ready now!" and he stepped forward and lifted his axe.

I wrung my hands over this absurd piece of Quixotism; but if he was determined on fighting, of course I could not stop him.

"Fight not, my white brother," said Ignosi, laying his hand affectionately on Sir Henry's arm; "thou hast fought enough, and if aught befell thee at his hands it would cut my heart in twain."

"I will fight, Ignosi," was Sir Henry's answer.

"It is well, Incubu; thou art a brave man. It will be a good fight. Behold, Twala, the Elephant is ready for thee."

The ex-king laughed savagely, and stepped forward and faced Curtis. For a moment they stood thus, and the setting sun caught their stalwart frames and clothed them both in fire. They were a well-matched pair.

Then they began to circle round each other, their battle-axes raised.

Suddenly Sir Henry sprang forward and struck a fearful blow at Twala, who stepped to one side. So heavy was the stroke that the striker half overbalanced himself, a circumstance of which his antagonist took a prompt advantage. Circling his heavy battle-axe round his head, he brought it down with tremendous force. My heart jumped into my mouth; I thought that the affair was already finished. But no; with a quick upward movement of the left arm Sir Henry interposed his shield between himself and the axe, with the result that its outer edge was shorn clean off, the axe falling on his left shoulder, but not heavily enough to do any serious damage. In another second Sir Henry got in another blow, which was also received by Twala upon his shield. Then followed blow upon blow, which were, in turn, either received upon the shield or avoided. The excitement grew intense; the regiment which was watching the encounter forgot its discipline, and, drawing near, shouted and groaned at every stroke. Just at this time, too, Good, who had been laid upon the ground by me, recovered from his faint, and, sitting up, perceived what was going on. In an instant he was up, and, catching hold of my arm, hopped about from place to place on one leg, dragging me after him, yelling out encouragements to Sir Henry—

"Go it, old fellow!" he halloed. "That was a good one! Give it him amidships," and so on.

Presently Sir Henry, having caught a fresh stroke upon his shield, hit out with all his force. The stroke cut through Twala's shield and through the tough chain armour behind it, gashing him in the shoulder. With a yell of pain and fury Twala returned the stroke with interest, and, such was his strength, shore right through the rhinoceros' horn handle of his antagonist's battle-axe, strengthened as it was with bands of steel, wounding Curtis in the face.

A cry of dismay rose from the Buffaloes as our hero's broad axe-head fell to the ground; and Twala, again raising his weapon, flew at him with a shout. I shut my eyes. When I opened them again, it was to see Sir Henry's shield lying on the ground, and Sir Henry himself with his great arms twined round Twala's middle. To and fro they swung, hugging each other like bears, straining with all their mighty muscles for dear life, and dearer honour. With a supreme effort Twala swung the Englishman clean off his feet, and down they came together, rolling over and over on the lime paving, Twala striking out at Curtis' head with the battle-axe, and Sir Henry trying to drive the tolla he had drawn from his belt through Twala's armour.

It was a mighty struggle, and an awful thing to see.

"Get his axe!" yelled Good; and perhaps our champion heard him.

At any rate, dropping the tolla, he made a grab at the axe, which was fastened to Twala's wrist by a strip of buffalo hide, and still rolling over and over, they fought for it like wild cats, drawing their breath in heavy gasps. Suddenly the hide string burst, and then, with a great effort, Sir Henry freed himself, the weapon remaining in his grasp. Another second and he was up upon his feet, the red blood streaming from the wound in his face, and so was Twala. Drawing the heavy tolla from his belt, he staggered straight at Curtis and struck him upon the breast. The blow came home true and strong, but whoever it was made that chain armour understood his art, for it withstood the steel. Again Twala struck out with a savage yell, and again the heavy knife rebounded, and Sir Henry went staggering back. Once more Twala came on, and as he came our great English-man gathered himself together, and, swinging the heavy axe round his head, hit at him with all his force. There was a shriek of excite-ment from a thousand throats, and, behold! Twala's head seemed to spring from his shoulders, and then fell and came rolling and bounding along the ground towards Ignosi, stopping just at his feet. For a second the corpse stood upright, the blood spouting in foun-tains from the severed arteries; then with a dull crash it fell to the earth, and the gold torque from the neck went rolling away across the pavement. As it did so Sir Henry, overpowered by faintness and loss of blood, fell heavily across it.

In a second he was lifted up, and eager hands were pouring water on his face. Another minute, and the great grey eyes opened wide.

He was not dead.

Then I, just as the sun sank, stepping to where Twala's head lay in the dust, unloosed the diamond from the dead brows, and handed it to Ignosi.

"Take it," I said, "lawful King of the Kukuanas."

Ignosi bound the diadem upon his brows, and then advancing placed his foot upon the broad chest of his headless foe and broke out into a chant, or rather a pæan of victory, so beautiful, and yet so utterly savage, that I despair of being able to give an adequate idea of it. I once heard a scholar with a fine voice read aloud from the Greek poet Homer, and I remember that the sound of the rolling lines seemed to make my blood stand still. Ignosi's chant, uttered as it was in a language as beautiful and sonorous as the old Greek, pro-duced exactly the same effect on me, although I was exhausted with toil and many emotions.

"*Now*," he began, "*now is our rebellion swallowed up in victory, and our evil-doing justified by strength.*

"*In the morning the oppressors rose up and shook themselves, they bound on their plumes and made them ready for war.*

"*They rose up and grasped their spears: the soldiers called to the* captains, 'Come, lead us'—and the captains cried to the king, 'Direct thou the battle.'

"They rose up in their pride, twenty thousand men, and yet a twenty thousand.

"Their plumes covered the earth as the plumes of a bird cover her nest, they shook their spears and shouted, yea, they hurled their spears into the sunlight; they lusted for the battle and were glad.

"They came up against me; their strong ones came running swiftly to crush me; they cried, 'Ha! ha! he is as one already dead.'

"Then breathed I on them, and my breath was as the breath of a storm, and lo! they were not.

"My lightnings pierced them; I licked up their strength with the lightning of my spears; I shook them to the earth with the thunder of my shouting.

"They broke—they scattered—they were gone as the mists of the morning.

"They are food for the crows and the foxes, and the place of battle is fat with their blood.

"Where are the mighty ones who rose up in the morning?

"Where are the proud ones who tossed their plumes and cried, 'He is as one already dead?'

"They bow their heads, but not in sleep; they are stretched out, but not in sleep.

"They are forgotten; they have gone into the blackness, and shall not return; yea, others shall lead away their wives, and their children shall remember them no more.

"And I—I! the king—like an eagle have I found my eyrie.

"Behold! far have I wandered in the night time, yet have I returned to my little ones at the daybreak.

"Creep ye under the shadow of my wings, O people, and I will comfort ye, and ye shall not be dismayed.

"Now is the good time, the time of spoil.

"Mine are the cattle in the valleys, the virgins in the kraals are mine also.

"The winter is overpast, the summer is at hand.

"Now shall Evil cover up her face, and Prosperity shall bloom in the land like a lily.

"*Rejoice, rejoice, my people! let all the land rejoice in that the tyranny is trodden down, in that I am the king.*"

He paused, and out of the gathering gloom there came back the deep reply—

"*Thou art the king.*"

Thus it was that my prophecy to the herald came true, and within the forty-eight hours Twala's headless corpse was stiffening at Twala's gate.

Chapter 15

Good Falls Sick

AFTER THE FIGHT WAS ended, Sir Henry and Good were carried into Twala's hut, where I joined them. They were both utterly exhausted by exertion and loss of blood, and, indeed, my own condition was little better. I am very wiry, and can stand more fatigue than most men, probably on account of my light weight and long training; but that night I was fairly done up, and, as is always the case with me when exhausted, that old wound the lion gave me began to pain me. Also my head was aching violently from the blow I had received in the morning, when I was knocked senseless. Altogether, a more miserable trio than we were that evening it would have been difficult to discover; and our only comfort lay in the reflection that we were exceedingly fortunate to be there to feel miserable, instead of being stretched dead upon the plain, as so many thousands of brave men were that night, who had risen well and strong in the morning. Somehow, with the assistance of the beautiful Foulata, who, since we had been the means of saving her life, had constituted herself our handmaiden, and especially Good's, we managed to get off the chain shirts, which had certainly saved the lives of two of us that day, when we found that the flesh underneath was terribly bruised, for though the steel links had prevented the weapons from entering, they had not prevented them from bruising. Both Sir Henry and Good were a mass of bruises, and I was by no means free. As a remedy Foulata brought us some pounded green leaves, with an aromatic odour, which, when applied as a plaster, gave us considerable relief. But though the bruises were painful, they did not give us such anxiety as Sir Henry's and Good's wounds. Good had a hole right through the fleshy part of his "beautiful white leg," from which he had lost a great deal of blood; and Sir Henry had a deep cut over the jaw, inflicted by Twala's battle-axe. Luckily Good was a very decent surgeon, and as soon as his small box of medicines was forthcoming, he, having thoroughly cleansed the wounds, managed to stitch up first Sir

Henry's and then his own pretty satisfactorily, considering the imperfect light given by the primitive Kukuana lamp in the hut. Afterwards he plentifully smeared the wounds with some antiseptic ointment, of which there was a pot in the little box, and we covered them with the remains of a pocket-handkerchief which we possessed.

Meanwhile Foulata had prepared us some strong broth, for we were too weary to eat. This we swallowed, and then threw ourselves down on the piles of magnificent karrosses, or fur rugs, which were scattered about the dead king's great hut. By a very strange instance of the irony of fate, it was on Twala's own couch, and wrapped in Twala's own particular karross, that Sir Henry, the man who had slain him, slept that night.

I say slept; but after that day's work sleep was indeed difficult. To begin with, in very truth the air was full

> "Of farewells to the dying
> And mournings for the dead."[1]

From every direction came the sound of the wailing of women whose husbands, sons, and brothers had perished in the fight. No wonder that they wailed, for over twenty thousand men, or nearly a third of the Kukuana army, had been destroyed in that awful struggle. It was heart-rending to lie and listen to their cries for those who would never return; and it made one realise the full horror of the work done that day to further man's ambition. Towards midnight, however, the ceaseless crying of the women grew less frequent, till at length the silence was only broken at intervals of a few minutes by a long, piercing howl that came from a hut in our immediate rear, and which I afterwards discovered proceeded from Gagool wailing for the dead king Twala.

After that I got a little fitful sleep, only to wake from time to time with a start, thinking that I was once more an actor in the terrible events of the last twenty-four hours. Now I seemed to see that warrior, whom my hand had sent to his last account, charging at me on the mountain-top; now I was once more in that glorious ring of Greys, which made its immortal stand against all Twala's regiments, upon the little mound; and now again I saw Twala's plumed and gory head roll past my feet with gnashing teeth and glaring eye. At last, somehow or other, the night passed away; but when dawn broke I found that my companions had slept no better than myself. Good, indeed, was in a high fever, and very soon afterwards began to grow light-headed, and also, to my alarm, to spit blood, the result, no doubt, of some internal injury inflicted by the desperate efforts made by the Kukuana warrior on the previous day to get his big spear through the chain armour. Sir Henry, however, seemed pretty fresh, notwithstanding his wound on the face, which made eating difficult and laughter an impossibility, though he was so sore and stiff that he could scarcely stir.

About eight o'clock we had a visit from Infadoos, who seemed but little the worse—tough old warrior that he was—for his exertions on the previous day, though he informed us he had been up all night. He was delighted to see us, though much grieved at Good's condition, and shook hands cordially; but I noticed that he addressed Sir Henry with a kind of reverence, as though he were something more than man; and indeed, as we afterwards found out, the great Englishman was looked on throughout Kukuanaland as a supernatural being. No man, the soldiers said, could have fought as he fought, or could, at the end of a day of such toil and bloodshed, have slain Twala, who, in addition to being the king, was supposed to be the strongest warrior in Kukuanaland, in single combat, sheering through his bull-neck at a stroke. Indeed, that stroke became proverbial in Kukuanaland, and any extraordinary blow or feat of strength was thenceforth known as "Incubu's blow."

Infadoos told us also that all Twala's regiments had submitted to Ignosi, and that like submissions were beginning to arrive from chiefs in the country. Twala's death at the hands of Sir Henry had put an end to all further chance of disturbance; for Scragga had been his only son, and there was no rival claimant left alive.

I remarked that Ignosi had swum to the throne through blood. The old chief shrugged his shoulders. "Yes," he answered; "but the Kukuana people can only be kept cool by letting the blood flow sometimes. Many were killed indeed, but the women were left, and others would soon grow up to take the places of the fallen. After this the land would be quiet for awhile."

Afterwards, in the course of the morning, we had a short visit from Ignosi, on whose brows the royal diadem was now bound. As I contemplated him advancing with kingly dignity, an obsequious guard following his steps, I could not help recalling to my mind the tall Zulu who had presented himself to us at Durban some few months back, asking to be taken into our service, and reflecting on the strange revolutions of the wheel of fortune.

"Hail, O king!" I said, rising.

"Yes, Macumazahn. King at last, by the grace of your three right hands," was the ready answer.

All was, he said, going on well; and he hoped to arrange a great feast in two weeks' time in order to show himself to the people.

I asked him what he had settled to do with Gagool.

"She is the evil genius of the land," he answered, "and I shall kill her, and all the witch doctors with her! She has lived so long that none can remember when she was not old, and always she it is who has trained the witch-hunters, and made the land evil in the sight of the heavens above."

"Yet she knows much," I replied; "it is easier to destroy knowledge, Ignosi, than to gather it."

"It is so," he said, thoughtfully. "She, and she only, knows the secret of the 'Three Witches' yonder, whither the great road runs, where the kings are buried, and the silent ones sit."

"Yes, and the diamonds are. Forget not thy promise, Ignosi; thou must lead us to the mines, even if thou hast to spare Gagool alive to show the way."

"I will not forget, Macumazahn, and I will think on what thou sayest."

After Ignosi's visit I went to see Good, and found him quite delirious. The fever from his wound seemed to have taken a firm hold of his system, and to be complicated by an internal injury. For four or five days his condition was most critical; indeed, I firmly believe that had it not been for Foulata's indefatigable nursing he must have died.

Women are women, all the world over, whatever their colour. Yet somehow it seemed curious to watch this dusky beauty bending night and day over the fevered man's couch, and performing all the merciful errands of the sick-room as swiftly, gently, and with as fine an instinct as a trained hospital nurse. For the first night or two I tried to help her, and so did Sir Henry so soon as his stiffness allowed him to move, but she bore our interference with impatience, and finally insisted upon our leaving him to her, saying that our movements made him restless, which I think was true. Day and night she watched and tended him, giving him his only medicine, a native cooling drink made of milk, in which was infused the juice of the bulb of a species of tulip, and keeping the flies from settling on him. I can see the whole picture now as it appeared night after night by the light of our primitive lamp, Good tossing to and fro, his features emaciated, his eyes shining large and luminous, and jabbering nonsense by the yard; and seated on the ground by his side, her back resting against the wall of the hut, the soft-eyed, shapely Kukuana beauty, her whole face, weary as it was, animated by a look of infinite compassion—or was it something more than compassion?

For two days we thought that he must die, and crept about with heavy hearts. Only Foulata would not believe it.

"He will live," she said.

For three hundred yards or more around Twala's chief hut, where the sufferer lay, there was silence; for by the king's order all who lived in the habitations behind it had, except Sir Henry and myself, been removed, lest any noise should come to the sick man's ears. One night, it was the fifth night of his illness, as was my habit, I went across to see how he was getting on before turning in for a few hours.

I entered the hut carefully. The lamp placed upon the floor showed the figure of Good, tossing no more, but lying quite still.

So it had come at last! and in the bitterness of my heart I gave something like a sob.

"Hush—h—h!" came from the patch of dark shadow behind Good's head.

Then, creeping closer, I saw that he was not dead, but sleeping soundly, with Foulata's taper fingers clasped tightly in his poor white hand. The crisis had passed, and he would live. He slept like that for eighteen hours; and I scarcely like to say it, for fear I should not be believed, but during the entire period did that devoted girl sit by him, fearing that if she moved and drew away her hand it would wake him. What she must have suffered from cramp, stiffness, and weariness, to say nothing of want of food, nobody will ever know;

but it is a fact that, when at last he woke, she had to be carried away—her limbs were so stiff that she could not move them.

After the turn had once been taken, Good's recovery was rapid and complete. It was not till he was nearly well that Sir Henry told him of all he owed to Foulata; and when he came to the story of how she sat by his side for eighteen hours, fearing lest by moving she should wake him, the honest sailor's eyes filled with tears. He turned and went straight to the hut where Foulata was preparing the mid-day meal (we were back in our old quarters now), taking me with him to interpret in case he could not make his meaning clear to her, though I am bound to say she understood him marvelously as a rule, considering how extremely limited was his foreign vocabulary.

"Tell her," said Good, "that I owe her my life, and that I will never forget her kindness."

I interpreted, and under her dark skin she actually seemed to blush.

Turning to him with one of those swift and graceful motions that in her always reminded me of the flight of a wild bird, she answered softly, glancing at him with her large brown eyes—

"Nay, my lord; my lord forgets! Did he not save *my* life, and am I not my lord's handmaiden?"

It will be observed that the young lady appeared to have entirely forgotten the share which Sir Henry and myself had had in her preservation from Twala's clutches. But that is the way of women! I remember my dear wife was just the same. I retired from that little interview sad at heart. I did not like Miss Foulata's soft glances, for I knew the fatal amorous propensities of sailors in general, and Good in particular.

There are two things in the world, as I have found it, which cannot be prevented: you cannot keep a Zulu from fighting, or a sailor from falling in love upon the slightest provocation!

It was a few days after this last occurrence that Ignosi held his great "indaba" (council), and was formally recognised as king by the "indunas" (head men) of Kukuanaland. The spectacle was a most imposing one, including, as it did, a great review of troops. On this day the remaining fragment of the Greys were formally paraded, and in the face of the army thanked for their splendid conduct in the great battle. To each man the king made a large present of cattle, promoting them one and all to the rank of officers in the new corps of Greys which was in process of formation. An order was also promulgated throughout the length and breadth of Kukuanaland that, whilst we honoured the country with our presence, we three were to be greeted with the royal salute, to be treated with the same ceremony and respect that was by custom accorded to the king, and the power of life and death was publicly conferred upon us. Ignosi, too, in the presence of his people, reaffirmed the promises that he had made, to the effect that no man's blood should be shed without trial, and that witch-hunting should cease in the land.

When the ceremony was over, we waited upon Ignosi, and informed him that we were now anxious to investigate the mystery of the mines to which Solomon's Road ran, asking him if he had discovered anything about them.

"My friends," he answered, "this have I discovered. It is there that the three great figures sit, who here are called the 'Silent Ones,' and to whom Twala would have offered the girl, Foulata, as a sacrifice. It is there, too, in a great cave deep in the mountain, that the kings of the land are buried; there shall ye find Twala's body, sitting with those who went before him. There, too, is a great pit, which, at some time, long-dead men dug out, mayhap for the stones ye speak of, such as I have heard men in Natal speak of at Kimberley. There, too, in the Place of Death is a secret chamber, known to none but the king and Gagool. But Twala, who knew it, is dead, and I know it not, nor know I what is in it. But there is a legend in the land that once, many generations gone, a white man crossed the mountains, and was led by a woman to the secret chamber and shown the wealth, but before he could take it she betrayed him, and he was driven by the king of the day back to the mountains, and since then no man has entered the chamber."

"The story is surely true, Ignosi, for on the mountains we found the white man," I said.

"Yes, we found him. And now I have promised ye that if ye can find that chamber, and the stones are there——"

"The stone upon thy forehead proves that they are there," I put in, pointing to the great diamond I had taken from Twala's dead brows.

"Mayhap; if they are there," he said, "ye shall have as many as ye can take hence—if, indeed, ye would leave me, my brothers."

"First we must find the chamber," said I.

"There is but one who can show it to thee—Gagool."

"And if she will not?"

"Then shall she die," said Ignosi, sternly. "I have saved her alive but for this. Stay, she shall choose," and calling to a messenger he ordered Gagool to be brought.

In a few minutes she came, hurried along by two guards, whom she was cursing as she walked.

"Leave her," said the king to the guards.

As soon as their support was withdrawn, the withered old bundle, for she looked more like a bundle than anything else, sank into a heap on to the floor, out of which her two bright wicked eyes gleamed like a snake's.

"What will ye with me, Ignosi?" she piped. "Ye dare not touch me. If ye touch me I will blast ye as ye sit. Beware of my magic."

"Thy magic could not save Twala, old she-wolf, and it cannot hurt me," was the answer. "Listen: I will this of thee, that thou reveal where is the chamber where are the shining stones."

"Ha! ha!" she piped, "none know but I, and I will never tell thee. The white devils shall go hence empty-handed."

"Thou wilt tell me. I will make thee tell me."

"How, O king? Thou art great, but can thy power wring the truth from a woman?"

"It is difficult, yet will I do it."

"How, O king?"

"Nay, thus; if thou tellest not thou shalt slowly die."

"Die!" she shrieked, in terror and fury; "ye dare not touch me—man, ye know not who I am. How old think ye am I? I knew your fathers, and your fathers' fathers' fathers. When the country was young I was here, when the country grows old I shall still be here. I cannot die unless I be killed by chance, for none dare slay me."

"Yet will I slay thee. See, Gagool, mother of evil, thou art so old thou canst no longer love thy life. What can life be to such a hag as thee, who hast no shape, nor form, nor hair, nor teeth—hast naught, save wickedness and evil eyes? It will be mercy to slay thee, Gagool."

"Thou fool," shrieked the old fiend, "thou accursed fool, thinkest thou that life is sweet only to the young? It is not so, and naught thou knowest of the heart of man to think it. To the young, indeed, death is sometimes welcome, for the young can feel. They love and suffer, and it wrings them to see their beloved pass to the land of shadows. But the old feel not, they love not, and, *ha! ha!* they laugh to see another go out into the dark; *ha! ha!* they laugh to see the evil that is done under the sun. All they love is life, the warm, warm sun, and the sweet, sweet air. They are afraid of the cold, afraid of the cold and the dark, *ha! ha! ha!*" and the old hag writhed in ghastly merriment on the ground.

"Cease thine evil talk and answer me," said Ignosi, angrily. "Wilt thou show the place where the stones are, or wilt thou not? If thou wilt not thou diest, even now," and he seized a spear and held it over her.

"I will not show it; thou darest not kill me, darest not. He who slays me will be accursed for ever."

Slowly Ignosi brought down the spear till it pricked the prostrate heap of rags.

With a wild yell she sprang to her feet, and then again fell and rolled upon the floor.

"Nay, I will show it. Only let me live, let me sit in the sun and have a bit of meat to suck, and I will show thee."

"It is well. I thought I should find a way to reason with thee. To-morrow shalt thou go with Infadoos and my white brothers to the place, and beware how thou failest, for if thou showest it not, then shalt thou slowly die. I have spoken."

"I will not fail, Ignosi. I always keep my word: *ha! ha! ha!* Once a woman showed the place to a white man before, and behold evil befell him," and here her wicked eyes glinted. "Her name was Gagool too. Perchance I was that woman."

"Thou liest," I said, "that was ten generations gone."

"Mayhap, mayhap; when one lives long one forgets. Perhaps it was my mother's mother who told me, surely her name was Gagool also. But mark, ye will find in the place where the bright playthings are, a bag of hide full of stones. The man filled that bag, but he never took it away. Evil befell him, I say, evil befell him! Perhaps it was my mother's mother who told me. It will be a merry journey—we can see the bodies of those who died in the battle as we go. Their eyes will be gone by now, and their ribs will be hollow. *Ha! ha! ha!*"

Chapter 16

The Place of Death

IT WAS ALREADY DARK on the third day after the scene described in the previous chapter, when we camped in some huts at the foot of the "Three Witches," as the triangle of mountains were called to which Solomon's great road ran. Our party consisted of our three selves and Foulata, who waited on us—especially on Good—Infadoos, Gagool, who was borne along in a litter, inside which she could be heard muttering and cursing all day long, and a party of guards and attendants. The mountains, or rather the three peaks of the mountains, for the whole mass evidently consisted of a solitary upheaval, were, as I have said, in the form of a triangle, of which the base was towards us, one peak being on our right, one on our left, and one straight in front of us. Never shall I forget the sight afforded by those three towering peaks in the early sunlight of the following morning. High, high above us, up into the blue air, soared their twisted snow-wreaths. Beneath the snow the peaks were purple with heaths, and so were the wild moors that ran up the slopes towards them. Straight before us the white ribbon of Solomon's great road stretched away uphill to the foot of the centre peak, about five miles from us, and there stopped. It was its terminus.

I had better leave the feelings of intense excitement with which we set out on our march that morning to the imagination of those who read this history. At last we were drawing near to the wonderful mines that had been the cause of the miserable death of the old Portuguese Dom, three centuries ago, of my poor friend, his ill-starred descendant, and also, as we feared, of George Curtis, Sir Henry's brother. Were we destined, after all that we had gone through, to fare any better? Evil befell them, as that old fiend Gagool said, would it also befall us? Somehow, as we were marching up that last stretch of beautiful road, I could not help feeling a little superstitious about the matter, and so I think did Good and Sir Henry.

For an hour and a half or more we tramped on up the heather-fringed road, going so fast in our excitement that the bearers with Gagool's hammock could scarcely keep pace with us, and its occupant piped out to us to stop.

"Go more slowly, white men," she said, projecting her hideous shrivelled countenance between the curtains, and fixing her gleaming eyes upon us; "why will ye run to meet the evil that shall befall ye, ye seekers after treasure?" and she laughed that horrible laugh which always sent a cold shiver down my back, and which for awhile quite took the enthusiasm out of us.

However, on we went, till we saw before us, and between ourselves and the peak, a vast circular hole with sloping sides, three hundred feet or more in depth, and quite half a mile round.

"Can't you guess what this is?" I said to Sir Henry and Good, who were staring in astonishment down into the awful pit before us.

They shook their heads.

"Then it is clear that you have never seen the diamond mines at Kimberley. You may depend on it that this is Solomon's Diamond Mine; look there," I said, pointing to the stiff blue clay which was yet to be seen among the grass and bushes which clothed the sides of the pit, "the formation is the same. I'll be bound that if we went down there we should find 'pipes' of soapy brecciated rock. Look, too," and I pointed to a series of worn flat slabs of rock which were placed on a gentle slope below the level of a watercourse which had in some past age been cut out of the solid rock; "if those are not tables once used to wash the 'stuff,' I'm a Dutchman."

At the edge of this vast hole, which was the pit marked on the old Don's map, the great road branched into two and circumvented it. In many places this circumventing road was built entirely of vast blocks of stone, apparently with the object of supporting the edges of the pit and preventing falls of reef. Along this road we pressed, driven by curiosity to see what the three towering objects were which we could discern from the hither side of the great hole. As we got nearer we perceived that they were colossi of some sort or another, and rightly conjectured that these were the three "Silent Ones" that were held in such awe by the Kukuana people. But it was not until we got quite close that we recognised the full majesty of these "Silent Ones."

There upon huge pedestals of dark rock, sculptured in unknown characters, twenty paces between each, and looking down the road which crossed some sixty miles of plain to Loo, were three colossal seated forms—two males and one female—each measuring about twenty feet from the crown of the head to the pedestal.

The female form, which was nude, was of great though severe beauty, but unfortunately the features were injured by centuries of exposure to the weather, Rising from each side of her head were the points of a crescent. The two male colossi were, on the contrary, draped, and presented a terrifying cast of features, especially the one to our right, which had the face of a devil. That to our left was serene in countenance, but the calm upon it was dreadful. It was the calm of inhuman cruelty, the cruelty, Sir Henry remarked, that the ancients attributed to beings potent for good, who could yet watch the sufferings of humanity, if not with rejoicing, at least without suffering themselves. The three formed a most awe-inspiring trinity, as they sat there in their solitude and gazed out across the plain for ever. Contemplating these "Silent Ones," as the Kukuanas called them, an intense curiosity again seized us to know whose were the hands that had shaped them, who was it that had dug the pit and made the road. Whilst I was gazing and wondering, it suddenly occurred to me (being familiar with the Old Testament) that Solomon went astray after strange gods, the names of three of whom I remembered—"Ashtoreth the goddess of the Zidonians, Chemosh the god of the Moabites, and Milcom the god of the children of Ammon"—and I suggested to my companions that the three figures before us might represent these false divinities.

"Hum," said Sir Henry, who was a scholar, having taken a high degree in classics at college, "there may be something in that; Ashtoreth of the Hebrews was the Astarte of the Phœnicians, who were the great traders of Solomon's time. Astarte, who afterwards was the Aphrodite of the Greeks, was represented with horns like the half-moon, and there on the brow of the female figure are distinct horns. Perhaps these colossi were designed by some Phœnician official who managed the mines. Who can say?"

Before we had finished examining these extraordinary relics of remote antiquity, Infadoos came up, and, having saluted the "Silent Ones" by lifting his spear, asked us if we intended entering the "Place of Death" at once, or if we would wait till after we had taken food at mid-day. If we were ready to go at once, Gagool had announced her willingness to guide us. As it was not more than eleven o'clock, we—driven to it by a burning curiosity—announced our intention of proceeding instantly, and I suggested that, in case we should be detained in the cave, we should take some food with us. Accordingly Gagool's litter was brought up, and that lady herself assisted out of it; and meanwhile Foulata, at my request, stored some "biltong," or dried game-flesh, together with a couple of gourds of water in a reed basket. Straight in front of us, at a distance of some fifty paces from the backs of the colossi, rose a sheer wall of rock, eighty feet or more in height, that gradually sloped up till it formed the base of the lofty snow-wreathed peak, which soared up into the air three thousand feet above us. As soon as she was clear of her hammock, Gagool cast one evil grin upon us, and then, leaning on a stick, hobbled off towards the sheer face of the rock. We followed her till we came to a narrow portal solidly arched, that looked like the opening of a gallery of a mine.

Here Gagool was waiting for us, still with that evil grin upon her horrid face.

"Now, white men from the stars," she piped; "great warriors, Incubu, Bougwan, and Macumazahn the wise, are ye ready? Behold, I am here to do the bidding of my lord the king, and to show ye the store of bright stones."

"We are ready," I said.

"Good! good! Make strong your hearts to bear what ye shall see. Comest thou too, Infadoos, who didst betray thy master?"

Infadoos frowned as he answered—

"Nay, I come not, it is not for me to enter there. But thou, Gagool, curb thy tongue, and beware how thou dealest with my lords. At thy hands will I require them, and if a hair of them be hurt, Gagool, be'st thou fifty times a witch, thou shalt die. Hearest thou?"

"I hear, Infadoos; I know thee, thou didst ever love big words; when thou wast a babe I remember thou didst threaten thine own mother. That was but the other day. But fear not, fear not, I live but to do the bidding of the king. I have done the bidding of many kings, Infadoos, till in the end they did mine. *Ha! ha!* I go to look upon their faces once more, and Twala's too! Come on, come on, here is the lamp," and she drew a great gourd full of oil, and fitted with a rush wick, from under her fur cloak.

"Art thou coming, Foulata?" asked Good in his villainous Kitchen Kukuana, in which he had been improving himself under that young lady's tuition.

"I fear, my lord," the girl answered, timidly.

"Then give me the basket."

"Nay, my lord, whither thou goest, there will I go also."

"The deuce you will!" thought I to myself; "that will be rather awkward if ever we get out of this."

Without further ado Gagool plunged into the passage, which was wide enough to admit of two walking abreast, and quite dark, we following her voice as she piped to us to come on, in some fear and trembling, which was not allayed by the sound of a sudden rush of wings.

"Hullo! what's that?" halloed Good; "somebody hit me in the face."

"Bats," said I; "on you go."

When we had, so far as we could judge, gone some fifty paces, we perceived that the passage was growing faintly light. Another minute, and we stood in the most wonderful place that the eyes of living man ever lit on.

Let the reader picture to himself the hall of the vastest cathedral he ever stood in, windowless indeed, but dimly lighted from above (presumably by shafts connected with the outer air and driven in the roof, which arched away a hundred feet above our head), and he will get some idea of the size of the enormous cave in which we stood, with the difference that this cathedral designed of nature was loftier and wider than any built by man. But its stupendous size was the least of the wonders of the place, for running in rows down its length were gigantic pillars of what looked like ice, but were, in reality, huge stalactites. It is impossible for me to convey any idea of the overpowering beauty and grandeur of these pillars of white spar, some of which were not less than twenty feet in diameter at the base, and sprang up in lofty and yet delicate beauty sheer to the distant roof. Others again were in process of formation. On the rock floor there was in these cases what looked, Sir Henry said, exactly like a broken column in an old Grecian temple, whilst high above, depending from the roof, the point of a huge icicle could be dimly seen. And even as we gazed we could hear the process going on, for presently with a tiny splash a drop of water would fall from the far-off icicle on to the column below. On some columns the drops only fell once in two or three minutes, and in these cases it would form an interesting calculation to discover how long, at that rate of dripping, it would take to form a pillar, say eighty feet high by ten in diameter. That the process was, in at least one instance, incalculably slow, the following instance will suffice to show. Cut on one of these pillars we discovered a rude likeness of a mummy, by the head of which sat what appeared to be one of the Egyptian gods, doubtless the handiwork of some old-world labourer in the mine. This work of art was executed at about the natural height at which an idle fellow, be he Phœnician workman or British cad, is in the habit of trying to immortalise himself at the expense of nature's masterpieces, namely, about five feet from the ground; yet at the time that we saw it, which *must* have been nearly three thousand years after the date of the execution of the drawing, the column was only eight feet high, and was still in process of formation, which gives a rate of growth of a foot to a thousand years, or an inch and a fraction to a century. This we knew because, as we were standing by it, we heard a drop of water fall.

Sometimes the stalactites took strange forms, presumably where the dropping of the water had not always been on the same spot. Thus, one huge mass, which must have weighed a hundred tons or so, was in the form of a pulpit, beautifully fretted over outside with what looked like lace. Others resembled strange beasts, and on the sides of the cave were fan-like ivory tracings, such as the frost leaves upon a pane.

Out of the vast main aisle, there opened here and there smaller caves, exactly, Sir Henry said, as chapels open out of great cathedrals. Some were large, but one or two—and this is a wonderful instance of how nature carries out her handiwork by the same unvarying laws, utterly irrespective of size—were tiny. One little nook, for instance, was no larger than an unusually big doll's house, and yet it might have been the model of the whole place, for the water dropped, the tiny icicles hung, and the spar columns were forming in just the same way.

We had not, however, as much time to examine this beautiful place as thoroughly as we should have liked to do, for unfortunately Gagool seemed to be indifferent to stalactites, and only anxious to get her business over. This annoyed me the more, as I was particularly anxious to discover, if possible, by what system the light was admitted into the place, and whether it was by the hand of man or of nature that this was done, also if it had been used in any way in ancient times, as seemed probable. However, we consoled ourselves with the idea that we would examine it thoroughly on our return, and followed on after our uncanny guide.

On she led us, straight to the top of the vast and silent cave, where we found another doorway, not arched as the first was, but square at the top, something like the doorways of Egyptian temples.

"Are ye prepared to enter the Place of Death?" asked Gagool, evidently with a view to making us feel uncomfortable.

"Lead on, Macduff,"[1] said Good, solemnly, trying to look as though he was not at all alarmed, as indeed did we all except Foulata, who caught Good by the arm for protection.

"This is getting rather ghastly," said Sir Henry, peeping into the dark doorway. "Come on, Quatermain—*seniores priores.** Don't keep the old lady waiting!" and he politely made way for me to lead the van, for which I inwardly did not bless him.

Tap, tap, went old Gagool's stick down the passage, as she trotted along, chuckling hideously; and still overcome by some unaccountable presentiment of evil, I hung back.

"Come, get on, old fellow," said Good, "or we shall lose our fair guide."

Thus adjured, I started down the passage, and after about twenty paces found myself in a gloomy apartment some forty feet long, by thirty broad, and thirty high, which in some past age had evidently been hollowed, by hand-labour, out of the mountain. This apartment was not nearly so well lighted as the vast stalactite ante-cave, and at the first glance all I could make out was a massive stone table running its length, with a colossal white figure at its head, and life-sized white figures all round it. Next I made out a brown thing,

---

*Elders first (Latin).

seated on the table in the centre, and in another moment my eyes grew accustomed to the light, and I saw what all these things were, and I was tailing out of it as hard as my legs would carry me. I am not a nervous man, in a general way, and very little troubled with superstitions, of which I have lived to see the folly; but I am free to own that that sight quite upset me, and had it not been that Sir Henry caught me by the collar and held me, I do honestly believe that in another five minutes I should have been outside that stalactite cave, and that the promise of all the diamonds in Kimberley would not have induced me to enter it again. But he held me tight, so I stopped because I could not help myself. But next second his eyes got accustomed to the light, too, and he let go of me, and began to mop the perspiration off his forehead. As for Good he swore feebly, and Foulata threw her arms round his neck and shrieked.

Only Gagool chuckled loud and long.

It *was* a ghastly sight. There at the end of the long stone table, holding in his skeleton fingers a great white spear, sat *Death* himself, shaped in the form of a colossal human skeleton, fifteen feet or more in height. High above his head he held the spear, as though in the act to strike; one bony hand rested on the stone table before him, in the position a man assumes on rising from his seat, whilst his frame was bent forward so that the vertebræ of the neck and the grinning, gleaming skull projected towards us, and fixed its hollow eye-places upon us, the jaws a little open, as though it were about to speak.

"Great heavens!" said I, faintly, at last, "what can it be?"

"And what are *those things?*" said Good, pointing to the white company round the table.

"And what on earth is *that thing?*" said Sir Henry, pointing to the brown creature seated on the table.

"Hee! hee! hee!" laughed Gagool. "To those who enter the Hall of the Dead, evil comes. Hee! hee! hee! ha! ha!"

"Come, Incubu, brave in battle, come and see him thou slewest;" and the old creature caught his coat in her skinny fingers, and led him away towards the table. We followed.

Presently she stopped and pointed at the brown object seated on the table. Sir Henry looked, and started back with an exclamation; and no wonder, for there seated, quite naked, on the table, the head which Sir Henry's battle-axe had shorn from the body resting on its knees, was the gaunt corpse of Twala, last king of the Kukuanas. Yes, there, the head perched upon the knees, it sat in all its ugliness, the vertebræ projecting a full inch above the level of the shrunken flesh of the neck, for all the world like a black double of Hamilton Tighe.*[2] Over the whole surface of the corpse there was gathered a thin, glassy film, which made its appearance yet more appalling, and for which we were, at the moment, quite unable to account, till we presently observed that from the roof of the chamber the water fell steadily, *drip! drop! drip!* on to the neck of the corpse, from whence it ran down over the entire surface, and finally escaped into the rock through a tiny hole in the table. Then I guessed what it was—*Twala's body was being transformed into a stalactite.*

A look at the white forms seated on the stone bench that ran around that ghastly board confirmed this view. They were human forms indeed, or rather had been human forms; now they were *stalactites.* This was the way in which the Kukuana people had from time immemorial preserved their royal dead. They petrified them. What the exact system was, if there was any, beyond placing them for a long period of years under the drip, I never discovered, but there they sat, iced over and preserved for ever by the silicious fluid. Anything more awe-inspiring than the spectacle of this long line of departed royalties, wrapped in a shroud of ice-like spar, through which the features could be dimly made out (there were twenty-seven of them, the last being Ignosi's father), and seated round that inhospitable board, with Death himself for a host, it is impossible to imagine. That the practice of thus preserving their kings must have been an ancient one is evident from the number, which, allowing for an average reign of fifteen years, would, supposing that every king who reigned was placed here—an improbable thing, as some are sure to have perished in battle far from home—fix the date of its commencement at four and a quarter centuries back. But the colossal Death, who sits at the head of the board, is far older than that, and unless I am much mistaken, owes his origin to the same artist who designed the three colossi. He was hewn out of a single stalactite, and, looked at as a work of art, was most admirably conceived

---

*"Now haste ye, my handmaidens, haste and see / How he sits there and glowers with his head on his knee." [Haggard's note]. The lines are from *The Ingoldsby Legends.*

and executed. Good, who understood anatomy, declared that so far as he could see the anatomical design of the skeleton was perfect down to the smallest bones.

My own idea is, that this terrific object was a freak of fancy on the part of some old-world sculptor, and that its presence had suggested to the Kukuanas the idea of placing their royal dead under its awful presidency. Or perhaps it was placed there to frighten away any marauders who might have designs upon the treasure chamber beyond. I cannot say. All I can do is to describe it as it is, and the reader must form his own conclusion.

Such, at any rate, was the White Death, and such were the White Dead!

Chapter 17

Solomon's Treasure Chamber

WHILE WE HAD BEEN engaged in getting over our fright, and in examining the grisly wonders of the place, Gagool had been differently occupied. Somehow or other—for she was marvellously active when she chose—she had scrambled on to the great table, and made her way to where our departed friend Twala was placed, under the drip, to see, suggested Good, how he was "pickling," or for some dark purpose of her own. Then she came hobbling back, stopping now and again to address a remark (the tenor of which I could not catch) to one or other of the shrouded forms, just as you or I might greet an old acquaintance. Having gone through this mysterious and horrible ceremony, she squatted herself down on the table immediately under the White Death, and began, so far as I could make out, to offer up prayers to it. The spectacle of this wicked old creature pouring out supplications (evil ones, no doubt) to the arch enemy of mankind, was so uncanny that it caused us to hasten inspection.

"Now, Gagool," said I, in a low voice—somehow one did not dare to speak above a whisper in that place—"lead us to the chamber."

The old creature promptly scrambled down off the table.

"My lords are not afraid?" she said, leering up into my face.

"Lead on."

"Good, my lords;" and she hobbled round to the back of the great Death. "Here is the chamber; let my lords light the lamp, and enter," and she placed the gourd full of oil upon the floor, and leaned herself against the side of the cave. I took out a match, of which we still had a few in a box, and lit the rush wick, and then looked for the doorway, but there was nothing before us but the solid rock. Gagool grinned. "The way is there, my lords."

"Do not jest with us," I said, sternly.

"I jest not, my lords. See!" and she pointed at the rock.

As she did so, on holding up the lamp we perceived that a mass of stone was slowly rising from the floor and vanishing into the rock above, where doubtless there was a cavity prepared to receive it. The mass was of the width of a good-sized door, about ten feet high and not less than five feet thick. It must have weighed at least twenty or thirty tons, and was clearly moved upon some simple balance principle, probably the same as that upon which the opening and shutting of an ordinary modern window is arranged. How the principle was set in motion, of course none of us saw; Gagool was careful to avoid that; but I have little doubt that there was some very simple lever, which was moved ever so little by pressure on a secret spot, thereby throwing additional weight on to the hidden counterbalances, and causing the whole huge mass to be lifted from the ground. Very slowly and gently the great stone raised itself, till at last it had vanished altogether, and a dark hole presented itself to us in the place which it had filled.

Our excitement was so intense, as we saw the way to Solomon's treasure chamber at last thrown open, that I for one began to tremble and shake. Would it prove a hoax after all, I wondered, or was old Da Silvestra right? and were there vast hoards of wealth stored in that dark place, hoards which would make us the richest men in the whole world? We should know in a minute or two.

"Enter, white men from the stars," said Gagool, advancing into the doorway; "but first hear your servant, Gagaoola the old. The bright stones that ye will see were dug out of the pit over which the Silent Ones are set, and stored here, I know not by whom. But once has this place been entered since the time that those who stored in the stones departed in haste, leaving them behind. The report of the treasure went down among the people who lived in the country from age to age, but none knew where the chamber was, nor the secret of the door. But it happened that a white man reached this country from over the mountains, perchance he too came 'from the stars,' and was well received of the king of the day. He it is who sits yonder," and she pointed to the fifth king at the table of the dead. "And it came to pass that he and a woman of the country who was with him came to this place, and that by chance the woman learnt the secret of the door—a thousand years might ye search, but ye should never find it. Then the white man entered with the woman, and found the stones, and filled with stones the skin of a small goat, which the woman had with her to hold food. And as he was going from the chamber he took up one more stone, a large one, and held it in his hand." Here she paused.

"Well," I asked, breathless with interest as we all were, "what happened to Da Silvestra?"

The old hag started at the mention of the name.

"How knowest thou the dead man's name?" she asked, sharply; and then, without waiting for an answer, went on—

"None know what happened; but it came about that the white man was frightened, for he flung down the goat-skin, with the stones, and fled out with only the one stone in his hand, and that the king took, and it is the stone that thou, Macumazahn, didst take from Twala's brows."

"Have none entered here since?" I asked, peering again down the dark passage.

"None, my lords. Only the secret of the door hath been kept, and every king hath opened it, though he hath not entered. There is a saying, that those who enter there will die within a moon, even as the white man died in the cave upon the mountain, where ye found him, Macumazahn. *Ha! ha!* mine are true words."

Our eyes met as she said it, and I turned sick and cold. How did the old hag know all these things?

"Enter, my lords. If I speak truth the goat-skin with the stones will lie upon the floor; and if there is truth as to whether it is death to enter here, that will ye learn afterwards. Ha! ha! ha!" And she hobbled through the doorway, bearing the light with her; but I confess that once more I hesitated about following.

"Oh, confound it all!" said Good, "here goes. I am not going to be frightened by that old devil;" and followed by Foulata, who, however, evidently did not at all like the job, for she was shivering with fear, he plunged into the passage after Gagool—an example which we quickly followed.

A few yards down the passage, in the narrow way hewn out of the living rock, Gagool had paused, and was waiting for us.

"See, my lords," she said, holding the light before her, "those who stored the treasure here fled in haste, and bethought them to guard against any who should find the secret of the door, but had not the time," and she pointed to large square blocks of stone, which had, to the height of two courses (about two feet three), been placed across the passage with a view to walling it up. Along the side of the passage were similar blocks ready for use, and, most curious of all, a heap of mortar and a couple of trowels, which, so far as we had time to examine them, appeared to be of a similar shape and make to those used by workmen to this day.

Here Foulata, who had throughout been in a state of great fear and agitation, said that she felt faint and could go no farther, but would wait there. Accordingly we set her down on the unfinished wall, placing the basket of provisions by her side, and left her to recover.

Following the passage for about fifteen paces farther, we suddenly came to an elaborately painted wooden door. It was standing wide open. Whoever was last there had either not had the time, or had forgotten, to shut it.

Across the threshold lay a skin bag, formed of a goat-skin, that appeared to be full of pebbles.

"Hee! hee! white men," sniggered Gagool, as the light from the lamp fell upon it. "What did I tell ye, that the white man who came here fled in haste, and dropped the woman's bag—behold it!"

Good stooped down and lifted it. It was heavy and jingled.

"By Jove! I believe it's full of diamonds," he said, in an awed whisper; and, indeed, the idea of a small goat-skin full of diamonds is enough to awe anybody.

"Go on," said Sir Henry, impatiently. "Here, old lady, give me the lamp," and taking it from Gagool's hand, he stepped through the doorway and held it high above his head.

We pressed in after him, forgetful, for the moment, of the bag of diamonds, and found ourselves in Solomon's treasure chamber.

At first, all that the somewhat faint light given by the lamp revealed was a room hewn out of the living rock, and apparently not more than ten feet square. Next there came into sight, stored one on the other as high as the roof, a splendid collection of elephant-tusks. How many of them there were we did not know, for of course we could not see how far they went back, but there could not have been less than the ends of four or five hundred tusks of the first quality visible to our eyes. There, alone, was enough ivory before us to make a man wealthy for life. Perhaps, I thought, it was from this very store that Solomon drew his material for his "great throne of ivory,"[1] of which there was not the like made in any kingdom.

On the opposite side of the chamber were about a score of wooden boxes, something like Martini-Henry ammunition boxes,[2] only rather larger, and painted red.

"There are the diamonds," cried I; "bring the light."

Sir Henry did so, holding it close to the top box, of which the lid, rendered rotten by time even in that dry place, appeared to have been smashed in, probably by Da Silvestra himself. Pushing my hand through the hole in the lid I drew it out full, not of diamonds, but of gold pieces, of a shape that none of us had seen before, and with what looked like Hebrew characters stamped upon them.

"Ah!" I said, replacing the coin, "we shan't go back empty-handed, anyhow. There must be a couple of thousand pieces in each box, and there are eighteen boxes. I suppose it was the money to pay the workmen and merchants."

"Well," put in Good, "I think that is the lot; I don't see any diamonds, unless the old Portuguese put them all into this bag."

"Let my lords look yonder where it is darkest, if they would find the stones," said Gagool, interpreting our looks. "There my lords will find a nook, and three stone chests in the nook, two sealed and one open."

Before interpreting this to Sir Henry, who had the light, I could not resist asking how she knew these things, if no one had entered the place since the white man, generations ago.

"Ah, Macumazahn, who watchest by night," was the mocking answer, "ye who live in the stars, do ye not know that some have eyes that can see through rock?"

"Look in that corner, Curtis," I said, indicating the spot Gagool had pointed out.

"Hullo, you fellows," he said, "here's a recess. Great heavens! look here."

We hurried up to where he was standing in a nook, something like a small bow window. Against the wall of this recess were placed three stone chests, each about two feet square. Two were fitted with stone lids, the lid of the third rested against the side of the chest, which was open.

"*Look!*" he repeated, hoarsely, holding the lamp over the open chest. We looked, and for a moment could make nothing out, on account of a silvery sheen that dazzled us. When our eyes got used to it, we saw that the chest was three-parts full of uncut diamonds, most of them of considerable size. Stooping, I picked some up. Yes, there was no mistake about it, there was the unmistakable soapy feel about them.

I fairly gasped as I dropped them.

"We are the richest men in the whole world," I said. "Monte Christo[3] is a fool to us."

"We shall flood the market with diamonds," said Good.

"Got to get them there first," suggested Sir Henry.

And we stood with pale faces and stared at each other, with the lantern in the middle, and the glimmering gems below, as though we were conspirators about to commit a crime, instead of being, as we thought, the three most fortunate men on earth.

"Hee! hee! hee!" went old Gagool behind us, as she flitted about like a vampire bat. "There are the bright stones that ye love, white men, as many as ye will; take them, run them through your fingers, *eat* of them, hee! hee! *drink* of them, ha! ha!"

There was something so ridiculous at that moment to my mind in the idea of eating and drinking diamonds, that I began to laugh outrageously, an example which the others followed, without knowing why. There we stood and shrieked with laughter over the gems which were ours, which had been found for *us* thousands of years ago by the patient delvers in the great hole yonder, and stored for *us* by Solomon's long-dead overseer, whose name, perchance, was written in the characters stamped on the faded wax that yet adhered to the lids of the chest. Solomon never got them, nor David, nor Da Silvestra, nor anybody else. *We* had got them; there before us were millions of pounds' worth of diamonds, and thousands of pounds' worth of gold and ivory, only waiting to be taken away.

Suddenly the fit passed off, and we stopped laughing.

"Open the other chests, white men," croaked Gagool, "there are surely more therein. Take your fill, white lords!"

Thus adjured, we set to work to pull up the stone lids on the other too, first—not without a feeling of sacrilege—breaking the seals that fastened them.

Hoorah! they were full too, full to the brim; at least, the second one was; no wretched Da Silvestra had been filling goat-skins out of that. As for the third chest, it was only about a fourth full, but the stones were all picked ones; none less than twenty carats, and some of them as large as pigeon-eggs. Some of these biggest ones, however, we could see by holding them up to the light, were a little yellow, "off coloured," as they call it at Kimberley.

What we did *not* see, however, was the look of fearful malevolence that old Gagool favoured us with as she crept, crept like a snake, out of the treasure chamber and down the passage towards the massive door of solid rock.

*   *   *   *   *

Hark! Cry upon cry comes ringing up the vaulted path. It is Foulata's voice!

"*Oh, Bougwan! help! help! the rock falls!*"

"Leave go, girl! Then——"

"*Help! help! she has stabbed me!*"

By now we are running down the passage, and this is what the light from the lamp falls on. The door of rock is slowly closing down; it is not three feet from the floor. Near it struggle Foulata and Gagool. The red blood of the former runs to her knee, but still the brave girl holds the old witch, who fights like a wild cat. Ah! she is free! Foulata falls, and Gagool throws herself on the ground, to twist herself like a snake through the crack of the closing stone. She is under—ah, God! too late! too late! The stone nips her, and she yells in agony. Down, down, it comes, all the thirty tons of it, slowly pressing her old body against the rock below. Shriek upon shriek, such as we never heard, then a long sickening *crunch*, and the door was shut just as we, rushing down the passage, hurled ourselves against it.

It was all done in four seconds.

Then we turned to Foulata. The poor girl was stabbed in the body, and could not, I saw, live long.

"Ah! Bougwan, I die!" gasped the beautiful creature. "She crept out—Gagool; I did not see her, I was faint—and the door began to fall; then she came back, and was looking up the path—and I saw her come in through the slowly falling door, and caught her and held her, and she stabbed me, and I *die*, Bougwan."

"Poor girl! poor girl!" Good cried; and then, as he could do nothing else, he fell to kissing her.

"Bougwan," she said, after a pause, "is Macumazahn there? it grows so dark, I cannot see."

"Here I am, Foulata."

"Macumazahn, be my tongue for a moment, I pray thee, for Bougwan cannot understand me, and before I go into the darkness—I would speak a word."

"Say on, Foulata, I will render it."

"Say to my lord, Bougwan, that—I love him, and that I am glad to die because I know that he cannot cumber his life with such as me, for the sun cannot mate with the darkness, nor the white with the black.

"Say that at times I have felt as though there were a bird in my bosom, which would one day fly hence and sing elsewhere. Even now, though I cannot lift my hand, and my brain grows cold, I do not feel as though my heart were dying; it is so full of love that could live a thousand years, and yet be young. Say that if I live again, mayhap I shall see him in the stars, and that—I will search them all, though perchance I should there still be black and he would—still be white. Say—nay, Macumazahn, say no more, save that I love—— Oh, hold me closer, Bougwan, I cannot feel thine arms—oh! oh!"

"She is dead—she is dead!" said Good, rising in grief, the tears running down his honest face.

"You need not let that trouble you, old fellow," said Sir Henry.

"Eh!" said Good; "what do you mean?"

"I mean that you will soon be in a position to join her. *Man, don't you see that we are buried alive?*"

Until Sir Henry uttered these words, I do not think the full horror of what had happened had come home to us, preoccupied as we were with the sight of poor Foulata's end. But now we understood. The ponderous mass of rock had closed, probably for ever, for the only brain which knew its secret was crushed to powder beneath it. This was a door that none could hope to force with anything short of dynamite in large quantities. And we were the wrong side of it!

For a few minutes we stood horrified there over the corpse of Foulata. All the manhood seemed to have gone out of us. The first shock of this idea of the slow and miserable end that awaited us was overpowering. We saw it all now; that fiend Gagool had planned this snare for us from the first. It would have been just the jest that her evil mind would have rejoiced in, the idea of the three white men, whom, for some reason of her own, she had always hated, slowly perishing of thirst and hunger in the company of the treasure they had coveted. I saw the point of that sneer of hers about eating and drinking the diamonds now. Perhaps somebody had tried to serve the poor old Don in the same way, when he abandoned the skin full of jewels.

"This will never do," said Sir Henry, hoarsely; "the lamp will soon go out. Let us see if we can't find the spring that works the rock."

We sprang forward with desperate energy, and standing in a bloody ooze, began to feel up and down the door and the sides of the passage. But no knob or spring could we discover.

"Depend on it," I said, "it does not work from the inside; if it did Gagool would not have risked trying to crawl underneath the stone. It was the knowledge of this that made her try to escape at all hazards, curse her."

"At all events," said Sir Henry, with a hard little laugh, "retribution was swift; hers was almost as awful an end as ours is likely to be. We can do nothing with the door; let us go back to the treasure room." We turned and went, and as we did so I perceived by the unfinished wall across the passage the basket of food which poor Foulata had carried. I took it up, and brought it with me back to that accursed treasure chamber that was to be our grave. Then we went back and reverently bore in Foulata's corpse, laying it on the floor by the boxes of coin.

Next we seated ourselves, leaning our backs against the three stone chests of priceless treasures.

"Let us divide the food," said Sir Henry, "so as to make it last as long as possible." Accordingly we did so. It would, we reckoned, make four infinitesimally small meals for each of us, enough, say, to support life for a couple of days. Besides the "biltong," or dried gameflesh, there were two gourds of water, each holding about a quart.

"Now," said Sir Henry, "let us eat and drink, for to-morrow we die."

We each ate a small portion of the "biltong," and drank a sip of water. We had, needless to say, but little appetite, though we were sadly in need of food, and felt better after swallowing it. Then we got up and made a systematic examination of the walls of our prison-house, in the faint hope of finding some means of exit, sounding them and the floor carefully.

There was none. It was not probable that there would be one to a treasure chamber.

The lamp began to burn dim. The fat was nearly exhausted.

"Quatermain," said Sir Henry, "what is the time—your watch goes?"

I drew it out, and looked at it. It was six o'clock; we had entered the cave at eleven.

"Infadoos will miss us," I suggested. "If we do not return to-night, he will search for us in the morning, Curtis."

"He may search in vain. He does not know the secret of the door, not even where it is. No living person knew it yesterday, except Gagool. To-day no one knows it. Even if he found the door he could not break it down. All the Kukuana army could not break through five feet of living rock. My friends, I see nothing for it but to bow ourselves to the will of the Almighty. The search for treasure has brought many to a bad end; we shall go to swell their number."

The lamp grew dimmer yet.

Presently it flared up and showed the whole scene in strong relief, the great mass of white tusks, the boxes full of gold, the corpse of poor Foulata stretched before them, the goat-skin full of treasure, the dim glimmer of the diamonds, and the wild, wan faces of us three white men seated there awaiting death by starvation.

Suddenly it sank, and expired.

Chapter 18

We Abandon Hope

I CAN GIVE NO adequate description of the horrors of the night which followed. Mercifully they were to some extent mitigated by sleep, for even in such a position as ours, wearied nature will sometimes assert itself. But I, at any rate, found it impossible to sleep much. Putting aside the terrifying thought of our impending doom—for the bravest man on earth might well quail from such a fate as awaited us, and I never had any great pretensions to be brave—the *silence* itself was too great to allow of it. Reader, you may have lain awake at night and thought the silence oppressive, but I say with confidence that you can have no idea what a vivid tangible thing perfect silence really is. On the surface of the earth there is always some sound or motion, and though it may in itself be imperceptible, yet does it deaden the sharp edge of absolute silence. But here there was none. We were buried in the bowels of a huge snow-clad peak. Thousands of feet above us the fresh air rushed over the white snow, but no sound of it reached us. We were separated by a long tunnel and five feet of rock even from the awful chamber of the dead; and the dead make no noise. The crashing of all the artillery of earth and heaven could not have come to our ears in our living tomb. We were cut off from all echoes of the world—we were as already dead.

And then the irony of the situation forced itself upon me. There around us lay treasures enough to pay off a moderate national debt, or to build a fleet of ironclads,[1] and yet we would gladly have bartered them all for the faintest chance of escape. Soon, doubtless, we should be glad to exchange them for a bit of food or a cup of water, and, after that, even for the privilege of a speedy close to our sufferings. Truly wealth, which men spend all their lives in acquiring, is a valueless thing at the last.

And so the night wore on.

"Good," said Sir Henry's voice at last, and it sounded awful in the intense stillness, "how many matches have you in the box?"

"Eight, Curtis."

"Strike one, and let us see the time."

He did so, and in contrast to the dense darkness the flame nearly blinded us. It was five o'clock by my watch. The beautiful dawn was now blushing on the snow-wreaths far over our heads, and the breeze would be stirring the night mists in the hollows.

"We had better eat something and keep up our strength," said I.

"What is the good of eating?" answered Good; "the sooner we die and get it over the better."

"While there is life there is hope," said Sir Henry.

Accordingly we ate and sipped some water, and another period of time passed, when somebody suggested that it might be as well to get as near to the door as possible and halloa, on the faint chance of somebody catching a sound outside. Accordingly Good, who, from long practice at sea, has a fine piercing note, groped his way down the passage and began, and I must say he made a most diabolical noise. I never heard such yells; but it might have been a mosquito buzzing for all the effect it produced.

After awhile he gave it up, and came back very thirsty, and had to have some water. After that we gave up yelling, as it encroached on the supply of water.

So we all sat down once more against our chests of useless diamonds in that dreadful inaction, which was one of the hardest circumstances of our fate; and I am bound to say that, for my part, I gave way in despair. Laying my head against Sir Henry's broad shoulder I burst into tears; and I think I heard Good gulping away on the other side, and swearing hoarsely at himself for doing so.

Ah, how good and brave that great man was! Had we been two frightened children, and he our nurse, he could not have treated us more tenderly. Forgetting his own share of miseries, he did all he could to soothe our broken nerves, telling stories of men who had been in somewhat similar circumstances, and miraculously escaped; and when these failed to cheer us, pointing out how, after all, it was only anticipating an end that must come to us all, that it would soon be over, and that death from exhaustion was a merciful one (which is not true). Then, in a diffident sort of a way, as I had once before heard him do, he suggested that we should throw ourselves on the mercy of a higher Power, which for my part I did with great vigour.

His is a beautiful character, very quiet, but very strong.

And so somehow the day went as the night had gone (if, indeed, one can use the terms where all was densest night), and when I lit a match to see the time it was seven o'clock.

Once more we ate and drank, and as we did so an idea occurred to me.

"How is it," said I, "that the air in this place keeps fresh? It is thick and heavy, but it is perfectly fresh."

"Great heavens!" said Good, starting up, "I never thought of that. It can't come through the stone door, for it is air-tight, if ever a door was. It must come from somewhere. If there were no current of air in the place we should have been stifled when we first came in. Let us have a look."

It was wonderful what a change this mere spark of hope wrought in us. In a moment we were all three groping about the place on our hands and knees, feeling for the slightest indication of a draught. Presently my ardour received a check. I put my hand on something cold. It was poor Foulata's dead face.

For an hour or more we went on feeling about, till at last Sir Henry and I gave it up in despair, having got considerably hurt by constantly knocking our heads against tusks, chests, and the sides of the chamber. But Good still persevered, saying, with an approach to cheerfulness, that it was better than doing nothing.

"I say, you fellows," he said, presently, in a constrained sort of voice, "come here."

Needless to say we scrambled over towards him quick enough.

"Quatermain, put your hand here where mine is. Now, do you feel anything?"

"I *think* I feel air coming up."

"Now listen." He rose and stamped upon the place, and a flame of hope shot up in our hearts. *It rang hollow.*

With trembling hands I lit a match. I had only three left, and we saw that we were in the angle of the far corner of the chamber, a fact that accounted for our not having noticed the hollow ring of the place during our former exhaustive examination. As the match burnt we scrutinised the spot. There was a join in the solid rock floor, and, great heavens! there, let in level with the rock, was a stone ring. We said no word, we were too excited, and our hearts beat too wildly with hope to allow us to speak. Good had a knife, at the back of which was one of those hooks that are made to extract stones from horses' hoofs. He opened it, and scratched away at the ring with it. Finally he got it under, and levered away gently for fear of breaking the hook. The ring began to move. Being of stone, it had not got set fast in all the centuries it had lain there, as would have been the case had it been of iron. Presently it was upright. Then he got his hands into it and tugged with all his force, but nothing budged.

"Let me try," I said, impatiently, for the situation of the stone, right in the angle of the corner, was such that it was impossible for two to pull at once. I got hold and strained away, but with no results.

Then Sir Henry tried and failed.

Taking the hook again, Good scratched all round the crack where we felt the air coming up.

"Now, Curtis," he said, "tackle on, and put your back into it; you are as strong as two. Stop," and he took off a stout black silk handkerchief, which, true to his habits of neatness, he still wore, and ran it through the ring. "Quatermain, get Curtis round the middle and pull for dear life when I give the word. *Now.*"

Sir Henry put out all his enormous strength, and Good and I did the same, with such power as nature had given us.

"Heave! heave! it's giving," gasped Sir Henry; and I heard the muscles of his great back cracking. Suddenly there came a parting sound, then a rush of air, and we were all on our backs on the floor with a great flag-stone on the top of us. Sir Henry's strength had done it, and never did muscular power stand a man in better stead.

"Light a match, Quatermain," he said, as soon as we had picked ourselves up and got one breath; "carefully, now."

I did so, and there before us was, God be praised! the *first step of a stone stair.*

"Now what is to be done?" asked Good.

"Follow the stair, of course, and trust to Providence."

"Stop!" said Sir Henry; "Quatermain, get the bit of biltong and the water that is left; we may want them."

I went creeping back to our place by the chests for that purpose, and as I was coming away an idea struck me. We had not thought much of the diamonds for the last twenty-four hours or so; indeed, the idea of diamonds was nauseous, seeing what they had entailed upon us; but, thought I, I may as well pocket a few in case we ever should get out of this ghastly hole. So I just stuck my fist into the first chest and filled all the available pockets of my old shooting coat, topping up—this was a happy thought—with a couple of handfuls of big ones out of the third chest.

"I say, you fellows," I sung out, "won't you take some diamonds with you? I've filled my pockets."

"Oh! hang the diamonds!" said Sir Henry. "I hope that I may never see another."

As for Good, he made no answer. He was, I think, taking a last farewell of all that was left of the poor girl who loved him so well. And, curious as it may seem to you, my reader, sitting at home at ease and reflecting on the vast, indeed the immeasurable, wealth which we were thus abandoning, I can assure you that if you had passed some twenty-eight hours with next to nothing to eat and drink in that place, you would not have cared to cumber yourself with diamonds whilst plunging down into the unknown bowels of the earth, in the wild hope of escape from an agonising death. If it had not, from the habits of a lifetime, become a sort of second nature with me never to leave anything worth having behind, if there was the slightest chance of my being able to carry it away, I am sure I should not have bothered to fill my pockets.

"Come on, Quatermain," said Sir Henry, who was already standing on the first step of the stone stair. "Steady, I will go first."

"Mind where you put your feet; there may be some awful hole underneath," said I.

"Much more likely to be another room," said Sir Henry, as he slowly descended, counting the steps as he went.

When he got to "fifteen" he stopped. "Here's the bottom," he said. "Thank goodness! I think it's a passage. Come on down."

Good descended next, and I followed last, and on reaching the bottom lit one of the two remaining matches. By its light we could just see that we were standing in a narrow tunnel, which ran right and left at right angles to the staircase we had descended. Before we could make out any more, the match burnt my fingers and went out. Then arose the delicate question of which way to turn. Of course, it was impossible to know what the tunnel was or where it ran to, and yet to turn one way might lead us to safety, and the other to destruction. We were utterly perplexed, till suddenly it struck Good that when I had lit the match the draught of the passage blew the flame to the left.

"Let us go against the draught," he said; "air draws inwards, not outwards."

We took this suggestion, and feeling along the wall with the hand, whilst trying the ground before us at every step, we departed from that accursed treasure chamber on our terrible quest. If ever it should be entered again by living man, which I do not think it will be, he will find a token of our presence in the open chests of jewels, the empty lamp, and the white bones of poor Foulata.

When we had groped our way for about a quarter of an hour along the passage, it suddenly took a sharp turn, or else was bisected by another, which we followed, only in course of time to be led into a third. And so it went on for some hours. We seemed to be in a stone labyrinth which led nowhere. What all these passages are, of course I cannot say, but we thought that they must be the ancient workings of a mine, of which the various shafts travelled hither and thither as the ore led them. This is the only way in which we could account for such a multitude of passages.

At length we halted, thoroughly worn out with fatigue, and with that hope deferred which maketh the heart sick,[2] and ate up our poor remaining piece of biltong, and drank our last sup of water, for our throats were like lime-kilns. It seemed to us that we had escaped Death in the darkness of the chamber only to meet him in the darkness of the tunnels.

As we stood, once more utterly depressed, I thought I caught a sound, to which I called the attention of the others. It was very faint and very far off, but it *was* a sound, a faint, murmuring sound, for the others heard it too, and no words can describe the blessedness of it after all those hours of utter, awful stillness.

"By heaven! it's running water," said Good. "Come on."

Off we started again in the direction from which the faint murmur seemed to come, groping our way as before along the rocky walls. As we went it got more and more audible, till at last it seemed quite loud in the quiet. On, yet on; now we could distinctly make out the unmistakable swirl of rushing water. And yet how could there be running water in the bowels of the earth? Now we were quite near to it, and Good, who was leading, swore that he could smell it.

"Go gently, Good," said Sir Henry, "we must be close." *Splash!* and a cry from Good.

He had fallen in.

"Good! Good! where are you?" we shouted, in terrified distress. To our intense relief, an answer came back in a choky voice.

"All right; I've got hold of a rock. Strike a light to show me where you are."

Hastily I lit the last remaining match. Its faint gleam discovered to us a dark mass of water running at our feet. How wide it was we could not see, but there, some way out, was the dark form of our companion hanging on to a projecting rock.

"Stand clear to catch me," sung out Good. "I must swim for it."

Then we heard a splash, and a great struggle. Another minute and he had grabbed at and caught Sir Henry's outstretched hand, and we had pulled him up high and dry into the tunnel.

"My word!" he said, between his gasps, "that was touch and go. If I hadn't caught that rock, and known how to swim, I should have been done. It runs like a mill-race, and I could feel no bottom."

It was clear that this would not do; so after Good had rested a little, and we had drunk our fill from the water of the subterranean river, which was sweet and fresh, and washed our faces, which sadly needed it, as well as we could, we started from the banks of this African Styx,[3] and began to retrace our steps along the tunnel, Good dripping unpleasantly in front of us. At length we came to another tunnel leading to our right.

"We may as well take it," said Sir Henry, wearily; "all roads are alike here; we can only go on till we drop."

Slowly, for a long, long while, we stumbled, utterly weary, along this new tunnel, Sir Henry leading now.

Suddenly he stopped, and we bumped up against him.

"Look!" he whispered, "is my brain going, or is that light?"

We stared with all our eyes, and there, yes, there, far ahead of us, was a faint glimmering spot, no larger than a cottage window pane. It was so faint that I doubt if any eyes, except those which, like ours, had for days seen nothing but blackness, could have perceived it at all.

With a sort of gasp of hope we pushed on. In five minutes there was no longer any doubt: it *was* a patch of faint light. A minute more and a breath of real live air was fanning us. On we struggled. All at once the tunnel narrowed. Sir Henry went on his knees. Smaller yet it grew, till it was only the size of a large fox's earth—it was *earth* now, mind you; the rock had ceased.

A squeeze, a struggle, and Sir Henry was out, and so was Good, and so was I, and there above us were the blessed stars, and in our nostrils was the sweet air; then suddenly something gave, and we were all rolling over and over and over through grass and bushes, and soft, wet soil.

I caught at something and stopped. Sitting up I halloed lustily. An answering shout came from just below, where Sir Henry's wild career had been stopped by some level ground. I scrambled to him, and found him unhurt, though breathless. Then we looked for Good. A little way off we found him too, jammed in a forked root. He was a good deal knocked about, but soon came to.

We sat down together there on the grass, and the revulsion of feeling was so great, that I really think we cried for joy. We had escaped from that awful dungeon, that was so near to becoming our grave. Surely some merciful Power must have guided our footsteps to the jackal hole at the termination of the tunnel, (for that is what it must have been). And see, there on the mountains, the dawn we had never thought to look upon again was blushing rosy red.

Presently the grey light stole down the slopes, and we saw that we were at the bottom, or rather, nearly at the bottom, of the vast pit in front of the entrance to the cave. Now we could make out the dim forms of the three colossi who sat upon its verge. Doubtless those awful passages, along which we had wandered the live-long night, had originally been, in some way, connected with the great diamond mine. As for the subterranean river in the bowels of the mountain, Heaven only knows what it was, or whence it flows, or whither it goes. I for one have no anxiety to trace its course.

Lighter it grew, and lighter yet. We could see each other now, and such a spectacle as we presented I have never set eyes on before or since. Gaunt-cheeked, hollow-eyed wretches, smeared all over with dust and mud, bruised, bleeding, the long fear of imminent death yet written on our countenances, we were, indeed, a sight to frighten the daylight. And yet it is a solemn fact that Good's eye-glass was still fixed in Good's eye. I doubt whether he had ever taken it out at all. Neither the darkness, nor the plunge in the subterranean river, nor the roll down the slope, had been able to separate Good and his eye-glass.

Presently we rose, fearing that our limbs would stiffen if we stopped there longer, and commenced with slow and painful steps to struggle up the sloping sides of the great pit. For an hour or more we toiled steadfastly up the blue clay, dragging ourselves on by the help of the roots and grasses with which it was clothed.

At last it was done, and we stood on the great road, on the side of the pit opposite to the colossi.

By the side of the road, a hundred yards off, a fire was burning in front of some huts, and round the fire were figures. We made towards them, supporting one another, and halting every few paces. Presently, one of the figures rose, saw us, and fell on to the ground, crying out for fear.

"Infadoos, Infadoos! it is us, thy friends."

We rose; he ran to us, staring wildly, and still shaking with fear.

"Oh, my lords, my lords, it is indeed you come back from the dead!—come back from the dead!"

And the old warrior flung himself down before us, and clasped Sir Henry's knees, and wept aloud for joy.

Chapter 19

Ignosi's Farewell

TEN DAYS FROM THAT eventful morning found us once more in our old quarters at Loo; and, strange to say, but little the worse for our terrible experience, except that my stubbly hair came out of that cave about three shades greyer than it went in, and that Good never was quite the same after Foulata's death, which seemed to move him very greatly. I am bound to say that, looking at the thing from the point of view of an oldish man of the world, I consider her removal was a fortunate occurrence, since, otherwise, complications would have been sure to ensue. The poor creature was no ordinary native girl, but a person of great, I had almost said stately, beauty, and of considerable refinement of mind. But no amount of beauty or refinement could have made an entanglement between Good and herself a desirable occurrence; for, as she herself put it, "Can the sun mate with the darkness, or the white with the black?"

I need hardly state that we never again penetrated into Solomon's treasure chamber. After we had recovered from our fatigues, a process which took us forty-eight hours, we descended into the great pit in the hope of finding the hole by which we had crept out of the mountain, but with no success. To begin with, rain had fallen, and obliterated our spoor; and what is more, the sides of the vast pit were full of ant-bear and other holes. It was impossible to say to which of these we owed our salvation. We also, on the day before we started back to Loo, made a further examination of the wonders of the stalactite cave, and, drawn by a kind of restless feeling, even penetrated once more into the Chamber of the Dead; and, passing beneath the spear of the white Death, gazed, with sensations which it would be quite impossible for me to describe, at the mass of rock which had shut us off from escape, thinking, the while, of the priceless treasures beyond, of the mysterious old hag whose flattened fragments lay crushed beneath it, and of the fair girl of whose tomb it was the portal. I say gazed at the "rock," for examine as we would, we could find no traces of the join of the sliding door; nor, indeed, could we hit upon the secret, now utterly lost, that worked it, though we tried for an hour or more. It was certainly a marvellous bit of mechanism, characteristic, in its massive and yet inscrutable simplicity, of the age which produced it; and I doubt if the world has such another to show.

At last we gave it up in disgust; though, if the mass had suddenly risen before our eyes, I doubt if we should have screwed up courage to step over Gagool's mangled remains, and once more enter the treasure chamber, even in the sure and certain hope of unlimited diamonds. And yet I could have cried at the idea of leaving all that treasure, the biggest treasure probably that has ever in the world's history been accumulated in one spot. But there was no help for it. Only dynamite could force its way through five feet of solid rock. And so we left it. Perhaps, in some remote unborn century, a more fortunate explorer may hit upon the "Open Sesame,"[1] and flood the world with gems. But, myself, I doubt it. Somehow, I seem to feel that the millions of pounds' worth of gems that lie in the three stone coffers will never shine round the neck of an earthly beauty. They and Foulata's bones will keep cold company till the end of all things.

With a sigh of disappointment we made our way back, and next day started for Loo. And yet it was really very ungrateful of us to be disappointed; for, as the reader will remember, I had, by a lucky thought, taken the precaution to fill the pockets of my old shooting coat with gems before we left our prison-house. A good many of these fell out in the course of our roll down the side of the pit, including most of the big ones, which I had crammed in on the top. But, comparatively speaking, an enormous quantity still remained, including eighteen large stones ranging from about one hundred to thirty carats in weight. My old shooting coat still held enough treasure to make us all, if not millionaires, at least exceedingly wealthy men, and yet to keep enough stones each to make the three finest sets of gems in Europe. So we had not done so badly.

On arriving at Loo, we were most cordially received by Ignosi, whom we found well, and busily engaged in consolidating his power, and reorganising the regiments which had suffered most in the great struggle with Twala.

He listened with breathless interest to our wonderful story; but when we told him of old Gagool's frightful end, he grew thoughtful.

"Come hither," he called, to a very old Induna (councillor), who was sitting with others in a circle round the king, but out of ear-shot. The old man rose, approached, saluted, and seated himself.

"Thou art old," said Ignosi.

"Ay, my lord the king!"

"Tell me, when thou wast little, didst thou know Gagaoola the witch doctress?"

"Ay, my lord the king!"

"How was she then—young, like thee?"

"Not so, my lord the king! She was even as now; old and dried, very ugly, and full of wickedness."

"She is no more; she is dead."

"So, O king! then is a curse taken from the land."

"Go!"

"*Koom!* I go, black puppy, who tore out the old dog's throat. *Koom!*"

"Ye see, my brothers," said Ignosi, "this was a strange woman, and I rejoice that she is dead. She would have let ye die in the dark place, and mayhap afterwards she had found a way to slay me as she found a way to slay my father, and set up Twala, whom her heart loved, in his place. Now go on with the tale; surely there never was the like!"

After I had narrated all the story of our escape, I, as we had agreed between ourselves that I should, took the opportunity to address Ignosi as to our departure from Kukuanaland.

"And now, Ignosi, the time has come for us to bid thee farewell, and start to seek once more our own land. Behold, Ignosi, with us thou camest a servant, and now we leave thee a mighty king. If thou art grateful to us, remember to do even as thou didst promise: to rule justly, to respect the law, and to put none to death without a cause. So shalt thou prosper. To-morrow, at break of day, Ignosi, wilt thou give us an escort who shall lead us across the mountains? Is it not so, O king?"

Ignosi covered his face with his hands for awhile before answering.

"My heart is sore," he said at last; "your words split my heart in twain. What have I done to ye, Incubu, Macumazahn, and Bougwan, that ye should leave me desolate? Ye who stood by me in rebellion and in battle, will ye leave me in the day of peace and victory? What will ye—wives? Choose from out the land! A place to live in? Behold, the land is yours as far as ye can see. The white man's houses? Ye shall teach my people how to build them. Cattle for beef and milk? Every married man shall bring ye an ox or a cow. Wild game to hunt? Does not the elephant walk through my forests, and the river-horse* sleep in the reeds? Would ye make war? My Impis (regiments) wait your word. If there is anything more that I can give, that will I give ye."

"Nay, Ignosi, we want not these things," I answered; "we would seek our own place."

"Now do I perceive," said Ignosi, bitterly, and with flashing eyes, "that it is the bright stones that ye love more than me, your friend. Ye have the stones; now would ye go to Natal and across the moving black water and sell them, and be rich, as it is the desire of a white man's heart to be. Cursed for your sake be the stones, and cursed he who seeks them. Death shall it be to him who sets foot in the place of Death to seek them. I have spoken, white men; ye can go."

I laid my hand upon his arm. "Ignosi," I said, "tell us, when thou didst wander in Zululand, and among the white men in Natal, did not thine heart turn to the land thy mother told thee of, thy native land, where thou didst see the light, and play when thou wast little, the land where thy place was?"

"It was even so, Macumazahn."

"Then thus does our heart turn to our land and to our own place."

Then came a pause. When Ignosi broke it, it was in a different voice.

"I do perceive that thy words are, now as ever, wise and full of reason, Macumazahn; that which flies in the air loves not to run along the ground; the white man loves not to live on the level of the black. Well, ye must go, and leave my heart sore, because ye will be as dead to me, since from where ye will be no tidings can come to me.

"But listen, and let all the white men know my words. No other white man shall cross the mountains, even if any may live to come so far. I will see no traders with their guns and rum. My people shall fight with the spear, and drink water, like their forefathers before

---

*Literal translation of the Greek *hippopotamus*.

them. I will have no praying-men to put fear of death into men's hearts, to stir them up against the king, and make a path for the white men who follow to run on. If a white man comes to my gates I will send him back; if a hundred come, I will push them back; if an army comes, I will make war on them with all my strength, and they shall not prevail against me. None shall ever come for the shining stones; no, not an army, for if they come I will send a regiment and fill up the pit, and break down the white columns in the caves and fill them with rocks, so that none can come even to that door of which ye speak, and whereof the way to move it is lost. But for ye three, Incubu, Macumazahn, and Bougwan, the path is always open; for behold, ye are dearer to me than aught that breathes.

"And ye would go. Infadoos, my uncle, and my Induna, shall take thee by the hand and guide thee, with a regiment. There is, as I have learnt, another way across the mountains that he shall show ye. Farewell, my brothers, brave white men. See me no more, for I have no heart to bear it. Behold, I make a decree, and it shall be published from the mountains to the mountains, your names, Incubu, Macumazahn, and Bougwan, shall be as the names of dead kings, and he who speaks them shall die.* So shall your memory be preserved in the land for ever.

"Go now, ere my eyes rain tears like a woman's. At times when ye look back down the path of life, or when ye are old and gather yourselves together to crouch before the fire, because the sun has no more heat, ye will think of how we stood shoulder to shoulder in that great battle that thy wise words planned, Macumazahn, of how thou wast the point of that horn that galled Twala's flank, Bougwan; whilst thou stoodst in the ring of the Greys, Incubu, and men went down before thine axe like corn before a sickle; ay, and of how thou didst break the wild bull's (Twala's) strength, and bring his pride to dust. Fare ye well for ever, Incubu, Macumazahn, and Bougwan, my lords and my friends."

He rose, looked earnestly at us for a few seconds, and then

---

*This extraordinary and negative way of showing intense respect is by no means unknown among African people, and the result is that, as is usual, the name in question has a significance, the meaning has to be expressed by an idiom or another word. In this way a memory is preserved for generations, or until the new word supplants the old one. [Haggard's note] threw the corner of his karross over his head, so as to cover his face from us.

We went in silence.

Next day at dawn we left Loo, escorted by our old friend Infadoos, who was heart-broken at our departure, and the regiment of Buffaloes. Early as the hour was, all the main street of the town was lined with multitudes of people, who gave us the royal salute as we passed at the head of the regiment, while the women blessed us as having rid the land of Twala, throwing flowers before us as we went. It really was very affecting, and not the sort of thing one is accustomed to meet with from natives.

One very ludicrous incident occurred, however, which I rather welcomed, as it gave us something to laugh at.

Just before we got to the confines of the town, a pretty young girl, with some beautiful lilies in her hand, came running forward and presented them to Good (somehow they all seemed to like Good; I think his eye-glass and solitary whisker gave him a fictitious value), and then said she had a boon to ask.

"Speak on."

"Let my lord show his servant his beautiful white legs, that his servant may look on them, and remember them all her days, and tell of them to her children; his servant has travelled four days' journey to see them, for the fame of them has gone throughout the land."

"I'll be hanged if I do!" said Good, excitedly.

"Come, come, my dear fellow," said Sir Henry, "you can't refuse to oblige a lady."

"I won't," said Good, obstinately; "it is positively indecent."

However, in the end he consented to draw up his trousers to the knee, amidst notes of rapturous admiration from all the women present, especially the gratified young lady, and in this guise he had to walk till we got clear of the town.

Good's legs will, I fear, never be so greatly admired again. Of his melting teeth, and even of his "transparent eye," they wearied more or less, but of his legs, never.

As we travelled, Infadoos told us that there was another pass over the mountains to the north of the one followed by Solomon's great road, or rather that there was a place where it was possible to climb down the wall of cliff that separated Kukuanaland from the desert, and was broken by the towering shapes of Sheba's Breasts. It appeared, too, that rather more than two years previously a party of Kukuana hunters had descended this path into the desert in search of ostriches, whose plumes were much prized among them for war head-dresses, and that in the course of their hunt they had been led far from the mountains, and were much troubled by thirst. Seeing, however, trees on the horizon, they made towards them, and discovered a large and fertile oasis of some miles in extent, and plentifully watered. It was by way of this oasis that he suggested that we should return, and the idea seemed to us a good one, as it appeared that we should escape the rigours of the mountain pass, and as some of the hunters were in attendance to guide us to the oasis, from which, they stated, they could perceive more fertile spots far away in the desert.*

Travelling easily, on the night of the fourth day's journey we found ourselves once more on the crest of the mountains that separate Kukuanaland from the desert, which rolled away in sandy billows at our feet, and about twenty-five miles to the north of Sheba's Breasts.

At dawn on the following day, we were led to the commencement of a precipitous descent, by which we were to descend the precipice, and gain the desert two thousand and more feet below.

Here we bade farewell to that true friend and sturdy old warrior, Infadoos, who solemnly wished all good upon us, and nearly wept with grief. "Never, my lords," he said, "shall mine old eyes see the like of ye again. Ah! the way that Incubu cut his men down in the battle! Ah! for the sight of that stroke with which he swept off my brother Twala's head! It was beautiful—beautiful! I may never hope to see such another, except perchance in happy dreams."

We were very sorry to part from him; indeed, Good was so moved

---

*It often puzzled all of us to understand how it was possible that Ignosi's mother, bearing the child with her, should have survived the dangers of the journey across the mountains and the desert, dangers which so nearly proved fatal to ourselves. It has since occurred to me, and I give the idea to the reader for what it is worth, that she must have taken this second route, and wandered out like Hagar into the desert.[2] If she did so, there is no longer anything inexplicable about the story, since she may well, as Ignosi himself related, have been picked up by some ostrich hunters before she or the child were exhausted, and led by them to the oasis, and thence by stages to the fertile country, and so on by slow degrees southwards to Zululand.—A. Q. [Haggard's note]

that he gave him as a souvenir—what do you think?—an *eye-glass*. (Afterwards we discovered that it was a spare one.) Infadoos was delighted, foreseeing that the possession of such an article would enormously increase his prestige, and after several vain attempts actually succeeded in screwing it into his own eye. Anything more incongruous than the old warrior looked with an eye-glass I never saw. Eyeglasses don't go well with leopard-skin cloaks and black ostrich plumes.

Then, having seen that our guides were well laden with water and provisions, and having received a thundering farewell salute from the Buffaloes, we wrung the old warrior's hand, and began our downward climb. A very arduous business it proved to be, but somehow that evening we found ourselves at the bottom without accident.

"Do you know," said Sir Henry that night, as we sat by our fire and gazed up at the beetling cliffs above us, "I think that there are worse places than Kukuanaland in the world, and that I have spent unhappier times than the last month or two, though I have never spent such queer ones. Eh! you fellows?"

"I almost wish I were back," said Good, with a sigh.

As for myself, I reflected that all's well that ends well; but in the course of a long life of shaves, I never had such shaves as those I had recently experienced. The thought of that battle still makes me feel cold all over, and as for our experience in the treasure chamber——!

Next morning we started on a toilsome march across the desert, having with us a good supply of water carried by our five guides, and camped that night in the open, starting again at dawn on the morrow.

By mid-day of the third day's journey we could see the trees of the oasis of which the guides spoke, and by an hour before sundown we were once more walking upon grass and listening to the sound of running water.

Chapter 20

Found

AND NOW I COME to perhaps the strangest thing that happened to us in all that strange business, and one which shows how wonderfully things are brought about.

I was walking quietly along, some way in front of the other two, down the banks of the stream, which ran from the oasis till it was swallowed up in the hungry desert sands, when suddenly I stopped and rubbed my eyes, as well I might. There, not twenty yards in front, placed in a charming situation, under the shade of a species of fig tree, and facing to the stream, was a cosy hut, built more or less on the Kafir principle of grass and withes, only with a full-length door instead of a bee-hole.

"What the dickens," said I to myself, "can a hut be doing here!" Even as I said it, the door of the hut opened, and there limped out of it *a white man* clothed in skins, and with an enormous black beard. I thought that I must have got a touch of the sun. It was impossible. No hunter ever came to such a place as this. Certainly no hunter would ever settle in it. I stared and stared, and so did the other man, and just at that juncture Sir Henry and Good came up.

"Look here, you fellows," I said, "is that a white man, or am I mad?"

Sir Henry looked, and Good looked, and then all of a sudden the lame white man with the black beard gave a great cry, and came hobbling towards us. When he got close, he fell down in a sort of faint.

With a spring Sir Henry was by his side.

"Great Powers!" he cried, "*it is my brother George!*"

At the sound of the disturbance, another figure, also clad in skins, emerged from the hut, with a gun in his hand, and came running towards us. On seeing me he too gave a cry.

"Macumazahn," he hallooed, "don't you know me, Baas? I'm Jim the hunter. I lost the note you gave me to give to the Baas, and we have been here nearly two years." And the fellow fell at my feet, and rolled over and over, weeping for joy.

"You careless scoundrel!" I said; "you ought to be well hided."

Meanwhile the man with the black beard had recovered and got up, and he and Sir Henry were pump-handling away at each other, apparently without a word to say. But whatever they had quarrelled about in the past (I suspect it was a lady, though I never asked), it was evidently forgotten now.

"My dear old fellow," burst out Sir Henry at last, "I thought that you were dead. I have been over Solomon's Mountains to find you, and now I come across you perched in the desert, like an old Aasvögel (vulture)."

"I tried to go over Solomon's Mountains nearly two years ago," was the answer, spoken in the hesitating voice of a man who has had little recent opportunity of using his tongue, "but when I got here, a boulder fell on my leg and crushed it, and I have been able to go neither forward nor back."

Then I came up. "How do you do, Mr. Neville?" I said; "do you remember me?"

"Why," he said, "isn't it Quatermain, eh, and Good too? Hold on a minute, you fellows, I am getting dizzy again. It is all so very strange, and, when a man has ceased to hope, so very happy."

That evening, over the camp fire, George Curtis told us his story, which, in its way, was almost as eventful as our own, and amounted shortly to this. A little short of two years before, he had started from Sitanda's Kraal, to try and reach the mountains. As for the note I had sent him by Jim, that worthy had lost it, and he had never heard of it till to-day. But, acting upon information he had received from the natives, he made, not for Sheba's Breasts, but for the ladder-like descent of the mountains down which we had just come, which was clearly a better route than that marked out in old Dom Silvestra's plan. In the desert he and Jim suffered great hardships, but finally they reached this oasis, where a terrible accident befell George Curtis. On the day of their arrival, he was sitting by the stream, and Jim was extracting the honey from the nest of a stingless bee, which is to be found in the desert, on the top of the bank immediately above him. In so doing he loosed a great boulder of rock, which fell upon George Curtis' right leg, crushing it frightfully. From that day he had been so dreadfully lame, that he had found it impossible to go either forward or back, and had preferred to take the chances of dying on the oasis to the certainty of perishing in the desert.

As for food, however, they had got on pretty well, for they had a good supply of ammunition, and the oasis was frequented, especially at night, by large quantities of game, which came thither for water. These they shot, or trapped in pitfalls, using their flesh for food, and, after their clothes wore out, their hides for covering.

"And so," he ended, "we have lived for nearly two years, like a second Robinson Crusoe and his man Friday, hoping against hope that some natives might come here and help us away, but none have come. Only last night we settled that Jim should leave me, and try to reach Sitanda's Kraal and get assistance. He was to go to-morrow, but I had little hope of ever seeing him back again. And now *you*, of all people in the world, *you*, who I fancied had long ago forgotten all about me, and were living comfortably in old England, turn up in a promiscuous way and find me where you least expected. It is the most wonderful thing I ever heard of, and the most merciful too."

Then Sir Henry set to work and told him the main facts of our adventures, sitting till late into the night to do it.

"By Jove!" he said, when I showed him some of the diamonds; "well, at least you have got something for your pains, besides my worthless self."

Sir Henry laughed. "They belong to Quatermain and Good. It was part of the bargain that they should share any spoils there might be."

This remark set me thinking, and having spoken to Good I told Sir Henry that it was our unanimous wish that he should take a third share of the diamonds, or if he would not, that his share should be handed to his brother, who had suffered even more than ourselves on the chance of getting them. Finally, we prevailed upon him to consent to this arrangement, but George Curtis did not know of it till some time afterwards.

*   *   *   *   *

And here, at this point, I think I shall end this history. Our journey across the desert back to Sitanda's Kraal was most arduous, especially as we had to support George Curtis, whose right leg was very weak indeed, and continually throwing out splinters of bone; but we did accomplish it somehow, and to give its details would only be to reproduce much of what happened to us on the former occasion.

Six months from the date of our re-arrival at Sitanda's, where we found our guns and other goods quite safe, though the old scoundrel in charge was much disgusted at our surviving to claim them, saw us all once more safe and sound at my little place on the Berea, near Durban, where I am now writing, and whence I bid farewell to all who have accompanied me throughout the strangest trip I ever made in the course of a long and varied experience.

Just as I had written the last word, a Kafir came up my avenue of orange trees, with a letter in a cleft stick, which he had brought from the post. It turned out to be from Sir Henry, and as it speaks for itself I give it in full.

"Brayley Hall, Yorkshire

"MY DEAR QUATERMAIN,—

"I sent you a line a few mails back to say that the three of us, George, Good, and myself, fetched up all right in England. We got off the boat at Southampton, and went up to town You should have seen what a swell Good turned out the very next day, beautifully shaved, frock coat fitting like a glove, brand new eye-glass, &c &c. I went and walked in the park with him, where I met some people I know, and at once told them the story of his 'beautiful white legs.'

"He is furious, especially as some ill-natured person has printed it in a society paper.

"To come to business, Good and I took the diamonds to Streeter's to be valued, as we arranged, and I am really afraid to tell you what they put them at, it seems so enormous. They say that of course it is more or less guess-work, as such stones have never to their knowledge been put on the market in anything like such quantities It appears that they are (with the exception of one or two of the largest) of the finest water, and equal in every way to the best Brazilian stones. I asked them if they would buy them, but they said that it was beyond their power to do so, and recommended us to sell by degrees, for fear we should flood the market. They offer, however, a hundred and eighty thousand for a small portion of them.

"You must come home, Quatermain, and see about these things, especially if you insist upon making the magnificent present of the third share, which does *not* belong to me, to my brother George. As for Good, he is *no good*. His time is too much occupied in shaving, and other matters connected with the vain adorning of the body. But I think he is still down on his luck about Foulata. He told me that since he had been home he hadn't seen a woman to touch her, either as regards her figure or the sweetness of her expression.

"I want you to come home, my dear old comrade, and buy a place near here. You have done your day's work, and have lots of money now, and there is a place for sale quite close which would suit you admirably. Do come; the sooner the better; you can finish writing the story of our adventures on board ship. We have refused to tell the story till it is written by you, for fear that we shall not be believed If you start on receipt of this, you will reach here by Christmas, and I book you to stay with me for that. Good is coming, and George, and so, by the way, is your boy Harry (there's a bribe for you). I have had him down for a week's shooting, and like him. He is a cool young hand; he shot me in the leg, cut out the pellets, and then remarked upon the advantage of having a medical student in every shooting party.

"Good-bye, old boy; I can't say any more, but I know that you will come, if it is only to oblige

"Your sincere friend,
"HENRY CURTIS.

"*P.S.—The tusks of the great bull that killed poor Khiva have now been put up in the hall here, over the pair of buffalo horns you gave me, and look magnificent; and the axe with which I chopped off Twala's head is stuck up over my writing table. I wish we could have managed to bring away the coats of chain armour.*

"H.C."

To-day is Tuesday. There is a steamer going on Friday, and I really think I must take Curtis at his word, and sail by her for England, if it is only to see my boy Harry and see about the printing of this history, which is a task I do not like to trust to anybody else.

THE END.

Endnotes

Introduction

1. (p. 7) *Kukuanaland:* In his 1905 New Illustrated Edition of *King Solomon's Mines*, Haggard revealed that the fictitious Kukuanaland is based on Matabeleland, the southwestern part of today's Zimbabwe between the Zambezi and Limpopo Rivers, inhabited by the Ndebele people.
2. (p. 7) *Chaka:* Known as "Great Zulu Warrior" and "The Black Napoleon," the warrior king Chaka (1786–1828)—also known as Shaka Zulu built the Zulu tribe (of modern-day KwaZulu/Natal province) into a powerful nation skilled at hand-to-hand combat and united southern Africa's tribes against colonial rule. For more information, see Carolyn Hamilton, *Terrific Majesty: The Powers of Shaka Zulu and the Limits of Historical Invention* (Cambridge, MA: Harvard University Press, 1998).

Chapter 1

1. (p. 9) *the old Colony:* The Cape Colony was part of South Africa during the nineteenth-century British occupation. Originally founded in 1652 by the Dutch, the Cape Colony was taken over in 1806 by Britain, who ruled until it became known as the Cape Province after the Union of South Africa was formed in 1910.
2. (p. 9) *"Ingoldsby Legends":* Stories in prose and verse, many of them grotesque and humorous, by Canon Richard Harris Barham (1788–1845) were collected as *The Ingoldsby Legends* in 1840. Highly popular in Victorian times and after, *The Ingoldsby Legends* is now sadly out of print.
3. (p. 10) *Khiva's and Ventvögel's sad deaths:* Haggard named Khiva and Ventvögel in his novel in tribute to two of his real-life servants who were murdered in 1877.
4. (p. 11) *Bamangwato:* This region in present-day Botswana just north of South Africa (formerly the British protectorate of Bechuanaland) was established in 1780 by the Bamangwato tribe, which now calls itself the Bangwato.
5. (p. 11) *the Diamond Fields:* In 1869 diamonds were discovered in Barkley West, on the Vaal River in South Africa, a region that came to be known as the Diamond Fields. The city of Kimberly, which became the diamond

211

capital, quickly grew up. As recently as 1964, a new mine opened in the region.

6. (p. 13) *the tenth commandment:* Haggard mentions the biblical commandment (Exodus 20:17) against envy: "Thou shalt not covet thy neighbour's house, thou shalt not covet thy neighbour's wife, nor his manservant, nor his maidservant, nor his ox, nor his ass, nor any thing that is thy neighbour's" (King James Version; henceforth, KJV).

7. (p. 14) *Sir Garnet:* Viscount Garnet Joseph Wolseley (1833–1913) was the most renowned and successful soldier of the Victorian era. The librettist W. S. Gilbert is said to have used Wolseley as "the very model of a modern major-general" in Gilbert and Sullivan's *The Pirates of Penzance* (1879). See Halik Kochanski, *Sir Garnet Wolseley: Victorian Hero* (London: Hambledon Press, 1999).

8. (p. 14) *Madeira chair:* Wickerwork chair originally made on the island of Madeira, which lies some 350 miles from the African coast and was discovered by the Portuguese in 1418. Madeira wickerwork is made from a local willow-like bush, the *vime*, whose flexible branches are used in making chairs, tables, and baskets. Madeira wicker was widely exported beginning around 1850.

9. (p. 15) *Inyati:* This remote site in what today is Zimbabwe was in Haggard's time a station of the London Missionary Society, which attempted to convert the local peoples.

Chapter 2

1. (p. 18) *The Legend of Solomon's Mines:* Haggard here refers to the long-standing legend that the biblical King Solomon's gold was brought to him by the Queen of Sheba from the land of Ophir. In 2002 London-based Afghan travel writer Tahir Shah published *In Search of King Solomon's Mines* (London: John Murray), which suggests that Ophir was present-day Ethiopia. Shah's quixotic travel narrative is an entertaining, although quite different, elaboration on some of the same myths that preoccupied Haggard a century earlier.

2. (p. 18) *the Zambesi Falls:* The Zambesi (more often spelled Zambezi) River divides Zambia from Zimbabwe. Along the river are a series of waterfalls, including the majestic Victoria Falls, a tourist attraction long before 1904, when the Victoria Falls Hotel and Victoria Falls Railway Station, both still extant, were built to accommodate visitors. Haggard may have intended to

refer to these powerful falls, whose waters descend from a maximum height of 355 feet, at an average rate of 33,000 cubic feet per second.

3. (p. 19) *the Ophir of the Bible:* In the Bible's first book of Kings (1 Kings 9:28; 1 Kings 22:48; etc.), Ophir is the destination for which King Solomon's ships set out from the Gulf of Aqabah, to return with gold, gems, and other riches. Writers have claimed at various times that Ophir was really located in India, the Far East, Africa, and Arabia, and the debate continues.

4. (p. 19) *Mashukulumbwe country:* To the west of present-day Zimbabwe, the Mashukulumbwe tribe acquired their name, which means "underdogs," after a defeat in battle, according to Robert Baden-Powell's *African Adventures* (London: C. A. Pearson, 1937, chapter 11). The Suliman Mountains that Haggard mentions are fictitious.

5. (p. 19) *Manica country:* Manica is in the middle of present-day Mozambique, between the Zambezi and Luenha Rivers in the north and the Save River in the south. Near Manica, in the mountains near Zimbabwe, a gold rush attracted Europeans around 1900. Panning for gold continues today in local rivers.

6. (p. 20) *Delagoa Portugee:* This phrase refers to a member of the Portuguese community in Delagoa Bay, an inlet of the Indian Ocean on the east coast of southern Africa, at the northern limit of a series of lagoons lining the coast from Saint Lucia Bay in present-day Mozambique.

7. (p. 21) *Boer tobacco pouch:* The Western Australian Museum Archaeology Collection owns a Boer tobacco pouch made of woven fabric, originating from the Transvaal, South Africa (see http://museum.wa.gov.au/w099/10633.HTM). Pouches of more exotic material are also mentioned in other sources: In chapter 1 of Haggard's novel *Finished* (London: Ward, Lock, 1917), Allan Quatermain is offered a pouch for Boer tobacco "made of lion skin of unusually dark colour." Haggard offers his own translations for the local words *Swart-vet-pens* and *rimpi*.

8. (p. 24) *a Bechuana:* The Bechuana are a southern African Bantu people who in Haggard's time lived in Bechuanaland (present-day Botswana), as well as Basutoland (present-day Lesotho), the Orange River Colony, and the western and northern districts of the Transvaal. Today they are also known by other names, including Tswana, Batswana, and Botswana.

Chapter 3

1. (p. 27) *East London:* Located in South Africa's Eastern Cape province, East London is a scenic coastal city on the Indian Ocean with easy access to

beaches where dolphins and whales still abound. Nearby Eastern Beach has developed a tourist industry attracting surfers to sites like the Nahoon Reef.

2. (p. 28) *the English Mail:* Ships from Great Britain carrying mail were given the ship prefix RMS (Royal Mail Ship) and were operated by such firms as the Royal Mail Steam Packet Company (RMSP). Tourism to South Africa developed by the turn of the century.

3. (p. 28) *Berea:* The old historical area of Durban, known as Berea, is a large and bustling port. Durban, whose Zulu name is Tekweni, lies in the province of KwaZulu-Natal, the ancestral home of the Nguni people. Durban is named after Sir Benjamin D'Urban, the first colonial governor in the early nineteenth century.

4. (p. 31) *Sikukuni's:* Also spelled Secocoeni, Sikukuni was the name of a powerful native chief in the eastern Transvaal. The following extract is from chapter 1 of Haggard's *Cetywayo and His White Neighbours: or, Remarks on Recent Events in Zululand, Natal, and the Transvaal* (London: Trubner and Company, 1882):

> Secocoeni, the powerful chief of the Bapedi, one of the tribes whose territories border on the Transvaal, came to a difference with the Boers over another border question. There is good ground for supposing that Cetywayo incited him to withstand the Boer demands; it is certain that during the course of the war that followed he assisted him with advice, and more substantially still, with Zulu volunteers.
>
> To be brief, the Secocoeni war resulted in the discomfiture of the Transvaal forces. Another result of this struggle was to throw the whole state into the most utter confusion, of which the Dutch burghers, always glad of an opportunity to defy the law, took advantage to refuse to pay taxes. National bankruptcy ensued, and confusion grew worse confounded.
>
> Cetywayo took note of all this, and saw that now was his opportunity to attack. The Boers had suffered both in morale and prestige from their defeat by Secocoeni, who was still in arms against them; whilst the natives were proportionately elated by their success over the dreaded white men.

5. (p. 31) *Griqua:* The Griqua people of southern Africa, also known as the Cape Hottentot people, are indigenous to sub-Saharan Africa. Displaced over the years from their tribal land (today's Rooiberg and Luiperdskop), the Griqua have recently reacquired some of their land, and a Griqua Cultural Heritage Site is being planned. For more information, the Griqua National Conference may be reached by phone/fax in South Africa, +27 27 213 4848.

6. (p. 32) *bump of caution:* This is an ironic reference to the much-derided pseudo-science of phrenology, established by Viennese physician Franz Joseph Gall (1758–1828), to derive a subject's character based on the bumps on his or her head. According to phrenologists, bumps on the back of the head express such qualities as love of children, love of women, love of fame, pride, constancy of affection, and caution or cowardice.

7. (p. 34) *full choke both barrels:* Choke is a constriction at or near the muzzle of a shotgun barrel that affects the way shot is dispersed, a refinement developed by the nineteenth-century gun makers Fred Kimball in the United States and W. W. Greener in England. A hunting gun with two barrels permits two different loads of ammunition with two different chokes. The first barrel might have a more open choke, allowing for a wide pattern of shot dispersal during a first, close-range shot. The barrel fired afterward can be full-choked, for a tighter, longer-range pattern to hit the prey as it tries to escape. A gun that is full-choked both barrels may be intended for two long-distance shots, perhaps at turkeys or other flying birds.

8. (p. 35) *that unlucky Zulu War:* The 1879 Zulu War (also called the Anglo-Zulu War) was fought between the Zulu nation, under their king Cetshwayo (also spelled Cetywayo and Cetewayo; c.1826–1884), and the British army. In 1877 the Transvaal became part of the British Empire, and the British became involved in a longstanding struggle between the Zulus and the Boers. In 1878 Sir Henry Bartle Frere, British commissioner for South Africa, used a minor border incident to demand that Cetywayo disband his army, which Cetywayo refused to do. In January 1879 British troops invaded Zululand, where Lord Frederic Chelmsford's forces were defeated at the battle of Isandlwana. Further bloody battles ensued in the following months, until Cetywayo was captured by the British on August 28 and exiled to London. The Zulu War officially ended on September 1, 1879, and the victorious British divided Zululand among thirteen chiefs, which led to further conflicts.

9. (p. 35) *Lukanga River:* This vast wetland with swamp, open water, and seasonally flooded plains in Zambia is more commonly referred to as the Lukanga Swamp. It usually drains into the Kafue River, although on occasion the Kafue drains into the Lukanga system.

10. (p. 36) *moocha:* In his *Smith and the Pharaohs, and Other Tales* (Bristol: J. W. Arrowsmith, 1920; chapter 12), Haggard defines a *moocha* as a "waist-belt of catskins" worn by tribesmen. In his novel *Heu-Heu; or, The Monster* (London: Hutchinson, 1924; chapter 2) Haggard also describes a *moocha* as a hide "tied round [the stomach] by the leg skins, which hide seemed to have been dressed."

Chapter 4

1. (p. 38) *Lobengula:* Lobengula (c.1833–1894) was king of Matabeleland (in present-day Zimbabwe). He resisted unsuccessfully against European colonizers after he sold the mineral rights for his land and the British South Africa Company began extensive mining.

2. (p. 38) *the poisonous herb called "tulip":* The one-leaved Cape tulip (*Homeria flaccida*) and the two-leaved Cape tulip (*Homeria miniata*), members of the iris family (Iridaceae), are toxic weeds native to southern Africa. To the untutored eye they may be confused with lilies, but all parts of the Cape tulip are poisonous to livestock and humans. They cause heart and kidney failure, among other symptoms. Biosecurity technicians are particularly vigilant in preventing their growth.

3. (p. 40) *tambouki grass:* This plant (*Andropogon gayanus*), also called tambuki grass and gamba grass, is a dense grass found in tropical Africa that favors monsoonal climates and is used for cattle grazing and hay. It is described as "tall and resinous tambouki grass" in Haggard's short story "Hunter Quatermain's Story," reprinted in *Hunter Quatermain's Story: The Uncollected Adventures of Allan Quatermain* (London: Peter Owen, 2003).

4. (p. 41) *daccha:* This substance is also called *dagga,* the Dutch term for *Cannabis sativa* (marijuana), a common intoxicant in Africa by the time British colonists arrived. Use of cannabis or *dagga* was considered by Europeans to demoralize the native manual laborers. In 1870 a law was passed in South Africa prohibiting the "smoking, use, or possession by the sale, barter, or gift" of marijuana on the part of any "coolies." The law had little effect, and in 1887 an investigative committee, the Wragg Commission, discovered that native workers were still using cannabis. See Ernest L.

Abel, *Marihuana: The First Twelve Thousand Years* (New York: Plenum Press, 1980).

5. (p. 44) *I gave mine its quietus:* That is, I killed it. This line is likely a reference to Hamlet's "To be or not to be" soliloquy: "When he himself might his quietus make with a bare bodkin" (Shakespeare, *Hamlet*, act 3, scene 1).

6. (p. 44) *the Prince Imperial:* Napoléon Eugene Louis Jean Joseph (1856–1879) the prince imperial of France, the only son of the late Emperor Napoleon III, was among those killed in the British army's abortive invasion of Zululand in 1879 (see endnote 8, chapter 3). After studying at the Royal Military Academy at Woolwich, U.K., the Prince Imperial went to Africa with the permission of Queen Victoria to pursue his military and political ambitions. See Donald Featherstone, *Captain Carey's Blunder: The Death of the Prince Imperial, June 1879* (London: Leo Cooper, 1973).

Chapter 5

1. (p. 47) *ant-bear:* The aardvark (*Orycteropus afer*), also called the earth pig or the ant bear, is found throughout Africa. It feeds on termites by night and sleeps in burrows by day. It digs its own holes for shelter and also takes over termite nests. In one of these, Quatermain and his fellow travelers buried the remains of Khiva.

2. (p. 47) *karoo shrub:* In South Africa's Western Cape province, the Great Karoo is a majestic arid zone, the largest plateau of its kind outside Asia. Its name is derived from the Khoi word *karusa*, meaning dry and barren. The region has a rich variety of shrubs and succulent plants (plants with thick, fleshy, water-storing leaves, like cacti).

3. (p. 54) *"Girl I left behind me":* A time-honored soldier's marching song that originated around the year 1800. Its last verse reads:

> My mind her image still retains,
> Whether asleep or waking;
> I hope to see my dear again,
> For her my heart is breaking:
> But if e'er I chance to go that way,
> And that she has not resign'd me;
> I'll reconcile my mind and stay,
> With the girl I left behind me.

Chapter 30 of William Makepeace Thackeray's novel *Vanity Fair* (1847–1848) is entitled "The Girl I Left Behind Me." Thackeray wrote: "So it is in the world. Jack or Donald marches away to glory with his knapsack on his shoulder, stepping out briskly to the tune of 'The Girl I left Behind Me.' It is she who remains and suffers,—and has the leisure to think, and brood, and remember."

4. (p. 55) *quagga:* This subspecies of plains zebra (*Equus quagga*) of interior regions of southern Africa was hunted to extinction. The last extant quagga mare died at the Amsterdam Zoo on August 12, 1883. The quagga was yellowish-brown with stripes on its head and neck. A selective breeding program, the Quagga Project, began in 1987 to retrieve quagga genes in order to produce a quagga comparable to those preserved in museums. For more information, see www.museums.org.za/sam/quagga/quagga.htm.

5. (p. 56) *they came, "not as single spies, but in battalions":* This is a reference not to the Old Testament but to Shakespeare's *Hamlet* (act 4, scene 5): "When sorrows come, they come not single spies, but in battalions." The misattribution is one of Haggard's jokes about Quatermain's limited grasp of literature; his knowledge was restricted to the Bible and *The Ingoldsby Legends.*

6. (p. 57) *The Black Hole of Calcutta:* "Black hole" was the common name for a military detention cell until the nineteenth century. In 1756 Siraj-ud-Dawlah, the nawab of Bengal, occupied Fort William in Calcutta and imprisoned British soldiers in a small, airless space. Many died by the following day, providing effective anti-Indian propaganda for the British. The exact number of dead is still debated by historians.

Chapter 6

1. (p. 59) *Jackdaw of Rheims:* In this verse chapter from *The Ingoldsby Legends,* by Canon Richard Harris Barham (1788–1845), a cardinal's ring disappears. The cardinal curses the thief, and the rundown appearance of the jackdaw—a crow-like bird—identifies him as the culprit.

2. (p. 60) *Springbok spoor:* The springbok (*Antidorcas marsupialis*) is a southern African gazelle noted for its leaps. Spoor is the trail of a wild animal.

3. (p. 61) *the world-famed one at Cape Town:* Haggard compares the fictitious mountains of Sheba's breasts to Cape Town's well-known landmark Table Mountain. At 3,563 feet above sea level and made of sandstone, Table Mountain offers magnificent views and has inspired a variety of local legends.

4. (p. 62) *biltong:* The name of this southern African dried meat specialty, made from ostrich or other game, comes from the Dutch *bil,* meaning "rump," and *tong,* meaning "strip."

5. (p. 63) *the Island of Ascension:* Ascension Island, in the south Atlantic Ocean, is covered with jagged lumps of black volcanic clinker.

6. (p. 64) *like Nebuchadnezzar:* Nebuchadnezzar was a Babylonian king who, according to the biblical book of Daniel (4:33) "was driven from men, and did eat grass as oxen, and his body was wet with the dew of heaven, till his hairs were grown like eagles' feathers, and his nails like birds' claws" (KJV). This was in punishment for his prideful self-sufficiency and rejection of the Almighty's authority.

Chapter 7

1. (p. 73) *champaign country:* From the Old French word *champaigne* (or in modern French, *campagne*), this phrase denotes flat, open country, as John Milton described in the third book of *Paradise Regained*: "Fair champaign, with less rivers interveined."

2. (p. 75) *the great road over the St. Gothard in Switzerland:* The Saint Gothard Pass in the Alps joins Switzerland and Italy, and provides many picturesque views. Travel across the pass was difficult during snowy winter months until 1882, when the Saint Gothard railway tunnel was constructed.

3. (p. 82) *the Bayéte of the Zulus: Bayete Nkosi* was the greeting ("We greet you! Hail!") used by the Zulu nation to address their mighty leader King Chaka (see note 2 to the Introduction). Today a company in Cape Town, South Africa, Bayete Products (see www.bayetefootwear.co.za) sells Bayete sandals, thongs, and handbags. Other companies in South Africa's hospitality industry use the word, like Bayete Zulu Safaris (www.bayetezulusafaris.ix.co.za) and the Bayete Bed & Breakfast in Durban (www.savenues.com/kznlbayete.htm).

Chapter 8

1. (p. 84) *civil war:* A series of civil wars mark the history of the Zulus. In the Zulu Civil War of 1840, the Zulu leader Dingane was defeated by his brother Mpande. The Zulu Civil War of 1856 pitted two brothers, Cetshwayo and Mbulazi, in a battle over succession rights; Cetshwayo vanquished and executed his brother. See Jeff Guy, *The Destruction of the Zulu Kingdom: Civil War in Zululand, 1879–1884*, (London: Longman, 1979);

also Ian Knight, *The Anatomy of the Zulu Army: From Shaka to Cetshwayo, 1818–1879* (London: Greenhill Books, 1995).

2. (p. 87) *Sakabwla:* This is probably a misprint for Sakabula, the Zulu name for the long-tailed widow bird (*Euplectes progne*). Sakabula means "show-off'; the birds' 20-inch red and yellow tail feathers are strikingly deployed to attract female birds. Zulu soldiers tied ostrich, blue crane, and sakabula feathers to their headdresses to add height and make themselves more terrifying to enemies.

Chapter 9

1. (p. 93) *Unlimited Loo:* Loo, a game for five or more players, became popular in England starting in the seventeenth century. There were two forms. In the quiet domestic game called Limited Loo, the money added to the pool was a modest and fixed amount; Limited Loo is mentioned in some Jane Austen novels, including *Pride and Prejudice.* In Unlimited Loo, the amount of the pool can increase rapidly, leading to great wins and great losses in a short time. It may have been this version of the game that Alexander Pope cited in his poem "The Rape of the Lock" (1712) (canto 3): "Ev'n mighty Pam [the Jack], that Kings and Queens o'erthrew / And mow'd down armies in the fights of Lu."

2. (p. 95) *a splendid tiger-skin karross:* In southern Africa, a *karross* (or *kaross*) is a sleeveless cloak made of sheepskin or other animal hide, with the hair left on. *Karross* is also used to describe leopard-skin cloaks worn by tribal chiefs. The etymology of the word is uncertain; it may be related to the Dutch word *kuras* or the English *cuirass* (a protective breastplate).

Chapter 10

1. (p. 103) *the Amazulu:* The original name for the Zulu people, *amaZulu* means "the people of heaven."

2. (p. 108) *kerries:* More often spelled *kierie,* this Afrikaans word describes a club used in battle. Along with spear, bow, and arrows, the kierie was part of Zulu tribal regalia. A knobkerrie—in Afrikaans *knopkierie*—joined *knop* ("knob") to *kierie* ("club") to describe a shorter, knobbed club made of wood; Zulu warriors battered enemies with these clubs at close range or, if farther away, threw them.

3. (p. 110) *a black Madame Defarge:* A character in Charles Dickens's *A Tale of Two Cities* (1859), Madame Defarge sits knitting in her wine shop, con-

sumed with hatred for the French aristocracy, upon whom she wreaks vengeance.

Chapter 11

1. (p. 122) *Arthur's appeal to the ruffians:* In act 4, scene 1 of Shakespeare's *King John*, the title character conspires with a chamberlain to murder a young prince and sends two ruffians to burn out the boy's eyes with red-hot irons. Prince Arthur pleads persuasively, and they do not blind him: "Will you put out mine eyes? / These eyes that never did nor never shall / So much as frown on you." Charles Dickens, in chapter 14 of *A Child's History of England* (1851–1853), also addressed the subject:

> Then, the King took secret counsel with the worst of his nobles how the Prince was to be got rid of. Some said, 'Put out his eyes and keep him in prison.' . . . King John, feeling that in any case, whatever was done afterwards, it would be a satisfaction to his mind to have those handsome eyes burnt out that had looked at him so proudly while his own royal eyes were blinking at the stone floor, sent certain ruffians to Falaise to blind the boy with red-hot irons. But Arthur so pathetically entreated them, and shed such piteous tears, and so appealed to HUBERT DE BOURG (or BURGH), the warden of the castle, who had a love for him, and was an honourable, tender man, that Hubert could not bear it. To his eternal honour he prevented the torture from being performed, and, at his own risk, sent the savages away.

Chapter 12

1. (p. 128) *"Dilly, Dilly, come and be killed":* The British nursery song "Oh, what have you got for dinner, Mrs. Bond?" contains the lines:

> There's beef in the larder, and ducks in the pond;
> Dilly, dilly, dilly, dilly, come to be killed,
> For you must be stuffed and my customers filled!

Dylan Thomas memorably used this old song in his "play for voices" *Under Milk Wood* (1954), in which a loft hawk calls, "dilly dilly, come and be killed." C. S. Lewis, near the end of his essay "On Obstinacy in Belief," (reprinted in *The World's Last Night, and Other Essays*, New York: Harcourt, 1960) points out the flaws in ungrounded faith: "The ducks who come to the call 'Dilly, dilly, come and be killed' have confidence in the farmer's wife."

Chapter 13

1. (p. 135) *gatling:* In 1862, inspired by the American Civil War, the North Carolina-born gun maker Richard Jordan Gatling (1818–1903) patented a mechanical gun with multiple barrels on a revolving frame that could fire hundreds of rounds per minute. By 1882 a newer model could fire up to 1,200 rounds per minute. The Gatling gun plays a role in Mark Twain's *A Connecticut Yankee in King Arthur's Court* (1889), in which the narrator Hank Morgan invents his own Gatling gun, which shoots out money.

Chapter 14

1. (p. 145) *the three Romans:* The allusion is to legendary heroes of ancient Rome. According to the historian Livy, Horatius Cocles ("Horatio the one-eyed") and two companions defended the Sublician bridge against an army of Etruscans led by Lars Porsena, while the Roman army hastily destroyed the bridge. Having succeeded, Horatius jumped into the River Tiber and swam to shore safely: *Tum Cocles Tiberine pater inquit te sancte precor haec arma et hunc militem propitio flumine accipias* ("Then Cocles shouted, 'Father Tiber, I respectfully beg you to receive these arms and this soldier in a benevolent flood'") (Livy, *History of Rome*, 2:10). Thomas Macaulay, in his *Lays of Ancient Rome* (1842), translated the same words in quatrain form, in stanza 59 of "Horatius: A Lay Made about the Year of the City CCCLX":

> "Oh, Tiber! father Tiber!
> To whom the Romans pray,
> A Roman's life, a Roman's arms,
> Take thou in charge this day!"

2. (p. 149) *as I think the "Ingoldsby Legends" beautifully puts it:* In fact, the lines are from canto 6, stanza 34 of the long poem *Marmion: A Tale of Flodden Field* (1808), by Sir Walter Scott:

> The stubborn spearmen still made good
> Their dark impenetrable wood,
> Each stepping where his comrade stood,
> The instant that he fell.

The historical battle of Flodden (1513), which pitted Scotland against England, was won by England with heavy losses on both sides. The same canto of Scott's work contains the famous lines: "O, what a tangled web we weave, / When first we practise to deceive! (*Marmion*, canto 6, stanza 17). Once again Quatermain refers to his favorite "Ingoldsby Legends" (see note 2 for chapter 1).

3. (p. 152) *"fallen from his high estate"*: The quotation is from the poem "Alexander's Feast," by British poet John Dryden (1631–1700), describing King Darius defeated by Alexander the Great and forsaken by his people:

> Fallen, fallen, fallen, fallen,
> Fallen from his high estate,
> And welt'ring in his blood;
> Deserted, at his utmost need,
> By those his former bounty fed;
> On the bare earth expos'd he lies,
> With not a friend to close his eyes (lines 77–83).

Chapter 15

1. (p. 160) *"Of farewells to the dying / And mournings for the dead"*: From the poem "Resignation," by American poet Henry Wadsworth Longfellow (1807–1882). The entire quatrain reads:

> The air is full of farewells to the dying,
> And mournings for the dead;
> The heart of Rachel, for her children crying,
> Will not be comforted! (lines 5–8).

The reference to Rachel is taken from the biblical book of Jeremiah, in which Rachel mourns for her children (Jeremiah 31:15). This indirect biblical allusion fits Haggard's characterization of Quatermain as knowing only two books, the Bible and *The Ingoldsby Legends* (see note 2 for chapter 1).

Chapter 16

1. (p. 174) *"Lead on, Macduff"*: This is a common misquotation of "Lay on, Macduff," from the last scene of Shakespeare's *Macbeth*, when Macbeth and his enemy Macduff are fighting. Macduff gives Macbeth a chance to

surrender, but Macbeth refuses: "Lay on, Macduff, / And damned be him that first cries, 'Hold, enough!'" (act 5, scene 8). "Lay on" meant to attack.

2. (p. 176) *Hamilton Tighe:* From "The Legend of Hamilton Tighe" in *The Ingoldsby Legends* (see note 2 for chapter 1). Tighe was a murdered sailor whose ghost appeared, holding his head in his lap, much to the dismay of his killer, a sailor named Hairy-faced Dick (who "hath a swarthy hue, / Between a gingerbread-nut and a Jew").

Chapter 17

1. (p. 182) *great throne of ivory:* King Solomon's ornate throne is described in the Old Testament (1 Kings 10:18–20 and 2 Chronicles 9:17–20).

2. (p. 182) *Martini-Henry ammunition boxes:* Martini-Henry breech-loading rifles were used by British soldiers in many Victorian wars and are now avidly collected and reproduced (see www.martinihenry.com and *www.users.bigpond.com/digger18/main.htm*). Also see Dennis Lewis's book *Martini-Henry .450 Rifles & Carbines* (Latham, NY: Excalibur, 1996).

3. (p. 183) *Monte Christo:* This is the anglicized spelling of the protagonist's name in Alexandre Dumas's popular novel *The Count of Monte Cristo* (1844), in which Edmond Dantès, unjustly imprisoned, is told of treasure left on the Island of Monte Cristo. Dantès eventually escapes prison, locates the treasure, takes the title count of Monte Cristo, and buys a house in the wealthy Paris suburb of Auteuil. From there he focuses on taking revenge against his past abusers.

Chapter 18

1. (p. 188) *a fleet of ironclads:* In 1822 French general Henri J. Paixhans suggested that the French navy build ironclad ships. In 1859 France launched the first ironclad warship, *Gloire*. Ironclad warships became more visible during the American Civil War, when in 1862 the battle of Hampton Roads between USS *Monitor* and CSS *Virginia* was the first-ever between ironclad vessels. In terms of cost, according to the Web site of the Vicksburg National Military Park (www.nps.gov/vick/visctr/sitebltn/age_iron.htm) the ironclad USS *Cairo* commissioned in 1862, cost $101,000 to build. The *Monitor*, also commissioned in 1862, cost $195,000. The "fleet of ironclads" Quatermain mentions could thus easily have cost more than a million dollars in nineteenth-century currency.

2. (p. 193) *that hope deferred which maketh the heart sick:* From the Old Testament book of Proverbs 13:12: "Hope deferred maketh the heart sick: but

when the desire cometh, it is a tree of life" (KJV). In this context "hope deferred" refers to the continuing suspense and difficulties experienced by Quatermain and his friends. The implicit mention of the biblical tree of life from the book of Genesis suggests a lost Eden, like Africa itself.

3. (p. 194) *African Styx:* In Greek mythology, the Styx River surrounded Hades (Hell); it is mentioned in Homer's *Iliad* and *Odyssey* and much later literature. Haggard's metaphor of an African Styx is complex, since the river in question will return Quatermain and crew to modern urban civilization, rather than to Hell. However, in the ethos of many Victorian travelers, there are many similarities between the two places.

Chapter 19

1. (p. 198) *"Open Sesame":* The phrase is the password that opens a cave of treasures in the story of "Ali Baba and the Forty Thieves" from *The Thousand and One Nights.* Haggard would have known *The Arabian Nights' Entertainments* (the work's alternate name) in the celebrated Victorian translation (1885–1888) by Sir Richard Burton. In the story, Ali Baba's brother Kasim forgets the magic words and tries "Open, Barley!" without success, followed by "the names of all manner of grains save sesame." According to one etymology, the term "Open, Sesame" is inspired by the way sesame seeds pop open easily when ripe.

2. (p. 203) *wandered out like Hagar into the desert:* In the Old Testament book of Genesis 16:1–16, Hagar is the Egyptian maid of Sarah, the prophet Abraham's wife. Sarah is sterile and arranges for Hagar to bear her husband a son, Ishmael. Hagar and Ishmael are sent into the wilderness, where they are protected by God. Mention of this biblical story of redemption after wanderings seems fitting near the end of the adventures described in *King Solomon's Mines.*

Inspired by King Solomon's Mines

Lost World and Lost Race Literature

Not only was *King Solomon's Mines* (1885) a popular success upon its initial publication in England; it also helped inspire a new genre of writing. Along with its sequel *Allan Quatermain* (1887) and the mythical *She: A History of Adventure* (1887), *King Solomon's Mines* inaugurated the flowering of what are known as Lost World and Lost Race novels. Haggard himself wrote fourteen Quatermain novels and forty-five other books before his death in 1925.

Lost World and Lost Race novels depict Europeans in conflict with foreign people and unknown, dangerous environments. Nineteenth-century British imperialism whetted the reading public's appetite for these books, creating curiosity about the exotic nations their country was colonizing. Vividly written accounts set in Africa, India, and other lands real and imagined, Lost World and Lost Race novels range from high-minded critiques of British imperialism to swashbuckling tales. They continue to be read today.

In Haggard's *Nada the Lily* (1892), the Zulu hero Umslopogaas lives with a wolf pack. Rudyard Kipling said that this book inspired his two *Jungle Books* (1894, 1895), which Kipling set in the wilds of India, where he was born. Brought together by a shared interest in the legacy of colonialism, Kipling and Haggard became good friends. Kipling helped Haggard brainstorm plots for *When the World Shook* (1919) and the posthumously published *Allan and the Ice-Gods* (1927).

Many Lost World and Lost Race novels are simple adventure stories, but a handful wrestle with the ethical implications of Britain's exploitation of the native people in the countries it occupied. H. G. Wells turned the tables on British imperialists in *The War of the Worlds* (1898), which portrays Earth as the victim of uninvited colonization by hostile aliens from Mars. In his novella *Heart of Darkness* (1902), Joseph Conrad told the story of the sailor Marlow, who made a harrowing journey up the Congo River; Marlow describes in exacting detail the savagery and squalor perpetrated by white explorers who, like Quatermain, try to profit from Africa's natural riches. In _Nostromo_ (1904), Conrad again depicted the corruption and destruction brought by colonialism; the title character is charged with, and eventually loses his life, protecting the bounty of an Englishman's silver mines.

Even the creator of Sherlock Holmes was influenced by the craze for Lost World and Lost Race fiction. Sir Arthur Conan Doyle set his _The Lost World_ (1912), the first of his five Professor Challenger stories, on a volcanic plateau. In a hidden Amazon rainforest, George E. Challenger's expedition uncovers the ultimate lost race—dinosaurs—and soon the creatures threaten his life. Writing about Challenger, Doyle's second most famous creation, provided the author with a much-needed break from writing the Holmes mysteries.

In America, Edgar Rice Burroughs successfully perpetuated the Haggard legacy with _Tarzan of the Apes_ (1914), the story of a British nobleman orphaned in Africa and raised by wild animals. The plot is reminiscent of Haggard's work as well as of Kipling's _Jungle Books_. In _Return of Tarzan_ (1915), the hero grows tired of the civilized city life to which he has been restored, just as Haggard's hero does in later installments of the Quatermain saga. Tarzan appears in more than twenty sequels, several of which describe his encounter with the fabled lost city of Opar. In a second adventure series that employs many conventions of the Lost World genre, Burroughs's character John Carter travels to Mars and throughout outer space.

Science-fiction author Michael Crichton could be called the H. Rider Haggard of today. His _Congo_ (1980) is a Victorian adventure novel in the style of _King Solomon's Mines_. In the opening pages, a group of eight explorers searching for the lost city of Zinj are slaughtered by an unknown menace. Crichton traces the journey of the recovery team, who uncover hidden diamonds, angry natives, and unnamable horrors.

Author Alan Moore, another fan of adventure yarns, borrows Haggard's hero Allan Quatermain, as well as characters from Bram Stoker's _Dracula_, H. G. Wells's _The Invisible Man_, Jules Verne's _Twenty Thousand Leagues under the Sea_, and other best-sellers of the nineteenth century for his graphic two-volume novel set in the Victorian era, _The League of Extraordinary Gentlemen_ (2000). Quatermain is the leader of a group that tries to stop a villain from firebombing the East End of London. In the end, the villain turns out to be none other than Professor Moriarty—Sherlock Holmes's nemesis. In the second volume, Moore has Burroughs's Mars expert John Carter assist his other heroes in an interplanetary conflict straight out of Wells's *The War of the Worlds*.

In 2003 London-based travel writer Tahir Shah, an ethnic Afghan, published the entertaining true story of his search for treasure in Africa, In *Search of King Solomon's Mines*. Armed with a map bought at a flea market in Jerusalem, Shah hires a superstitious Ethiopian cabdriver as his guide through the capital city of Addis Ababa and its rural surroundings. The resulting rollicking travelogue, a humorous version of Haggard's adventure tales, provides an interesting rendition of Ethiopian history.

Haggard's Sequels to King Solomon's Mines

Allan Quatermain—the first and what some believe to be the best sequel to *King Solomon's Mines*—finds its hero mourning the loss of his son Harry. Weary of effete, civilized Britain, Quatermain returns to Africa to get in touch with his primitive self. Accompanied by Sir Henry Curtis, Captain John Good, and the Zulu guide Umslopogaas, Quatermain searches for a mythical race of white Africans. A civil war erupts when the adventurers discover the civilization of Zu-Vendis and its two queens both fall in love with Curtis. After the war Quatermain discovers that an assassin has been dispatched to murder the winning monarch. Adventure ensues as Quatermain rushes across the country to save her.

Over the next forty years, Haggard continued to write sequels to *King Solomon's Mines*, which include *Maiwa's Revenge* (1888), *Allan's Wife* (1889), *Marie* (1912), *Child of Storm* (1913), *The Holy Flower* (1915), *The Ivory Child* (1916), *Finished* (1916), *The Ancient Allan* (1920), *She and Allan* (1921), *Heu-Heu; or, The Monster* (1924), *The Treasure of the Lake* (1926), and *Allan and the Ice-Gods* (1927).

She: A History of Adventure

Haggard's fantasy-adventure *She* has left an impact on literature equal to that of his Quatermain saga. Psychologist Carl Jung considered the title character—also known as Ayesha or "She-Who-Must-Be-Obeyed"—an archetype of woman that exists in the subconscious of all men. Immortal and all-powerful, Ayesha is also fickle and unforgiving.

The search for inner Africa as described by Haggard fascinated Jung and his mentor Sigmund Freud. *She* was one of Jung's favorite books, and he wrote about it throughout his career. In his *Interpretation of Dreams* (1899), Freud calls *She* "a strange work, but full of hidden meaning." Freud found Haggard's novel therapeutic enough to recommend it to a patient, as he recounts in *Interpretation.*

She and its three sequels sold almost as well as *King Solomon's Mines* and were equally important in the development of Lost World and Lost Race novels. Many authors of fantasy novels took cues from Haggard's creations, including C. S. Lewis, who wrote "The Mythopoeic Gift of Rider Haggard," an article addressing the author's myth-making ability. Lewis's *The Chronicles of Narnia* series (1950–1956) draws noticeably on the tales of Haggard, as does *The Lord of the Rings* (1954–1956), by Lewis's friend J. R. R. Tolkien.

Hundreds of writers have imitated Haggard over the years, but only French author Pierre Benoit has been openly criticized for thematic similarities. Benoit sued reviewer Henry Magden when the latter claimed that the subterranean Queen Antinea from Benoit's book *L'Atlantide* (1919) too closely resembled the title character of *She.* Benoit lost the case, although it was never proven that he had even read *She* before writing *L'Atlantide*, whose ruthless Antinea labels and preserves her dead lovers in a mysterious metal from Atlantis. *L'Atlantide*, which was translated into more than fifteen languages, became a classic in its own right and won the Grand Prize of the French Academy.

Film

More than thirty films have been made from the works of H. Rider Haggard, including six versions of *King Solomon's Mines*, two of *Allan Quatermain*, and twelve of *She.* The 1937 *King Solomon's Mines*, directed by Robert Stevenson, cast African-American screen and theater legend Paul Robeson as Umbopo. The special effects, especially the bubbling lava, are impressive for this early film, which also includes excellent fight scenes. As with most film adaptations of the book, this version also inserts a white female love interest. Sir

Cedric Hardwicke plays Allan Quatermain, Robert Adams is King Twala, and John Loder portrays Sir Henry Curtis.

A 1950 remake of *King Solomon's Mines* by MGM, directed by Compton Bennett and Andrew Morton, is the first color adaptation of Haggard's novel. Stewart Granger and Deborah Kerr play Quatermain and Elizabeth Curtis, a wealthy Englishwoman whose husband has disappeared while searching for African diamond mines. The film earned three Oscar nominations and won two awards, including Best Cinematography. More recently, *King Solomon's Mines* (2004) was revised as a television miniseries starring Patrick Swayze and Alison Doody.

The best-known films inspired by *King Solomon's Mines* are those of the Indiana Jones trilogy, co-written by George Lucas and directed by Steven Spielberg. Allan Quatermain is clearly the prototype for Harrison Ford's Indiana Jones, the swaggering, khaki-clad explorer in the broad-brim hat. The first film, *Raiders of the Lost Ark* (1981), introduces Indy, a professor and archaeologist who leaves the university to try to prevent the Nazis from obtaining the Ark of the Covenant, an ancient artifact that would allow the Nazis to raise an invincible army. Several tricks seem cribbed from the 1950 version of *King Solomon's Mines*, including the use of a falling boulder to block the mouth of a cave. The movie then cycles through multiple action-adventure situations: booby traps, snake pits, duels, chase scenes, and explosions. *Raiders of the Lost Ark* won four Academy Awards and sparked two less successful adaptations of Haggard's work, a 1985 version of *King Solomon's Mines* and *Allan Quatermain and the Lost City of Gold* (1987), both starring Richard Chamberlain and Sharon Stone.

Indiana Jones and the Temple of Doom (1984) has an occult twist, with many scenes that seem inspired by a 1935 film version of *She*. Kate Capshaw plays Willie, the love interest who constantly bickers with Indy. Jonathan Ke Quan plays Short Round, Indy's tiny Asian sidekick who accompanies Indy as he attempts to wrest five mystical gems from the underground caves of the Kali-worshiping Thuggee cult. Gruesome incidents abound, including a feast of monkey brains and a priest ripping the heart out of a living human sacrifice.

Sean Connery—who is Allan Quatermain in the 2003 film version of *The League of Extraordinary Gentlemen*—plays Indy's father,

Henry Jones, in *Indiana Jones and the Last Crusade* (1989), a prequel to the first two Indiana Jones films. Kidnappers abduct the elder Jones, a medievalist who knows the location of the Holy Grail, the cup used by Jesus at the Last Supper that is purported to grant eternal life. Indy embarks on a search for both his father and the Holy Grail, encountering tanks, zeppelins, and biplanes along the way. The film's opening sequence—featuring a twelve-year-old Indiana Jones, played by River Phoenix—reveals the origins of the scar on Indy's chin, his signature hat, and his fear of snakes.

Comments & Questions

In this section, we aim to provide the reader with an array of perspectives on the text, as well as questions that challenge those perspectives. The commentary has been culled from sources as diverse as reviews contemporaneous with the work, letters written by the author, literary criticism of later generations, and appreciations written throughout the work's history. Following the commentary, a series of questions seeks to filter H. Rider Haggard's King Solomon's Mines *through a variety of points of view and bring about a richer understanding of this enduring work.*

Comments

THE SPECTATOR

There can be no doubt that it is more difficult for the novelist of to-day to write a fresh and novel book of adventure than it was for his predecessors. The possible combinations of human life are in theory infinite, but the practical and probable are limited. Mr. Haggard's main idea is one of these; for treasures have doubtless often been buried, and sometimes been found. But it is not novel. It has been used before, and pretty frequently; and used, too, in something of the same way that Mr. Haggard uses it. The frontispiece, with its mysterious markings, which is, we are told, the map of the way which a discoverer must travel, reminds us at once of the paper by which, in the "Gold-Bug" of Poe, the whereabouts of the buccaneer's buried store of gold is identified. But Mr. Haggard's invention is not at fault, and enables him to invest the central incident of his story with a certain weird originality which takes away all idea from the reader that he has been reading the same things before. It was a happy thought, in the first place, to make the treasure King Solomon's. That is a name to conjure with as well in the West as in the East; and though we do not remember that diamonds figure in the Scripture catalogue of that potentate's wealth, we are ready to believe that his treasury was rich beyond the dreams of avarice. It may even be said that the Scriptural associations of the name give a certain verisimilitude to the story, something in the same way in

233

which the sailor's introduction of Pharaoh's chariot-wheels did to his yarn about the Red Sea. But there is more than this. It is an absolute stroke of genius when, in the ice-cavern, the discoverers find frozen into permanence the actual form of the old Portuguese adventurer of three hundred years before, and can even trace—so unchanged is the figure—the very wound in his arm from which he drew the blood wherewith he was to trace the map that was to guide some more fortunate adventurer. We felt when we reached that point that we were in the hands of a story-teller of no common powers; nor did the rest of the narrative, so skilfully and so high is the interest piled up, at all disappoint our expectations. The descriptions of battles do not easily admit of striking variations; yet no one will hesitate to allow this merit to the great fight between King Twala and King Ignosi, with the forlorn-hope of the Greys, who go into battle two thousand strong and come out with sixty, and the truly Homeric duel between King Twala and Sir Henry Curtis. It reeks, perhaps, a little too much of blood, but it is as effective a piece of writing as we have seen for a long time. The final scene in the cave, too, is very thrilling, the apparent hopelessness of the situation and the final escape being equally well managed.

—November 7, 1885

THE NATION

'King Solomon's Mines' is a capital boy's books, to which the purely fabulous foundation is no drawback. The marvellous adventures of Captain Good and his friends in the land that lay beyond the "Suliman Mountains" appeal, through devices familiar and novel, to the healthy boy's ardor for fighting savages and coming off victorious, with the spoils of Golconda to boot.

—February 4, 1886

FORTNIGHTLY REVIEW

Mr. Haggard, in dedicating his novel of Allan Quatermain to his son, expresses the hope that he and other boys may find in it something that will help them to "attain to the state and dignity of English gentlemen." That there is anything in the temper and tendency of Mr. Haggard's books positively inimical to the pursuit of such an ideal we do not go so far as roundly to assert. . . .

We may observe that the repugnance inspired by the details of Mr. Haggard's murdering and massacring passages is sometimes still further aggravated by a tone of levity and even facetiousness accompanying the ghastly recital. One of his characters, a great amateur in homicide, with a hundred murders on his hands, deprecates some modes of killing a man as being not sufficiently "sportsmanlike." This person's favourite method is then circumstantially described, with a certain gusto suggestive of admiration—the admirer being Allan Quatermain, the autobiographic hero of two of the novels. For our own part, we are not so sensitive to the humorous side of carnage as Mr. Haggard appears to be, and we confess we find in it little to amuse. . . .

[*King Solomon's Mines*] exhibits some of Mr. Haggard's choicest flowers of humour. Captain Good is caught by a party of savages at a time when he happens to be divested of his nether garment, and to keep up the first impression thus produced upon their untutored minds, he goes for several days without that article of clothing. This incident, amplified by various detail, is quite the strong feature and pivot of interest throughout several chapters, Mr. Haggard being evidently delighted with such fair fruit of his humorous invention. We are sure it is meant for humour; not, indeed, because we ourselves find anything very amusing in it, but because we know of nothing else that it can be meant for. Though it affects us rather sadly, we think it can hardly be intended as an experiment in pathos. . . .

If it suited us to condescend to such humble particularities, we could produce from Mr. Haggard's writings an array of sentences betokening an ignorance of the principles of syntax which might discredit any schoolboy. We care not to pursue such small game. For after all, individual solecisms sink into insignificance beside the collective folly and futility of these books. As the world is said to be wiser than its wisest man, so Mr. Haggard's writings in their totality are worse than the worst things which they contain.

We have spoken with a degree of severity which will perhaps be attributed to private animus. We not only disclaim any such motive, we go farther, and do not hesitate to say that it is to the very fact of the utter absence of all personal considerations that our severity is due. The intrusion of such considerations would have brought human compunctions and relentings—would have begotten an unwillingness to deliver the maximum sentence which we believe such eminent offenses against good taste and good sense demand. It is only by rigidly shutting our eyes to everything but the general and public aspect of the case that we are enabled to go through the performance of such an unpleasant judicial duty. It is not that we grudge Mr. Haggard his undeserved success, but that we grudge the comparative neglect of meritorious fiction which the rage for meretricious fiction implies. We believe Mr. Haggard's own inmost literary conscience will ratify our pronouncement. He is a clever man, well able to take the measure of his own charlatanry—very likely the last person in the world to mistake his own charlatanry for genius. He is a clever man, for to gauge public taste is not done by a sort of fluke, but argues very considerable if not always scrupulous talents; and he has accurately gauged the taste of a section of the reading public, which the triumph of his experiment proves to be a large section. But that taste—the taste for such an ill-compounded *mélange* of the sham-real and the sham-romantic—is a deplorable symptom. There is among the very poor in our large cities a class of persons who nightly resort to the gin-shop to purchase a mixture of every known liquor, the heterogeneous rinsings of a hundred glasses. The flavour of this unnameable beverage defies imagination, but the liquor has for its lovers one transcendent virtue—it distances all rivalry in the work of procuring swift and thorough inebriation. Its devotees would not thank you for a bottle of the finest Château Yquem, when the great end and aim of drinking—the being made drunk—can be reached by such an infinitely readier agency. The taste for novels like Mr. Rider Haggard's is quite as truly the craving for coarse and violent intoxicants because they coarsely and violently intoxicate. But the victims of this thirst are without the excuse which the indigent topers to whom we liken them may plead. The poor tippler might say that he bought his unutterable beverage because he could not afford a better. But the noblest vintages of literature may be purchased as cheaply as their vilest substitutes. When we have abundance of exquisite grapes in our vineyards, is it not almost incredible that persons who pretend to some connoisseurship should be content to besot themselves with a thick, raw concoction, destitute of fragrance, destitute of sparkle, destitute of everything but the power to induce a crude inebriety of mind and a morbid

state of the intellectual peptics? It is indeed almost incredible, but
the pity of it is, it is true.

—September 1, 1888

JAMES KENNETH STEPHEN

> Will there never come a season
> Which shall rid us from the curse
> Of a prose which knows no reason
> And an unmelodious verse;
> When the world shall cease to wonder
> At the genius of an Ass,
> And a boy's eccentric blunder
> Shall not bring success to pass;
>
> When mankind shall be delivered
> From the clash of magazines,
> And the inkstand shall be shivered
> Into countless smithereens;
> When there stands a muzzled stripling,
> Mute, beside a muzzled bore:
> When the Rudyards cease from kipling,
> And the Haggards Ride no more.
>
> —from "To R. K." (1891)

MORTON NORTON COHEN

Haggard adds to the impact of his adventures by putting them in the
form of memoirs; by writing errors into the text so that he, as editor, may correct them in footnotes; by introducing a mass of metic-
ulous detail in describing far-away places, the people who inhabit
them, the costumes they wear, even the utensils they eat with. The
formula is a psychological powerhouse, and in Haggard's hands it
seldom fails, no matter how steep his tale or how flat his minor characters, to draw the reader into a strange and distant world.

—from *Rider Haggard: His Life and Works* (1960)

C. S. LEWIS

The real defects of Haggard are two. First, he can't write. Or rather
(I learn from Mr. Cohen) won't. Won't be bothered. Hence the

clichés, jocosities, frothy eloquence. When he speaks through the mouth of Quatermain he makes some play with the unliterary character of the simple hunter. It never dawned on him that what he wrote in his own person was a great deal worse—'literary' in the most damning sense of the word.

Secondly, the intellectual defects. . . . Though Haggard had sense, he was ludicrously unaware of his limitations.

—from *On Stories and Other Essays on Literature* (1966)

Questions

1. Does *King Solomon's Mines* appeal to anything beyond the perpetual male adolescent that seems to be lodged somewhere within all of us?

2. What is an adventure? Why do we want to have one (in our imaginations if not in the flesh)?

3. Would *King Solomon's Mines* be a better novel if a feisty and beautiful woman had been a participant in the adventures?

4. It is no longer common for adventure novelists to set their fictions in Africa. Any ideas about why?

5. In the treatment of Africans in the novel, is there anything beyond the old racist stereotypes?

6. What would you say has kept this novel popular, widely read and translated, and often imitated for more than 100 years?

For Further Reading

Editions of Haggard's Works

The Annotated "She": A Critical Edition of H. Rider Haggard's Victorian Romance. Edited, with an introduction and notes, by Norman Etherington. Bloomington: Indiana University Press, 1991. An expert on Haggard provides much helpful documentation.

Diary of an African Journey: The Return of Rider Haggard. Edited, with an introduction and notes, by Stephen Coan. New York: New York University Press, 2001. A perspicacious look at the latest views on Haggard.

King Solomon's Mines. Edited, with an introduction, by Dennis Butts. Oxford: Oxford University Press, 1989. Good, succinct notes.

King Solomon's Mines. Edited by James Danly. Introduction by Alexandra Fuller. New York: Modern Library, 2002. Extensive notes.

King Solomon's Mines. Edited by Gerald Monsman. Peterborough, Ontario: Broadview Press, 2002. An intelligent workbook format with additional texts relating to the novel.

The Private Diaries of Sir H. Rider Haggard, 1914–1925. Edited by D. S. Higgins. London: Cassell, 1980.

Biographical Studies

Cohen, Morton Norton. *Rider Haggard: His Life and Work.* Second edition. London: Macmillan, 1968. The standard biography, written with great affection for Haggard.

Etherington, Norman. *Rider Haggard.* Boston: Twayne Publishers, 1984. A useful summary.

Haggard, H. Rider. *The Days of My Life: An Autobiography.* Edited by C. J. Longman. London and New York: Longmans, Green, 1926. Haggard's own view, which is surprisingly reliable.

Haggard, Lilias Rider. *The Cloak That I Left: A Biography of the Author Henry Rider Haggard, K.B.I., by His Daughter Lilias Rider Haggard.* London: Hodder and Stoughton, 1951. The view of Haggard's daughter, an essential source for all biographers.

Manthorpe, Victoria. *Children of the Empire: The Victorian Hag-gards.* London: Victor Gollancz, 1996. More on Haggard's family circle.

Pocock, Tom. *Rider Haggard and the Lost Empire.* London: Weiden-feld and Nicolson, 1993. An enthusiastic look at Haggard and his times.

Criticism

Chrisman, Laura. *Rereading the Imperial Romance: British Imperial-ism and South African Resistance in Haggard, Schreiner, and Plaatje.* Oxford: Clarendon Press, 2000. A useful comparative study.

Fraser, Robert. *Victorian Quest Romance: Stevenson, Haggard, Kipling, and Conan Doyle.* Plymouth, UK: Northcote House, in association with the British Council, 1998. Haggard among his literary friends and competitors.

Katz, Wendy Roberta. *Rider Haggard and the Fiction of Empire: A Critical Study of British Imperial Fiction.* Cambridge: Cambridge University Press, 1987. A well-researched view of Haggard as racist and imperialist.

Leibfried, Philip. *Rudyard Kipling and Sir Henry Rider Haggard on Screen, Stage, Radio, and Television.* Jefferson, NC: McFarland, 1999. A reliable study of Haggard's impact on the mass media.

Low, Gail Ching-Liang. *White Skins/Black Masks: Representation and Colonialism.* London: Routledge, 1995. A general study that in-cludes discussion of Haggard's work.

Siemens, Lloyd, with Roger Neufeld. *The Critical Reception of Sir Henry Rider Haggard: An Annotated Bibliography, 1882–1991.* Greensboro: University of North Carolina at Greensboro Press, 1991. How journalists and others have reacted to Haggard.

Stiebel, Lindy. *Imagining Africa: Landscape in H. Rider Haggard's African Romances.* Westport, CT, and London: Greenwood Press, 2001. An in-depth look at Africa as Haggard understood it.

Whatmore, D. E. *H. Rider Haggard: A Bibliography.* Westport, CT: Meckler Publishing, 1987. A good starting point for any student of Haggard's work.

Adventures of Huckleberry Finn	Mark Twain	1-59308-000-X	$4.95
The Adventures of Tom Sawyer	Mark Twain	1-59308-068-9	$4.95
Aesop's Fables	Aesop	1-59308-062-X	$5.95
The Age of Innocence	Edith Wharton	1-59308-074-3	$4.95
Alice's Adventures in Wonderland and Through the Looking Glass	Lewis Carroll	1-59308-015-8	$5.95
Anna Karenina	Leo Tolstoy	1-59308-027-1	$8.95
The Art of War	Sun Tzu	1-59308-016-6	$3.95
The Awakening and Selected Short Fiction	Kate Chopin	1-59308-001-8	$4.95
The Call of the Wild and White Fang	Jack London	1-59308-002-6	$4.95
Candide	Voltaire	1-59308-028-X	$4.95
A Christmas Carol, The Chimes and The Cricket on the Hearth	Charles Dickens	1-59308-033-6	$5.95
The Collected Poems of Emily Dickinson	Emily Dickinson	1-59308-050-6	$5.95
The Complete Sherlock Holmes, Volume I	Sir Arthur Conan Doyle	1-59308-034-4	$7.95
The Complete Sherlock Holmes, Volume II	Sir Arthur Conan Doyle	1-59308-040-9	$7.95
The Count of Monte Cristo	Alexandre Dumas	1-59308-088-3	$5.95
Cyrano de Bergerac	Edmond Rostand	1-59308-075-1	$3.95
David Copperfield	Charles Dickens	1-59308-063-8	$7.95
The Death of Ivan Ilych and Other Stories	Leo Tolstoy	1-59308-069-7	$7.95
Don Quixote	Miguel de Cervantes	1-59308-046-8	$9.95
Dracula	Bram Stoker	1-59308-004-2	$4.95
Emma	Jane Austen	1-59308-089-1	$4.95
Ethan Frome and Selected Stories	Edith Wharton	1-59308-090-5	$5.95
Frankenstein	Mary Shelley	1-59308-005-0	$3.95
Great Expectations	Charles Dickens	1-59308-006-9	$4.95
Grimm's Fairy Tales	Jacob and Wilhelm Grimm	1-59308-056-5	$7.95
Gulliver's Travels	Jonathan Swift	1-59308-057-3	$3.95
Heart of Darkness and Selected Short Fiction	Joseph Conrad	1-59308-021-2	$4.95
The House of Mirth	Edith Wharton	1-59308-104-9	$4.95
Howards End	E. M. Forster	1-59308-022-0	$6.95
The Hunchback of Notre Dame	Victor Hugo	1-59308-047-6	$5.95
The Idiot	Fyodor Dostoevsky	1-59308-058-1	$7.95
The Importance of Being Earnest and Four Other Plays	Oscar Wilde	1-59308-059-X	$6.95
The Inferno	Dante Alighieri	1-59308-051-4	$6.95
Jane Eyre	Charlotte Brontë	1-59308-007-7	$4.95
Jude the Obscure	Thomas Hardy	1-59308-035-2	$6.95
The Jungle	Upton Sinclair	1-59308-008-5	$4.95

(continued)

BARNES & NOBLE CLASSICS